Tim LaHaye is a noted author, minister, and nationally recognized speaker on Bible prophecy. He is founder and president of Tim LaHaye Ministries and a cofounder of the Pre-Trib Research Center. A pastor for thirty-nine years, Dr. LaHaye has written more than fifty nonfiction books and coauthored the Left Behind series, the most successful Christian fiction venture in publishing history, with Jerry Jenkins. LaHaye and his wife, Beverly, who have been married for more than fifty years, live in Southern California. You can visit his website at www.TimLaHaye.com.

Jerry B. Jenkins, formerly vice president for publishing and currently writer-at-large for the Moody Bible Institute of Chicago, is the author of more than 150 books, including the Left Behind series with Tim LaHaye. Dr. Jenkins's writing has appeared in *Time, Reader's Digest, Parade,* and *Guideposts,* and dozens of other Christian periodicals. He owns Jenkins Entertainment, a filmmaking company based in Los Angeles, as well as the Christian Writers Guild, which aims to train tomorrow's professional Christian writers and has nearly two thousand members worldwide. A sought-after marriage and family speaker, Jenkins lives with his wife, Dianna, in Colorado Springs. You can visit his website at www.JerryJenkins.com.

BOOKS IN THE JESUS CHRONICLES

John's Story: The Last Eyewitness
Mark's Story: The Gospel According to Peter

THE JESUS CHRONICLES

Book Two

MARK'S STORY

THE GOSPEL ACCORDING TO PETER

TIM LAHAYE *and* JERRY B. JENKINS

BERKLEY PRAISE, NEW YORK

BERKLEY PRAISE
Published by The Berkley Publishing Group
A Division of Penguin Group (USA) Inc.
375 Hudson Street, New York, New York 10014, USA
Penguin Group (Canada), 90 Eglinton Avenue East, Suite 700, Toronto, Ontario M4P 2Y3, Canada
(a division of Pearson Penguin Canada Inc.)
Penguin Books Ltd., 80 Strand, London WC2R 0RL, England
Penguin Group Ireland, 25 St. Stephen's Green, Dublin 2, Ireland (a division of Penguin Books Ltd.)
Penguin Group (Australia), 250 Camberwell Road, Camberwell, Victoria 3124, Australia
(a division of Pearson Australia Group Pty. Ltd.)
Penguin Books India Pvt. Ltd., 11 Community Centre, Panchsheel Park, New Delhi—110 017, India
Penguin Group (NZ), 67 Apollo Drive, Rosedale, North Shore 0632, New Zealand
(a division of Pearson New Zealand Ltd.)
Penguin Books (South Africa) (Pty.) Ltd., 24 Sturdee Avenue, Rosebank, Johannesburg 2196, South Africa

Penguin Books Ltd., Registered Offices: 80 Strand, London WC2R 0RL, England

PRINTING HISTORY
Putnam Praise hardcover edition / October 2007
Berkley Praise trade paperback edition / February 2009

Berkley Praise trade paperback ISBN: 978-0-425-21890-7

The Library of Congress Control Number for the Putnam Praise hardcover edition is: 2007932396

NKJV

NEW KING JAMES VERSION®
Build Your Life On It.™

147514730

TO OUR GRANDCHILDREN AND OUR GREAT-GRANDCHILDREN

May God grant you the strength

to bear the torch,

for as long as He tarries.

ONE

The ghastliest night of young John Mark's life began with intriguing news from his mother, which portended excitement but certainly not treachery and violence.

Having finished the laborious search of the house for leaven, and suffering the deep hunger pangs of the Fast of the Firstborn, the sixteen-year-old looked forward to that evening's Passover feast, despite the fact that it would be the first without his late father. He had been killed nearly a year before.

"We will enjoy our meal later," his mother said as they sat in the first-floor great room of their expansive home just inside the walls of Jerusalem. The city was teeming with like-minded pilgrims, eager to celebrate the same event. "But first we have been assigned a very important undertaking of hospitality."

"Who will be our guests?"

"Well, they will not be here to visit. We are to serve them."

"The servants will serve them, you mean?"

"Mark, I said what I meant. The servants will help, but it falls to us to serve them. I, by offering the dining room upstairs. You, by overseeing the servants in administering the meal."

"Who will cook it?"

"The guests themselves."

"I'm confused."

"All will become clear. First you are to carry a water pitcher near the Water Gate. From there, two men will follow you—"

"Must it be a pitcher, Mother? Women carry pitchers. I'd be happy to carry water in a wineskin—"

His mother held up a hand. "Please, Mark. Listen first, question second. The Teacher gave me these instructions Himself, and so—"

"Oh! I hoped He and His friends were in town! They will be our visitors?"

"—and so we will follow His wishes to the letter. Peter and John will follow you from the gate to—"

"I love Peter! He—"

His mother stopped Mark with a look. "From the gate to our home, where you will show them to the upper room. You will then make yourself scarce until you are needed, and you will make certain the servants are diligently attending to our friends."

John Mark had long been intrigued by the occasional visits of Jesus and His disciples. Some had been friends of his parents. About a week after his father had been crushed under a runaway wagon near the Fish Gate, Peter arrived to just spend time with Mark. The sting of the sudden loss permeated the day they spent near Peter's home in Capernaum on the northern tip of the Sea of Galilee, but seeing Peter's fishing operation—his boat now run by others—allowed something else, finally, to occupy Mark's mind at least briefly.

While Peter showed Mark how he skillfully manned the nets,

hurling them far and wide to catch sardines and musht and biny, he regaled him with astonishing accounts of his travels with Jesus. The thick, robust Peter—who seemed the closest to Jesus, and a leader among His disciples—had even left his wife, Esther, and their young children at home to follow the Teacher. Mark and Peter had become fast friends, Mark deeply admiring the fisherman's fierce gaze, his direct speech, and his lusty appetite for life. Although no one could ever replace his father, Mark could not imagine what might have become of him without Peter as his friend and mentor, seemingly appearing whenever he needed him most in his grief and groundlessness.

The band of men—all of them, even the Master Himself—were of lowly estate compared to Mark's family. And yet he enjoyed hearing them talk and laugh and sing, growling out hymns and psalms. Of late, however, danger seemed to follow them. They were no longer so boisterous and happy. Where once they had followed an evening of teaching and parables with humor and teasing, now they often arrived furtively, separately, and spoke in low tones.

Jesus' fame had spread throughout all of Judea with fantastic stories abounding of His healing the sick, even raising the dead. Some said He was Messiah—even Mark's mother believed that, though Mark himself wasn't so sure. Was it possible that a mere man he knew personally could be the One whose coming was foretold in ancient texts Mark studied every day?

It didn't seem likely, and yet Peter too believed this with all his heart. Often Peter's eyes grew so bright with the tales that Mark had to wonder how much of it was true.

Mark himself wasn't above crafting a tall tale. One of the great regrets of Mark's young life was having been caught in a bald-faced lie to his mother. Once, when his cousin Joses was visiting from Cyprus, Mark had claimed the lanky, dark-haired boy's handcrafted toy as his own. When Joses told his aunt Mary, she demanded the truth from Mark, adding, "Only you will know if you're being honest with me."

"I know," he said, "and I am! I made this myself."

In less than an hour Mark's highly developed conscience convicted him, forcing him to confess and willingly accept his mother's punishment. He returned the toy, of course, and endured a brief but stinging session with the rod. His mother directed Mark back to the Psalms and the laments of his hero David, who often had to plead for God's forgiveness.

"I CANNOT STRESS ENOUGH how important it is to not draw attention to Peter and John," his mother said now. "The Teacher Himself asked that no one outside our household know that they will be here."

"I am not to greet them?"

She shook her head. "That you are carrying a pitcher will be their sign to follow you."

"But they know me already!"

"You are not to speak to them until you have arrived back here."

MARK FELT CONSPICUOUS filling the pitcher with water from the well not far from the Water Gate. He prayed no one would recognize him and demand to know why he was doing the work of a woman.

At the appointed hour, Peter and John approached, Peter with a dead lamb over his shoulders, dried blood staining his garment. Mark could tell by how the men looked at each other, nodding and raising their brows, that they were surprised it was he they were to follow.

Neither spoke as they followed at a distance, until they came within the shadows afforded by the olive trees lining the portal of Mark's home.

"Mary," they said in unison when Mark's mother appeared. She directed them to the great room, where a servant took the lamb, and Mary signaled Mark to fill a basin with water and also to pour them cups to drink. As they drank, she washed their feet with the water from the basin.

Peter said, "The Teacher asks, 'Where is the guest room in which I may eat the Passover with My disciples?' "

Mary nodded to her son as she finished drying the men's feet. They stepped into their sandals and followed Mark up an outer staircase to the spacious area atop the house, made airy by arched openings in the walls. The servants had already set the large dining table up there with the finest candles and dishware in the house and encircled it with reclining couches.

Not far from a grate over a fire of coals, the lamb lay on a wooden preparation table, upon which were also arrayed knives, bread dough, wine, and bitter herbs. Peter whispered to a servant, "And for the haroset?"

"Yes!" Mark said, embarrassed. "Fetch the ingredients, now!" he ordered the servant.

The man hurried off, and Peter drew Mark aside. "Son, a word," he said. "Remember that these are serving not only you, but also us and the Teacher. They deserve our respect."

"But Mother had instructed them to have ready everything you need to prepare the—"

"We are all but men, John Mark. Capable of mistakes."

"But we want everything perfect for—"

"And it will be. That is why we are here now. By the time the others arrive, all will be made ready."

Mark felt his face redden. "Forgive me."

Peter threw an arm around Mark. "Fret not. I too have had to learn to treat all the way the Master treats me. It has been a hard lesson."

Standing so close to Peter, Mark could tell he had strapped a heavy sword and scabbard inside his tunic. "You carry a weapon?"

Peter held a finger to his lips. "One cannot be too careful."

The servant returned with dried fruit, spices, pomegranates, nuts, dates, and a goblet of vinegar. He bowed, eyes downcast, and appeared surprised when young Mark thanked him profusely.

"Now leave us," Peter said, "as we prepare the meal."

AS THE OTHER DISCIPLES began to arrive—in pairs or small groups—the servants were pressed into assisting Mary and Mark in welcoming them, washing their feet, giving them water, and directing them upstairs. Simon, Thomas, and Philip arrived together, and several minutes later Matthew and Judas Iscariot. James—the brother of John—Andrew, the other Judas, and Bartholomew were next, and finally the other James accompanied Jesus.

Mark had long been fascinated by these men, all about twice his age save John, just ten years older. Some—like Judas Iscariot and Andrew—were friendlier than others. Some—like Matthew—kept to themselves. Though Mark knew Peter best, he also found Judas and Andrew personable and animated. He was drawn to Jesus, as most seemed to be, and yet Mark also felt most self-conscious when he had the Teacher's attention. The Man seemed to study his face and truly listen to every word, somehow making Mark feel as if he had hardly anything of import to say. He also felt somehow unworthy in the Man's presence, as if Jesus knew what kind of a person Mark really was. Had his mother told Him of his propensity for deceit? For conceit? Of his impatience? His temper?

This evening, however, Mark didn't have to worry about Jesus' searching eyes. The Teacher and all the rest seemed pensive and secretive.

For a man so revered and reviled, so appealing and yet feared, Jesus certainly did not appear out of the ordinary. Yes, He carried Himself with a quiet confidence and authority, and if Mark could believe Peter's stories, Jesus was nothing if not fearless. He was by no means the tallest of the thirteen. That honor fell to the reserved Matthew. Nor was He attractive, as were Bartholomew and John. Jesus was vigorous and appeared strong-looking—no surprise for a man who had been a carpenter. But to have become the center of so much attention? It didn't make sense to Mark, at least from the Man's appearance. Listening to Him, though, was another matter. The young man relished the opportunity, after his duties had been fulfilled, to sit at the top of the stairs, just out of sight behind the door, and simply listen.

By the end of the evening, he would hear and see more than he had ever dreamed—even in his worst nightmare.

TWO

John Mark, you are the master of this house now," his mother said as they lit the candles and sat to celebrate their own Passover Seder. Her eyes bore a faraway look. "And yet you are also the one to ask the ceremonial questions tonight."

"I know."

Mark longed to get back upstairs. He did not want to abandon his mother on this special night, especially when she seemed wistful, but often when such emotion gripped her, she wanted to be alone.

As they began their ritual, a servant who had been assigned to the upper room rushed past, begging the mistress's pardon. "The Teacher has requested another pitcher, basin, and towel," he said.

Mark's mother appeared confused. "He is aware we have washed everyone's feet, is He not?"

The servant looked nonplussed as well.

"Carry on, carry on," she said quickly. "Give Him whatever He asks. Mark, we must hurry, so you can supervise the servants."

Though they wasted little time between the fifteen separate elements of the observance, it was impossible to finish in less than half an hour. Mother and son served each other, and it fell to Mark to ask and answer the traditional questions and also to recite the story of the Passover. How Mark missed his father! He could only imagine how difficult this was for his mother.

"This night is different from all other nights because once we were slaves to Pharaoh in Egypt, but God took us out with a mighty hand and an outstretched arm. If God had not brought our ancestors out of Egypt, then we, and our children, and our children's children, would still be slaves in the land of Egypt."

Mark had to admit he was distracted by a single voice from above. During brief silences between his questions and his mother's responses, he tried to make out what the Teacher was saying. Jesus was earnest, that was clear, and His tone was urgent. But Mark would have to ask Peter what was said. He could not tell whether their seder had begun or whether Jesus was merely teaching, as He often did.

The singing of traditional Psalms was one of Mark's favorite parts of the Passover observance. His mother's eyes filled as they quietly harmonized.

"I love the Lord, because He has heard my voice and my supplications. Because He has inclined His ear to me, therefore I will call upon Him as long as I live. The pains of death surrounded me, and the pangs of Sheol laid hold of me; I found trouble and sorrow. Then I called upon the name of the Lord: 'O Lord, I implore You, deliver my soul!'

"Gracious is the Lord, and righteous; yes, our God is merciful. The Lord preserves the simple; I was brought low, and He saved me. Return to your rest, O my soul, for the Lord has dealt bountifully with you. For You have delivered my soul from death, my eyes from tears, and my feet from falling."

John Mark believed in God, loved Him, and prayed for the coming Messiah. He thrilled to the stories of old, how God had delivered His chosen people time and again despite their failings. Mark knew what it meant to fail, to not be the man he believed God—and his mother—wanted and expected him to be. Besides the constant need to put his wishes above others', he frequently had to seek forgiveness for being selfish, cross, or disobedient.

"I will offer to You the sacrifice of thanksgiving, and will call upon the name of the Lord. I will pay my vows to the Lord now in the presence of all His people, in the courts of the Lord's house, in the midst of you, O Jerusalem. Praise the Lord!

"Praise the Lord, all you Gentiles! Laud Him, all you peoples! For His merciful kindness is great toward us, and the truth of the Lord endures forever. Praise the Lord!"

Even as they sang the beautiful old passages from the Torah, Mark's mind wandered, and he was eager to finish and listen in on the disciples and the One they called their Master.

Mark had to admit that having in their own home the Man some believed was Messiah Himself made him doubt it all the more. What was the likelihood that after all these years, Messiah would come in Mark's lifetime, know his mother, and visit their home? Interesting and fascinating as he found the Man and His friends, the very idea seemed preposterous. And while Peter's stories included acts that would certainly qualify the Man as the Chosen One, Mark also knew that grown men loved to exaggerate, to thrill gullible young people.

Jesus was surely a wonderful man, and His disciples obviously believed in Him and were devoted to Him. But Mark would have to see one of His miracles himself to even consider that Jesus of Nazareth might be the promised deliverer and king.

With the singing of the psalms completed, Mark began helping his mother and the servants to clear their table, but she urged him to hurry upstairs. "The Teacher informed me that He and His disciples may stay very late and that I should not feel obligated to wait up for them. Please give Him my regards, as I do feel I will turn in early."

"Shall I stay with you, Mother?" Mark said, willing, but hopeful she would decline his offer. "Are you all right?"

"No, please. Memories tonight are sweet and painful, but I will feel most comforted if I know you are seeing to our guests."

AS MARK MOUNTED the steps he could hear Jesus speaking again. Near the top he was met by the servants coming down. "Where are you going?" he whispered.

"He has excused us, master," one said, carrying a pitcher, a basin, and a towel.

"What's this?"

"He washed their feet. The Teacher."

"Did He not know that we already—"

"He knew."

"Very well. Remain nearby to restore the room when they have left. I will signal you."

Mark sat on the top step, where he would remain out of sight behind the door and yet be able to hear. He tucked his knees up to his chest and wrapped his arms around them, for he was wearing only a thin linen garment, and the night was growing chilly.

He listened intently. For whatever reason, Jesus had washed His disciples' feet. They continued to murmur about it and one or two seemed to be weeping.

Then Mark heard the Master speak.

Jesus said, "Assuredly, I say to you, one of you who eats with Me will betray Me."

"What?"

Mark recognized the sorrowful voice of Peter, echoed by many others. They all seemed to protest at once, then asked Jesus one by one, "Is it I?"

Jesus spoke quietly. "It is one of the twelve, who dips with Me in the dish."

Several gasped at that, and it was all Mark could do to keep from peeking around the corner to see who it was. Jesus continued, "The Son of Man indeed goes just as it is written of Him, but woe to that man by whom the Son of Man is betrayed! It would have been good for that man if he had never been born."

Suddenly came the sound of rushing footsteps, and Mark pressed himself back against the wall as a figure swept from the room and clambered down the steps. Judas Iscariot! Could it be? Mark stopped himself from calling out, knowing he would give himself away, and he so wanted to hear more.

There was more murmuring, and finally silence, save for the sounds of bowls being passed and cups lifted and set down on the table. Jesus quietly prayed, thanking God for their bread. Then He said something so strange that Mark thought he had not heard correctly: "Take, eat; this is My body."

Jesus gave thanks for the wine and said to His disciples, "This is My blood of the new covenant, which is shed for many. Assuredly, I say to you, I will no longer drink of the fruit of the vine until that day when I drink it new in the kingdom of God."

What was He saying? Mark was a diligent student, but he could make no sense of this. And then he heard one, a voice he did not recognize, ask which of the disciples should be considered the greatest. Jesus said, "The kings of the Gentiles exercise lordship over them, and those who exercise authority over them are called 'benefactors.' But not so among you; on the contrary, he who is greatest among you, let him be as the younger, and he who governs as he who serves. For who is greater, he who sits at the table, or he who serves? Is it not he who sits at the table? Yet I am among you as the One who serves."

Was that why He, the Teacher Himself, the one they called Master and even Lord, had washed their feet? No wonder they found this Man astounding.

Jesus continued, "If I then have washed your feet, you also ought to wash one another's feet. For I have given you an example, that you should do as I have done to you. Most assuredly, I say to you, a servant is not greater than his master; nor is he who is sent greater than he who sent him. If you know these things, blessed are you if you do them.

"But you are those who have continued with Me in My trials. And I bestow upon you a kingdom, just as My Father bestowed one upon Me, that you may eat and drink at My table in My kingdom, and sit on thrones judging the twelve tribes of Israel.

"You call Me Teacher and Lord, and you say well, for so I am."

What in the name of heaven did He mean? The disciples had to be wondering the same, but when Jesus continued, He sounded just as perplexing. "Most assuredly, I say to you that you will weep and lament, but the world will rejoice; and you will be sorrowful, but your sorrow will be turned into joy."

Why would they weep? What was to become of Him? Mark rose and stole into the room, quickly moving to the back as if tending to details. When no one seemed to notice, and Jesus did not quit speaking, the lad lowered himself out of sight where he could see the Teacher and most of His disciples.

"I do not speak concerning all of you," Jesus said. "I know whom I have chosen. Now I tell you before it comes, so that when it does come to pass, you may believe that I am He. Most assuredly, I say to you, he who receives whomever I send receives Me; and he who receives Me receives Him who sent Me."

Jesus was making astounding claims about Himself, but maybe Mark was just too young to understand. He would have to ask Peter what he thought of all this. If anyone understood, Peter would.

Jesus said, "Little children, I shall be with you a little while longer. You will seek Me; and as I said to the Jews, 'Where I am going, you cannot come,' so now I say to you. A new commandment I give to you, that you love one another as I have loved you. By this all will know that you are My disciples."

Mark could see their consternation. They could not have understood this any more than he did.

"Let not your heart be troubled; you believe in God, believe also in Me. In My Father's house are many mansions; if it were not so, I would have told you. I go to prepare a place for you. And if I go and prepare a place for you, I will come again and receive you to Myself; that where I am, there you may be also. And where I go you know, and the way you know."

They did? Mark certainly didn't. He was relieved when Thomas said, "Lord, we do not know where You are going, and how can we know the way?"

Jesus said, "I am the way, the truth, and the life. No one comes to the Father except through Me. If you had known Me, you would have known My Father also; and from now on you know Him and have seen Him."

He was claiming to be the Son of God!

Philip said, "Lord, show us the Father, and it is sufficient for us."

Jesus cocked his head and smiled. "Have I been with you so long, and yet you have not known Me, Philip? He who has seen Me has seen the Father; so how can you say, 'Show us the Father'? Do you not believe that I am in the Father, and the Father in Me? The words that I speak to you I do not speak on My own authority; but the Father who dwells in Me does the works. Believe Me that I am in the Father and the Father in Me, or else believe Me for the sake of the works themselves."

Had Mark seen all the works Peter told of, he would have found it easier to believe this. Now he didn't know what to think. This Teacher was fascinating, captivating even, but could this be true?

"Most assuredly, I say to you, he who believes in Me, the works that I do he will do also; and greater works than these he will do, because I go to My Father. And whatever you ask in My name, that I will do, that the Father may be glorified in the Son. If you ask anything in My name, I will do it."

Was that a promise just for the disciples, or might it be something Mark could try too? He might just have to put Jesus to the test.

"If you love Me, keep My commandments. And I will pray the Father, and He will give you another Helper, that He may abide with you forever—the Spirit of truth, whom the world cannot receive, because it neither sees Him nor knows Him; but you know Him, for He dwells with you and will be in you. I will not leave you orphans; I will come to you."

Who dwells with them and will be in them? Jesus Himself? Or another? Mark was getting more confused by the moment.

"A little while longer and the world will see Me no more, but you will see Me. Because I live, you will live also. At that day you will know that I am in My Father, and you in Me, and I in you."

Mark's mind was reeling. The world will see Him no more? But the disciples will? And they will live?

"He who has My commandments and keeps them, it is he who loves Me. And he who loves Me will be loved by My Father, and I will love him and manifest Myself to him."

The other Judas said, "Lord, how is it that You will manifest Yourself to us, and not to the world?"

Jesus said, "If anyone loves Me, he will keep My word; and My Father will love him, and We will come to him and make Our home with him. He who does not love Me does not keep My words; and the word which you hear is not Mine but the Father's who sent Me."

He was speaking the words of God? Mark wanted to know Jesus enough to love Him and keep His word.

"These things I have spoken to you while being present with you. But the Helper, the Holy Spirit, whom the Father will send in My name, He will teach you all things, and bring to your remembrance all things that I said to you."

So *that* is who will be in the disciples. A spirit?

"Peace I leave with you, My peace I give to you; not as the world gives do I give to you. Let not your heart be troubled, neither let it be afraid. You have heard Me say to you, 'I am going away and coming back to you.' If you loved Me, you would rejoice because I said, 'I am going to the Father,' for My Father is greater than I.

"And now I have told you before it comes, that when it does come to pass, you may believe.

"I am the vine, you are the branches. He who abides in Me, and I in him, bears much fruit; for without Me you can do nothing. If anyone does not abide in Me, he is cast out as a branch and is withered; and they gather them and throw them into the fire, and they are burned. If you abide in Me, and My words abide in you, you will ask what you desire, and it shall be done for you. By this My Father is glorified, that you bear much fruit; so you will be My disciples."

For the first time, after all the hours he'd spent with Peter and the years he'd spent studying the Scriptures, John Mark wished he could be a disciple of Jesus. Was He the Christ, the Messiah? Mark had no idea. But He spoke with such authority and depth.

"As the Father loved Me, I also have loved you; abide in My love. If you keep My commandments, you will abide in My love, just as I have kept My Father's commandments and abide in His love.

"These things I have spoken to you, that My joy may remain in you, and that your joy may be full. This is My commandment, that you love one another as I have loved you. Greater love has no one than this, than to lay down one's life for his friends. You are My friends if you do whatever I command you. No longer do I call you servants, for a servant does not know what his master is doing; but I have called you friends, for all things that I heard from My Father I have made known to you. You did not choose Me, but I chose you and appointed you that you should go and bear fruit, and that your fruit should remain, that whatever you ask the Father in My name He may give you. These things I command you, that you love one another.

"These things I have spoken to you, that you should not be made to stumble. They will put you out of the synagogues; yes, the time is coming that whoever kills you will think that he offers God service. And these things they will do to you because they have not known the Father nor Me. But these things I have told you, that when the time comes, you may remember that I told you of them."

This Man knows the future? How long would it be before Mark could know for sure?

"I still have many things to say to you, but you cannot bear them now. However, when He, the Spirit of truth, has come, He will guide you into all truth; for He will not speak on His own authority, but whatever He hears He will speak; and He will tell you things to come.

"A little while, and you will not see Me; and again a little while, and you will see Me, because I go to the Father."

A little while? Again, Mark felt lost, and he could tell by their murmuring and their looks that the disciples did too. Yet it was as if Jesus read their minds.

"Are you inquiring among yourselves about what I said? Most assuredly, I say to you that you will weep and lament, but the world will rejoice; and you will be sorrowful, but your sorrow will be turned into joy. You now have sorrow; but I will see you again and your heart will rejoice, and your joy no one will take from you.

"[T]he time is coming when I will no longer speak to you in figurative language, but I will tell you plainly about the Father. I came forth from the Father and have come into the world. Again, I leave the world and go to the Father."

Well, Mark decided, that couldn't have been more clear. And apparently Peter agreed. He said, "See, now You are speaking plainly, and using no figure of speech! Now we are sure that You know all things, and have no need that anyone should question You. By this we believe that You came forth from God."

Jesus said, "Do you now believe? Indeed the hour is coming, yes, has now come, that you will be scattered, each to his own, and will leave Me alone. And yet I am not alone, because the Father is with Me. These things I have spoken to you, that in Me you may have peace. In the world you will have tribulation; but be of good cheer, I have overcome the world."

As Mark watched, transfixed, Jesus looked up and said, "Father, the hour has come. Glorify Your Son, that Your Son also may glorify You, as You have given Him authority over all flesh, that He should give eternal life to as many as You have given Him. And this is eternal life, that they may know You, the only true God, and Jesus Christ whom You have sent. I have glorified You on the earth. I have finished the work which You have given Me to do. And now, O Father, glorify Me together with Yourself, with the glory which I had with You before the world was.

"I pray for these, My friends. Holy Father, keep through Your name those whom You have given Me, that they may be one as We are. Those whom You gave Me I have kept; and none of them is lost except the son of perdition, that the Scripture might be fulfilled. But now I come to You, and these things I speak in the world, that they may have My joy fulfilled in themselves. I have given them Your word; and the world has hated them because they are not of the world, just as I am not of the world. I do not pray that You should take them out of the world, but that You should keep them from the evil one.

"I do not pray for these alone, but also for those who will believe in Me through their word; that they all may be one, as You, Father, are in Me, and I in You; that they also may be one in Us, that the world may believe that You sent Me. And the glory which You gave Me I have given them, that they may be one just as We are one: I in them, and You in Me; that they may be made perfect in one, and that the world may know that You have sent Me, and have loved them as You have loved Me."

Mark sat shivering, mesmerized by the puzzling, troubling statements of the Teacher. Mark realized that if this had been his own rabbi, holding forth on some teaching, he might have dozed. But the Teacher said such amazing things.

When Jesus finished praying, He said, "After we sing, I would that you would join me at the Mount of Olives." He led the disciples in a hymn, the very one Mark and his mother had sung to finish their seder.

As Jesus and the remaining eleven made their way down the steps, Mark followed unnoticed and instructed the servants to finish tending to the upper room. He tiptoed past his mother's quiet bedroom and crept into the night, after the group. A cold breeze was blowing, but Mark didn't dare return home for his cloak, as he did not want to rouse his mother, nor did he want to lose sight of the men.

Jesus, clearly having announced Himself as Messiah, would be betrayed? Mark could not have been deterred from following the men even if his mother has risen and forbidden it. The frigid wind be cursed. The Mount of Olives was not far.

THREE

Mark wondered whether Jesus and His men would break up into small groups again so as to not draw attention to themselves. But as they made their way through the city toward the gate, it became plain that no one took notice of them. Jerusalem was as crowded as Mark had ever seen it, with people dancing and singing and conversing around makeshift fires.

From several paces behind, Mark could not tell for sure, but it appeared Jesus and His disciples did not speak until they had exited the city to the east, heading toward the hillside that bore countless groves of olive trees. Mark followed them across a brook—little more than a stream this time of year—which ran through the Kidron Valley, the valley that separated the Mount of Olives and the Temple Mount.

Mark took advantage of the sound of the water to draw closer to the group without being noticed and was able to hear Jesus say, "All of you will be made to stumble because of Me this night, for it is written: *'I will strike the Shepherd, and the sheep will be scattered.'* But after I have been raised, I will go before you to Galilee."

After He has been raised? Again Mark wondered if he had heard correctly. Was Jesus to die and then rise? Were it not for the goose bumps on his skin, Mark would have wondered if this was a dream. Had he and his mother entertained deity? Could it be true? Could a Man he knew personally be the Chosen One of God?

Peter said, "Master, even if all are made to stumble, I will not be."

Mark wanted to be just like Peter, resolute and true.

But the comment made Jesus stop and face Peter. Mark hung back in the shadows, worried one of them might see him.

Jesus spoke quietly, sadness in his tone. "Assuredly, I say to you that even this night, before the rooster crows twice, you will deny Me three times."

Deny his mentor, his master? Mark couldn't imagine that of Peter, let alone how it must have made the man feel to hear that from Jesus.

Peter raised his voice. "If I have to die with You, I will not deny You!"

That was the Peter that Mark knew. And the rest of the disciples crowded around Jesus, all saying likewise. "Not me! I will stand with you!"

Mark followed them to an expansive area filled with gardens, and Jesus led them to a beautiful and fragrant section called Gethsemane, enclosed by a low stone wall. As they entered the gate, He said, "Peter, James, John, come with me. The rest of you sit here while I pray."

The other eight sat chatting among themselves, but Mark was drawn to Jesus. He wanted to hear anything He might say to His closest confidants, and he also wanted to hear the Teacher pray.

Mark crouched low behind the wall, keeping out of sight of the other disciples, as he scurried along, trying to follow Jesus and His men. When they moved farther east into the garden, he scaled the wall and angled close enough to hear them and see their silhouettes in the moonlight. Hiding behind a large poplar, Mark tried to control his shuddering. He rubbed his arms while otherwise trying to remain as still as possible.

Peter and John and John's brother James had fallen silent and appeared embarrassed. It was as if they didn't know what to say or do as Jesus began to fret. There was no other way to describe it. The Teacher covered His face with His hands, then stared into the heavens. Mark heard Him sigh and then groan. He sat on a large outcropping of rock, then stood and paced.

Jesus turned to His friends. "My soul is exceedingly sorrowful, even to death. Stay here and watch."

The three looked at one another as He moved away, and Mark pressed his hand over his mouth to muffle his own gasp as Jesus fell to the ground. "If it is possible," He said, weeping, "allow this hour to pass from Me."

What did the Man so fear? Mark could not imagine. Jesus had three friends only a few feet away, at least one of them armed, and not a stone's throw away sat eight more. And yet He lay prostrate, forehead resting on his hands in the dirt. "Abba, Father, all things are possible for You. Take this cup away from Me; nevertheless, not what I will, but what You will."

Mark was startled when Jesus suddenly rose and turned. Had he been found out? The lad held his breath as Jesus returned to His friends. "Simon," he said, calling Peter by his formal name, "are you sleeping? Could you not watch one hour?"

Peter stood quickly. "Lord, I am here." James and John sat up.

"Watch and pray," Jesus said, "lest you enter into temptation. The spirit indeed is willing, but the flesh is weak."

As Jesus moved away again, the three disciples whispered among themselves. "James," Peter said, "nudge me if I doze again, please. And John, be sure James stays alert."

Mark was riveted by this mysterious Man the disciples seemed to so love. He fell to the ground again and repeated the same prayer, panting, groaning, crying. Whatever it was He felt compelled to accomplish, He wished He didn't have to, and yet time and again He told God He was willing.

Having seemed to gain no peace about it, He slowly rose and returned to Peter and James and John. Mark was astonished to see that they had all dozed off again, and he considered tossing a pebble into their midst to alert them before they were found out.

"My friends," Jesus said sadly, making the three rouse awkwardly, but none had an excuse.

Yet a third time Jesus stepped away from them and collapsed into prayer, this time sweating so heavily that Mark saw the moisture cascading from His beard and onto His hands. Suddenly He rose and rushed back to the three. His tone had changed from sadness to anger.

"Are you still sleeping? It is enough! The hour has come; behold, the Son of Man is being betrayed into the hands of sinners. Rise, let us be going. See, My betrayer is at hand."

And there stood Judas Iscariot, trailed by a great multitude with swords and clubs! He approached Jesus with arms outstretched saying, "Rabbi, Rabbi!" and kissed Him.

"Friend," Jesus said with great sorrow, "why have you come? You would betray the Son of Man with a kiss?"

In the flickering light of many torches, Mark could see fear in Judas's eyes as he backed away. Jesus stepped forward to the crowd. "Whom are you seeking?" He said.

"Jesus of Nazareth."

"I am He."

With His admission, the first line of the throng fell backward onto the ground. Then He said again, "Whom are you seeking?"

They warily staggered to their feet and one said, "Jesus of Nazareth."

"I have told you that I am He. Therefore, if you seek Me, let these go their way."

Surely, Mark thought, Jesus' friends would not desert Him, not leave Him to this mob of soldiers and religious leaders! He thrilled to see his hero, Peter, draw his sword, lunge forward, and flail at a servant who stood next to a high priest. The blade sliced off the man's ear, and he dropped to his knees, screaming.

"Malchus!" the priest cried out, and others moved to aid him.

Jesus said, "Peter, put your sword into the sheath. Shall I not drink the cup which My Father has given Me?" He put His hands on the injured man's head, and immediately his ear was restored.

Malchus stood, staring at his bloody hand. Mark was astonished. *This must be a dream!*

Jesus spoke to the mob. "Have you come out, as against a robber, with swords and clubs to take Me? I was daily with you in the temple teaching, and you did not seize Me. But the Scriptures must be fulfilled."

The detachment of troops and the captain and the officers of the Jews arrested Jesus and bound Him. Mark watched intently to see what Peter would do, and his mouth fell open when the fisherman backed away and fled with James and John. The three raced to their compatriots, and all the disciples ran off into the darkness. Surely Peter would plot with them and return to again defend his Master.

Jesus was left utterly devoid of friends, His only acquaintance the one who had betrayed Him with a kiss. Mark's heart seemed to burst for this Man of whom Peter had spoken so highly. How could Peter defend Him with the sword one minute and run in the next?

Mark didn't know what had gotten into him, but as the throng surrounded Jesus and led Him back toward the city, he moved out of hiding and followed them, his thin linen garment his only shield against the night. What he hoped to accomplish he had no idea, but it certainly seemed wrong to abandon one's friend.

Somehow Mark had missed that a few soldiers had been dispatched to track the disciples, and having failed, now returned. "You there!" one said, as they closed on him. Mark, young and fast, panicked and ran, knowing he could elude them if only he could avoid their grasp.

One grabbed the edge of his garment just as Mark was gaining speed, and the man's yank turned the boy in a circle. Another clutched his tunic at the neck. Mark imagined himself dragged before the magistrates, and while he was not one of Jesus' disciples, nor could he fathom any fault being brought against him, he would then have to face his own mother. How would he explain where he had been and what he had been doing?

He thrashed and spun and kept running, his garment ripped entirely from his body. And as he leapt the stone wall naked, he heard the soldiers laugh and one say, "Let him go! He's just a child!"

Mark stayed in the shadows, trembling and frantic that no one see him. He had never been naked outside his own home, and with all the tourists and pilgrims milling about the city gates, he had no idea where to go. Cowering in a shallow ditch not a hundred yards from the eastern gate, he watched as the procession of soldiers and Jewish leaders led Jesus toward the city. He squinted in the darkness at familiar forms, wondering if it was possible that Peter and John followed at a distance.

Mark didn't know where James or the other eight were, but he thrilled to the possibility that Peter and John had not abandoned Jesus after all. Oh, that they would defend their Teacher! He crept toward the city wall, madly searching for something, anything with which to cover himself. Just as he heard a group of laughing men and women approach, Mark came upon a pile of refuse with dogs yammering about. He pulled a huge expanse of scratchy wool from a mound of rags and quickly wrapped himself.

Immediately the uncomfortable material at least blocked the cold wind, and while the covering was twice as large as he needed, Mark was grateful to finally be dressed. He tied the excess in a bulky knot behind him and hurried to follow the soldiers and Jesus. Sure enough, trailing at a distance crept Peter and John, keeping out of sight of those accompanying Jesus. The procession attracted the attention of many crowding the gate.

As the soldiers and leaders arrived at the courtyard of the high priest, they were allowed in one at a time by a young woman who guarded the door. She turned away many she apparently did not recognize. Peter stayed back when she greeted John by name and held the door open for him.

It appeared to Mark that John was at first unaware that Peter had been left outside. He returned and spoke to the girl, pointing at Peter. "He is with me."

As she allowed Peter in, the servant girl said, "You are not also one of this Man's disciples, are you?"

Mark was crestfallen when Peter said, "I am not." It was all he could do to choke back tears as the fisherman he so admired showed such cowardice.

Mark elbowed his way through the crowd and peered through the gate as the servants and officers built a fire of coals. How he wished he could join them and warm himself. Peter stood among them, rubbing his hands over the fire.

The curious crowd pressed Mark up against the bars of the gate as the high priest asked Jesus about His disciples and His doctrine. Jesus said, "I spoke openly to the world. I always taught in synagogues and in the temple, where the Jews always meet. I have said nothing in secret, so why do you ask Me? Ask those who have heard Me. They know what I said."

One of the officers slapped Jesus hard. "Do You answer the high priest like that?"

Jesus said, "If I have spoken evil, tell me; but if I have spoken the truth, why do you strike Me?"

Mark's attention was turned back to Peter when someone said, "Say, you are not also one of His disciples, are you?"

"I am not!" he said, cursing. Mark covered his mouth as sobs invaded his throat. How could such a brave, robust, honorable man so coarsely and blatantly lie?

A servant of the high priest leaned close and studied Peter's face. "That was my cousin whose ear you cut off! Did I not see you in the garden with Him?"

"I know nothing of what you speak," Peter said, again swearing. "You are mistaken."

And immediately a rooster crowed.

Mark could take no more. He dared not be out any later, for if his mother awakened to find him gone, she would be terribly vexed. Bitterly disappointed, he set off toward home, running the whole way with tears coursing down his face.

He had heard Jesus speak of Himself as the Son of God, finger His own betrayer before the betrayal, pray to His Father, and restore a man's destroyed ear. Surely He had to be who His disciples and Mark's mother believed He was. How then could His friends desert Him? And what would become of Him? Mark had so admired Peter. And now he didn't ever want to see the man again.

FOUR

Breathless and still weeping, Mark quieted himself as he slipped into his room and quickly shed the woolen covering. He replaced it with a nightshirt and curled up on his mat. But the lad did not even try to close his eyes. He should have been drowsy, exhausted even. But he was able to comprehend nothing of what he had seen this fateful night, and his mind whirled.

Mark knew his mother would sense that something deeply troubled him. What would he tell her at daybreak? Dare he tell about Peter? Was it fair to influence his mother's thinking about a friend? And yet it was the truth! Peter had proven a coward and a liar.

Mark was not aware of finally having drifted off, but at the crack of dawn he roused, still sick in his soul. He smelled breakfast cooking and knew his mother would be up. She never slept while her servants were working. He could not imagine eating, but knew he should and that his mother would likely insist on it.

When he returned from relieving himself, Mark found her in his room. She looked worse than he felt. "I have bad news for you," she said. "Jesus has been arrested and faces sentencing today."

Mark fought to hold his tongue but failed. "Where did you hear this?"

"A messenger arrived this morning. Jesus' disciples are asking if they may hide out in our upper room."

"Hide out? What are they afraid of?"

"The Romans and the Pharisees, of course."

The young man sank onto his cot and sighed. "Why are they not standing with Him, testifying for Him, defending Him?"

"And how do you know they are not?"

"You said yourself they seek a hiding place."

His mother's gaze had fallen upon his woolen covering, bunched up in the corner. She raised it and spread it wide. "What is this?" she said. "And where is your tunic from yesterday?"

"Oh, Mother!" Mark said, dissolving into tears. He held his head in his hands as he recounted the events from the night before. "I know you must punish me for being away without your knowledge. But I felt I just had to."

His mother turned ashen, her lips quivering as she sat next to him. "You were foolhardy," she said in a monotone, her eyes far away. "But I am grateful you are safe."

Had she heard a word he'd said? And when she returned to herself, would he still be punished? His transgression seemed inconsequential compared with what he had reported.

"I confess I would have been hard-pressed to keep from following them myself," she said.

"Verily?" he said.

His mother nodded. "And Jesus foretold all that happened?"

"Yes! Mother, I would not have believed it had I not seen and heard it for myself! And Peter! I hate him!"

His mother's gaze returned to him. She laid a shaky hand on his. "You mustn't be so hard on him. Put yourself in his place."

"I wish I could! If I believed in Jesus the way he claims to, I would never have forsaken Him!"

She seemed to study him until he had to look away. "May you forever retain such passion. I would like to believe I too would have stood by my Lord."

"Mother, when Peter denied knowing Jesus, he was so angry he cursed. I hope he—"

She held up a hand and shook her head. "I cannot imagine his fear."

"Fear is right. I have lost all respect for him."

Mark stood and gathered the scratchy covering, bundling it to discard it. "I don't care to ever see him again, let alone speak to him."

"Jesus must be our concern now, son. But remember, Peter is your elder, due your respect."

"Respect for what? Cowardice? Disloyalty?"

"You maintain he should not have deserted his friend."

"Of course!"

"And yet you are doing the same to him."

"But Jesus did not deserve what Peter did to him!"

She stood and embraced the boy and he was struck that her frail frame seemed to shudder uncontrollably. "And if I were you," she said, "I would take care not to put myself in a position to say who deserves your wrath."

Mark's mother was called away by a servant with news that some of the disciples had arrived. Mark was hardly in a mood to see them, for fear that Peter might be among them and he would be unable to hide his disgust. He busied himself with chores, only to learn that Peter was not among the few who soon sat retelling his mother everything of the night before.

To Mark, John was the only disciple not worthy of reproof, and indeed he heard from a servant that John was still in the city. More than once Mark had heard John referred to as the disciple Jesus loved, and now he could see why.

Soon Mark's curiosity got the better of him and he made his way to the great room, where James, the son of Zebedee and brother of John, was telling his mother more of the story. The four who had accompanied him looked pale and stunned, as if still afraid and uncertain about their future.

"In the early morning they bound the Teacher and led Him from the high priest Caiaphas's to the Praetorium to face Governor Pilate. It seemed all the chief priests and elders of the people were plotting to put Jesus to death."

"To death?" Mark's mother said, covering her mouth. "Whatever for?"

"They claim all kinds of charges, from blasphemy to insurrection—crimes against the Jews *and* the Romans. The chief priests and all the council sought testimony against Jesus to put Him to death, but found none, because while many bore false witness against Him, their testimonies did not agree. But some rose up and said, 'We heard Him say, "I will destroy this temple made with hands, and within three days I will build another made without hands." ' But not even then did their testimony agree.

"The high priest himself asked Jesus, 'Do You answer nothing? What is it these men testify against You?' But Jesus kept silent. Again the high priest asked Him, 'Are You the Christ, the Son of the Blessed?'

"Jesus said, 'I am. And you will see the Son of Man sitting at the right hand of the Power, and coming with the clouds of heaven.' "

"He said that?" Mark's mother said, eyes wide.

"He did. And the high priest tore his own clothes and said, 'What further need do we have of witnesses? You have heard the blasphemy! What do you think?' And they all condemned Him to be deserving of death. Some spat on Him and others blindfolded Him and beat Him, saying, 'Prophesy!' "

Mark's mother stared at the floor and shook her head. "And what has become of Judas?"

The disciples looked at one another, and Bartholomew spoke. "Word is that he tried to return to the chief priests and elders his payment, saying, 'I have sinned by betraying innocent blood.' They would have none of it and said, 'What is that to us? You see to it!' Some say he threw the coins in the temple and went and hanged himself."

"Oh, no!"

"Madam," Thomas said, "the man betrayed our Lord for thirty pieces of silver."

Mary spied her son in the corner. "Mark, I'd rather you not hear all this."

"I could have seen it all last night!" he said. "Nothing could shock me now! To have seen Peter deny Jesus with curses . . ."

James held up a hand. "Mark, my brother assures me that Peter is abject with sorrow and remorse. We must be sympathetic and—"

"Sympathetic! He *should* be abject!"

"Son, like all of us, he fears for his life."

"John doesn't!"

"But John and I know the high priest, Mark. That is the only reason he and I were able to move about freely in that company."

"So John was there the whole night?"

"He is still there, son."

"And?"

"He reports that as the Master stood before the governor, Pilate asked Him directly, 'Are You the King of the Jews?' "

"Did Jesus deny it?" Mark said. "I would wager He is not afraid for His life."

"You are correct. Jesus said, 'It is as you say.' "

"That's courage!" Mark said.

"Indeed. And it is why we put our trust in the Lord, and not in mere men. While Jesus was being accused of all manner of sin by the chief priests and elders, He answered nothing more. Pilate said, 'Do You not hear how many things they testify against You?' But He answered him not one word, so that the governor marveled greatly."

"What does Pilate care about this discord among the Jews?" Mark's mother said. "Why does he not just return to Caesarea and leave us to our own troubles?"

"I'm sure he would prefer nothing more. But the people cried out for Jesus' execution. Then Pilate entered the Praetorium again, called Jesus, and said to Him, 'Are You the King of the Jews?'

"Jesus said, 'Are you speaking for yourself about this, or did others tell you this?'

"Pilate said, 'Am I a Jew? Your own nation and the chief priests have delivered You to me. What have You done?'

"Jesus said, 'My kingdom is not of this world. If My kingdom were of this world, My servants would fight so that I should not be delivered to the Jews; but now My kingdom is not from here.' "

Mark was stunned to remember that Jesus had predicted His friends would not defend Him. "Tell me the rest."

"Pilate said, 'Are You a king then?'

"Jesus said, 'You say rightly that I am a king. For this cause I was born, and for this cause I have come into the world, that I should bear witness to the truth. Everyone who is of the truth hears My voice.'

"Pilate said, 'What is truth?' And he went out again to the Jews and said, 'I find no fault in Him at all.' "

"So why didn't he let Jesus go?"

James glanced at the others. "As you know, at the feast the governor is accustomed to releasing to the multitude one prisoner whom they wish."

"Had you all been there," Mark said, "you could have insisted it be Jesus."

"Did *anyone* call for His release?" his mother said.

James looked away. "You are familiar with Barabbas?"

"Of course," she said. "The notorious prisoner. Surely the people did not—"

"They did, ma'am. Pilate said, 'Whom do you want me to release to you? Barabbas, or Jesus, who is called Christ?' I believe he knew they had handed Him over because of envy. But somehow the chief priests and elders persuaded the multitudes that they should ask for Barabbas and destroy Jesus. They cried out, 'Release Barabbas!'

"Pilate said, 'What then shall I do with Jesus?'

"They all said, 'Let Him be crucified!'

"The governor said, 'Why, what evil has He done?'

"But they cried out all the more, saying, 'Let Him be crucified!'

"Finally Pilate shrugged and took water and washed his hands before the multitude, saying, 'I am innocent of the blood of this just Person. You see to it.'

"The people responded, 'His blood be on us and on our children!' "

Thomas and Bartholomew leaned to peer out the window as others arrived. "The other James and Peter," Thomas said, and Mark stood and rushed from the room before they were welcomed. But he could not force himself far enough away to be unable to hear their account. Indeed, Peter sounded like a defeated man.

"Tell us," John's brother said.

Peter recited the latest news in a flat tone, and Mark found himself angrier with the man than before.

"After Pilate released Barabbas to the crowd—and to much cheering, I might add—he scourged Jesus and delivered Him to be crucified."

"And what did you do about that?" Mark demanded, reentering.

Peter looked up, stricken. "What could I do?" he said, voice thick with emotion. "The soldiers took Jesus into the Praetorium and gathered the whole garrison around Him. They stripped Him and put a scarlet robe on Him."

"Peter, please," Mark's mother said. "Not in front of the boy."

"He denied his friend in front of me, Mother! Do you think this could be worse? I want to hear it all!"

Peter hung his head. "It's true. I denied my Lord three times, just as He said I would. I am ashamed unto death."

"And yet it is not you who are to die, is it?" Mark said.

Peter shook his head miserably. John's brother put a hand on his shoulder. "We must hear the rest, Simon."

Peter cleared his throat, his voice now weak and raspy. "They twisted a crown from thorns and pressed it on His head, putting a reed in His right hand. And they bowed before Him and mocked Him, saying, 'Hail, King of the Jews!' They spat on Him and took the reed and struck Him on the head. And when they had mocked Him, they took the robe off Him, put His own clothes on Him, and led Him away."

"To be crucified?" Mark said.

Peter nodded, still averting his eyes. "As they dragged him out, they found a man of Cyrene—some said his name was also Simon—and compelled him to bear Jesus' cross. They were on their way to Golgotha, the Place of a Skull, when we fled."

"You fled yet again," Mark said, tears streaming. "You might as well have been the one carrying His cross! Who is with Him now? Anyone who cares for Him?"

Peter rubbed his face. "John is there, with Jesus' mother and Mary of Magdala. And several women from Galilee."

"I must go!" Mark's mother said, standing. "Someone take me!"

But the disciples sat unmoving.

"Is my son right? Are you all cowards? I shall go myself then!" She grabbed a shawl and ran from the house.

"None of you?" Mark said, glaring at them. "Hide in the upper room then! Learn from John, the youngest among you, and from the women, what has become of your Teacher, your Master, your Lord."

And he ran to escort his mother to the place of death, less than half a mile to the north of their home.

When he caught her just past Herod's Palace, she stopped and turned to face him. "Only you," she said, seeming to grasp what he had been trying to tell her about the disciples and their weakness.

"Only me, and I will not be turned away."

"You are a man today, Mark, but I will allow you to come only on your solemn promise that you keep your distance. The authorities do not care about me, but men who go there will be subject to arrest."

"I am not afraid."

She looked at him with such earnestness that he could not look away or deny her. "Your solemn promise, John Mark."

"I promise."

FIVE

When Mark and Mary reached the awful plateau, a crowd had gathered, and Mark knew he could mingle without being detected. But when they came to the edge of the scene, his mother turned to him. "No farther."

He nodded and watched her proceed directly to John and to Jesus' mother and the other women—including John's mother. They huddled a distance from where three crosses lay in the dust. The women embraced and consoled one another. Mark was so proud of John and his courage.

It was about nine in the morning when two other condemned men were nailed to their crosses and raised to where they would die. Jesus cried out when the spikes pierced His flesh and His cross was raised and then sunk with a thud into the earth between the two. Horrified and repulsed, Mark did not know where he found the fortitude to watch, and yet he could not turn away.

As the Teacher hung there, gasping, chest heaving, shoulders straining to pull Himself high enough for each breath, one of the guards leaned a crude ladder against the cross and mounted it, nailing above His head the accusation against Him: THIS IS JESUS THE KING OF THE JEWS.

Jesus peered down at His mother. "Woman," He said, "behold your son!" He turned to John. "Behold your mother!"

Many who watched blasphemed Him, wagging their heads and saying, "You who destroy the temple and build it in three days, save Yourself! If You are the Son of God, come down from the cross!"

Even the rulers in the crowd called out, "He saved others; let Him save Himself if He is the Christ, the chosen of God."

The soldiers also mocked Him, saying, "If You are the King of the Jews, save Yourself."

Jesus said, "Father, forgive them, for they do not know what they do."

Mark, fists clenched, jaw set, trembled with rage as the chief priests mocked Jesus right with the scribes and elders, "He saved others; Himself He cannot save. If He is the King of Israel, let Him now come down from the cross, and we will believe Him. He trusted in God; let God deliver Him now if He will have Him; for He said, 'I am the Son of God.' "

Even the robber hanging on one side of Him reviled Him. "If You are the Christ, save Yourself and us."

The other said, "Do you not even fear God, seeing you are under the same condemnation? And we indeed justly, for we receive the due reward of our deeds; but this Man has done nothing wrong." He said to Jesus, "Lord, remember me when You come into Your kingdom."

Jesus said, "Assuredly, I say to you, today you will be with Me in Paradise."

As Mark stood sobbing, desperate to do something, imagining sacrificing himself to charge the soldiers and try to lead others to pull Jesus from the death tree, darkness as of the night settled over all the land. He had promised his mother, and he could not leave her without a loved one. Mark pulled his cloak tight around his neck and shivered, straining to see, somehow compelled to know when Jesus breathed his last. This was all beyond his comprehension, more than he could fathom. He remained there three hours, which seemed like twelve, and at about noon Jesus cried out with a loud voice, "My God, My God, why have You forsaken Me?"

And all Mark could think was that it was not His Father who had forsaken Jesus, but His friends. One had betrayed Him, one had denied Him, nine more had abandoned Him, and one faithful friend remained.

"I thirst!" Jesus cried.

Someone ran and found a sponge, soaked it with something, and put it on a reed, offering it up to Him. But Jesus turned away and cried out again with a loud voice, "It is finished! Father, into Your hands I commit My spirit." And He fell silent and still.

Mark dropped to his knees, burying his face in his hands. What was he to make of this horror? What had Jesus done but heal the sick and raise the dead? He had taught and thrilled people with news of the coming kingdom and of heaven. Were the skeptics right? If He was truly the Son of God, could He not have defeated all these who would destroy Him and avoided this gruesome death?

Just as Mark was pleading with God to show Himself, the ground shook and threw him flat, legs and arms spread wide, trying to hold on as the earth rolled and roiled. Massive rocks and boulders split, resounding like thunder.

Mark struggled to his feet and peered over the crowd to the crosses, where a centurion and his men fought to stay mounted on horses that stamped and reared. The centurion cried out, "Truly this was the Son of God!"

The entire crowd now appeared terrified and began beating their chests and streaming away. John and Mary and all Jesus' acquaintances remained at a distance, watching, but they covered their eyes when soldiers came and broke the legs of the criminals on either side of Him. When the soldiers came to Jesus they seemed to determine that He was already dead, so they did not break His legs. But one of the soldiers pierced His side with a spear, and blood and water poured out.

As the crowd disappeared, all who were left were the soldiers and the women with John, who remained until evening. Mark stayed behind them, out of his mother's sight, for fear she would insist he return home. They seemed to be talking among themselves about what to do next when a horse and wagon arrived, bearing a man John greeted warmly. It was Joseph of Arimathea. He had surreptitiously met with Jesus and the disciples at Mark's home more than once. Word was that he was a member of the Jewish council but a secret follower of Jesus—secretly for fear of the Jews.

"I asked the governor to be entrusted with the body," he said, and produced a document he showed to the guards. A centurion confirmed it bore the seal of Pilate, and Joseph was allowed to lower the body of Jesus. As the women wailed, Joseph carefully wrapped Him in a clean linen cloth and bore Him slowly to a nearby garden cemetery. Mary Magdalene and another Mary—not John's mother—followed, with Mark far behind.

Soon another man arrived, Nicodemus, a ruler of the Jews, bearing about a hundred pounds of myrrh and aloes. He and Joseph packed the spices around the body and rewrapped Jesus with strips of cloth. They then dressed him in a white burial robe and laid the body in a tomb Joseph said had recently been hewn out of the rock for his own family.

The two Marys asked Joseph if they could observe the tomb and how His body was laid, then said they were going to prepare spices and fragrant oils with which they would anoint Him following the Sabbath.

Joseph and Nicodemus squatted at the base of a colossal stone that lay in a slanted trough just above the opening of the tomb. A wood chock kept it from rolling down. They pressed their full weight against it and were able to budge it an inch or so off the chock so Nicodemus could kick the wood out of the way. They quickly stepped away from the stone, and it rolled in front of the door.

The two men grimly departed.

THE WALK BACK TO his home was the longest of Mark's life. He had not eaten all day, and yet he felt not a pang of hunger. Upon his arrival his mother had a servant wash his feet. She embraced him, weeping, but he was uncertain whether he would ever shed tears again.

He nodded toward the upper room. "Are they there?"

"Yes," she said, "but please don't go up. As you can imagine, they are heartbroken."

"Guilty is what they are."

"They feel it too, Mark. Your reproach will accomplish nothing."

He went to his room, eager to confront Jesus' so-called friends—especially Peter. But he also grieved with them and for them. For whatever mistakes they had made, Mark could not doubt their bereavement. These men had committed their very lives to the Teacher, at least up until He needed them most.

Restless, Mark finally mounted the steps, not knowing what he would say or do. As he reached the top, rather than show himself, he sat just outside the door where he had sat just the night before. All he heard was weeping and groaning and the sobbing of full-grown men. Their despair reached his heart in spite of everything, and he could no longer corral his own tears.

So much for the Messiah and the coming kingdom. All was lost.

. . .

THE NEXT DAY, the Sabbath, was the worst Mark could imagine. Even the servants seemed subdued as they cooked and delivered meals to him and his mother and the disciples. Mark felt sick to his very bones, and yet his mother persuaded him to eat so as not to make things worse. When finally he forced down some olives and then grapes, his appetite—and his imagination—was stirred. As he ate, something drew him to the tomb.

About an hour after sundown, Mark asked his mother if she wanted to go with him. "It's truly quite a beautiful spot," he said.

"Maybe in time," she said. "Just now I cannot bring myself to go. The pain is too fresh."

Mark recalled that it had taken some time for her to visit even his father's grave. "Do you mind if I go? I will not tarry long."

"Please don't. I will worry after you."

"Don't go, or don't tarry?"

"You may go. But please, return swiftly."

MARK TOOK HIS HEAVIEST cloak and ventured out. While it felt good to be away from the morose atmosphere at home, every step through the city brought back memories of the horrifying events that filled the last several hours.

Mark was stunned to enter the area of the garden tomb and see through the branches of the olive trees flames from torches in front of the grave. As he drew nearer, he heard men talking. Peering into the clearing he discovered Roman soldiers arrayed before the heavy stone Joseph and Nicodemus had rolled in front of the opening.

Some of the men stood at the ready, but most milled about, looking bored. Something about how they carried themselves made Mark approach them without fear. He stepped into the clear and pretended to be younger than his sixteen years. He idly found a pebble, which he threw far above the trees.

"Hey, there!" he called to the soldiers, pitching his voice higher than normal and waving.

Some smiled at him. Most ignored him. He moved closer. "What are you doing?"

"Just following orders," one said. "Guarding the tomb."

Mark scowled as if deeply puzzled. "Why guard a tomb? Keeping people out, or keeping someone in?"

The guard laughed. "We wondered the same. Truth is, somebody reminded the governor that this character predicted he would rise from the dead after three days. Pilate wants to make sure his friends don't come and steal his body, then claim he arose. We even sealed the stone with heavy wax and the governor's mark. We'll know if anyone tries to budge it. It would take several men to move it from that decline."

Mark found a spot to sit where he could dangle his legs.

"You want to be a soldier when you grow up?" the guard said.

"I don't know. Maybe."

Sure, that's exactly what a Jewish boy wanted to become. A Roman soldier.

Mark couldn't bring himself to tell his mother what he had seen. No doubt she would see this as a desecration of the grave. Fortunately, the soldier had made it clear that this duty was to last only three days, so by the time his mother did feel up to visiting, the men guarding the tomb would be gone.

The lad did not know what to make of the governor's fear that someone would claim Jesus had risen from the dead. He lay back on his cot that night, as miserable as he had ever been. This was worse than the death of his father, which, while tragic and unfair, had plainly been an accident. Mark covered his eyes with the heels of his hands and pleaded with God to somehow comfort his heart and help him understand all that had come to pass. Had Jesus really been the Son of God? And if so, how was it that God had allowed Him to be slain by mere men?

Above him Mark heard the slow plodding of the disciples. Voices were muffled, and there was not one sound of a psalm or hymn. What was to become of these men? Would they all return to their homes in Galilee and their former occupations?

They seemed paralyzed with grief, but even worse, fear. That still angered Mark, but he could hardly blame them. Most were recognizable. They all could be identified by someone as a follower of Jesus, who was now seen as a rabble-rouser, a rebel, a troublemaker for both the Jews and the Romans. If He had been deemed worthy of execution, what about them?

The disciples themselves had made no claims of deity, but Jesus had told both the high priest and the governor himself that they had correctly deduced that He was a king.

And what would become of John Mark? Just a few days before, he had allowed himself to imagine growing older, maturing, becoming an adult friend of Peter and the disciples and, yes, even Jesus Himself. Now his future seemed bleak and foreboding.

Very late that night Mark roused at the sound of John returning. John asked a servant to awaken Mark's mother, and apologized profusely.

"Not at all, sir," she said, appearing pale and shaken. "What is it, John?"

He reported that the other women were attending Jesus' mother, "allowing me to return to the disciples. But Mary of Magdala wants to visit the tomb in the morning. I wondered if you would care to join her. I cannot bear the idea of going."

"Nor can I," Mark's mother said. "Unless she would otherwise be alone."

"No, others have agreed to go and help anoint the body."

"Then I would beg your pardon and prefer not to."

"I understand."

And with that, John bade her leave and mounted the stairs to the upper room. Mark could tell that the rest were gathering to hear the latest from John. Mark thought about the Roman guards at the tomb. Surely the women would be troubled to discover them there. He set out his sandals and tunic and cloak, planning to go along and help talk the guards into breaking the seal on the stone and allowing the women in. Would the guard he had talked to recognize him and suspect him of having been sympathetic to the condemned?

Mark drifted off, confident that going was the right thing.

SIX

"They won't believe us!"

"I hardly believe it myself!"

"I *don't* believe it!"

"But they were angels!"

Mark's eyes popped open at the sound of the excited women's voices. They flew past his window and lifted their skirts as they raced up the stairs. And he realized he had slept past dawn and missed his opportunity to go with them to the tomb.

What could they hardly believe, and what was that about angels? Whatever it was, they felt it justified racing straight to the upper room without even announcing themselves to the mistress of the house. Now they were rapping at the door above, and Mark heard murmuring and footsteps. He grabbed his cloak and slung it over his shoulders as he too headed upstairs.

By the time he arrived, the disciples—plus several of their greater company from Galilee who had come for Passover—were covering themselves and rubbing their eyes, seeming overwhelmed by Mary of Magdala, another Mary, and several others.

"What is it?" Peter said.

John, the last to rouse, squinted at the women as he approached, pulling on his sandals. They all seemed to talk at once until John held up a hand. "Please, please," he said. "Sit and tell us all that has happened."

The others looked to Mary Magdalene. "I hardly know where to begin," she said, "and if we hadn't seen it with our own eyes, we would not believe it ourselves. We went to the sepulcher just before dawn with our spices and oils, prepared to anoint Jesus' body but wondering whether—even with all of us working together—we could roll away the huge stone. We arrived to find it already rolled away."

"Oh, no!" a disciple said. "What more can these people do to us, to Him?"

"Was the body still there?" someone else said.

Mary Magdalene took a deep breath. "We entered the tomb to see and were met there by two angels who—"

"Angels!" Peter roared. "How do you know they were angels and not grave robbers? They could have been—"

The women shook their heads, and Mary of Magdala said, "Their countenance was like lightning and their raiment white as snow. We were scared speechless and hid our faces, but these men actually spoke to us!"

"They spoke? What did they say?"

The women all began to talk again, but finally Mary silenced the others. "They told us not to be afraid and that they knew we sought Jesus, who was crucified."

"You're dreaming," someone said. "Why defile our memory of the Lord with fanciful tales?"

"Let me speak," Mary said.

"Yes, let her finish!" John said.

"One of the angels said, 'He is not here, for He has risen, as He said. Remember how He told you when you were yet in Galilee that the Son of Man must be delivered into the hands of sinful men and be crucified, but the third day would rise again. Behold the place where they laid Him.' We looked, and He was not there."

"Nonsense!"

"Foolishness!"

"Believe it or not at your own peril," Mary said, "but the angels told us to come and tell you that you would soon see Him."

"Idle tales!" someone raged, but Mark noticed Peter and John lock eyes. Then they burst from the room and flew down the stairs.

Mark turned to follow them but ran into his own mother. How much had she heard? Apparently enough to know that she didn't want him following Peter and John. No matter how much he pleaded, she was resolute. "Son, you will stay right here with me until they return with a report."

Mary Magdalene, however, slipped away alone and headed from the house.

MARK'S MOTHER INSISTED that he and the servants prepare breakfast and serve everyone while waiting for John and Peter to return. It was all Mark could do to concentrate, but he had to admit he found himself agreeing with the disciples who chose not to believe the women's report. He didn't know what to think. He wanted to believe this, but it was so far-fetched! But could they all have conspired on such a tale, deluded by their grief and hope? Had Jesus predicted His own resurrection? And if so, why couldn't Mark believe it any more than His friends chose to?

As they sat eating in the upper room, it was clear the other women were offended by the men's skepticism. And yet it did not seem to dampen their enthusiasm. Mark made sure he stayed close enough to hear them recite over and over the astounding events of the early dawn.

Presently a servant stood in the doorway. "The men have returned!"

As one, those in the upper room rose, and Peter and John stomped up the stairs. Peter proved mute due to breathlessness. John, gasping and grinning ear to ear, held up a hand for silence.

"It's true, beloved! It's true!"

Peter, catching his breath, gushed, "The youngster beat me to the tomb, but I ducked in ahead of him. The grave clothes remain intact, but the body is gone!"

"Are you sure?"

"I say He is risen!" John said.

"We don't know that," Peter said.

"Did you see angels too?"

"Can it be?"

One of the women asked if either of the men had seen Mary of Magdala.

"We thought she was here," Peter said.

So the women left to search for her.

As the disciples talked excitedly among themselves, Mary Magdalene arrived and stood in the doorway at the top of the stairs. The men fell silent and stared at her.

"I saw the Lord," she said, barely above a whisper.

Thomas rushed to her and helped her sit. "What? Tell us everything!"

"I was crying outside the tomb, fearing we had all been mistaken and that someone had taken Jesus' body. But as I stooped to look into the tomb, the angels were still there—one on each end of where He had lain—and they asked why I was weeping. I said, 'Because they have taken my Lord, and I know not where they have laid Him.'

"I backed away and turned to see a man I assumed to be the gardener standing there. He said, 'Woman, why are you weeping? Whom are you seeking?'

"I said, 'Sir, if You have carried Him away, tell me where You have laid Him, and I will take Him away.' "

Mary stopped and pressed her lips together, fighting tears. "Then He said to me, 'Mary!' and I knew. I said, 'Teacher!' He told me not to cling to Him, for He had not yet ascended to the Father, but He said, 'Go to My brethren and say to them, "I am ascending to My Father and your Father, and to My God and your God." ' "

Mark had never seen anyone so radiant as Mary. John had been excited, thrilled to find the empty tomb. Peter still seemed to doubt. But Mary said she had talked with Jesus! Mark wanted to believe her so badly.

Just then the other women who had been at the tomb arrived with a similar story. "Jesus met us on the road," they said. "He told us to rejoice! We fell and held His feet and worshiped Him. He said, 'Do not be afraid,' and told us to tell you that you will soon see Him too."

THE REST OF THE DAY was spent reviewing all the accounts, the eleven disciples and many of their associates from Galilee arguing among themselves how much could be believed and what should be discounted. Many ventured out, hoping to see Jesus, but most of the eleven, fearing they would be recognized, stayed in the upper room.

Late that evening, all those who were closest to Jesus—save Thomas—sat around the table, eating and trying to make sense of the day's events. There was a knock on the door, and two of the Galileans entered with haste.

"We must tell you what happened!" one named Cleopas said. "We were walking the seven miles to Emmaus—conversing and wondering aloud about all that has happened—when a man drew near and walked with us. We did not know him. He said, 'What kind of conversation is this that you are sad?'

"I said, 'Are You the only stranger in Jerusalem and know not the things which have happened?'

"He said, 'What things?'

"I said, 'The things concerning Jesus of Nazareth, who was a Prophet mighty in deed and word before God and all the people, and how the chief priests and our rulers delivered Him to be condemned to death, and crucified Him.' I told him we had been hoping that it was He who would redeem Israel, but that it had already been three days since these things happened. I added that certain women of our company, who arrived at the tomb early, astonished us with their report that they did not find His body, but that they had also seen a vision of angels who said He was alive. I told him that certain of those with us went to the tomb and found it just as the women had said, but that they did not see Jesus.

"And then, gentlemen, this stranger said, 'O foolish ones, and slow of heart to believe in all that the prophets have spoken! Ought not the Christ to have suffered these things and to enter into His glory?' And beginning at Moses and all the Prophets, he expounded to us all the Scriptures concerning the Christ.

"When we drew near to Emmaus we begged that he abide with us, for it was toward evening and the day was far spent. And he stayed with us and sat at the table with us. My friends, when he took the bread and blessed it and broke it and gave it to us, our eyes were opened and we knew Him. It was the Lord. And He soon vanished from before our very eyes.

"We said to one another, 'Did not our hearts burn within us while

He talked with us on the road, and while He opened the Scriptures to us?' We rose up immediately and rushed here to tell you, the Lord is risen indeed!"

It had to be true, Mark thought. It just had to be. And yet he could tell from the looks of the disciples that even they weren't sure. But as they all sat pondering, suddenly Jesus Himself stood in the midst of them and said, "Peace to you."

Mark froze, terrified that he was seeing a spirit.

Jesus said, "Why are you troubled? And why do doubts arise in your hearts? Behold My hands and My feet, that it is I Myself. Handle Me and see, for a spirit does not have flesh and bones as you clearly see I have."

He showed them His hands and His feet, but Mark sat like all the rest, overjoyed but still finding it hard to believe. And Jesus said, "Have you any food here?"

John immediately rose and gave Him a piece of a broiled fish and some honeycomb, and He ate. Mark noticed Peter, pale and wide-eyed, and yet appearing afraid to meet Jesus' gaze. Everyone else just stared, unmoving.

"These are the words I spoke to you while I was still with you," Jesus said, "that all things must be fulfilled which were written in the Law of Moses and the Prophets and the Psalms concerning Me. As the Father has sent Me, I also send you." And He breathed on them and said, "Receive the Holy Spirit. If you forgive the sins of any, they are forgiven them; if you retain the sins of any, they are retained."

And Jesus disappeared from their midst.

Soon Thomas arrived.

"We have seen the Lord!" the others told him.

He looked warily at them and shook his head. "Unless I see in His hands the print of the nails, and put my finger into the print of the nails, and put my hand into His side, I will not believe."

Mark was at first nearly as disappointed in Thomas as he had been with Peter. But he had to admit that even he would not have been able to take the word of these men and women he knew and admired and trusted. Had he not seen the risen Jesus with his own eyes, neither would he have believed it.

SEVEN

For the next week the excited disciples didn't dare venture far from Mark's mother's home. Jerusalem abounded with rumors and danger, and much of the disciples' time was spent planning their return to Galilee. Mark, unknown to the authorities as an associate of the crucified Jesus, ran errands with the servants, buying foodstuffs and taking care of the disciples' needs. His heart was full to bursting, since he himself had seen the risen Jesus and knew he could never again be dissuaded from believing.

EIGHT DAYS AFTER JESUS had appeared to them in the upper room, the disciples were again inside, this time with Thomas present. With the door shut, Jesus once again appeared in their midst and said, "Peace to you!"

He said to Thomas, "Reach your finger here, and look at My hands; and reach your hand here, and put it into My side. Do not be unbelieving, but believing."

Thomas, clearly overcome, fell to his knees and said, "My Lord and my God!"

Jesus said, "Thomas, because you have seen Me, you have believed. Blessed are those who have not seen and yet have believed."

And again He was gone.

THE DISCIPLES FINALLY packed up and stole away to Galilee in the middle of a balmy night, and Mark felt terribly alone. Many evenings he sat up with his mother, pondering over what had happened during the previous several days. His spirit had been so invigorated that he found it almost impossible to sleep. He had become a believer in Jesus the Christ, and yet he had no idea what that meant for his future.

"This has made everything I do seem wholly insignificant," Mark said.

"Oh, on the contrary," his mother said. "I should think it would make you want to study all the more and be prepared to live for God as never before."

"But reading ancient texts and memorizing seems so mundane and boring. I want to be a disciple. Why don't they tell the world what they know of Jesus, that they saw Him risen, and that He truly is the Son of God?"

"You would do that?"

"I would love to!"

"But didn't the Lord Himself tell them to remain in Jerusalem until it was time to return to Galilee and see Him again, where they would be endued with power? Perhaps that is a prerequisite to their telling anyone of Him."

"I wish I were older, like Joses. Then I would travel with the disciples." Mark's cousin Joses had moved to Israel when he reached adulthood.

"I am glad you are not. I need you here."

Mark grew thoughtful. "What of Peter?" he said.

"What do you mean?"

"He denied the Lord, but then saw Him alive. Yet Peter seemed to hide from Him."

"Wouldn't you, Mark? When he and John saw the empty tomb, John believed. Peter withheld judgment until he saw the Lord with his own eyes."

"If I were him, I would want to plead for the Lord's forgiveness."

"I'm sure Jesus knows his heart."

"Mother, you must let me go to Galilee. How can I miss what is to come?"

"I will do nothing of the sort. You have already been exposed to much more than anyone your age should be. It is time for you to continue to study and learn and grow, preparing yourself for whatever God might have in mind for your adulthood."

Mark could think of little worse. He prayed more than ever, and he did apply himself seriously to his studies—but then he always had. Daily he listened for any news from Galilee about the disciples or about Jesus, but all he heard were the claims of the Roman guards who swore they had fallen asleep and that Jesus' friends had stolen His body.

FINALLY, forty days after Jesus' resurrection, the day came when Mark's mother interrupted his studying to tell him he had a visitor.

"Who?"

"Listen to me, John Mark. It is Peter. Now, don't look at me that way. His feet are being washed as we speak, and I want you to hear him out. The disciples are back from Jerusalem, but he came here first, expressly to see you and talk to you. Give him the benefit of the doubt, will you?"

Mark wasn't sure he could, but he promised to try.

Peter greeted him with an embrace that Mark barely returned. The fisherman asked if they could speak privately, then led Mark to the upper room.

"Amazing things were shared here, were they not?" Peter said.

Mark nodded. "I shall never forget."

"Nor I. Son," Peter said, pointing to a bench, "please sit and hear me. I am deeply troubled in my spirit about the impression I left on you."

Mark could only nod.

"I can only imagine what you thought of me after we had become so close. Or had I misunderstood our esteem for each other? I certainly more than held you in high regard, son."

"I treasured our friendship," Mark managed, unable to look at the man. "But—"

"However disappointed you were in me, multiply it a hundredfold and imagine what I thought of myself. When the Lord said I would deny Him, I would have bet my life I would not have. I believed in Him and loved Him with my whole heart, and yet I let fear for my own life rule me."

"Have you been able to apologize to Him?"

"I have. Let me tell you what has happened since last we saw you. As you know, the Lord told us to return to Galilee, but when we arrived, we didn't know what we were to do. I have never been one for sitting around. So one day when I was with Thomas, Nathanael, the brothers James and John, and a couple of the others, I decided that while we waited, I would go fishing on the Sea of Galilee. The rest seemed to like that idea, so we went out and immediately climbed into a small boat. We fished the rest of the day and all that whole night, but we caught nothing."

"Nothing?"

"Not one fish, can you imagine? Fishermen we were, but we failed miserably! We even joked about being so out of practice, but soon it became serious. We had not even caught anything to eat. Well, when the first light of the sun appeared on the horizon, I saw a man on the shore. He called out to us the strangest question. He said, 'Children, have you any food?' Can you imagine, calling grown men children? We told him we had caught no fish. And he said, 'Cast the net on the right side of the boat, and you will find some.'

"Let me tell you the truth, John Mark: I followed his suggestion on a lark. Do you think we veterans of the sea had not cast on both sides of the boat all night? Of course we had. But to humor the stranger, and because certainly nothing else had worked, I supervised the casting of the nets on the right side.

"Oh, son, I wish you had been there with us! The multitude of fish was so great we could not, even all seven of us, draw the nets back in! I tore off my cloak, and we pulled and strained and laughed at our good fortune. Then I noticed John studying the shore. He said, 'Peter, it is the Lord!'

"Was it possible? I had not recognized Him or His voice, but how I had missed Him and longed to see Him! I threw on my cloak and leapt overboard, splashing and swimming until I could touch bottom, then slogging the rest of the way—about two hundred cubits—to the shore. The others arrived in the boat, dragging the net with all those fish.

"They could see as well as I that Jesus had started a fire of coals with fish and bread already cooking. He said, 'Bring some of which you have just caught.' I went and helped drag the net to land, and do you know, Mark, we counted one hundred fifty-three large fish, and yet our net was not broken.

"Jesus said, 'Come and eat breakfast,' yet none of us dared ask Him who He was, though we knew it was the Lord. This was the third time

Jesus showed Himself to us after He was raised from the dead. He took the bread and gave it to us, and likewise the fish."

Mark just sat shaking his head.

"Now, son, let me tell you what happened when we had finished eating. I had wanted to embrace Jesus and to fall on my face before Him, pleading His pardon for my egregious sin. But He turned to me and said, 'Simon, son of Jonah, do you love Me more than these?'

"Why, I was so overjoyed to be asked that I said, 'Yes, Lord, You know that I love You.'

"And He said, 'Feed My lambs.'

"Then, a second time He said to me, 'Simon, son of Jonah, do you love Me?'

"I said, 'Yes, Lord. You know that I love You.'

"He said to me, 'Tend My sheep.'

"And yet a third time, He said, 'Simon, son of Jonah, do you love Me?'

"Mark, by now I was grieved because He had asked me three times. I cried, 'Lord, You know all things; You know that I love You.'

"Jesus said to me, 'Feed My sheep. Most assuredly, I say to you, when you were younger, you girded yourself and walked where you wished; but when you are old, you will stretch out your hands, and another will gird you and carry you where you do not wish. Follow Me.'

"Mark, I was puzzled. When I was old another would gird me and carry me where I did not wish? That made me wonder about John, and I said, 'But Lord, what about this man?'

"Jesus made it clear to me that John's future was none of my business. He said, 'If I will that he remain till I come, what is that to you? You follow Me.' "

"What do you make of the conversation?" Mark said. "Did you feel He had forgiven you?"

Peter nodded. "All I know is that I denied Him thrice, and thrice He asked me to affirm that I loved Him. And I do."

"Where is He now, sir?"

"He has returned to the Father. But not before He left us with His power and His charge. A few days later—just yesterday, in fact—Jesus told us to meet Him again on the Mount of Olives. When all eleven of us saw Him, we worshiped Him, but some still seemed to be doubting."

"After all this?"

"As I have often said, Mark, we are but mere men. But it was there that He commanded us not to depart from Jerusalem, but to wait for the promise of the Father, 'which,' He said, 'you have heard from Me; for John truly baptized with water, but you shall be baptized with the Holy Spirit not many days from now.' "

"What does that mean, Peter, baptized with the Holy Spirit?"

"Well, we don't know yet, do we? Believe me, I will let you know. While we were with Him, we asked if He was about to restore the kingdom to Israel."

"That's what everyone who believed Him to be the Promised One has been wondering. What did He say?"

"He told us it was not for us to know times or seasons, which He implied were under the purview of the Father. But He said, 'You shall receive power when the Holy Spirit has come upon you; and you shall be witnesses to Me in Jerusalem, and in all Judea and Samaria, and to the end of the earth. All authority has been given to Me in heaven and on earth. Go therefore and make disciples of all the nations, baptizing them in the name of the Father and of the Son and of the Holy Spirit, teaching them to observe all things that I have commanded you. He who believes and is baptized will be saved; but he who does not believe will be condemned.'

"And it was then that He seemed to open our understanding so that we might be able to comprehend as never before the truth of the Holy Scriptures. Our eyes were opened, and He said, 'Thus it is written, and thus it was necessary for the Christ to suffer and to rise from the dead the third day, and that repentance and remission of sins should be preached in His name to all nations, beginning at Jerusalem. And you are witnesses of these things.'

"He then lifted His hands and blessed us, saying, 'Lo, I am with you always, even to the end of the age.'

"While we watched, He was taken up, and a cloud received Him out of our sight. And while we were staring toward heaven as He went up, two men appeared in white apparel, saying, 'Men of Galilee, why do you stand gazing up into heaven? This same Jesus, who was taken up from you into heaven, will so come in like manner as you saw Him go into heaven.'

"We returned straightaway with great joy the half-mile journey to Jerusalem. Your mother has again graciously invited us to lodge in the upper room, but daily we will be continually in the temple, praising and blessing God."

"And you do not fear the authorities?"

Peter smiled and stood, putting a hand on Mark's shoulder. "Tell me, young one: had you experienced what we have, would you fear any man?"

EIGHT

As Mark accompanied Peter to the portal of his home to bid him adieu, the lad had to admit to himself that, yes, had he been through what Peter and the others had, he would not likely ever feel fear again. But what intrigued him most about Peter's account was Jesus' reference to the remission of sins. If anyone needed that, Mark did. And his daily Scripture readings referred to it constantly.

Peter hesitated, plainly with something on his mind.

"John Mark," he said, "this evening the other disciples and I will return here for a season with much business to attend to. We greatly anticipate—with some consternation, of course—this spiritual baptism the Lord referenced. But, son, you and I will be seeing much of each other again, and I would that we might repair the friendship we once enjoyed. I know I disappointed you. I failed you and of course the Master, and—"

"You need say no more, sir. I confess I was disillusioned, but I don't know whence came the foolish idea that I might have acted any differently under the circumstances. That the Lord Himself appears to have forgiven you and assigned you to minister to people in His name, well, that is more than enough for me."

"I covet the respect I once felt from you, John Mark."

"That you have, sir."

And they embraced.

LATER THAT DAY Peter returned to the upper room with James, John, and Andrew; Philip and Thomas; Bartholomew and Matthew; James the son of Alphaeus and Simon the Zealot; and Judas the son of James. Not long later arrived several of the women from Galilee, plus Mary the mother of Jesus, along with His brothers.

While Mark and his mother and their servants slipped in and out with refreshments, the disciples and their friends continued with one accord in prayer and supplication. Mark was most impressed by the earnestness and devotion of these and continually told his mother how privileged he felt—and believed she should feel—that God had entrusted them with the hospitality of these special people.

That evening John Mark's own studies took on entirely new meaning for him. "Mother," he said, "suddenly I am being led to passages and prophecies that all seem to speak of Messiah. And it is clear they all refer to Jesus."

"You should tell Peter. He once confided to me that he wished you would teach him, as he is uneducated but very curious about the Scriptures."

For the next few days, whenever Peter had a spare moment, Mark showed him what he was studying and answered many questions. Peter read slower than Mark, so the lad tried to teach him as much as he knew about each passage. Like Mark, Peter was most intrigued by references to the Messiah. But the boy could not bring himself to ask about the remission of sins. He didn't want Peter to think less of him.

A FEW DAYS LATER Peter informed Mark and his mother that he would like to invite more than a hundred clandestine believers to join those already meeting in the upper room. "Not to lodge here, of course, Mary, but to meet with us on some important matters."

"Well, certainly," she said. "Mark and the servants can stock up on supplies, and—"

"We wish not to be a burden, friend. They will not be with us long."

The next day about a hundred twenty crowded the upper room, and Mark and his mother were welcomed to sit in. Peter, who seemed to have been reinstated by the disciples to his natural place of leadership, stood in the midst of the throng and said, "Men and brethren, this Scripture had to be fulfilled, which the Holy Spirit spoke before by the mouth of David concerning Judas, who became a guide to those who arrested Jesus; for he was numbered with us and obtained a part in this ministry: (Now this man purchased a field with the wages of iniquity; and falling headlong, he burst open in the middle and all his entrails gushed out. And the field where Judas killed himself has already become known to all dwelling in Jerusalem as the Field of Blood.) It is written in the book of Psalms: *'Let his dwelling place be desolate, and let no one live in it'*; and, *'Let another take his office.'* "

This last caused much murmuring among the assembled, and Peter continued. "Therefore, of these men who have accompanied us all the time that the Lord Jesus went in and out among us, beginning from the baptism of John to that day when He was taken up from us, one of these must become a witness with us of His resurrection."

The gathered proposed two names: Joseph called Barsabas, who was surnamed Justus, and Matthias. Peter led them in prayer, saying, "You, O Lord, who know the hearts of all, show which of these two You have chosen to take part in this ministry and apostleship from which Judas by transgression fell, that he might go to his own place."

The disciples cast lots, and the lot fell on Matthias. And so he became the twelfth apostle.

TEN DAYS AFTER JESUS had ascended into Heaven and thus fifty days since Passover, the time came for the Jewish celebration of the Feast of Weeks or Harvest, also known as Pentecost. It followed Passover by "seven weeks of weeks," or forty-nine days. This fiftieth day signified one of three annual feast days, during which the entire nation of Israel was to come to Jerusalem.

Mark loved all the ceremonial feast days, for Jerusalem came alive with pilgrims from all over Asia and Israel—including his cousin Joses, now a grown man with curly hair and a full beard. Most exciting to Mark was that the disciples were again joined by the hundred twenty or so, and Peter announced that they would be meeting the next morning in a building not far from the temple.

Mark pleaded with both his mother and Peter to be allowed to attend, and while his mother left it up to Peter, the latter informed Mark that the meeting involved "private matters." Mark was disappointed, but through messengers, he and Joses agreed to meet near the temple. At least Mark would be in the city, for he found it impossible to stay far from Peter and John and the rest of the disciples.

While searching for Joses he kept in sight the building where the disciples were meeting. All those who joined them seemed to display the same resolve in their countenances, and Mark was struck that—as Peter often said—they seemed of one accord.

About an hour later the entire assemblage poured out of the meeting room and down the stairs into the crowded city. To a man and woman, they beamed, and they all seemed to be speaking in different languages. What was this?

Mark rushed to Peter. "What is going on?"

The apostle could barely contain himself. "While we were praying and singing, suddenly there came a sound from the sky like a mighty wind, and it filled the entire place! There appeared atop each of our heads divided tongues as of fire. Immediately we all began to speak with other tongues, as the Spirit gave us utterance. John Mark, you know I am not an educated man, and yet I too have been blessed with this ability!"

Mark noticed that the milling crowds from every nation were confused, because they seemed to hear this group speak in their own languages.

They marveled, saying to one another, "Look, are not all these who speak Galileans? And how is it that we hear, each in our own language in which we were born?"

Peter said, "Look! Parthians and Medes and Elamites, those from Mesopotamia, Judea and Cappadocia, Pontus and Asia, Phrygia and Pamphylia, Egypt and the parts of Libya adjoining Cyrene, visitors from Rome, both Jews and proselytes, Cretans and Arabs—they all hear us speaking in their own tongues of the wonderful works of God!"

All looked amazed and perplexed, saying to one another, "Whatever could this mean?" Others, mocking, said, "They must be full of new wine."

But Peter, standing up with the eleven, raised his voice and said,

"Men of Judea and all who dwell in Jerusalem, let this be known to you, and heed my words. For these are not drunk, as you suppose, since it is only nine o'clock in the morning! But this is what was spoken by the prophet Joel: *'And it shall come to pass in the last days, says God, that I will pour out of My Spirit on all flesh; your sons and your daughters shall prophesy, your young men shall see visions, your old men shall dream dreams. And on My menservants and on My maidservants I will pour out My Spirit in those days; and they shall prophesy. I will show wonders in heaven above and signs in the earth beneath: Blood and fire and vapor of smoke. The sun shall be turned into darkness, and the moon into blood, before the coming of the great and awesome day of the Lord. And it shall come to pass that whoever calls on the name of the Lord shall be saved.'* "

Mark was so proud of Peter he feared he would burst. They had only recently come across this passage, and now Peter was able to quote it from memory, and all around were able to understand him, apparently in their own languages. Who was this man who had so fearfully denied his Lord and now boldly proclaimed the truth about Him?

"Men of Israel," Peter cried out, "hear these words: Jesus of Nazareth, a Man attested by God to you by miracles, wonders, and signs which God did through Him in your midst, as you yourselves also know—Him, being delivered by the determined purpose and foreknowledge of God, you have taken by lawless hands, have crucified, and put to death; whom God raised up, having loosed the pains of death, because it was not possible that He should be held by it.

"For David says concerning Him: *'I foresaw the Lord always before my face, for He is at my right hand, that I may not be shaken. Therefore my heart rejoiced, and my tongue was glad; moreover my flesh also will rest in hope. For You will not leave my soul in Hades, nor will You allow Your Holy One to see corruption. You have made known to me the ways of life; You will make me full of joy in Your presence.'*

"Men and brethren, let me speak freely to you of the patriarch David, that he is both dead and buried, and his tomb is with us to this day. Therefore, being a prophet, and knowing that God had sworn with an oath to him that of the fruit of his body, according to the flesh, He would raise up the Christ to sit on his throne, he, foreseeing this, spoke concerning the resurrection of the Christ, that His soul was not left in Hades, nor did His flesh see corruption.

"This Jesus God has raised up, of which we are all witnesses. Therefore being exalted to the right hand of God, and having received from the Father the promise of the Holy Spirit, He poured out this which you now see and hear. For David did not ascend into the heavens, but he says himself: *'The Lord said to my Lord, "Sit at My right hand, till I make Your enemies Your footstool."'*

"Therefore let all the house of Israel know assuredly that God has made this Jesus, whom you crucified, both Lord and Christ."

More quoting of the Scriptures! And as Mark watched, astonished, the crowd appeared troubled and cut to the heart. They approached Peter and the rest of the apostles and said, "Men and brethren, what shall we do?"

Peter said, "Repent, and let every one of you be baptized in the name of Jesus Christ for the remission of sins; and you shall receive the gift of the Holy Spirit. For the promise is to you and to your children, and to all who are afar off, as many as the Lord our God will call."

With many other words he testified and exhorted them, saying, "Be saved from this perverse generation."

Mark wanted above all this remission of sins, forgiveness, and the Holy Spirit. He could not keep from joining the throng that crowded around Peter and the rest, lining up to repent and be baptized. He had long considered himself a secret believer in the Christ, of course, but now he wanted everyone to know he was counting himself among all the souls who were added to this new church that day.

And while Mark milled about with all these new believers in

Christ—Peter would inform him later that they numbered three thousand—who should appear in the crowd but his cousin Joses, in his Levite garb, taller and thinner since Mark had last seen him. Joses embraced Mark and exulted that he too had become a believer in Christ.

For the next several days the new Christians excitedly assembled with the disciples for teaching in doctrine, for fellowship, for the breaking of bread, and for prayer. Joses quickly established himself with the disciples as devout and sincere, and—like Mark—a student of the Scriptures.

Many wonders and signs were done through the apostles, and all who believed shared with one another all that they owned as anyone had need. Every day they met in the temple and broke bread from house to house, eating with gladness and what Peter told Mark appeared to be simplicity of heart, praising God.

Most impressive was that these people were so happy, they didn't initially even run into trouble with Jewish leaders or the Romans. They seemed to have favor with all.

Daily Joses and Mark met in the city and wondered at the power of God that had been showered upon the apostles for the bold proclamation of the truth of Christ.

And every day more were saved and added to the church.

NINE

Mark felt free, forgiven, filled; he suddenly found himself immersed in the things of God. Joses stayed with him and his mother for several days, and the cousins enjoyed following the disciples all over the city and seeing and hearing what was going on. They spent their evenings poring over ancient texts and marveling at how the Scriptures were replete with references to the Messiah.

Joses seemed unable to quit grinning. "How can anyone doubt that Jesus fulfills all the prophecies of the Chosen One?" he said.

Because Joses was there, Mark's mother was less concerned about Mark being away from home and in the middle of everything going on in the city. "The authorities must be up in arms," she said, "with so many becoming Christians."

"Not so far," her nephew said. "Everyone seems so happy and joyous that the religious leaders and the Romans probably see no reason to interfere."

It seemed that every day, Peter took one or more of the disciples with him to the temple for one of three prayer times—at nine in the morning, noon, and three in the afternoon. One day Mark and Joses followed as Peter and John approached the temple for the three o'clock session. As they watched, a lame beggar at the temple's Beautiful Gate sat pleading for alms from all who entered. Mark had seen this man, who appeared to be in his early forties, in the same spot every day for his entire life and recalled that when he was a child, his mother lectured him about not staring at the man's gnarled feet and grotesquely malformed ankles.

Seeing Peter and John, the man whined, "Please, sirs, for a humble man, crippled from birth . . ."

The disciples stopped, and Peter stooped to gaze at the man. "Look at us," Peter said.

The beggar's face lit and he reached for whatever Peter and John would offer.

But Peter said, "Silver and gold I do not have, but what I do have I give you: In the name of Jesus Christ of Nazareth, rise up and walk."

And with that Peter took the man by the hand and lifted him. As Mark watched, the man's feet and ankles were immediately restored, and he leapt up and walked into the temple with them.

"Praise God!" he cried. "Praise God!"

Instantly a crowd pressed in, people murmuring and amazed. "It's the one who sat begging alms at the gate of the temple!" they called out, and first hundreds, then thousands gathered to see. The healed man clung to Peter and John, and as they moved onto Solomon's Porch, Mark and Joses found themselves in the middle of a massive crowd that pointed and cheered, clearly stunned.

Peter extended his arms to quiet them. "Men of Israel, why do you marvel at this? Or why look so intently at us, as though by our own power or godliness we had made this man walk? The God of Abraham, Isaac, and Jacob, the God of our fathers, glorified His Servant Jesus, whom you delivered up in the presence of Pilate, though he was determined to let Him go. But you denied the Holy One and the Just, and asked for a murderer to be granted to you, and killed the Prince of life, whom God raised from the dead, of which we are witnesses. And it is faith in His name that has made this man strong. Yes, the faith which comes through Jesus has given him this perfect soundness in the presence of all of you.

"Yet now, brethren, I know that you did this to Jesus in ignorance, as did also your rulers. But those things God foretold through His prophets, that the Christ would suffer, He has thus fulfilled. Repent therefore and be converted, that your sins may be blotted out, so that times of refreshing may come from the presence of the Lord, and that He may send Jesus Christ, who was preached to you before. For Moses truly said to the fathers, *'The Lord your God will raise up for you a Prophet like me from your brethren. Him you shall hear in all things, whatever He says to you. And it shall be that every soul who will not hear that Prophet shall be utterly destroyed from among the people.'*

"Yes, all the prophets from Samuel and those who follow foretold these days. You are sons of the prophets and of the covenant God made with our fathers, saying to Abraham, *'And in your seed all the families of the earth shall be blessed.'* To you first, God, having raised up His Servant Jesus, sent Him to bless you, in turning away every one of you from your iniquities."

Again Mark was amazed that this was the same man who had been so fearful at the time of the arrest of Jesus. This weak, very human fisherman now seemed to speak with the very authority of God. But what was this? Here came the priests, the captain of the temple, and the Sadducees!

"Stop! Stop!" they shouted, stepping in front of Peter and John. "Dare you teach the people that in Jesus there is resurrection from the dead?"

"Let them speak!" the crowd roared. "We believe! We believe!"

And as the officials grabbed Peter and John and hauled them away, many who heard believed. As Mark watched, others of the disciples began working their way through the crowds, which by now had grown to many thousands, and began praying with new believers.

"Mark," Joses said, "there must be five thousand men alone here who have become believers!"

That night in the upper room the remaining disciples prayed for Peter and John and their announced public trial the next day. Mark's mother was troubled. "You and Joses will tell me everything that happens tomorrow, will you not?"

Wild animals could not have kept Mark away. What could the authorities do to such bold men who were clearly acting under the power of God and seeing thousands join their number daily?

The next day Mark made sure that he and Joses were there early when the rulers, elders, and scribes, as well as Annas the high priest, Caiaphas, and the family of the high priest gathered and set Peter and John in their midst. Not far away, Mark noticed, the healed beggar stood tall and beamed.

The authorities demanded of Peter and John, "By what power or by what name have you done this?"

Mark looked at Joses, who raised his brows. The question could not have been more perfect if Peter himself had written it! Peter, his voice ringing out, said, "Rulers of the people and elders of Israel, if we this day are judged for a good deed done to a helpless man, by which he was made well, let it be known to you all, and to all the people of Israel, that this man stands here before you whole by the name of Jesus Christ of Nazareth, whom you crucified and whom God raised from the dead. He is, as the Scriptures say, the *'stone which was rejected by you builders, which has become the chief cornerstone.'* Nor is there salvation in any other, for there is no other name under heaven given among men by which we must be saved."

The authorities looked dumbfounded, scowling, squinting, and shaking their heads. Mark heard one mutter, "Are these not uneducated and untrained men? But what can we say when the man who has been healed stands right there?"

"Leave us to confer!" the high priest said, and Peter and John and the healed man, along with the crowd, moved away.

Moments later the rulers called them back in. The high priest cleared his throat. "Gentlemen, that a notable miracle has been done through you is evident to all who dwell in Jerusalem, and we cannot deny it. But we deduce that spreading such further among the people would accomplish no good purpose. Therefore, by the power vested in us, we command you in the name of God not to speak at all nor teach in the name of Jesus."

What? Mark wondered what possible bad thing could come of a miracle of healing.

Peter said, "Whether it is right in the sight of God to listen to you more than to God, you judge. For we cannot but speak the things which we have seen and heard."

The crowd roared, glorifying God because of the disciples and what they had done. It was clear the rulers were concerned about such support, but the high priest quieted them. "You have our ruling. Now you may go, but you must obey or dire consequences will result."

Peter and John were immediately surrounded by the other ten disciples, and many of the other more than a hundred from Galilee, plus Mark and Joses, pressed close. John led them all back to the upper room at Mark's home, then led them in prayer, saying, "Lord, You are God, who made heaven and earth and the sea, and all that is in them, who by the mouth of Your servant David have said, '*Why did the nations rage, and the people plot vain things? The kings of the earth took their stand, and the rulers were gathered together against the Lord and against His Christ.'*

"For truly against Your holy Servant Jesus, whom You anointed, both Herod and Pontius Pilate, with the Gentiles and the people of Israel, were gathered together to do whatever Your hand and Your purpose determined before to be done. Now, Lord, look on their threats, and grant to Your servants that with all boldness we may speak Your word, by stretching out Your hand to heal, and that signs and wonders may be done through the name of Your holy Servant Jesus."

When they had prayed, the upper room began to shake, and Mark felt power surge through him. He realized that all had experienced the same, and they rose from their knees filled with the Holy Spirit and eager to speak the word of God with boldness. They immediately took to the streets of Jerusalem again and began preaching the Word of God and the salvation of Christ.

Enthusiastic believers appeared again to support and encourage them, and multitudes more who believed seemed of one heart and one soul. As if they had all thought of it at once—though Mark knew God had put it in their hearts—everyone began to exclaim that nothing they possessed was their own, but that everything they owned should be shared in common.

Joses said, "Mark, I want to sell my land and give the proceeds to the disciples and their ministry."

Mark laughed, wondering if his mother would let him do the same with their estate.

Over the next several days the apostles gave witness to the resurrection of the Lord Jesus with great power, and grace was upon them all. Everyone knew the authorities had to be concerned, but for a time the Christians were protected, nor was anyone among them lacking. All who possessed lands or houses sold them and brought the proceeds and laid them at the apostles' feet, and they distributed to each as anyone had need. Peter informed Mark's mother that she had, in essence, already given her property to the Lord for the apostles' use, and so she should not trouble herself by trying to sell it.

When Joses came forward with the proceeds from the sale of his land, Peter embraced him and said, "From henceforth, young man, we shall call you Barnabas, which is translated 'Son of Encouragement.' "

TEN

This new movement, a church based on the teachings of the resurrected Jesus, swept the city of Jerusalem and now threatened the city's way of life. Everyone had to wonder how long it would be permitted to flourish. Mark assumed the others, as excited and enthusiastic as he, had to have at the back of their minds the danger posed by the local rulers. Peter and John had been warned, and yet from that time until now, they had done entirely the opposite of what they had been commanded by the authorities.

Meanwhile, the disciples and their many followers moved back and forth between the upper room and the temple to pray three times a day. On their way there and back they preached boldly the message of the Christ. More and more became believers and gave the disciples everything they owned.

One afternoon, following the return to the upper room of the disciples and more than a hundred others, a man who identified himself as Ananias poured out a bag of cash at the apostles' feet.

"My wife Sapphira and I," he said, "have decided to give you all the proceeds of the sale of a parcel of our land."

"Bless you," someone said, but Mark perked up when Peter seemed to cloud over while counting the money.

The room fell silent when Peter suddenly said, "Ananias, why has Satan filled your heart to lie to the Holy Spirit and keep back part of the price of the land for yourself? Was the land not your own?"

"Of course it was! I—"

"And after the parcel was sold, was not the profit in your personal control?"

"Certainly!"

"Why have you conceived this thing in your heart? You have not lied to men but to God."

Ananias dropped to the floor and died.

Terror seemed to sweep the room as Mark and Joses (now called Barnabas) enlisted other young men to help them wrap the body and carry it out to be buried.

About three hours later, Ananias's wife trotted up the stairs, asking Mark in passing, "Is my husband here?"

Mark froze, and before he could answer, Peter lifted the money her husband had donated and said, "Sapphira, tell me, is this the amount for which you sold the land?"

"Yes," she said, looking puzzled. "Exactly."

Peter said, "How is it that you and your husband have agreed together to test the Spirit of the Lord? Look, those who buried your husband are at the door, and they will carry you out."

Immediately she fell at his feet and breathed her last.

Great fear came upon the church and all those who heard about this.

Meanwhile, the apostles performed many signs and wonders among the people every day in Solomon's Porch—healing the lame and the deaf and blind, indeed doing, as Jesus had prophesied, greater things even than He had done. The welcoming of new believers suddenly stopped, however, as it seemed everyone—though they respected the Christ followers—was scared of what the authorities might do. Still, multitudes of both men and women brought the sick out into the streets on beds and couches, many saying they hoped that even the shadow of Peter passing by might fall on them.

Barnabas began working more closely with the disciples, and Mark was proud of his cousin—though in his heart of hearts had to admit he was envious. He felt privileged to be a close friend of Peter, but the chief disciple had become so busy that it seemed Barnabas got more time with him than Mark did. Barnabas helped keep order when a multitude gathered from the cities surrounding Jerusalem, bringing the sick and those tormented by unclean spirits. Every one of them was healed.

Finally the day came when the high priest and the Sadducees had had enough. They rose up, filled with indignation, and threw the apostles in prison. Barnabas barely avoided arrest, and he and Mark ran back to the upper room, where Mark's mother and many of the other believers prayed fervently for the imprisoned.

In the morning word came that Peter and John and the others were teaching again at the temple! How had they gotten out of prison? Mark and Barnabas ran the whole way, only to find that the disciples reported that in the middle of the night an angel of the Lord opened the prison doors and brought them out, telling them, "Go, stand in the temple and speak to the people all the words of life."

Even as Mark stood there, mouth agape, word came that the high priest and those with him had called together the council and all the elders of the children of Israel, and had sent notice to the prison to have the disciples brought before them. But the officers returned and reported, "We found the prison shut securely and the guards standing before the doors, but we found no one inside!"

The high priest, the captain of the temple, and the chief priests huddled, apparently trying to decide what to do, when someone came and told them, "The men you put in prison are in the temple teaching the people!"

As the officers approached, Mark heard the captain command his charges to avoid violence, "unless you want the crowds to stone us."

Peter and John kept the peace, surrendering to the guards and keeping the people quiet. And when they had been brought before the council, the high priest said, "Did we not strictly command you not to teach in this name? And look, you have filled Jerusalem with your doctrine, and intend to bring this Man's blood on us!"

Mark had to fight to keep from shouting and cheering when Peter stood and said, "We ought to obey God rather than men. The God of our fathers raised up Jesus, whom you murdered by hanging on a tree. Him God has exalted to His right hand to be Prince and Savior, to give repentance to Israel and forgiveness of sins. We are His witnesses to these things, and so also is the Holy Spirit whom God has given to those who obey Him."

The council glared and reddened, and the high priest rose and shook his fist in the faces of the disciples. "You are bringing about your own deaths!"

But one from the council stood, the Pharisee Gamaliel, whom Mark recognized as Barnabas's former teacher of the law. He was held in wide respect. "I suggest we excuse these men for a moment while we deliberate further on this matter."

The disciples were held under guard outside, but Mark found a place where he could hear the discussion. Gamaliel said, "Men of Israel, take heed what you intend to do regarding these men. For some time ago Theudas rose up, claiming to be somebody. A number of men, about four hundred, joined him. He was slain, and all who obeyed him were scattered and came to nothing. After this man, Judas of Galilee rose up in the days of the census and drew away many people after him. He also perished, and all who obeyed him were dispersed. And now I say to you, keep away from these men and let them alone; for if this plan or this work is of men, it will come to nothing; but if it is of God, you cannot overthrow it—and you just may find yourselves fighting against God Himself."

The disciples were summoned back in, and the high priest ordered them savagely flogged thirty-nine times each. "I command you once again that you should never again speak in the name of Jesus!"

Mark was shaken by the violence done to his friends, but when they left the presence of the council, he found them rejoicing! "Peter, how can you be happy after what has come to pass?"

"I rejoice that we were counted worthy to suffer shame for Jesus' name."

Daily in the temple, and in many homes, they continued to teach and preach Jesus as the Christ.

IT WAS ONLY NATURAL that as the number of disciples was multiplying, conflict might arise among them. Mark found this hugely disappointing, but Barnabas reminded him, as Peter often had, that these were all mere men.

There arose a complaint against the Hebrews among them by those who spoke Greek, because, they said, the widows among their number were being neglected in the daily distribution of food. Peter and the other eleven summoned the multitude of the disciples to the upper room, and Peter said, "It does not make sense that we should leave the preaching and teaching of the word of God in order to serve food. Therefore, brethren, we suggest that you select from among you seven men of good reputation, full of the Holy Spirit and wisdom, whom we may appoint over this business. That way, it will fall to them to be certain everyone is fairly served, and we will be allowed to give ourselves continually to prayer and to the ministry of the word."

"I like that idea!" Barnabas said, and the entire body seemed pleased with it too.

Mark was impressed that the first man they chose was Stephen, a man Barnabas had been telling him was full of faith and the Holy Spirit. They also selected a man named Philip, along with five others they set before the apostles. When the disciples had prayed for them, they laid hands on these seven and blessed them for the work upon which they were to embark.

Immediately the word of God seemed to spread even more quickly, and the number of disciples multiplied greatly in Jerusalem. And Barnabas certainly proved right about Stephen. He was full of faith and power and performed great wonders and signs among the people.

"He is a man of the Scriptures," Barnabas said. "A devout and diligent student."

Soon, however, there arose some from what was called the Synagogue of the Freedmen (Cyrenians, Alexandrians, and those from Cilicia and Asia), who seemed jealous of Stephen. Mark had heard him preach and saw that these Freedmen were not able to counter his wisdom or the Spirit by which he spoke. Soon they had induced people to start spreading rumors about him, saying, "We have heard him speak blasphemous words against Moses and God."

It wasn't long before they stirred up the people, the elders, and the scribes, and they seized Stephen and brought him before the council.

Some swore testimony that he spoke "blasphemous words against this holy place and the law; we have heard him say that this Jesus of Nazareth will destroy this place and change the customs Moses delivered to us."

Mark was impressed that not only did Stephen not appear frightened, but his countenance also appeared to glow, as if he had the face of an angel.

The high priest demanded of him, "Are these things so?"

Stephen stood respectfully and spoke calmly. "Brethren and fathers, listen: The God of glory appeared to our father Abraham when he was in Mesopotamia, before he dwelt in Haran, and said to him, *'Get out of your country and from your relatives, and come to a land that I will show you.'* Then he came out of the land of the Chaldeans and dwelt in Haran. And from there, when his father was dead, He moved him to this land in which you now dwell. And God gave him no inheritance in it, not even enough to set his foot on. But even when Abraham had no child, God promised to give it to him for a possession, and to his descendants after him.

"But God spoke in this way: that his descendants would dwell in a foreign land, and that they would be brought into bondage and oppressed four hundred years. *'And the nation to whom they will be in bondage I will judge,'* said God, *'and after that they shall come out and serve Me in this place.'* Then He gave him the covenant of circumcision; and so Abraham begot Isaac and circumcised him on the eighth day; and Isaac begot Jacob, and Jacob begot the twelve patriarchs."

Barnabas seemed to gaze at Stephen with the same admiration and awe Mark felt at the man's obvious command of history and the ancient Scriptures.

Stephen continued, still in a conciliatory tone, "And the patriarchs, becoming envious, sold Joseph into Egypt. But God was with him and delivered him out of all his troubles, and gave him favor and wisdom in the presence of Pharaoh, king of Egypt; and he made him governor over Egypt and all his house.

"Now a famine and great trouble came over all the land of Egypt and Canaan, and our fathers found no sustenance. But when Jacob heard that there was grain in Egypt, he sent out our fathers first. And the second time Joseph was made known to his brothers, and Joseph's family became known to the Pharaoh. Then Joseph sent and called his father Jacob and all his relatives to him, seventy-five people.

"So Jacob went down to Egypt; and he died, he and our fathers. And they were carried back to Shechem and laid in the tomb that Abraham bought for a sum of money from the sons of Hamor, the father of Shechem."

This was a story Mark was familiar with from his studies, as were Barnabas and many among the multitude. Still, Stephen made it compelling, and Mark could only imagine that others were hearing it afresh as he was.

"But when the time of the promise drew near which God had sworn to Abraham, the people grew and multiplied in Egypt till another king arose, who did not know Joseph. This man dealt treacherously with our people, and oppressed our forefathers, making them expose their babies, so that they might not live.

"At this time Moses was born, and was well pleasing to God; and he was brought up in his father's house for three months. But when he was set out, Pharaoh's daughter took him away and brought him up as her own son. And Moses was learned in all the wisdom of the Egyptians, and was mighty in words and deeds.

"Now when he was forty years old, it came into his heart to visit his brethren, the children of Israel. And seeing one of them suffer wrong, he defended and avenged him who was oppressed, and struck down the

Egyptian. For he supposed that his brethren would have understood that God would deliver them by his hand, but they did not understand. And the next day he appeared to two of them as they were fighting, and tried to reconcile them, saying, 'Men, you are brethren; why do you wrong one another?'

"But he who did his neighbor wrong pushed him away, saying, *'Who made you a ruler and a judge over us? Do you want to kill me as you did the Egyptian yesterday?'*

"Then, at this saying, Moses fled and became a dweller in the land of Midian, where he had two sons. And when forty years had passed, an Angel of the Lord appeared to him in a flame of fire in a bush, in the wilderness of Mount Sinai.

"When Moses saw it, he marveled at the sight; and as he drew near to observe, the voice of the Lord came to him, saying, *'I am the God of your fathers—the God of Abraham, the God of Isaac, and the God of Jacob.'* And Moses trembled and dared not look. *'Then the Lord said to him, "Take your sandals off your feet, for the place where you stand is holy ground. I have surely seen the oppression of My people who are in Egypt; I have heard their groaning and have come down to deliver them. And now come, I will send you to Egypt." '*

"This Moses whom they rejected, asking him, *'Who made you a ruler and a judge?'* is the one God sent to be a ruler and a deliverer by the hand of the Angel who appeared to him in the bush. He brought them out, after he had shown wonders and signs in the land of Egypt, and in the Red Sea, and in the wilderness forty years.

"This is that Moses who said to the children of Israel, *'The Lord your God will raise up for you a Prophet like me from your brethren. Him you shall hear.'* "

More than a mere recitation, this history lesson clearly was headed toward a meaningful conclusion. Stephen, Mark decided, had become a gifted teacher and preacher.

"This is he who was in the congregation in the wilderness with the Angel who spoke to him on Mount Sinai, and with our fathers, the one who received the living oracles to give to us, whom our fathers would not obey, but rejected. And in their hearts they turned back to Egypt, saying to Aaron, *'Make us gods to go before us; as for this Moses who brought us out of the land of Egypt, we do not know what has become of him.'*

"And they made a calf in those days, offered sacrifices to the idol, and rejoiced in the works of their own hands. Then God turned and gave them up to worship the host of heaven, as it is written in the book of the Prophets:

" *'Did you offer Me slaughtered animals and sacrifices during forty years in the wilderness, O house of Israel? You also took up the tabernacle of Moloch, and the star of your god Remphan, images which you made to worship; and I will carry you away beyond Babylon.'*

"Our fathers had the tabernacle of witness in the wilderness, as He appointed, instructing Moses to make it according to the pattern that he had seen, which our fathers, having received it in turn, also brought with Joshua into the land possessed by the Gentiles, whom God drove out before the face of our fathers until the days of David, who found favor before God and asked to find a dwelling for the God of Jacob. But Solomon built Him a house.

"However, the Most High does not dwell in temples made with hands, as the prophet says:

" *'Heaven is My throne, and earth is My footstool. What house will you build for Me? says the Lord, or what is the place of My rest? Has My hand not made all these things?'* "

Suddenly the mild-mannered Stephen stared at his listeners and appeared stern. "You stiff-necked and uncircumcised in heart and ears!" he said. "You always resist the Holy Spirit; as your fathers did, so do you. Which of the prophets did your fathers not persecute? And they killed those who foretold the coming of the Just One, of whom you now have become the betrayers and murderers, who have received the law by the direction of angels and have not kept it."

It became clear that those listening were sorely offended. They gnashed their teeth and shook their fists at Stephen. But his countenance appeared angelic again as he gazed into the sky. "Look!" he said, "I see the heavens opened and the Son of Man standing at the right hand of God!"

The crowd covered their ears, then charged him, grabbing him and dragging him out of the city. Mark and Barnabas could only run along behind in terror as the men slung off their cloaks and left them at the feet of a young man among them and found stones to throw.

"Beware that man," Barnabas said, pointing out the one watching the cloaks. "We were classmates under Gamaliel. His name is Saul, and he is a brilliant scholar and a hater of Christians."

The mob hurled their rocks at Stephen as he was calling out, "Lord Jesus, receive my spirit." As he was driven to his knees by the blows, he cried with a loud voice, "Lord, do not charge them with this sin." And soon he was dead.

ELEVEN

Mark stared, speechless and terrified, at the still form of the beloved Stephen. Was this to become the price for being a bold follower of Jesus? Mark could not imagine fear as great as the day he saw the Master Himself put to death in the most gruesome Roman way. But to see an acquaintance, a beloved coworker, stoned to death before his very eyes, allowed him a glimpse of the fear Peter must have felt when Jesus was arrested.

As Mark and his cousin stole away in silence, Barnabas pointed at Saul, who was smiling and clapping his compatriots on the back while helping them into their cloaks. A wiry little nondescript man. What kind of a monster was he?

Peter assigned devout men to carry Stephen to his burial, where he was both eulogized and bitterly mourned. Mark wished he had gotten to know Stephen better. It was obvious he had endeared himself to the disciples, and had been a fearless warrior for the faith. His stoning ignited great persecution against the church at Jerusalem. Many of the new believers escaped throughout the regions of Judea and Samaria, but the apostles remained.

Though Saul had merely looked on as Stephen was stoned to death, he now seemed suddenly emboldened and began to wreak havoc. He led bands of marauders from door to door throughout Jerusalem, demanding to know whether Christ followers were within. All over the city he gained a name for himself among the rulers for hauling off men and women to prison.

The disciples and Barnabas and Mark received word from many who had been scattered that they had gone everywhere preaching the word. Philip had departed to the city of Samaria and preached Christ. Apparently multitudes agreed with everything he said when they witnessed the miracles he performed. He cast unclean spirits out of many, and others who had been paralyzed and lame were healed. Peter said he had been told of great joy in that city.

But Philip also reported to the apostles that a certain man named Simon, who had previously practiced sorcery and astonished the people of Samaria, had gained a following who claimed, "This man has the great power of God." But when Philip preached concerning the kingdom of God and Jesus Christ, both men and women were baptized, and this Simon also believed and was baptized. He began to follow Philip and was amazed at the miracles and signs.

The apostles at Jerusalem urged Peter and John to go to Samaria to pray for the new believers that they might receive the Holy Spirit. When they returned, Peter gave an account to Mark and Barnabas that they had laid hands on the people and that the people had received the Holy Spirit.

"But this Simon," Peter said, "the former sorcerer, offered us money, saying, 'Give me this power also, that anyone on whom I lay hands may receive the Holy Spirit.'

"I told him, 'Your money perish with you, because you thought that the gift of God could be purchased with money! Your heart is not right in the sight of God. Repent therefore of this your wickedness, and pray God that the thought of your heart may be forgiven you. I see that you are poisoned by bitterness and bound by iniquity.'

"And Simon said, 'Pray to the Lord for me, that none of the things which you have spoken may come upon me.' "

OVER THE NEXT FOUR years such accounts made Mark want to be a true disciple, traveling and spreading the Gospel, but his mother would have none of it. "You are still but twenty years old and have much to learn, and I need you here."

"But Barnabas wants to do the same. Let me go with him if he is assigned."

"No! He is older and can choose for himself whether this is the life for him. You have many years ahead of you."

After this Mark pulled Peter aside and confided in him, "One day I would love to go with you when you are out and about teaching and preaching the things of God."

"God may just call you to such a ministry," Peter said. "When you are older, of course."

"You sound like my mother."

Peter smiled and put a hand on Mark's shoulder. "A wise woman."

"What I really long to hear, Peter, are your memories of Jesus. I met him only months before He died, but you knew Him three years. What was it like, being with Him from when first He began performing great signs and wonders?"

Peter's eyes seemed far away. "The miracles were one thing," he said. "But the teaching . . . Our times together, just listening to Him tell us of God and of Heaven, of the kingdom."

"You must write all that, Peter. The world must know."

"We are telling more and more every day."

"But it must be recorded."

"Mark, you know I am not a man of letters. That work is for a scholar, which you are becoming."

"But the account must be directly from an eyewitness like yourself."

"There were many others."

"Then they should write too. If I were able to travel with you, I could help."

Peter returned his gaze and grinned. "Always conniving to get your way. I shall leave it to you to talk your mother into this scheme. I daresay she requires your presence here for a few more years. Anyway, before I become a historian, we have pressing duties with all these new believers, not to mention our most devoted opponent."

"Saul."

"Saul of Tarsus," Peter said. "He seems full of the devil, more determined than ever to destroy us and everything we believe and teach. And with the Jews and Romans behind him, he seems to have all the authority he needs. We have just learned that he is still threatening to murder all disciples of the Lord. Word is that he has gone to the high priest and asked for letters from him to the synagogues of Damascus, so that if he finds any Christian believers there, men or women, he might bring them bound to Jerusalem. We must pray for this man."

"Pray for him?" Mark said.

Peter seemed to study John Mark. "We don't get as much time together as we once did, do we?"

"I didn't think you noticed."

"I noticed. Of course I have been busier than ever, but frankly you have seemed more interested in the activity than in true devotion to the cause."

Mark was stunned. "I apologize if I have left that impression. It does not represent how I truly feel. I long to know more of the Master's teaching. But I know how busy you are."

Peter pointed to a bench inviting Mark to sit, and took a seat beside him.

"The Lord taught us to pray for our enemies, and I cannot think of anyone who better embodies that description than this Saul. Your cousin tells me the man was born a Jew and studied with him under Gamaliel to become a Pharisee. He has Roman blood on his father's side. In short, he is uniquely qualified to counter the work of Christ and seems utterly determined to do so."

"And yet we are to pray for him? I should think we ought to pray against him."

"Well, of course, we pray for protection *from* him and that his schemes will fail. But Jesus would tell us that God loves Saul in spite of his sins and that we ought to pray for his soul. Imagine him as a believer."

"Talk about a miracle!"

"No more so than you or I becoming followers of the Lord, John Mark. We are but—"

"Mere men, I know."

"Try it, son. Try praying for the enemy. Pray for Saul."

PHILIP AND MANY OF the others eventually returned to Jerusalem, where they preached the gospel in many villages of the Samaritans. One day Philip told Peter this story in Mark's hearing:

"An angel of the Lord spoke to me, saying, 'Arise and go toward the south along the road which goes down from Jerusalem to Gaza.' So I went to the desert, and behold, a man of Ethiopia, a eunuch of great authority under Candace, the queen of the Ethiopians, who had charge of all her treasury and had come to Jerusalem to worship, was returning in his chariot. The Spirit told me, 'Go near and overtake this chariot.'

"So I ran to him and heard him reading the prophet Isaiah. I said, 'Do you understand what you are reading?'

"He said, 'How can I, unless someone guides me?' And he invited me to sit with him. The Scripture he read was this:

" '*He was led as a sheep to the slaughter; and as a lamb before its shearer is silent, so He opened not His mouth. In His humiliation His justice was taken away, and who will declare His generation? For His life is taken from the earth.*'

"The eunuch said, 'I ask you, of whom does the prophet say this, of himself or of some other man?'

"Well, as you can imagine, beginning with that Scripture, I preached to him, explaining that the passage clearly refers to Jesus of Nazareth, the Son of God, who was slain for our sins.

"He was immediately persuaded, and as we traveled down the road, we came to a body of water. And the eunuch said, 'What hinders me from being baptized?'

"I told him, 'If you believe with all your heart, you may.'

"And he said, 'I believe that Jesus Christ is the Son of God.'

"After I baptized him and we came up out of the water, the Spirit of the Lord caught me away so that the eunuch saw me no more. The Lord brought me to Azotus, where I preached, likewise in all the cities till I came to Caesarea."

Mark marveled at this and many other dramatic stories of the miracles of God and the mighty acts of the apostles. He despaired over having to wait and burned with longing to travel with these great men of God.

THREE YEARS LATER

{ SEVEN YEARS SINCE THE CRUCIFIXION }

TWELVE

I just feel it, Mother," Mark said one evening after a rare quiet dinner with only her. He was now well into his twenties. "It's as if the Lord Himself is making it impossible for me to sit still. I simply have to get going and do the work the disciples are doing."

"John Mark, I am pleased that you seem so earnest in your faith, and you know I share your belief in Jesus as the Messiah. But though you are no longer young, you are nowhere near finishing your studies."

"Mother, few of the disciples are learned men. Their passion, and the Holy Spirit, seem all they need."

"They are men of age now. And they too would tell you to take care of your widowed mother awhile longer and continue to prepare yourself for a life of service."

Mark had wearied of the discussion, which always seemed to end where they had ended the last time. In truth he was frustrated that his eagerness alone could not sway his mother. But deep inside, he feared she was right. What if he got out there on a missionary trip and grew homesick? He couldn't imagine it, but he would then become a burden to the very men he admired and wanted to help.

Perhaps what bothered Mark most was that his cousin Joses, now known to all—even his aunt Mary—as Barnabas, had clearly been accepted by the others as a fellow disciple. His opinions were sought and valued. And, sure, he was an adult as they were, but Mark believed himself every bit as knowledgeable about the Scriptures as Barnabas. And while he had never been tested as a preacher or as an evangelist, neither had Barnabas. He detected jealousy in his own heart, but he believed his motive for wanting to join the disciples was pure.

Rhoda, a servant girl assigned to the front gate, interrupted Mark and his mother. "Master," she said, "your cousin approaches."

Mark hurried to welcome Barnabas and wash his feet.

"Is Peter here? And the others?"

"They are not," Mark said. "You seem to have news."

"It is your great fortune they are not here to hear it first," Barnabas said, eagerly accepting a large cup of water. "You will not believe what I have to tell you."

"Then don't delay."

"You know Saul?"

"Barnabas! We all know Saul, though he seems to have disappeared for years. What of him?"

"He has become a believer."

"A believer in what? Rome? He was already that."

"John Mark, if he is to be believed, he has become one of us, a follower of Christ."

"Impossible. I don't believe it."

"As I predicted you wouldn't. But never say anything is impossible. What kind of evangelists would we be if we believed that?"

"How do you know this? Where did you hear it? From his own lips?"

"No, I have never met him, but the news is spreading quickly that three years ago he went from persecuting Christians to preaching Christ. Word from Damascus and elsewhere is that he was holding forth in the synagogues there, arguing that Jesus is Christ, the Son of God and the Messiah. The Jews were confounded and were heard to say, 'Is this not he who destroyed those who called on this name in Jerusalem, and has come here for that purpose, so that he might bring them bound to the chief priests?' "

"Barnabas, if this is true, it is a miracle of God!"

"Of course it is. And I intend to find out for myself."

"How?"

"Rumor has it that he is on his way to Jerusalem to meet with Peter. I intend to intercept him and ask him for myself. If someone Peter trusts does not vouch for such a man, Peter would never agree to meet with him anyway."

"But if it is a false report, you will be in danger."

"John Mark, surely after all this time you know that we need fear no man."

NOT MANY DAYS LATER, when Peter and James were in the upper room, Barnabas arrived at Mark's door with Saul himself in tow. Though older, of course, he appeared as Mark had remembered him at the sight of Stephen's stoning—small, dark, and intense.

"I have heard much about you, John Mark," he said, "and I greet you in the name of Jesus the Christ."

Mark found himself cordial but noncommittal, and after the men had been offered water to drink and had their feet washed, he led them to the upper room. Saul did not seem surprised at the guarded response from Peter and James. They bade him sit, but neither offered a hearty greeting or even a smile.

"You were an accomplice to the stoning of our friend," James said.

Saul responded, "And many more you know not of, to my abject shame."

"What business brings you to us?" Peter said.

Barnabas interrupted. "This eloquent and learned man is more than capable of speaking for himself, but he is here under my sponsorship, since I believe that you should hear from his own mouth the story of his encounter with God."

"We see you as the enemy of God," Peter said.

"And that I was," Saul said, "the chiefest of sinners. But now I beg your indulgence."

Peter nodded, and Saul began.

"Three years ago you may know I was on my way to Damascus, intending to root out believers in Christ and have them arrested. As you well know, I had been successful in doing this here in Jerusalem, and I had the authority, from the Pharisees and the Romans, to do the same throughout the region. But as my party and I traversed the road, suddenly a light shone around me from heaven. I fell to the ground and heard a voice saying, 'Saul, Saul, why are you persecuting Me?'

"I said, 'Who are You, Lord?'

"And the Lord said, 'I am Jesus, whom you are persecuting. It is hard for you to kick against the goads.' "

Mark could remain silent no longer. "Excuse me, sir, but you're saying Jesus Himself spoke to you from heaven?"

"I am, young man. Trembling and astonished, I said, 'Lord, what do You want me to do?'

"The Lord said, 'Arise and go into the city, and you will be told what you must do.'

"The men who journeyed with me stood speechless, hearing a voice but seeing no one. I arose from the ground, but when I opened my eyes I was blind! My friends led me by the hand into Damascus, where for three days I stayed at the house of a friend named Judas on the street called Straight, and I was without sight, and neither ate nor drank."

Mark could only imagine. He himself might have lost his appetite forever.

"There, as I was fervently praying, the Lord gave me a vision of a man named Ananias coming in and putting his hand on me, so that I might receive my sight. Who should appear at my door but a man named Ananias, who told me this incredible story. He said the Lord had spoken to him in a dream and told him to go to the street called Straight and inquire at the house of Judas for one called Saul of Tarsus, 'for behold, he is praying and in a vision he has seen a man named Ananias.' "

Peter and James looked as astonished as Mark felt. As bizarre as this was, it was just like something God would do.

Saul smiled. "Ananias told me that he answered the Lord, saying he had heard from many about me and how much harm I had done to the saints in Jerusalem. He even told the Lord that he knew I had authority from the chief priests to bind all who call on His name. But he said the Lord told him, 'Go, for he is a chosen vessel of Mine to bear My name before Gentiles, kings, and the children of Israel. For I will show him how many things he must suffer for My name's sake.' "

"Pardon me again, sir," Mark said, feeling Peter's glare and knowing he should hold his tongue. "But did you mean to say that the Lord told this Ananias that you were to bear His name before Gentiles?"

Saul narrowed his eyes at Mark. "And kings. If you think that astonishes you, imagine how I felt. Before the children of Israel I could understand, but I confess I was as worried about the 'suffering for His name's sake' part. If I had to endure what I had inflicted on Christ's followers—fair and just as that may be—I had a hard road ahead. But, brothers, Ananias laid his hands on me and said, 'Brother Saul, the Lord Jesus, who appeared to you on the road as you came, has sent me that you may receive your sight and be filled with the Holy Spirit.' And immediately there fell from my eyes something like scales, and I received my sight at once, arose, and was baptized."

Mark stole a glance at Peter, who raised a brow as if to remind his young charge that they had prayed for just this possibility.

"When I had eaten, I was strengthened. I spent several days with the disciples at Damascus, who immediately believed my report. They allowed me to preach Christ in the synagogues, that He is the Son of God. Everyone seemed amazed, for they knew who I was and who I had been. But I increased all the more in strength, and confounded the Jews in Damascus, proving that this Jesus is the Christ.

"Eventually the Jews plotted to kill me. The governor, under Aretas the king, was guarding the city with a garrison, desiring to arrest me, but I was let down in a basket through a window in the wall and escaped from his hands. For the last few years I have lived in seclusion, studying and preparing for ministry."

Mark sat shaking his head, more in wonder than doubt, but he feared Saul misunderstood.

"Gentlemen, hear me. I can only imagine your skepticism, and I cannot blame you. I was one who once had confidence in the flesh, and if anyone else thinks he may have confidence in the flesh, I more so: circumcised the eighth day, of the stock of Israel, of the tribe of Benjamin, a Hebrew of the Hebrews; concerning the law, a Pharisee; concerning zeal, persecuting the church; concerning the righteousness which is in the law, blameless.

"But what things were gain to me, these I have counted loss for Christ. Yet indeed I also count all things loss for the excellence of the knowledge of Christ Jesus my Lord, for whom I have suffered the loss of all things, and count them as rubbish, that I may gain Christ and be found in Him, not having my own righteousness, which is from the law, but that which is through faith in Christ, the righteousness which is from God by faith; that I may know Him and the power of His resurrection, and the fellowship of His sufferings, being conformed to His death, if, by any means, I may attain to the resurrection from the dead."

Mark was struck by the articulate mind of this man. He had said so much in so few words that Mark wanted to stop him so he could rehearse them in his head. But Saul continued:

"Not that I have already attained, or am already perfected; but I press on, that I may lay hold of that for which Christ Jesus has also laid hold of me. Brethren, I do not count myself to have apprehended; but one thing I do, forgetting those things which are behind and reaching forward to those things which are ahead, I press toward the goal for the prize of the upward call of God in Christ Jesus.

"Therefore let us, as many as are mature"—and here he glanced at Mark, making him redden—"have this mind; and if in anything you think otherwise, God will reveal even this to you. Nevertheless, to the degree that we have already attained, let us walk by the same rule, let us be of the same mind.

"For our citizenship is in heaven, from which we also eagerly wait for the Savior, the Lord Jesus Christ, who will transform our lowly body that it may be conformed to His glorious body, according to the working by which He is able even to subdue all things to Himself."

Mark felt as if he were listening to a sermon from Peter, yet this man had a different style, a rush of organization and logic that made him as compelling as Mark's mentor.

"Brothers, I implore you: I would that you would see me as one of you, a coworker in the kingdom of God through Christ."

Peter and James sat silent, trading glances. Mark was convinced, and he believed they had to be also. Soon Peter stood and reached for Saul, calling him "My brother," and embraced him, welcoming him to their work.

Soon Saul spoke boldly in Jerusalem in the name of the Lord Jesus, amazing all, especially the rulers and the Hellenists—the same ones Stephen had debated. Now Saul became their target, but when the disciples found out, they brought him to Caesarea and sent him back to his hometown of Tarsus for his own protection.

Mark heard nothing more of Saul for several years, but much discord arose among the brethren in Jerusalem to occupy the young man's time.

THIRTEEN

Soon it was reported that the new churches throughout all Judea, Galilee, and Samaria enjoyed peace and were edified. Peter said they were walking in the fear of the Lord and in the comfort of the Holy Spirit, and that's why they were multiplying.

Mark always loved when the disciples returned from their missionary trips, for they had story after story. Peter told of visiting the saints in Lydda, where he said he found a man named Aeneas, who had been bedridden and paralyzed eight years. "I said, 'Aeneas, Jesus the Christ heals you. Arise and make your bed.' And he arose immediately. Mark, do you know that all who dwelt at Lydda and Sharon saw him and turned to the Lord."

"All?"

"I speak the truth, son. Is there anyone you know who would not be persuaded if they saw a man ill for eight years suddenly become whole?"

Mark shook his head. "Peter, you must allow me to accompany you on one of these missions, and soon."

"You'll want even more to come along when you hear what took place at nearby Joppa. A disciple named Tabitha was full of good works and charitable deeds, but the news came to me that she had fallen ill and died. They had washed her and laid her in an upper room, and the disciples sent two men for me, most urgently imploring me not to delay.

"When I arrived, all the widows stood weeping, showing the tunics and garments Tabitha had made. I asked them all to leave, and I knelt and prayed. Then I said, 'Tabitha, arise.' And she opened her eyes, and when she saw me she sat up, alive. The news spread all through Joppa, and many believed on the Lord."

"So she was not dead, but merely very ill?"

"Oh, she was quite dead when I ministered to her. Surely you do not doubt the Lord's power after all you have seen."

"To be used in such a way—"

"You say well, 'to be used.' This is not of myself, hardly of my own power, of which I have none aside from the Holy Spirit. A few days later I was staying with a tanner named Simon, and I went up on the housetop to pray at about the sixth hour. I became very hungry, but while a meal was being made ready, I fell into a trance and saw heaven opened and an object like a great sheet bound at the four corners descending to me. In it were all kinds of four-footed animals, wild beasts, creeping things, and birds of the air. And a voice came to me and said, 'Rise, Peter; kill and eat.'

"But I said, 'Not so, Lord! For I have never eaten anything common or unclean.'

"And a voice spoke to me a second time, 'What God has cleansed you must not call common.' This happened three times, and the object was taken up into heaven again.

"Now while I was wondering what this vision meant, behold, some men stood before Simon's gate, and they called and asked whether I,

Peter, was lodging there. The Spirit said to me, 'Behold, three men are seeking you. Arise, go down and go with them, doubting nothing; for I have sent them.'

"I went down and said, 'I am he whom you seek. For what reason have you come?'

"And they said, 'Cornelius the centurion, a just man, one who fears God and has a good reputation among all the nation of the Jews, was divinely instructed by a holy angel to summon you to his house, and to hear words from you.' I invited them in and lodged them.

"The next day I went away with them, and some brethren from Joppa accompanied me. The following day we entered Caesarea, where Cornelius was waiting and had called together his relatives and close friends. As I was coming in, Cornelius fell at my feet and worshiped me. I said, 'Stand up; I myself am also a man.' You see, Mark, we must be diligent in realizing that all these signs and wonders come solely from the Lord."

"Is it possible he would ever bestow such on me?" Mark said.

"Why not? As I talked with Cornelius, I went in and found many who had come together. I said, 'You know how unlawful it is for a Jewish man to keep company with or go to one of another nation. But God has shown me that I should not call any man common or unclean. Therefore I came without objection as soon as I was sent for. I ask, then, for what reason have you sent for me?' "

"You have always maintained ceremonial distance from the Gentiles."

"I have. But Cornelius said, 'Four days ago I was fasting, and at the ninth hour I prayed in my house, and behold, a man stood before me in bright clothing, and said, "Cornelius, your prayer has been heard, and your alms are remembered in the sight of God. Send therefore to Joppa and call Simon here, whose surname is Peter. He is lodging in the house of Simon, a tanner, by the sea. When he comes, he will speak to you." So I sent to you immediately, and you have done well to come. Now therefore, we are all present before God, to hear all the things commanded you by God.'

"I said, 'In truth I perceive that God shows no partiality. But in every nation whoever fears Him and works righteousness is accepted by Him. The word which God sent to the children of Israel, preaching peace through Jesus Christ—He is Lord of all—that word you know, which was proclaimed throughout all Judea, and began from Galilee after the baptism which John preached: how God anointed Jesus of Nazareth with the Holy Spirit and with power, who went about doing good and healing all who were oppressed by the devil, for God was with Him. And we are witnesses of all things which He did both in the land of the Jews and in Jerusalem, He whom they killed by hanging on a tree. Him God raised up on the third day, and showed Him openly, not to all the people, but to witnesses chosen before by God, even to us who ate and drank with Him after He arose from the dead. And He commanded us to preach to the people, and to testify that it is He who was ordained by God to be Judge of the living and the dead. To Him all the prophets witness that, through His name, whoever believes in Him will receive remission of sins.' "

"You said all this to Gentiles?"

"Absolutely, and while I was still speaking, the Holy Spirit fell upon all those who heard the word. And those of the circumcision who believed were astonished, as many as came with me, because the gift of the Holy Spirit had been poured out on the Gentiles also. For they heard them speak with tongues and magnify God.

"I told them, 'Can anyone forbid water, that these should not be baptized who have received the Holy Spirit just as we have?' And I commanded them to be baptized in the name of the Lord."

. . .

MARK WAS NOT SURPRISED when controversy arose among the brethren in Jerusalem when they heard that Peter had preached the gospel of Christ to Gentiles. Some contended with him, saying, "You even ate with them!"

Peter told them of his vision while praying in the city of Joppa and how the Lord had instructed him, "What God has cleansed you must not call common." He told of Gentiles coming to faith, "and I remembered the word of the Lord, how He said, 'John indeed baptized with water, but you shall be baptized with the Holy Spirit.' If therefore God gave them the same gift as He gave us when we believed on the Lord Jesus Christ, who was I that I could withstand God?"

Those who heard this at first fell silent, then glorified God, saying, "Then God has also granted to the Gentiles repentance to life."

It seemed to Mark that the whole world was beginning to hear the gospel, as far as Phoenicia, Cyprus, and Antioch. But up until then, those scattered after the death of Stephen had been preaching the word to no one but the Jews. Now the hand of the Lord was with them, and a great number of Jews and Gentiles believed and turned to the Lord.

Mark knew he should be overjoyed for Barnabas when he was sent by the disciples to minister at Antioch in Syria, a prosperous and growing body consisting primarily of Gentiles. And part of Mark *was* excited for his cousin. But again, that he was still tied to his mother and his home made him envious of all Barnabas would experience. His cousin soon wrote to Mark that he had arrived to see the grace of God on the people and was glad to encourage them all that with purpose of heart they should continue with the Lord. When Mark showed the letter to Peter, the disciple said Barnabas was "a good man, full of the Holy Spirit and of faith." How Mark wished he could act out his faith in such a way that the same could be said of him.

Soon word came that Barnabas had found the work in Antioch so demanding for its fast growth that he had departed for Tarsus to ask Saul to join him. For a whole year they worked together in the church at Antioch and taught a great many people. Barnabas wrote Mark that their detractors referred to them derisively as "Christians."

The disciples in Jerusalem began sending prophets to Antioch. One, Agabus, prophesied a great famine throughout the world, so the disciples, each according to his ability, sent relief to the brethren dwelling in Judea. They had much of it delivered personally by Barnabas and Saul, so occasionally Mark got to see them.

MARK AND HIS MOTHER had for more than ten years since the death, burial, and resurrection of Jesus feared the prospect of living so close to the dwelling place of King Herod, and it wasn't long before he had plainly had enough of the Christians. After many warnings and threats and decrees, the wicked king finally acted and had James, the brother of John, arrested.

Peter seemed intensely stressed over this, and Mark found himself in the unusual position of trying to encourage his mentor. "Herod cannot hold a true man of God, let alone harm him," he said. "Remember how the Spirit released you and allowed you to preach in the face of prohibitions from the rulers."

"I'm praying," Peter said, "but let us not be naïve. Stephen was not spared, and Herod seems deeply angry, furious with us all. James would be a tremendous loss to our cause."

Mark, old enough now to be more familiar with Peter, threw an arm around the big man's shoulders. "Is it naïveté or faith to trust that God will spare our beloved brother?"

"We will know tomorrow," Peter said. "But we must not make ourselves conspicuous at the hearing."

"Everyone knows you, Peter. You will not be able to attend unless in disguise."

"Even then I would probably be noticed, Mark. Would you go for me and bring a report?"

"I will go for you and bring you James!"

"Please, son, do not take this matter with a light heart. If indeed you deliver our beloved brother back here, we will rejoice with great gladness. But until then, be sober and fervent in your prayers."

Mark spent the evening allowing himself to imagine that being there when James was spared might gain him even greater entrée into the disciples' inner circle. Would they ever see him as an equal brother, as they clearly saw Barnabas? Was it too much to ask that he be naturally included on some mission to spread the gospel?

Excitement made him feel like a lad again and cost him precious sleep. In the morning he hurried to the palace in a bulky, hooded robe that would make him less obvious in the milling crowd. When he saw the throng, clearly consisting mostly of angry men who too seemed to have run out of patience with the Christians, for the first time Mark allowed himself the dread Peter must have been feeling. There seemed an air of expectancy, a bloodlust. Mark was suddenly transported back to the stoning of Stephen and prayed he would not have to endure another such spectacle.

He knew James to be a bold witness, if not as frank and direct as Peter. The man had ministered to the poor and the lame, healing and preaching the gospel earnestly. Mark could only hope he would be given a chance to defend himself, for he could be as articulate as any of the disciples, and the Spirit would surely use his words to affect many.

But when James was dragged out to the public court—to the celebration of most of the crowd—it was clear he had already suffered. His face was purple and swollen and his robe matted with blood. He limped and winced, but often he raised his hands—roped at the wrists—and appeared to pray as he looked up.

When King Herod emerged with his entourage to the sound of blaring trumpets, the crowd went wild, cheering and clapping and shouting, "Hail to the king!"

They quickly fell silent when the scowling man held up a hand, then readjusted his cape across his shoulders. Servants held a shade over him to block the glaring morning sun.

"James bar Zebedee has been tried and found guilty of insurrection and disobeying the decrees of the throne, offenses punishable by death."

No! Lord, spare him! Perform a miracle! Free him!

As the bloodthirsty crowd roared anew, Herod intoned, "Without further ado, the crown directs the executioner to slay the guilty with the sword."

James did not move, let alone cower or recoil. With his eyes still toward heaven, he lowered his hands to his waist as soldiers approached from either side to hold his elbows and steady him. The executioner wielded a heavy, two-edged sword that shone under the cloudless sky. And with barely a pause, the man swung the blade two-handed, piercing James's chest with a vicious crack, exposing his heart. As the man of God dropped to his knees, the soldiers on either side, blood-spattered themselves now, held him steady as the killing blow caught him just above his left ear and the great weapon cleaved his skull all the way to his nose.

As the crowd surged and ranted, Mark burst into tears and ran for his home. He tore up the stairs to the upper room, where the disciples waited. "What news?" Peter said, his face showing that he knew from Mark's tears.

"Put to the death by the sword," Mark rasped, collapsing to a bench. The rest of the disciples, as one, fell to their knees, weeping and mourning. All Mark could think of, besides the horrific gore he had witnessed, was what this would mean to all their futures. The Jews in Jerusalem seemed overjoyed and sang the praises of the king, and rumors soon abounded that Peter would be next.

Mark and his mother and the rest prayed fervently for Peter's safety, but during the Days of Unleavened Bread, Peter was also seized and thrown into prison. The king announced that four squads of soldiers would guard him—two chained to him in the cell and two more outside his cell, rotating around the clock. Herod intended to bring him before the people after Passover.

The remaining disciples and several others of the brothers and sisters stole away to Mark's home, and he had never seen such fear since the crucifixion of Jesus. Dozens of the believers knelt with him and his mother and cried out to God in behalf of Peter.

While they were praying, Rhoda, the servant girl, burst into the house and said, "Peter stands before the gate!"

"What?" many said. "You're mad! You are beside yourself!"

"No, it's true! I recognized his voice. It is he!"

"No," others said, "it is his angel."

But Mark heard continuous knocking, and when he went to open the gate, he was astonished to see Peter himself. Many cried out, but Peter motioned to them to keep silent. They bade him come in and sit and asked what had happened.

"I was sleeping, bound with chains between two soldiers, and suddenly an angel of the Lord stood by me, and a light shone in the prison.

The angel struck me on the side and raised me up, saying, 'Arise quickly!' And my chains fell off my hands. The angel said, 'Gird yourself and tie on your sandals and follow me.'

"I thought I was seeing a vision until we were past the first and the second guard posts and came to the iron gate that leads to the city. It opened of its own accord, and we went out and went down one street, and immediately the angel departed from me. I realized then that the Lord had sent His angel and delivered me from the hand of Herod and from all the expectation of the Jewish people. Now go, please, and tell these things to Jesus' brother James and to the brethren."

At daybreak Jerusalem was alive with the news that when Herod searched for Peter and did not find him, he had the guards put to death. By now, of course, Peter had departed Jerusalem and would return only infrequently and in secret.

As for Herod, he had been feuding with the people of Tyre and Sidon, so they came to him asking for peace. Mark knew it was because they relied on the king for their supplies of food. Herod, arrayed in royal apparel, sat proudly on his throne and gave an oration to them. And the people kept shouting, "His is the voice of a god and not of a man!"

But as they watched, an angel of the Lord struck him, because he did not give glory to God. For five days Herod lay screaming in agony as he was eaten by worms and died.

MEANWHILE, THE WORD OF God grew and multiplied. Barnabas and Saul came from Antioch to Jerusalem with famine relief following the death of Herod, and when it came time for them to return to their church, they invited John Mark to go along. Finally he was of an age and maturity to be right for the job.

Full of wonder and excitement, Mark set out on his first ministry journey and was impressed to find in the church at Antioch that Barnabas and Saul had raised up several prophets and teachers. As they ministered and fasted, these prophets and teachers said that the Holy Spirit had instructed them to "separate to Me Barnabas and Saul for the work to which I have called them."

In an impressive service of commission Mark would never forget, the new leaders of the Antiochan church—having fasted and prayed and laid hands on them—sent Barnabas and Saul on their way, with Mark as their assistant. One of their main thrusts was to evangelize the Gentiles all over the world.

They left from the port city of Seleucia, about sixteen miles from Antioch at the mouth of the Orantes River. And from there they sailed to Cyprus, Barnabas's home country. When they arrived in Salamis, the chief port and commercial center, Saul suggested they first preach the word of God in the synagogues, setting a precedent they would follow for years.

Mark found himself deeply moved by the way God used his cousin and Saul, the former tormentor of the church, and he learned much from these men.

Barnabas, despite being a close relative Mark knew better than anyone, proved one of the most devout and earnest missionaries he had ever met. Mark found himself regretting any envy or jealousy he had ever felt as he watched Barnabas boldly preach the gospel and minister to the sick and lowly everywhere they went. He seemed tireless and wholly devoted to the cause. Plus, his bent toward encouragement caused him to continually compliment Saul on his preaching and arguing for the faith.

For his sake, Saul proved a brilliant apologist, though his tireless intensity wore on Mark. Yet somehow, despite that he was a dynamic and spellbinding speaker, the man never seemed happy or satisfied. There was always something to fear, to watch out for, to battle. Even late into the night, when the three would share a spare room in one or another of the saints' homes, Saul would still be talking, criticizing, suggesting long into the night. Often he would hold forth until both Barnabas and Mark were snoring, then he would shout to rouse them and insist that they listen and finish some conversation he found important.

Mark could not deny that Saul was devout and passionate and generally right, but his intensity wore on the young man.

And Mark also found himself drawn back to Jerusalem. He missed Peter and wanted to hear more of the early days of Jesus' ministry. Neither Barnabas nor Saul had been eyewitnesses to the miracles of Jesus, as Peter had. And surprising even himself after all the years he had spent longing to get away, Mark missed his mother. Soon he began longing to return home.

On the island of Paphos, the missionaries found a sorcerer, a Jewish false prophet named Bar-Jesus. He was with the proconsul (a Roman provincial governor), Sergius Paulus, an intelligent man. Paulus called for Barnabas and Saul, asking to hear the word of God. But the sorcerer opposed them, seeking to turn the proconsul away from the faith.

Saul, who had begun calling himself Paul (his Roman name), glared at Bar-Jesus and said, "O full of all deceit and all fraud, you son of the devil, you enemy of all righteousness, will you not cease perverting the straight ways of the Lord? And now, indeed, the hand of the Lord is upon you, and you shall be blind, not seeing the sun for a time."

Immediately the sorcerer went around seeking someone to lead him. At that the proconsul believed, being astonished at the teaching of the Lord.

Mark marveled at what he had witnessed, yet this did not change his mind about departing for Jerusalem. When he broached the subject with Barnabas, his cousin seemed puzzled but not opposed. "You must do as you believe the Lord leads you," he said.

But Paul was adamant that Mark remain with them. "We have need of you, and the Holy Spirit called you to accompany us. You must not desert us or your calling."

Mark certainly didn't consider it desertion, and by the time they set sail from Paphos and came to Perga in Pamphylia, he had made up his mind to leave. Paul told him in no uncertain terms that he felt betrayed and abandoned, and as much as this troubled Mark in his spirit, he believed he was doing the right thing. He left them there, boarding a ship bound for Israel.

FOURTEEN

"Of course I'm delighted you're back, John Mark," his mother said. "But what are your plans?"

"To assist the disciples here in Jerusalem in any way they need me and, I hope, to join Peter on his missionary journeys. He has been in Antioch and may go from there to Asia Minor and possibly even to Rome. Why do you look so concerned?"

"Well, is it all right with the disciples that you have returned? With Peter? You seemed so certain of your calling to go with Joses and with Saul."

"They are known as Barnabas and Paul now, Mother. And I did feel called to go with them to Antioch. But as you know, they were commissioned by the church to venture out, and—"

"And you wrote me that this invigorated you more than ever. What happened?"

"Nothing happened. For years I couldn't get your blessing to go, and now it seems you don't want me here."

"I want you where God wants you, son."

"And has He told you where that is?"

"There is no need to be testy with me, John Mark. I just want you to tell me if you had a falling-out with your cousin or with—"

"There was no discord until I announced my leaving. Paul believes he knows best. He has become very forthright."

"Become?" his mother said. "What was he when he was persecuting believers? I daresay he brought the same personality to the work of Christ. Perhaps that is not always a good thing?"

"I admire him, Mother. How could I not? But he pressed me the way he presses unbelievers. I'm not sure I was up to his passion."

"And that is why you're back?"

"I don't know why I'm back! But I look forward to spending more time with Peter."

Most disconcerting, despite his age, Mark found his mother always more wise and incisive than he. Had it been a mistake to return? Had he prayed enough over the decision? Much as he wanted her blessing, his mother always seemed right.

PETER RETURNED clandestinely between his trips, and Mark found him no less curious and cautious than his own mother. "There is much for you to do, Mark," he said. "And I am glad your return does not suggest an aversion to travel, for there are many places I need yet go, and perhaps it *is* time for me to give in and ask that you accompany me."

"Truly? I cannot imagine a higher privilege! And we can spend time the way we used to!"

"Well, not quite the way we once did. There will be little time for fishing together, I can tell you that. But you must know that I have already heard from Paul."

"I can't say that surprises me."

Peter shook his head. "He is not happy. I have found him quite gifted in intellect and persuasion, which is a benefit to the gospel. But he has been critical of me as well. Did you find him difficult?"

"Not really. Well, yes. I suppose I always felt a step, and a thought, behind, as if I were always being weighed in the balance and found wanting."

"Perhaps you should have stayed. If you see me as your elder, would you hear me if I insisted you return?"

Mark found a bench and dropped onto it. "Please don't, Peter. If I didn't believe I needed time here and with you, I would not have returned. Put me to work; allow me time with you. I'm not sure Paul would have me back anyway."

"He is a reasonable man."

Mark caught Peter's eye and grinned. "Is he? I aver that it is his very unreasonableness that made him both a feared opponent and a treasured ally of the gospel."

PETER AND MARK'S TRAVELS allowed them plenty of time to talk.

"Tell me of John the Baptist," Mark said one day as they sojourned between Pontus and Galatia.

"Ah, the Baptist. Until I met Jesus, John had to be the most remarkable person I had ever encountered."

"How so?"

"You have been a student of the Prophets, Mark. Remember this passage?

'Behold, I send My messenger before Your face, Who will prepare Your way before You. The voice of one crying in the wilderness: "Prepare the way of the Lord; make His paths straight."'

"John came baptizing in the wilderness and preaching a baptism of repentance for the remission of sins. People from all the land of Judea, and those from right there in Jerusalem, were baptized by him in the Jordan River, confessing their sins.

"He wore camel's hair for clothing with a leather belt around his waist, and he ate locusts and wild honey. And he preached, saying, 'There comes One after me who is mightier than I, whose sandal strap I am not worthy to stoop down and loose. I indeed baptized you with water, but He will baptize you with the Holy Spirit.' Oh, Mark, he was a dynamic, impassioned man. He cared not a whit what anyone thought of him, small or great. His entire life was dedicated to telling the world of the soon coming of his cousin, Jesus.

"The Master, you know, was from Nazareth of Galilee, and the day finally came when He Himself came to be baptized by John in the Jordan. What a sight! As He rose up out of the water, the heavens parted and the Spirit descended upon Him like a dove. Then a voice came from heaven, saying, 'You are My beloved Son, in whom I am well pleased.' "

"And that's when He began to gather you disciples and teach and heal?"

"No, that came later, Mark. Once the brothers James and John and I and a few others joined Him, we asked where He had gone after His baptism, as we did not see him for more than a month. He told us that the Spirit had driven Him into the wilderness with the wild beasts, where He was tempted by Satan for forty days. He said angels ministered to Him."

"Tempted by Satan? How?"

"He urged Jesus to turn stones to bread, offered Him all the kingdoms of the world if He would just serve him. Tried to get Him to leap off a high place to prove the angels would catch Him. But He resisted the devil."

"And when He returned from the wilderness, then His ministry began?"

Peter nodded. "It was after John was put in prison that Jesus came to Galilee, preaching the gospel of the kingdom of God, and saying, 'The time is fulfilled, and the kingdom of God is at hand. Repent, and believe in the gospel.' "

"You were with Him then?"

"Soon. In fact, my brother Andrew and I were the first disciples He called. He was walking by the Sea of Galilee as we were casting our fishing net, and he called out to us, 'Follow Me, and I will make you become fishers of men!'

"Fishers of *men*?"

"We were as astonished as you, Mark, but we looked at each other, and we knew."

"Knew?"

"That we had no choice. Others wondered what madness had entered us, but we immediately left our nets and followed Him. Next he called the brothers James and John, who were nearby mending their nets in a boat with their father Zebedee and some hired servants. They simply rose and left everything and everyone and followed after the Teacher."

"Why did you all do this? How did you know? Was it what He said or how He said it?"

Peter shrugged. "I don't know. God must have put it in our hearts. None of us were out of sorts or unhappy with our lives or looking for anything new or different. This man simply appeared and told us, didn't ask us, to follow Him, and the time was right. He carried Himself with such authority—and yet humility—that we somehow understood that we were to go with Him and that our lives would never be the same.

"On the Sabbath we followed him to my hometown, Capernaum, and immediately He entered the synagogue and began teaching! We weren't the only ones amazed, for He taught as one having authority, and not as the scribes."

"What did the authorities do?"

"At first nothing! I believe they understood that He had some wisdom beyond theirs, but there was a man there with an unclean spirit. And he cried out, 'Let us alone! What have we to do with You, Jesus of Nazareth? Did You come to destroy us? I know who You are—the Holy One of God!'

"But Jesus rebuked him, saying, 'Be quiet, and come out of him!' When the unclean spirit had convulsed him and cried out with a loud voice, he came out of him. Everyone questioned among themselves, 'What is this? What new doctrine is this? For with authority He commands even the unclean spirits, and they obey Him.'

"Mark, I believe the people there ran out and told everyone they knew, because immediately Jesus' fame spread throughout all the region around Galilee.

"As soon as we left the synagogue, Andrew and I invited him to our home, where my wife's mother lay sick with a fever. With James and John also bearing witness, Jesus took her by the hand and sat her up, and immediately the fever left her. Soon she was helping serve us.

"That evening, when the sun had set and Sabbath was over, people began showing up with all who were sick and those who were demon-possessed. It seemed the whole city was gathered at our door. Jesus healed many and cast out demons, but this time He did not allow the demons to speak.

"The next morning I rose long before daylight, but Jesus was nowhere to be found. I roused the others and we went searching for Him. We found Him in a solitary place praying. I said, 'Teacher, everyone is looking for You.'

"He said, 'Let us go into the next towns, that I may preach there also, because for this purpose I have come forth.'

"He preached in synagogues throughout all Galilee, casting out demons. And a leper came and knelt before Him, saying, 'If You are willing, You can make me clean.'

"I could tell the Lord was moved. He reached out and touched the man and said, 'I am willing; be cleansed.' And as soon as He had spoken, the leprosy left the man. Jesus said, 'See that you say nothing to anyone; but go your way, show yourself to the priest, and offer for your cleansing those things which Moses commanded, as a testimony to them.' "

"Peter, why did Jesus not want anyone to know?"

"I believe He knew it would create a sensation and that He would be mobbed, thus curtailing what He hoped to accomplish. Which was exactly what happened. The man began to proclaim it freely, and Jesus could no longer openly enter the city. He retreated to deserted places, but still people came to Him from every direction.

"Finally we sneaked him back to my home in Capernaum, but it wasn't long before word got out and so many gathered that there was no longer room to receive them, not even near the door. Jesus preached the gospel of the kingdom to them. While He was preaching, someone tore open the roof above Him and lowered a cot bearing a paralyzed man, because it was so crowded they could not otherwise get in. When Jesus saw their faith, He said to the paralytic man, 'Son, your sins are forgiven you.'

"Now, Mark, I recognized certain of the scribes who had come to hear Him, and I was alarmed when He suddenly turned His attention to them. He said, 'Why do you sit there reasoning in your hearts and wondering why I speak blasphemies like this? You're asking who can forgive sins but God alone. But I ask you, which is easier, to say to the paralytic, "Your sins are forgiven you," or to say, "Arise, take up your bed and walk"? So that you may know that the Son of Man has power on earth to forgive sins'—He turned to the paralytic—'I say to you, arise, take up your bed, and go to your house.'

"Immediately he arose, took up the bed, and went out in the presence of them all, so that all were amazed and glorified God, saying, 'We never saw anything like this!'

"Then He went out again by the sea, and the multitudes came to Him, and He taught them. When He passed by, He saw Levi the son of Alphaeus sitting at the tax office. And He said to him, 'Follow Me.' And he arose and followed Him. Levi, as you know, is the disciple we call Matthew.

"Now as we were dining in Matthew's house, the scribes and Pharisees saw Jesus and asked us, 'How is it that He eats and drinks with tax collectors and sinners?'

"Jesus said to them, 'Those who are well have no need of a physician, but those who are sick. I did not come to call the righteous, but sinners, to repentance.' "

"Astonishing," Mark said. "Now tell me—"

"Mark, I am happy to tell you of Jesus, but you need to know that my highest goal is to prepare you for ministry."

"Is not my work with your ministry?"

"It is, but you should be out spreading the gospel, and not just with me on the occasional journey."

"Learning the history of the Master when He was with us is wonderful training."

"Perhaps, as it informs your own work of spreading the gospel. But I would be remiss if I did not make clear that you are not here merely to listen to my stories."

"I have told you, sir, that it is my intention to help you write them one day."

"I am still not convinced of the need for that, but all in good time. Let us not interrupt the work of God by dwelling on mere memories."

"To you they may be mere memories, Peter. To me, they are life."

FIFTEEN

Changes in the leadership of both the Romans and Jews meant the disciples had little way of knowing from one regime to the next whether they were to be tolerated or in danger of imprisonment or worse. Mark realized that it fell to Peter to decide how overt the believers could be in ministering. The local rulers had little problem with the ones they mockingly called Christians, as long as they were helping the poor. It was when they preached and taught of the resurrection and deity of Jesus and led new people to come to faith that they aroused the suspicion and ire of the leadership.

Mark humored Peter by seeking news of the brethren spread abroad and their exploits in taking the gospel to the rest of the world. But then daily he begged for more and more stories from the time Peter had spent with Jesus.

"Is it true, as the others have often said, that Jesus seemed to speak in riddles?"

"Oh, certainly. Many times we had no idea what He meant. He often said that he who had ears would hear. In other words, someone listening with the ears of faith could understand. He loved to use figures of speech and see who was catching His intent.

"For instance, some of the disciples of John the Baptist—while he was in prison—were still observing the pharisaical two-day-a-week fast. We believed that the Law of Moses required fasting only on the Day of Atonement, but the Pharisees had added Monday and Thursday fasts as signs of piety. The Pharisees came to Jesus and said, 'Why do the disciples of John fast, but Your disciples do not fast?'

"Jesus said, 'Can the friends of the bridegroom fast while the bridegroom is with them? As long as they have the bridegroom with them they cannot fast. But the days will come when the bridegroom will be taken away from them, and then they will fast in those days. No one sews a piece of unshrunk cloth on an old garment; or else the new piece pulls away from the old, and the tear is made worse. And no one puts new wine into old wineskins; or else the new wine bursts the wineskins, the wine is spilled, and the wineskins are ruined. But new wine must be put into new wineskins.' "

Mark flinched and shook his head. "Did you have any idea what He was talking about?"

"Not then, of course. But now it is clear, is it not, that He was speaking of Himself? Needless to say, if we didn't understand, the Pharisees understood even less. And they soon seemed to spend all their time trying to trip Him up on matters of the law. We were walking through grain fields on the Sabbath, plucking the heads of grain. The Pharisees asked Jesus, 'Why do they do what is not lawful on the Sabbath?'

"He turned to them and said, 'Have you never read what David did when he was in need and hungry, he and those with him: how he went into the house of God in the days of Abiathar the high priest, and ate the showbread, which is not lawful to eat except for the priests, and also gave some to those who were with him? The Sabbath was made for man, and not man for the Sabbath. Therefore the Son of Man is also Lord of the Sabbath.' "

"I cannot imagine how the Pharisees took this. They must have been infuriated!"

"Had they realized what He was saying, they would have been more so. On the same day we were in the synagogue and Jesus saw a man with a withered hand. The Pharisees were there and watching Him closely, as if daring Him to do something else unlawful on the Sabbath. He asked the man with the withered hand to step forward and said to the Pharisees, 'Is it lawful on the Sabbath to do good or to do evil, to save life or to kill?'

"This time they knew enough to keep silent, which clearly made Jesus angry. He told the man to stretch out his hand, and as he did, the hand was restored, as whole as the other. The Pharisees immediately left, and Jesus told us they were plotting with the Herodians against Him, how they might destroy Him."

"But this was still early in His ministry, correct? It was not yet His time."

"Yes, they were unable to hurt Him then. We withdrew to the sea, and a great multitude from Galilee followed us from Judea and Jerusalem and Idumea and beyond the Jordan, and when they heard how many things He was doing, a great multitude from Tyre and Sidon also came to Him.

"He told us to keep a small boat ready for Him because of the multitude, lest they should crush Him. For He healed many, so that as many as had afflictions pressed about Him to touch Him. And the unclean spirits, whenever they saw Him, fell down before Him and cried out, saying, 'You are the Son of God.' But He sternly warned them that they should not make Him known.

"Now, Mark, you know that by this time more than seventy disciples followed Jesus. But one day He went up on the mountain and called to Him just the twelve He wanted close to Him, whom He would send out to preach and minister in His name. To us He gave the power to heal and to cast out demons. That included me, James and John—the sons of Zebedee—Andrew, Philip, Bartholomew, Matthew, Thomas, James the son of Alphaeus, Thaddaeus, Simon the Canaanite, and Judas Iscariot.

"The next time we ventured out, such a multitude came together that we could not so much as eat. And with Jesus' detractors saying He was a madman, eventually word of all this reached His family in Nazareth, and they came, intending to rescue Him.

"The scribes who came from Jerusalem accused Him of being possessed by Beelzebub, and said, 'By the ruler of the demons He casts out demons.'

"So He called them to Himself and said, 'How can Satan cast out Satan? If a kingdom is divided against itself, that kingdom cannot stand. And if a house is divided against itself, that house cannot stand. And if Satan has risen up against himself, and is divided, he cannot stand, but has an end. No one can enter a strong man's house and plunder his goods, unless he first binds the strong man. And then he will plunder his house.

"'Assuredly, I say to you, all sins will be forgiven the sons of men, and whatever blasphemies they may utter; but he who blasphemes against the Holy Spirit never has forgiveness, but is subject to eternal condemnation.' This He said because they accused Him of having an unclean spirit."

"So what about His family, having come all the way from Nazareth?"

"Well, a multitude sitting around Him said, 'Look, Your mother and Your brothers are outside seeking You.'

"He said, 'Who is My mother, or My brothers?' And He looked in a circle at those of us who sat closest about Him, and said, 'Here are My mother and My brothers! For whoever does the will of God is My brother and My sister and mother.' "

"What did you make of that, Peter? Was it terribly insulting to His family?"

"I don't believe they heard Him. He was telling us how important we were to Him. He was not demeaning His own. Often He spoke in parables to teach us while hiding His real meaning from others. For instance, again He began to teach by the sea. And a great multitude was gathered to Him, so that He got into a boat and sat in it on the sea; and the whole multitude was on the land facing the sea. Then He taught them many things by parables, saying, 'Listen! Behold, a sower went out to sow. And it happened, as he sowed, that some seed fell by the wayside; and the birds of the air came and devoured it. Some fell on stony ground, where it did not have much earth; and immediately it sprang up because it had no depth of earth. But when the sun was up it was scorched, and because it had no root it withered away. And some seed fell among thorns; and the thorns grew up and choked it, and it yielded no crop. But other seed fell on good ground and yielded a crop that sprang up, increased and produced: some thirtyfold, some sixty, and some a hundred.'

"And He said to them, 'He who has ears to hear, let him hear!' "

"Peter," Mark said, "did you have ears to hear?"

"No, sadly I did not. When we were alone with Him, we asked Him about the parable. He told us, 'To you it has been given to know the mystery of the kingdom of God; but to those who are outside, all things come in parables,

" 'so that *"Seeing they may see and not perceive, and hearing they may hear and not understand; lest they should turn, and their sins be forgiven them."* '

"He said, 'Do you not understand this parable? How then will you understand all the parables? The sower sows the word. And these are the ones by the wayside where the word is sown. When they hear, Satan comes immediately and takes away the word that was sown in their hearts.

" 'These likewise are the ones sown on stony ground who, when they hear the word, immediately receive it with gladness; and they have no root in themselves, and so endure only for a time. Afterward, when tribulation or persecution arises for the word's sake, immediately they stumble. Now these are the ones sown among thorns; they are the ones who hear the word, and the cares of this world, the deceitfulness of riches, and the desires for other things entering in choke the word, and it becomes unfruitful. But these are the ones sown on good ground, those who hear the word, accept it, and bear fruit: some thirtyfold, some sixty, and some a hundred.' "

"So He *was* explaining Himself to you."

"Yes. And He also asked us, 'Is a lamp brought to be put under a basket or under a bed? Is it not to be set on a lampstand? For there is nothing hidden which will not be revealed, nor has anything been kept secret but that it should come to light. If anyone has ears to hear, let him hear.

" 'Take heed what you hear. With the same measure you use, it will be measured to you; and to you who hear, more will be given. For whoever has, to him more will be given; but whoever does not have, even what he has will be taken away from him.

" 'The kingdom of God is as if a man should scatter seed on the ground, and should sleep by night and rise by day, and the seed should sprout and grow, he himself does not know how. For the earth yields crops by itself: first the blade, then the head, after that the full grain in the head. But when the grain ripens, immediately he puts in the sickle, because the harvest has come.'

"Jesus often tried to explain Himself and His teachings with comparisons. He said, 'To what shall we liken the kingdom of God? Or with what parable shall we picture it? It is like a mustard seed which, when it is sown on the ground, is smaller than all the seeds on earth; but when it is sown, it grows up and becomes greater than all herbs, and shoots out large branches, so that the birds of the air may nest under its shade.'

"And with many such parables He spoke the word to us as we were able to hear it. But without a parable He did not speak to them. Only when we were alone did He explain all things to us. That made us feel special, but we did not always understand either.

"That same day, when evening had come, He said, 'Let us cross over to the other side.' "

"He was exhausted?"

"I'm certain He was, for He fell fast asleep on a pillow in the stern. When we left, other boats followed, full of people clearly wanting to stay with Him. But as we sailed, a great windstorm arose and the waves beat into the boat and began filling it. We thought we were going to die! We awoke the Lord and said, 'Teacher, do You not care that we are perishing?'

"He arose and said to the sea, 'Peace, be still!' And the wind ceased and there was a great calm. He said to us, 'Why are you so fearful? How is it that you have no faith?'

"Mark, I tell you, we were scared to death. Who could this be, that even the wind and the sea obey Him?"

SIXTEEN

Mark was desperate to pursue this idea of the disciples themselves fearing Jesus because He was so powerful. But before he could continue the discussion—while working to keep from any curious eyes but Peter's his late-night scribbling by candlelight—a message reached Peter that rendered him sober and silent for most of the day. If he wasn't interacting with other church leaders or teaching bodies of believers, he seemed utterly preoccupied. Finally, at their evening meal, when it was just the two of them, Mark broke the silence.

"What is it, rabbi?"

Peter stared straight ahead and tore another piece of bread with his teeth. He chewed slowly, then wiped his mouth. "First, Mark, you're no longer a youngster, so I must remind you that I wish you would not address me that way."

"I'm sorry, sir, but I—"

"Indeed, despite our respective ages, you are the one far more educated. Now don't look so forlorn; I know you intend this as a term of respect and I appreciate it. But while I may have taught you a few things—"

"A *few*?"

"I am hardly your teacher, let alone your rabbi. The only one worthy of that appellation is the Spirit Himself. I daresay our friend Paul comes close, but I would not even refer to him as my rabbi."

"*He* might."

That elicited a wan smile from Peter.

"Well," Mark said, "as you have allowed that I am no longer a youngster, I must assert my right to at least call you my master. Not *the* Master, of course, I know that. But, master, tell me what has you so troubled today. Was the news from Capernaum? Is your family well?"

Peter stretched and sat back. "They are fine. I miss my wife, of course. No, the news is from Antioch."

"No illness among our brethren, I hope."

"Just controversy. It seems we are always swept up in these issues that distract us from our true mission. It's the Gentile question again, of course."

"I thought that was long settled."

Peter nodded sadly. "We could have only hoped. Let's walk, shall we?"

Mark was eager to get out into the dark, cool evening. Peter believed in walking after a meal, and Mark had quickly adopted the practice. As they strolled, Peter said, "You know that from the beginning, I—in fact all of us—felt called to preach the gospel to the Jew first. But God made it plain to me that His salvation also extended to the heathen, the pagan, the Gentile. Clearly we are not to saddle Gentile believers with our Jewish laws and practices."

"So you have always said."

"Do you not agree?"

"Of course. The work of my cousin and Paul in Antioch alone bears out the truth of what the Lord impressed upon you."

"And yet, as I say, that is where the trouble has arisen. Everywhere we have traveled outside Palestine, you and I have seen Jewish and Gentile believers on an equal plane. Though Paul has become known as the Apostle to the Gentiles, in fact we could all be so described. But now Judaizers in Antioch, extreme in their belief that all true converts must also—in essence—become Jewish, have set themselves against us. But primarily they oppose Paul. He and Barnabas are seeking support and, if necessary, some meeting of the minds on this."

Mark shook his head. "It seems to me that if you and Paul merely broadcast your decision on this, that would satisfy everyone and allow us to get back to what—as you say—should be our priority."

"The gospel, of course. All these side matters are just schemes of the evil one to distract us."

"What will you do?"

"I have learned to mull these things before coming to conclusions, but I can tell you I am willing to host a gathering of the leadership if it becomes necessary."

"That sounds like a lot of effort for what you call a distraction."

"It may be the only way to put it behind us. I will correspond with Paul, and we will do whatever is necessary." Peter's pace had quickened.

"I sense you are still vexed, master."

"There is nothing more I can do until I hear again from Paul."

"Then perhaps you would like to think—and talk—of something more pleasant."

Peter slowed and shook his head. "Your curiosity is insatiable."

"My apologies."

"No, I rather admire it. I have perhaps an hour's more worth of energy."

"I don't want to presume upon you, sir."

"Of course you do."

"Yes, I do. Tell me what happened after Jesus had calmed the sea."

"All right. But then I must turn in. You must promise not to plead for more."

"I promise."

"Well, we came to the other side of the sea, to the country of the Gadarenes, and when Jesus disembarked from the boat, immediately there met Him out of the tombs a man with an unclean spirit. No one could bind this man, the people said. He had even broken free of shackles and chains. Night and day he spent his time in the mountains and in the tombs, crying out and cutting himself with stones.

"When he saw Jesus from afar, he ran and worshiped Him, crying with a loud voice, 'What have I to do with You, Jesus, Son of the Most High God? I implore You by God that You do not torment me.'

"Jesus said, 'Come out of the man, unclean spirit! What is your name?'

" 'My name is Legion; for we are many. Please, Sir, do not send us out of the country. Send us to the large herd of swine over there, that we may enter them.'

"Jesus immediately sent the spirits into the swine. There were about two thousand of them, and the herd stampeded down the steep place into the sea and drowned.

"Well, as you can imagine, the swineherds fled and must have told the story everywhere, because soon it seemed that everyone around came to see what had happened. They came to Jesus and found the once demon-possessed man clothed and in his right mind."

"They must have been amazed, and thrilled."

"Actually, they were afraid. They began to plead with Him to depart from their region. As Jesus returned to the boat, the man who had been demon-possessed begged to come along, but Jesus said, 'Go home to your friends, and tell them what great things the Lord has done for you, and how He has had compassion on you.' We received word that he departed and proclaimed in Decapolis all that Jesus had done for him; and all marveled."

"Imagine the people so afraid of Jesus after He had done such a great thing."

Peter nodded. "And it was soon after that that He performed another miracle. When we had crossed over again to the other side, a great multitude gathered by the sea. Jairus, one of the rulers of the synagogue, fell at Jesus' feet and said, 'My little daughter lies at the point of death. Come and lay Your hands on her, that she may be healed, and she will live.' So Jesus went with him, and a great multitude followed and pressed about Him.

"Suddenly Jesus stopped and turned to me. He said, 'Power has gone out from me. Who touched My clothes?'

"I said, 'You see the multitude thronging You and You ask, "Who touched Me?" '

"He looked around to see who had done this thing, and a trembling woman came and fell before Him. 'It was I,' she said. 'I have suffered a flow of blood for twelve years, and have suffered many things from many physicians. I spent all I had and got no better, but rather grew worse. When I heard about You, I came behind You in the crowd and touched Your garment. I knew that if only I may touch Your clothes, I should be made well. Immediately the fountain of my blood has dried, and I feel in my body that I have been healed of the affliction.'

"Jesus said, 'Daughter, your faith has made you well. Go in peace, and be healed of your affliction.'

"Just then someone from Jairus's house told the ruler, 'Your daughter is dead. Why trouble the Teacher any further?'

"But Jesus told Jairus, 'Do not be afraid; only believe.' And He permitted no one to follow Him except the brothers James and John and me. When we reached Jairus's house we encountered a tumult of wailing mourners. Jesus said, 'Why make this commotion and weep? The child is not dead, but sleeping.'

"They ridiculed Him, but He forced them all outside. He took Jairus and his wife and the three of us and entered where the child was lying. He took her by the hand and said, 'Little girl, I say to you, arise.'

"Immediately the girl arose and walked, and her parents were overcome with great amazement. But Jesus commanded them strictly that no one should know it and said that something should be given her to eat."

Mark followed Peter as he turned back to where they were lodging. "Were you able to comprehend all this, sir? I fear I would have believed I was dreaming."

"At the time it was easy to believe it, because such things were happening every day. It was only after His resurrection and return to heaven that I was able to reflect on the wonder of it all. There were many, however, who did not believe or follow Him, even though they saw his signs and wonders and heard Him speak. After raising Jairus's daughter, He came to His own country, and we disciples followed Him. When the Sabbath had come, He began to teach in the synagogue. Many hearing Him were astonished, saying, 'Where did this Man get these things? And what wisdom is this which is given to Him, that such mighty works are performed by His hands! Is this not the carpenter, the Son of Mary, and brother of James, Joses, Judas, and Simon? And are not His sisters here with us?' It was as if they were offended.

"Jesus said, 'A prophet is not without honor except in his own country, among his own relatives, and in his own house.' Because of their disbelief, He could do no mighty work there, except that He laid His hands on a few sick people and healed them."

"What did He think of their skepticism?"

"He marveled at it, but still He went about the villages in a circuit, teaching. Soon He called us twelve to Himself and began to send us out two by two, and gave us power over unclean spirits. He commanded us to take nothing for our journeys except a staff—no bag, no bread, no copper in our money belts—but to wear sandals, and not to put on two tunics.

"He said, 'In whatever town you enter a house, lodge there till you depart from that town. And whoever will not receive you nor hear you, when you depart, shake off the dust under your feet as a testimony against them. Assuredly, I say to you, it will be more tolerable for Sodom and Gomorrah in the day of judgment than for that city!'

"So we went out and preached that people should repent. We cast out many demons, and anointed with oil many who were sick, and healed them."

"How could He get away with all this?"

"Oh, you may rest assured, King Herod heard of Him, for His name had become well known.

"Some said, 'It is Elijah.'

"Others said, 'It is the Prophet, or like one of the prophets.'

"But Herod said, 'This is John, whom I beheaded; he has been raised from the dead!' You know Herod himself had sent and laid hold of John and bound him in prison because the baptizer had said, 'It is not lawful for you to have your brother's wife.'

"Herod's sister-in-law, Herodias, held it against John and wanted to kill him, but she could not, for Herod feared John. The king knew John was a just and holy man, and he protected him.

"But on Herod's birthday he threw a feast for his nobles, the high officers, and the chief men of Galilee. And when Herodias's daughter herself came in and danced, and pleased Herod and those who sat with him, the king said to the girl, 'Ask me whatever you want, and I will give it to you. Whatever you ask me, I will give you, up to half my kingdom.'

"So she went out and said to her mother, 'What shall I ask?'

"And her mother said, 'The head of John the Baptist!'

"Immediately she came with haste to the king and said, 'I want you to give me at once the head of John the Baptist on a platter.'

"The king was exceedingly sorry, yet, because of the oaths and because of those who sat with him, he did not want to refuse her. Immediately the king sent an executioner and commanded John's head to be brought. And he went and beheaded him in prison, brought his head on a platter, and gave it to the girl. The girl gave it to her mother. When John's disciples heard of it, they came and took away his corpse and laid it in a tomb."

Even the retelling seemed to sadden Peter. He sat outside the inn where they were staying and said, "We gathered to Jesus and told Him all things, both what we had done and what we had taught. He said, 'Come aside by yourselves to a deserted place and rest awhile.' What a relief! So many of us had been coming and going, and we did not even have time to eat. So we departed with Him in the boat to a deserted place."

"And what happened there?"

"Something far too glorious to tell quickly. That's enough for tonight."

Mark was abjectly disappointed and knew he would find it hard to sleep with such a good story looming. But he had promised not to plead for more.

SEVENTEEN

Over the next few days Peter did not seem to be of a mind to reminisce. When not ministering in the region, he bounced ideas off Mark, seeming to experiment with various approaches to Paul and the others about the Gentile question.

"Perhaps it would be best if we maintained some distance between ourselves and Gentile believers."

"What kind of distance? And why? You yourself have championed the idea that we are as one in Christ."

"Oh, we are. No question about that. But I hate to offend strong Jewish believers by dining with Gentile brothers."

"But they are wrong to be offended."

Peter pressed his lips together. "I know," he said at last, "but am I not wrong to offend them?"

"Far be it from me to counsel you, master."

"Just answer the question, Mark. How do I justify offending brothers?"

"Will you not offend the Gentiles if you do not break bread with them? And how would you justify that? By saying you're keeping the peace with brothers who are in the wrong?"

Peter shook his head. "You see what Paul deals with every day?"

"Something tells me he is not conflicted over this."

"No doubt he knows his own mind, and so will everyone else in due time."

Within a few days Peter seemed less distracted, allowing that he had written both Paul and James—the brother of Jesus—who, along with John, was leading the church in Jerusalem. "I believe they will agree that we need a meeting of the minds on this. For it has to do with more than just following Jewish law. It concerns even circumcision. There are those among us who believe that Gentiles who become believers must be circumcised. Surely this is taking things too far."

Peter appeared more energized in his work while waiting for some response, and Mark was also able to ply from him more stories of Jesus. "I've waited patiently for the story you said was far too glorious to tell quickly."

"Indeed you have. Well, as you know, Jesus had been teaching in and around the area of the Sea of Galilee, and the multitudes just kept coming, running to Him from all the cities. I knew He had to be getting tired, but when He saw such vast crowds it was obvious He was moved with compassion for them. He told me, 'They are like sheep not having a shepherd.'

"All day long he taught them many things. When the day was far spent, we came to Him and said, 'This is a deserted place, and already the hour is late. Send the people away so they may go into the surrounding country and villages and buy themselves bread; for they have nothing to eat.' "

Peter chuckled at the memory. "Jesus said, '*You* give them something to eat.'

"I asked him if he really expected us to spend more than half a year's wages on bread for the crowd. He said, 'How many loaves do you have? Go and see.'

"Do you know, among the massive throng, all we came up with were five loaves of bread and two fish. But Jesus commanded everyone to sit on the grass in ranks, in hundreds and in fifties. He took those loaves and fish, looked up to heaven, blessed and broke the loaves, and gave them to us to set before the people."

Peter trembled, beaming at the memory. "He divided those two fish among them all, and not only did they all eat until they were full, but we also gathered up twelve baskets full of fragments."

Mark furrowed his brow. "How many people are we talking about?"

"Son, the men alone counted about five thousand."

"Amazing. And then did He finally get some rest?"

"Yes. He bade farewell to the crowd and sent them on their way, then instructed us to sail to the other side to Bethsaida, telling us He would be along later. I asked Him how He would get there, and He told me not to fret, that He wished to depart to the mountain to pray. Naturally I assumed He would hire another boat later.

"Now, Mark, this was not a long voyage, as you know, but all night the wind was against us and we began to despair. At about the fourth watch of the night, all of us were straining at rowing when the image of a man appeared to be walking right past us! We screamed in terror, assuming it a ghost. It stopped and turned toward us and said, 'Be of good cheer! It is I; do not be afraid.' It was Jesus! And when He climbed into the boat, the wind ceased. We were greatly amazed beyond measure and marveled. Feeding five thousand with one meager meal was nothing compared with this.

"We finally crossed over and anchored in Gennesaret, and when we disembarked in the morning, immediately people recognized Jesus.

They ran through that whole region and returned carrying on beds those who were sick. Wherever He went, into villages, cities, or the country, people laid the sick in the marketplaces and begged Him that they might just touch the hem of His garment. Now hear me, Mark: every person who touched Him was made well."

"No doubt Jesus was attracting the attention of the religious leaders again."

"Of course. The Pharisees and some scribes came to Him from Jerusalem. And when they saw some of us eating bread with unwashed hands, they found fault."

"You hadn't washed in the special way of the elders?"

"Correct, and as you know, the Pharisees and the rest of the Jews do not eat unless they do so. When they come from the marketplace, they do not eat unless they wash."

"Not to mention all the other rituals, like the washing of cups, pitchers, copper vessels, and couches."

"Precisely. So the Pharisees and scribes said, 'Why do Your disciples not walk according to the tradition of the elders, but eat bread with unwashed hands?'

"Jesus said, 'Well did Isaiah prophesy of you hypocrites, as it is written: *"This people honors Me with their lips, But their heart is far from Me. And in vain they worship Me, Teaching as doctrines the commandments of men."* ' "

"He said that to *them*?" Mark said. "They must have been furious!"

"Oh, He said more than that. He told them they had laid aside the commandment of God in order to hold the tradition of men. 'All too well you reject the commandment of God, that you may keep your tradition. For Moses said, *"Honor your father and your mother"*; and, *"He who curses father or mother, let him be put to death."* But you say, "If a man says to his father or mother, 'Whatever profit you might have received from me is Corban' " (that is a gift to God), then you no longer let him do anything for his father or his mother, making the word of God of no effect through your tradition which you have handed down. And many such things you do.'

"Then He called the multitude to Himself and said, 'Hear Me, everyone, and understand: There is nothing that enters a man from outside which can defile him; but the things which come out of him, those are the things that defile a man.' And He concluded again with His charge: 'If anyone has ears to hear, let him hear!'

"We disciples were puzzled too, and when Jesus finally slipped into a house away from the crowd, we questioned Him. He said, 'Are you thus without understanding also? Do you not perceive that whatever enters a man from outside cannot defile him, because it does not enter his heart but his stomach, and is eliminated, thus purifying all foods? What comes out of a man, that defiles a man. For from within, out of the heart of men, proceed evil thoughts, adulteries, fornications, murders, thefts, covetousness, wickedness, deceit, lewdness, an evil eye, blasphemy, pride, foolishness. All these evil things come from within and defile a man.' "

"What must it have been like to spend your days under the counsel of One so wise?"

"Mark, we had not an inkling of our privilege until He was gone from us. From there we went to the region of Tyre and Sidon and followed Him into a house where He hoped to have some privacy. But He could not be hidden. A Greek woman, a Syro-Phoenician by birth whose young daughter had an unclean spirit, heard about Him and came and fell at His feet. She pleaded with Him to come and cast the demon out of her daughter. Jesus said, 'Let the children be filled first, for it is not good to take the children's bread and throw it to the little dogs.' "

"What did He mean by that?"

"We had no idea, but she seemed to understand. She said, 'Yes, Lord, yet even the little dogs under the table eat from the children's crumbs.'

"Her persistence seemed to convince Him of her faith. He said, 'For this saying go your way; the demon has gone out of your daughter.'

"From there we traveled through the midst of the region of Decapolis to the Sea of Galilee. There some brought to Him one who was deaf and had a speech impediment, and they begged Him to put His hand on him. Jesus took him aside from the multitude and put His fingers in his ears, and He spat and touched his tongue. Then, looking up to heaven, He sighed and said, 'Be opened.'

"Immediately the man's ears were opened, and his tongue was loosed, and he spoke plainly.

"Jesus commanded the people that they should tell no one; but the more He commanded them, the more widely they proclaimed it. People were astonished beyond measure, saying, 'He has done all things well. He makes both the deaf to hear and the mute to speak.' "

"And that feeding of the five thousand men and their families was not the only time Jesus did that, was it?"

"Oh, no. Another time, soon after this, Jesus called us disciples to Him and said, 'I have compassion on the multitude, because they have now continued with Me three days and have nothing to eat. And if I send them away hungry to their own houses, they will faint on the way; for some of them have come from afar.'

"Of course we asked Him where we would find bread in the wilderness when we had only seven loaves and a few small fish. And this time there were about four thousand people. Again He commanded the multitude to sit, and He took what we had and gave thanks, broke the food into pieces, and gave it to us to distribute to them. They ate and were filled, and we took up seven large baskets of leftover fragments.

"After He sent the people on their way, we immediately sailed to the region of Dalmanutha. Again the Pharisees came to dispute with Him, seeking a sign from heaven, testing Him. He sighed deeply in His spirit and said, 'Why does this generation seek a sign? Assuredly, I say to you, no sign shall be given to this generation.'

"We climbed again into the boat and left for the other side, but we had forgotten to bring bread. All we had on board was one loaf. Jesus said, 'Take heed, beware of the leaven of the Pharisees and the leaven of Herod.'

"Well, we whispered among ourselves that He must have said this because we had forgotten the bread. But He approached from the other side of the boat and said, 'Why do you reason because you have no bread? Do you not yet perceive nor understand? Is your heart still hardened? Having eyes, do you not see? And having ears, do you not hear? And do you not remember? When I broke the five loaves for the five thousand, how many baskets full of fragments did you take up?'

"We said, 'Twelve.'

" 'Also, when I broke the seven for the four thousand, how many large baskets full of fragments did you take up?'

"And we said, 'Seven.'

" 'Then how is it you do not understand?' "

"I still don't understand, Peter. What was He saying?"

"I believe He was reminding us that He could supernaturally provide anything we needed and warning us not to let religiosity invade our faith. That was when we finally understood that He was not speaking of the leaven of bread, but of the false doctrines and practices of the Pharisees and the Sadducees. That is one of the reasons I feel so strongly that we must not yoke Gentile believers with our old laws."

"Tell me of another miracle."

"Very well. When we came to Bethsaida, some brought a blind man to Him and begged Him to touch him. He took the man by the hand

and led him out of town. Jesus spat on his eyes and put His hands on him, then asked if he saw anything.

"The man looked up and said, 'I see men like trees, walking.' I believe he was saying that he could see, but not distinctly. So Jesus put His hands on the man's eyes again, and he was restored and saw everyone clearly. Jesus sent him home, saying, 'Neither go into the town, nor tell anyone in the town.'

"How I wish I could have been there, Peter."

"Like me, you would never forget it."

EIGHTEEN

It seemed to Mark to take forever for the apostles and elders to agree to a large meeting regarding the Jewish-Gentile question. He and Peter had been traveling and ministering together for years, and it took more than fifteen years after the death, burial, and resurrection of Christ for a council of all parties to be convened in Jerusalem.

According to Peter, certain disciples of James—the brother of Jesus and the ruling elder of the church in Jerusalem—had gone to the church at Antioch and taught the brethren that unless they were circumcised according to the custom of Moses, they could not be saved. Mark naturally found Peter extremely vexed over this.

"I know better, because God has shown me. He called us to preach first to Israel, but when His own chosen people rejected Him, He sent us into all the world to preach the gospel to everyone."

"But you, like me, Peter, can at least understand the dilemma of the Judaizers."

"Of course I can! Like you, like all the disciples, I was raised a Jew. The laws of Moses have dominated my life. I was circumcised, and I followed all the rules and traditions. That's why it was such a revelation to me when the Spirit led me into the home of an actual Gentile, Cornelius, and further gave me utterance to lead him to faith in Christ. How dare these men make an abomination of the free gift of salvation, offered to all who believe?"

Word came that Paul and Barnabas had vigorously disputed the Jerusalem representatives, and based on Peter's letter and the insistence of James's disciples, it was determined that the two leaders in Antioch and certain others of them should go to Jerusalem and meet with the council of apostles and elders to settle the matter.

Mark had longed to return home and see his now frail mother. Old and infirm as she was, still she supervised the servants and hosted the Jerusalem Council in her upper room. Mark did not consider himself in any respect equal to the apostles and elders, and thus felt privileged just to be there. Paul and Mark's cousin greeted him, Barnabas perhaps a bit more warmly than Paul. But at one point Mark noticed that Peter and Paul quickly quieted as he passed by, and later Peter admitted he had been trying to disabuse Paul of his negative opinion of Mark.

The rare occasion of the council spurred talk on many subjects and doctrines, but of course the primary one concerned the obligation of Gentile believers in Christ. Barnabas and Paul were called upon to bring a report, and after Barnabas gave a general and encouraging update on the church at Antioch, Paul took the floor.

"We were generously sent here by the body of believers," he said, "and as we passed through Phoenicia and Samaria, we told of the widespread conversion of the Gentiles. This caused a great outpouring of joy from all the brethren. We most appreciate being received by the church here, especially by you apostles and the elders, and I ask that you bear with me as I tell you of many new Gentile converts."

Paul held forth for several minutes, telling thrilling stories of conversions—including that of Titus, who was one who had accompanied him and Barnabas. But soon Paul was interrupted by some of the sect of the Pharisees who believed in Jesus. They rose up, saying, "Paul, it is necessary for you and Barnabas to circumcise these new believers and to command them to keep the law of Moses."

Paul responded angrily and Barnabas tried to be more conciliatory. But the more the two sides argued, the louder the discussion became. Finally Peter stood, and Mark was proud to see that he still enjoyed deep respect and deference from all. They sat and quieted themselves.

"Men and brethren," he said, "you know that a good while ago God chose among us, that by my mouth the Gentiles should hear the word of the gospel and believe. So God, who knows the heart, acknowledged them by giving them the Holy Spirit, just as He did to us, and made no distinction between us and them, purifying their hearts by faith.

"Now therefore, why do you test God by putting a yoke on the neck of the disciples which neither our fathers nor we were able to bear? But we believe that through the grace of the Lord Jesus Christ we shall be saved in the same manner as they. Now please, remain silent and listen to Barnabas and Paul declaring how many miracles and wonders God has worked through them among the Gentiles."

Barnabas and Paul related more stories, and when they had finished, James said, "Men and brethren, listen to me: Simon has declared how God at the first visited the Gentiles to take out of them a people for His name. And with this the words of the prophets agree, just as it is written: *'After this I will return and will rebuild the tabernacle of David, which has fallen down; I will rebuild its ruins, and I will set it up; So that the rest of mankind may seek the Lord, even all the Gentiles who are called by My name, says the Lord who does all these things.'*

"Known to God from eternity are all His works. Therefore I judge that we should not trouble those from among the Gentiles who are turning to God, but that we write to them to abstain from things polluted by idols, from sexual immorality, from things strangled, and from blood.

"For Moses has had throughout many generations those who preach him in every city, being read in the synagogues every Sabbath."

The council then decided to send chosen men of their own company to Antioch with Paul and Barnabas to inform Gentile believers in Antioch, Syria, and Cilicia of what they had decided: that they need not be circumcised or subject to the whole law of Moses, but "since we have heard that some who went out from us have troubled you with words, unsettling your souls, saying, 'You must be circumcised and keep the law'—to whom we gave no such commandment—it seemed good to us, being assembled with one accord, to send chosen men to you with our beloved Barnabas and Paul, men who have risked their lives for the name of our Lord Jesus Christ.

"We have therefore sent Judas and Silas, who will also report the same things by word of mouth. For it seemed good to the Holy Spirit, and to us, to lay upon you no greater burden than these necessary things: that you abstain from things offered to idols, from blood, from things strangled, and from sexual immorality. If you keep yourselves from these, you will do well. Farewell."

Word soon came to Mark and to Peter that when Paul and Barnabas and the others had gathered the multitude together at Antioch and read the letter, all rejoiced over its encouragement. In a letter to Mark, Barnabas reported that Judas and Silas, themselves being prophets, also exhorted and strengthened the brethren. And after they had stayed there for a time, they were sent back with greetings from the brethren to the apostles. "Paul and I also remained here," Barnabas wrote, "teaching and preaching the word of the Lord, with many others also.

Recently Paul suggested to me, 'Let us now go back and visit our brethren in every city where we have preached the word of the Lord, and see how they are doing.'

"Mark, I told Paul that you should be invited to join us, but he insisted that we should not take with us one who had departed from us in Pamphylia and had not gone on with us to the work. I know that Peter spoke highly of you to Paul in Jerusalem, and so I persisted, but Paul was adamant. Sad to say, the contention became so sharp that we have parted from each other. I need you to sail with me to Cyprus, as Paul has chosen Silas and departed, being commended by the brethren to the grace of God to go through Syria and Cilicia, strengthening the churches. Would you come?"

Peter gave his blessing for Mark to join his cousin, then traveled with Mark as far as Antioch, where Peter would minister for a time in the absence of Paul and Barnabas and Silas. On that journey to Antioch, Mark beseeched Peter to tell more of his time with Jesus.

"We did have a most telling discussion one day. As we followed Him to the towns of Caesarea Philippi, on the road He said, 'Who do men say that I am?'

"We told Him, 'John the Baptist; but some say, Elijah; and others, one of the prophets.'

"He said, 'But who do you say that I am?' "

"He asked that straight out?"

"He did, and I quickly said, 'You are the Christ.' He looked at me knowingly, and I was certain I had spoken for us all. He strictly warned us that we should tell no one about Him."

"Why?"

"The people would have forced Him to become their king and to throw off the shackles of Rome. But that was not what He was about. He began to teach us that the Son of Man must suffer many things, and be rejected by the elders and chief priests and scribes, and be killed, and after three days rise again. He said all this openly to the point where I took Him aside and rebuked Him. But He turned around and looked at the other disciples, rebuking me and saying, 'Get behind Me, Satan! For you are not mindful of the things of God, but the things of men.'

"You can only imagine my humiliation. My motive had been pure. I loved Him. But I could not fathom His leaving us, especially by dying. But the next time He spoke to the multitudes, He said, 'Whoever desires to come after Me, let him deny himself, and take up his cross, and follow Me. For whoever desires to save his life will lose it, but whoever loses his life for My sake and the gospel's will save it. For what will it profit a man if he gains the whole world, and loses his own soul? Or what will a man give in exchange for his soul? For whoever is ashamed of Me and My words in this adulterous and sinful generation, of him the Son of Man also will be ashamed when He comes in the glory of His Father with the holy angels.'

"Did you understand all of this?"

"Not all. But I gathered that He was comparing this worldly life to the eternality of the soul. He confided to the twelve of us that 'there are some standing here who will not taste death till they see the kingdom of God present with power.' Mark, I was among those He was referring to, despite that He had just compared me to Satan. James and John were also with Him to see the kingdom of God present with power."

"What did he mean? You will not die until He returns again?"

"Oh, no, I did not take it that way at all, for He made clear that no man knows the day or the hour of His coming. If He made clear it was to happen in my lifetime, that would contradict His assertion that not even He knows when He's coming, but only the Father."

"Then what was he saying, Peter?"

"I believe when He referred to the kingdom of God sent with power he meant the great outpouring of the Holy Spirit at the time of Pentecost. Six days later Jesus took the three of us and led us up on a high mountain, where He was transfigured before us. His clothes shone exceedingly white like snow, such as no launderer on earth could whiten them. And suddenly there stood Elijah with Moses, and they talked with Jesus."

"You must have been terrified! What was happening to Him?"

"Oh, I was! We all were. Greatly afraid and not knowing what else to say, I said, 'Rabbi, it is good for us to be here; and let us make three tabernacles: one for You, one for Moses, and one for Elijah.'

"A cloud came and overshadowed us, and a voice came out of the cloud, saying, 'This is My beloved Son. Hear Him!' Suddenly, when we looked around, we saw no one anymore but Jesus."

"So these were spirits? Ghosts?"

"I believe they were the saints themselves, Mark."

"And you have no doubt you heard the voice of God from a cloud?"

"That is something one does neither mistake nor forget. As we came down from the mountain, Jesus commanded that we should tell no one what we had seen, till the Son of Man had risen from the dead. We kept this word ourselves, but we wondered what He meant about rising from the dead.

"We asked Him, 'Why do the scribes say that Elijah must come first?'

"He said, 'Indeed, Elijah is coming first and restores all things. And how is it written concerning the Son of Man, that He must suffer many things and be treated with contempt? But I say to you that Elijah has also come, and they did to him whatever they wished, as it is written of him.' "

"I'm terribly confused. Were you?"

"For a time, yes. But we concluded that He was speaking of John the

Baptizer having come in the spirit and power of Elijah. And he was put to death, just as the prophets foretold.

"When we rejoined the other disciples, Jesus saw a great multitude around them and scribes disputing with them. Immediately, when they saw Him, all the people were greatly amazed, and ran to Him, greeting Him.

"He asked the scribes, 'What are you discussing with them?'

"One from the crowd said, 'Teacher, I brought You my son, who has a mute spirit. And wherever it seizes him, it throws him down; he foams at the mouth, gnashes his teeth, and becomes rigid. So I spoke to Your disciples, that they should cast it out, but they could not.'

"Jesus looked terribly disappointed in the other nine disciples, not to mention the father of the mute boy and the scribes who were there only to test Him. He said, 'O faithless generation, how long shall I be with you? How long shall I bear with you? Bring him to Me.'

"As soon as the spirit saw Jesus, it convulsed the boy and he fell, foaming at the mouth.

"Jesus asked the boy's father, 'How long has this been happening to him?'

" 'From childhood,' he said. 'And often he has thrown him both into the fire and into the water to destroy him. But if You can do anything, have compassion on us and help us.'

"Jesus said, 'If you can believe, all things are possible to him who believes.'

"Immediately the father cried out with tears, 'Lord, I believe; help my unbelief!' "

"An honest, human man," Mark said.

"Oh, yes. And when Jesus saw more people come running, He said, 'Deaf and dumb spirit, I command you, come out of him and enter him no more!'

"Then the spirit cried out, convulsed the boy greatly, and came out of him. The boy lay there so still that many said, 'He is dead.' But Jesus took him by the hand and lifted him, and he arose."

"Why could not the other disciples cast out the demon?" Mark said.

"That's what they asked Jesus privately. He said, 'This kind can come out by nothing but prayer and fasting.'

"We departed from there and passed through Galilee, but He did not want anyone to know He was there. He told us, 'The Son of Man is being betrayed into the hands of men, and they will kill Him. And after He is killed, He will rise the third day.'

"Mark, we had no idea what He meant, and not one of us had the courage to ask."

As always, Mark marveled at the stories of the Master, but he was struck anew with the tragedy it would have been had the gospel of the kingdom been kept from the Gentiles. This would prove an endless debate among the faithful, but Mark was confident that he knew the mind of God on the matter, even if his understanding was based solely on Peter's story of Cornelius.

NINETEEN

As Mark and his beloved mentor drew within a day's journey from Antioch, Mark's eager anticipation of traveling again with his cousin was tempered only by his disappointment that there was so much more he yearned to hear from Peter about Jesus. Mark was in his forties by now, and Peter much older. Mark only hoped they would reunite someday and have time to finish the entire story. He still believed he could talk the old man into getting it all written.

On that final day of travel, Peter reminisced more about his time with the Master.

"Knowing how resolute Jesus was that no one should know He was in the area, my wife and I hosted Him at our home in Capernaum. Once we were safely inside, and the rest of the disciples with us, He did one of those frequently disconcerting things He was known for. He said, 'What was it you disputed among yourselves on the road?'

"None of us dared say, Mark, because we were so ashamed. I don't see the danger of this in you, but this may be instructive nonetheless for the next step in your ministry life. You see, we had been disputing among ourselves who was the greatest."

"Besides Jesus, you mean."

"Yes, sadly. Just among us. Now you know He was not much older than we were, except for John who was nearly ten years His junior. But Jesus was so wise that He often treated us as His children, which we, of course, were. He sat and called us about Him, and when we had settled at His feet, He said, 'If anyone desires to be first, he shall be last of all and servant of all.'

"Just as we were wondering what He meant, one of my little nephews toddled into the room and headed directly for Jesus. Children always seemed drawn to Him. Jesus took him in His arms in the midst of us and said, 'Whoever receives one of these little children in My name receives Me; and whoever receives Me, receives not Me but Him who sent Me.'

"John said, 'Teacher, we saw someone who does not follow us casting out demons in Your name, and we forbade him because he does not follow us.'

"But Jesus said, 'Do not forbid him, for no one who works a miracle in My name can soon afterward speak evil of Me. For he who is not against us is on our side. For whoever gives you a cup of water to drink in My name, because you belong to Christ, assuredly, I say to you, he will by no means lose his reward.

" 'But whoever causes one of these little ones who believe in Me to stumble, it would be better for him if a millstone were hung around his neck, and he were thrown into the sea. If your hand causes you to sin, cut it off. It is better for you to enter into life maimed, rather than having two hands, to go to hell, into the fire that shall never be quenched—where *"Their worm does not die and the fire is not quenched."*

" 'And if your foot causes you to sin, cut it off. It is better for you to enter life lame, rather than having two feet, to be cast into hell, into the fire that shall never be quenched—where *"Their worm does not die and the fire is not quenched."*

" 'And if your eye causes you to sin, pluck it out. It is better for you to enter the kingdom of God with one eye, rather than having two eyes, to be cast into hell fire—where *"Their worm does not die and the fire is not quenched."*

" 'For everyone will be seasoned with fire, and every sacrifice will be seasoned with salt. Salt is good, but if the salt loses its flavor, how will you season it? Have salt in yourselves, and have peace with one another.' "

Mark marveled. "I would have been entirely lost, Peter. In fact, I still am. What did you make of all that?"

"Well, we had been raised to believe that the greatest among us were rulers and leaders. He was now saying that the truly greatest was a servant. And to be sure, He was the greatest example of that I have ever known. I have come to believe that the greatest in the kingdom is the one willing to serve humbly."

"And what was He saying, using the child as an example?"

"I believe He was speaking of people new to the faith. They are young and defenseless and easily swayed, so woe to anyone who leads them astray."

Mark fell silent and stared into the distance.

"You're troubled," Peter said.

Mark nodded. "And you know why."

"Of course. For the same reason I was when first Jesus spoke of cutting off body parts rather than sinning. You and I are believers in the Christ, and yet as our colleague Paul preaches, we continue to fight the old man of sin. We are sinners. You don't want to have to cut off parts of you that seem to cause you to sin."

Mark cocked his head. "Obviously. So what was Jesus implying?"

"I think He used such a gruesome comparison to show how futile it is for us to try to do anything about our sin. No matter what we do, even mutilate ourselves, we cannot rid ourselves of it. We repent of our sins and accept His forgiveness and His payment for us on the cross. Of course at that time I didn't know or understand either."

That made Mark feel a little better. "Part of me wishes I had been a disciple, but another part of me knows I would have been the least among you."

"You were but in your teen years then, Mark. Imagine your mother allowing you to traipse around Judea and Galilee with us."

They shared a laugh.

"Did Jesus get some peace and rest at your house?"

"Some, but soon He arose from there and came to the region of Judea by the other side of the Jordan. And multitudes gathered to Him again, and as He was accustomed, He taught them again. Of course, when He was around and the crowds were following and—worse, to the leaders—listening, the Pharisees were never far.

"They came and asked Him, 'Is it lawful for a man to divorce his wife?' "

"They were testing Him," Mark said.

"Of course. And He answered, 'What did Moses command you?'

"They said, 'Moses permitted a man to write a certificate of divorce, and to dismiss her.'

"Jesus said, 'Because of the hardness of your heart he wrote you this precept. But from the beginning of the creation, God *"made them male and female. For this reason a man shall leave his father and mother and be joined to his wife, and the two shall become one flesh."* So then they are no longer two, but one flesh. Therefore what God has joined together, let not man separate.'

"Later, in private, we asked Him to elaborate. He said, 'Whoever divorces his wife and marries another commits adultery against her. And if a woman divorces her husband and marries another, she commits adultery.' "

"What did the Pharisees say to that?"

Peter smiled. "They seldom said anything. They had a lot of questions, all intended to trip Him up. But once He spoke, they had little to say.

"Later the crowds brought little children to Him, that He might touch them. To my shame, some of the other disciples and I rebuked those who brought them. Jesus was greatly displeased. He said, 'Let the little children come to Me, and do not forbid them; for of such is the kingdom of God. Assuredly, I say to you, whoever does not receive the kingdom of God as a little child will by no means enter it.' He took them in His arms, laid His hands on them, and blessed them.

"One day as He was going out on the road, a man came running, knelt before Him, and said, 'Good Teacher, what shall I do that I may inherit eternal life?'

"Jesus said, 'Why do you call Me good? No one is good but One, that is, God. You know the commandments: *"Do not commit adultery," "Do not murder," "Do not steal," "Do not bear false witness," "Do not covet," "Honor your father and your mother."* '

"The man said, 'Teacher, all these things I have kept from my youth.'

"Jesus looked lovingly at him, and said, 'One thing you lack: Go your way, sell whatever you have and give to the poor, and you will have treasure in heaven; and come, take up the cross, and follow Me.'

"The man's countenance fell and he left sorrowful. It was obvious from his dress that he had great possessions and was unwilling to sacrifice any.

"Jesus said to us, 'How hard it is for those who have riches to enter the kingdom of God!' We were astonished at His words, but again He said, 'Children, how hard it is for those who trust in riches to enter the kingdom of God! It is easier for a camel to go through the eye of a needle than for a rich man to enter the kingdom of God.'

"We were greatly puzzled, saying among ourselves, 'Who then can be saved?'

"Jesus said, 'With men it is impossible, but not with God; for with God all things are possible.'

"Mark, I felt I needed to remind Him. I said, 'See, we have left all and followed You.'

"Jesus said, 'Assuredly, I say to you, there is no one who has left house or brothers or sisters or father or mother or wife or children or lands, for My sake and the gospel's, who shall not receive a hundredfold now in this time—houses and brothers and sisters and mothers and children and lands, with persecutions—and in the age to come, eternal life. But many who are first will be last, and the last first.' "

"His message on humility and servanthood again."

"We would hear it over and over. But what troubled us most at that time was that He began warning us of ominous events. We were on the road to Jerusalem, and we were both amazed and afraid. He took us twelve aside again and began to tell us things that would happen to Him: 'Behold, we are going up to Jerusalem, and the Son of Man will be betrayed to the chief priests and to the scribes; and they will condemn Him to death and deliver Him to the Gentiles; and they will mock Him, and scourge Him, and spit on Him, and kill Him. And the third day He will rise again.' "

"He was that clear that early about His resurrection? How could you have all missed that, or forgotten it?"

"You see, Mark, it strikes me now that it was as if we were deaf. We hoped He was speaking in riddles again, because we could not comprehend, nor did we wish to, that He Himself might die. Yet everything He said came true exactly as He had told us.

"It wasn't long after that that it became clear I was not the only impudent one among us. James and John, the brothers He called the Sons of Thunder, came to Him, saying, 'Teacher, we want You to do for us whatever we ask.'

"He appeared amused. He said, 'What do you want Me to do for you?'

"They said, 'Grant us that we may sit, one on Your right hand and the other on Your left, in Your glory.' "

"This after all His teaching on servanthood and humility?"

Peter nodded. "Jesus said, 'You do not know what you ask. Are you able to drink the cup that I drink, and be baptized with the baptism that I am baptized with?'

"They said, 'We are able.'

"Jesus said, 'You will indeed drink the cup that I drink, and with the baptism I am baptized with you will be baptized; but to sit on My right hand and on My left is not Mine to give, but it is for those for whom it is prepared.'

"I don't mind telling you, Mark, the rest of us were greatly displeased with James and John. But Jesus called us to Himself and said, 'You know that those who are considered rulers over the Gentiles lord it over them, and their great ones exercise authority over them. Yet it shall not be so among you; but whoever desires to become great among you shall be your servant. And whoever of you desires to be first shall be slave of all. For even the Son of Man did not come to be served, but to serve, and to give His life a ransom for many.'

"Mark, that was the essence of what He taught and what He was all about. We did not know then that He would actually give His life a ransom for us."

"And not just you," Mark said, "but also the children of Israel. And most confounding and wonderful, to the Gentiles as well."

Peter nodded, but he had a faraway look that troubled Mark. Surely his mentor would never waver on that, as he was the first God called to violate the ancient traditions and break bread with Gentiles, eventually leading them to salvation.

TWO YEARS LATER

{ TWENTY-SEVEN YEARS SINCE THE CRUCIFIXION }

TWENTY

Mark and Barnabas had enjoyed a long season encouraging the Gentile believers in Barnabas's homeland. They built up the existing church and established more, teaching and training presbyters to lead new congregations. Meanwhile, Mark gladly received any news from Jerusalem and Antioch, especially from his beloved mentor. Lately, however, missives from Peter had become scarce and their tone subdued.

As the time drew near for Mark and Barnabas to return to the church at Antioch, Mark grew anxious over what they might encounter there. "The old controversy seems to be brewing again," he told Barnabas. "I thought the entirety of church leadership, from John and James in Jerusalem and Peter in Antioch to Paul as he travels abroad, were in agreement on this issue."

"Surely," Barnabas said, "they're not squabbling over the Gentile question yet again. The Jerusalem Council should have settled that. What is Peter saying?"

"Not much, actually. Only that he is feeling estranged from the Gentiles, that he has somehow offended them."

"I cannot imagine. He himself is the one who was told by the Spirit to expand the gospel to the Gentiles, and the majority of our church in Antioch is made up of them."

Mark showed Barnabas the latest letter from Peter, in which he conceded that attendance, on the part of both Jewish and Gentile believers, was declining. " 'The Jews have begun forming their own separate fellowship,' " he read aloud, " 'and the Gentiles feel I have sided with them. Perhaps I have.' "

Barnabas looked up. " 'Perhaps I *have*?' What could he be saying? Surely he has not succumbed to pressure from the Judaizers. He has long been a strong proponent of the Jewish and Gentile equality in Christ."

Mark cocked his head, recalling the conversation he and Peter had had years before.

"No?" Barnabas said.

Mark told him of Peter's comment that while he fully recognized that no Jewish law or tradition—like circumcision—was necessary for anyone to be saved, he also wondered if he was right to offend Jewish believers by dining with Gentiles.

"Him, of all people," Mark said.

"And yet he has always been a deep thinker, Mark. Some would question whether those who believe that anything must be added to salvation by faith through grace alone are even true believers. I, for one, am convinced that true believers can honestly disagree on such matters."

"But they are wrong, Barnabas!"

"Perhaps. I know where I stand, but dare I tell another where he should stand?"

"I know someone who would."

Barnabas laughed. "Yes, Paul would not countenance anything that appeared to add a jot or tittle to the gospel. You know he is also on his way back to Antioch."

"Verily?"

Barnabas nodded. "He is scheduled to arrive about a month after we do. By then I hope we'll have this settled."

"Again."

"Yes, it may never really be settled. But we must somehow aid our brother Peter in reuniting the brethren."

Mark began counting the days before their departure to Antioch. He was troubled that old quarrels were clearly troubling Peter. And most of all he longed for time with his mentor not clouded by such matters. How could he get the man to continue reminiscing about Jesus' ministry if he was distracted? It had been a long time since Mark had heard a firsthand account of Jesus' teachings, and he had been lugging around bits of notes from Peter's previous stories the whole time. Someday he would have to get the old man to take the time to tell him everything he could remember.

WHEN FINALLY MARK and Barnabas sailed from Salamis to Antioch in Syria, they were welcomed by a small party from the church who seemed less enthusiastic than normal. In the past Mark had always looked forward to arriving at new locations or ones he had not visited for a while, because the brothers and sisters were so solicitous and warm in their welcomes. Now he and Barnabas returned the embraces and kisses of the brethren, but it was plain in all their eyes that something was on their minds. It wasn't long before the man driving their horse-drawn wagon said he wished both Barnabas and Paul were back in charge of the church.

The man leaned over and said to Mark, "Not to slight you, sir, but as you are aware, we know these men from their years of service."

Mark smiled. "No offense taken. And you know me as the one who deserted Paul."

"That is long in the past and you were a youngster. For all we know, you were in the right. All reports of you since then have been favorable."

"You might wish to share that with Paul when he arrives next month."

"I will! But you should know, some of those good reports come from him."

"But I have not been with him for years."

"They are secondhand accounts, then, but only recently a message was delivered from him wherein he expressed his eagerness to return to old friends, and you were listed among them."

Mark whispered to Barnabas, "What do you make of that?"

Barnabas shrugged. "Perhaps even a man like Paul matures with age. I wonder," he added, turning back to the driver, "was I listed as well?"

The man laughed. "You were listed first, sir."

"Then perhaps he has forgiven us both."

SAD TO SAY, Mark found Peter looking even older than he should have after two years. The strain of leadership had clearly marked his face, particularly around his eyes. And his gray hair was nearly white now. He could not mask his sadness, even as he tried to smile broadly at his reunion with Mark and Barnabas. And he seemed reserved and quiet, particularly around Mark's cousin. It was as if he wanted to speak with Mark alone, but Barnabas was not getting the hint. He said, "So tell Mark and me what the problem is here."

Peter sat heavily and sighed. "I don't understand it myself," he said. "The whole ordeal has gotten away from me."

"What ordeal and how so?" Barnabas said.

"Some men came from Jerusalem and inserted themselves into the congregation and the work here. I watched them carefully, and they soon proved themselves diligent and devout, though they seemed standoffish toward the Gentile believers. When finally I confronted them about this, they admitted they were disciples of Jesus' brother James and had been sent to help but also to evaluate our work. It turns out, gentlemen, that they are Judaizers. They know better than to continue harping on the need for Gentile believers to be circumcised or to follow the whole of the law. I preach regularly on the truth that Jesus fulfilled the law and that salvation is by grace alone. But they chastised me for abandoning my heritage and my Jewish friends by rubbing in their noses the fact that I dined with Gentiles at nearly every meal."

"Those men cannot really be disciples of James!" Mark said. "The only prohibitions that survived the Jerusalem Council were his, and if he had required more, he would have said so. There is certainly no restriction against the brethren, Jew and Gentile, eating together. No one knows that better than you."

Peter looked away and shook his head. "And yet I do not want to offend."

"That doesn't sound like you," Mark said. "I know you've expressed it before in my hearing, but where is the man who said he would die for the Lord? Where is the man who stood up to the Pharisees and the Romans and told them he would obey the Lord rather than men, regardless of the consequences?"

"But I am not opposing Rome or religious Jews here. I have been put in a place where I must walk a line between devout brothers. I began dining with only the Gentiles once a day, and with the Jews at the other meal. Others began following my lead—"

"As men always have, Peter," Barnabas said. "That is why you must be so careful in what you say and what you do. I don't envy you."

"Eventually I began declining invitations to meals from the Gentiles, and the Jews appreciated this and expressed that my offense had abated. I have been unable to hide my reluctance to dine with the Gentiles, and I know that now *they* are offended."

Mark was frankly disappointed, almost as deeply as when he was a teenager and saw Peter deny the Lord. He jerked to attention when Barnabas said, "Well, they shouldn't be offended. They are being petty. We're merely talking about meals here. Who cares who eats with whom? Your motive is pure, sir, and I support you."

"You do?" Mark said, peering at Barnabas to see whether he was being genuine or using sarcasm to make the opposite point.

It was clear that Peter believed Barnabas and was encouraged. "Thank you for that, friend."

Mark held up his hands. "Have we not all benefited from seeing copies of some letters from Paul to various churches? I daresay his treatises on the equality of believers stems in large part from your own testimony, Peter, of how the Spirit revealed this truth to you at Cornelius's house."

"I do not dispute the equality of believers, Mark," Peter said. "I simply want to keep the peace."

"At the expense of truth?" Mark said. "I have learned much from you, master, and I hesitate to disagree or presume to counsel you, but—"

"And well you shouldn't," Barnabas said. He leaned toward Peter and spoke earnestly. "I admire your example in this, Peter. People look to you for leadership, and if you believe you should refrain from breaking bread with Gentiles, you must be allowed to follow your conscience. If you believe that my also refraining would be the most proper thing for someone in my station, I would accede to your request."

"And I do," Peter said, energized. "I'm asking that all the elders of this church avoid offense by dining only with those who share their birth race."

"You are not serious!" Mark said, standing. "We are one in Christ, neither Jew nor Greek, neither circumcised nor uncircumcised. If you must choose whom not to offend, choose those who believe the gospel! Will you discipline or cast me out if I choose to dine with any believer?"

Peter rubbed his face. "I would not want to offend you either, son."

"You don't want to offend anyone! And yet Paul rightly teaches that the truth of the cross offends. I do not know what has happened to you, Peter, but I cannot abide this. When you wonder what has happened to this body, you must search yourself and your motives. In your urgency to not offend anyone, you have offended all—the Gentiles by separating yourself from them despite that they are your brothers, and the Jews by encouraging them in this heresy. They may accept you and respect you, but they are wrong, as are you."

"You may be right."

"Oh, Peter, I would rather that you argue with me even in your error, for there is more respect due a man who knows his own mind, even if he is wrong. But you are both wrong and yet still unsure what to do about it."

The last thing Mark wanted to do was to humiliate his mentor and friend. Knowing that Peter either had no response, or at least no good one, Mark chose to storm out rather than embarrass the man further. He could only imagine what Peter and Barnabas were saying about him now. Mark couldn't wait until Paul arrived. Surely he had heard of what was going on and would not be content until the issue was dealt with in the open.

The question in Mark's mind was whether he could trust the report that it seemed Paul once again considered him a friend. He resolved to be in the welcoming party that greeted Paul's ship, for Mark wanted to be sure the apostle and missionary knew he was aligned with him on this matter.

Once Paul reached the church, sparks were sure to fly.

TWENTY-ONE

The next few weeks were the most conflicted of Mark's life. Besides news from Jerusalem that his mother was failing—and of course he wondered when he would be able to make the trip of three hundred or so miles to see her—the controversy in Antioch seemed to worsen every day. For the life of him, Mark could not understand Peter's seeming weakness in the face of Judaizer criticism. That his own cousin was now in league with Peter on this was all the more disconcerting. Peter and Barnabas were revered by the Jewish believers, and it soon became apparent that the few Gentiles who remained were putting all their hopes into the return of Paul and, thus, sanity.

Mark had given up trying to argue with Peter or Barnabas, though they met frequently for prayer and planning. Neither seemed willing to acknowledge that attendance was continuing to drop. If only they had raised the subject, Mark would have held forth with gusto on what was wrong. But when he had brought it up, following that first meeting on his and Barnabas's return from Cyprus, neither would even discuss it.

If Mark had learned anything from Peter, it was forthrightness. He spoke his mind, always—he hoped—respectfully. And he found it impossible to hide his concern over the church. Barnabas seemed to paste on a joyous smile whenever he was in Peter's presence, and the two appeared to be vigorously going about the work of evangelizing and equipping the saints as always. How they could persist in this with the church in turmoil was beyond Mark's comprehension. He believed they had to be dreading the return of Paul as much as he yearned for it.

As that day drew nearer, Peter seemed more on edge, and it was also clear that he was trying to reestablish his friendship with Mark. Praying and planning together was one thing, but Mark could not offer the same eye contact and emotional warmth as before, because he simply didn't feel the same. Oh, he loved the man and in most ways respected him as much as anyone he had ever met. Peter was the closest thing to a father Mark had enjoyed in more than twenty years. But this issue—though it was hardly personal—had come between them. And much as Peter had to enjoy Barnabas's support, it became apparent that he was eager to return to Mark's good graces.

Peter brought news to Mark of his mother. "Mary is still as robust as a woman her age and in her condition can be," he said. "And the latest message from her is that you must not make a special trip when there is so much to do here."

"She is only saying that, Peter. I would not forgive myself if I neglected her too long and missed seeing her once more before she died. Do you think that is a possibility?"

"Always. Of course we never know when God will call us to Himself. But my reading of this is that there is no reason to believe she will not linger many more months. Perhaps when Paul and others have arrived to help here, you will be free. We have amassed provisions for the poor in Judea and could assign you to supervise that effort."

"I would be grateful."

Mark noticed Peter looking at him expectantly, as if his kindnesses deserved the respect and admiration Mark had once proffered. Mark forced a smile and nodded his thanks.

"You haven't asked me for any stories lately, my son."

That appellation seemed foreign, now that they were all but estranged. "You've been so busy," Mark said. "I didn't want to impose."

"You have always said that," Peter said, smiling sadly. "And I suppose at times I treated your curiosity as a nuisance."

"You did."

"Forgive me. In truth it humored me, and while I didn't want to appear overly eager to reminisce, such memories always invigorated me too, and I enjoyed the telling."

Was he implying he wanted to tell Mark more even now? A meeting was planned for that very evening, and another the following afternoon. And Peter had appointments at the local synagogue, where he was to debate pharisaical scholars on the Messianic prophecies. "Surely you need time to prepare for all your—"

"You let me worry about my schedule, Mark. I thought you might like to hear a story from our travels with the Master near Jericho."

"Well, of course, if you're sure—"

"I'm sure. We were leaving that fabled city, made famous by Joshua, of course, and a great multitude followed us down the road. A blind man named Bartimaeus sat by the side of the road and demanded of passersby to know what the cause of all the commotion was. When someone told him it was Jesus of Nazareth passing, he cried out, 'Jesus, Son of David, have mercy on me!'

"Many tried to shush him, but he cried out all the more, 'Son of David, have mercy on me!'

"Jesus stopped and asked that the man be brought to him. Someone whispered to Bartimaeus, 'Be of good cheer. Rise, He is calling you.'

"Well, he threw aside his garment and came to Jesus, who said, 'What do you want Me to do for you?'

"Bartimaeus said, 'Rabboni, that I may receive my sight.'

"Jesus said, 'Go your way; your faith has made you well.' And immediately he received his sight and followed Jesus on the road."

As had always happened when Peter told stories of Jesus, everything else disappeared from Mark's mind and he imagined himself among the crowds. His sharp disagreement with Peter had faded, his lessened respect was forgotten. And he longed to hear more. But when he looked at the old man, he saw tears.

"What is troubling you, Peter?"

The man waved, lips trembling. Finally he managed, "It's just that I would love to tell you more, but after that miracle we were fewer than fifteen miles from Jerusalem."

"And the end."

"Yes, the end."

"Someday I need to record it in your words."

"And perhaps someday I will have the fortitude to bring it all to mind. But not today, not now."

Peter looked haggard, and Mark could tell that much more was bothering him than painful memories. The local crisis was coming to a head, and the prospect of facing Paul had to be weighing on the disciple. Yet still Peter sat, certainly not appearing in a hurry to get anywhere. Mark had long prided himself on judging another's true emotions, and he felt now that his mentor had more to say, so he said, "Was there no more happiness, no more joy in the journey before the dark days?"

"Well, yes," Peter said, perking up. "I could tell you of the adulation of the people, if you have time."

"If *I* have time? You are the one—"

"I have asked you to let me worry about that," Peter said, and he settled in to talk more. "As we drew near Jerusalem, we first came to Bethany, where Jesus' friends Martha and Mary and Lazarus lived. You know the story of Lazarus."

"Of course."

"Normally Jesus stayed with them and we nearby, but on this occasion we were just passing through. He pulled James and me aside and told us to proceed to Bethphage, a tiny village about a mile southeast of Jerusalem near the Mount of Olives. He told us we would find a donkey with a colt tied next to her, 'on which no one has sat. Loose it and bring it. And if anyone says to you, "Why are you doing this?" say, "The Lord has need of it," and immediately he will send it here.' "

"Now, Peter, when had Jesus had opportunity to arrange this?"

"Oh, He didn't! We had been with Him day and night for weeks. But we went our way and found the colt tied by the door outside on the street. As we were loosing it, some who stood there said, 'What are you doing, loosing the colt?' And I said what Jesus had told me to say, and they stepped aside. We led the colt to Jesus and draped our cloaks over it so He could sit on it.

"Thus we traveled on into Jerusalem, a strange sight, you must agree—twelve men trailing a famous man on a tiny donkey. Word spread quickly that Jesus was coming, and many spread their clothes on the road, and others cut down leafy branches from the trees and spread them on the road. We were soon surrounded by people of all ages crying out, 'Hosanna! *"Blessed is He who comes in the name of the Lord!"* Blessed is the kingdom of our father David that comes in the name of the Lord! Hosanna in the highest!' "

Peter's anguish seemed to have left him, and Mark saw in his eyes the thrill of the memory. When Peter became silent, Mark said, "What a time that must have been. The people seemed to know Jesus was the King."

"You know this fulfilled an ancient prophecy," Peter said.

Mark nodded, grateful that his mother had been steadfast in keeping him at his studies all those years, memorizing long passages. " '*Tell the daughter of Zion, "Behold, your King is coming to you, lowly, and sitting on a donkey, a colt, the foal of a donkey."* ' "

"From there," Peter said, "Jesus went into Jerusalem and into the temple. We watched him warily as He looked around. As the hour was already late, He led us back out to Bethany. When we returned the next day, He was hungry. Along the way he saw from afar a fig tree having leaves and told us He was going to see if perhaps He would find something on it to eat. When we reached it, He found nothing but leaves, for it was not the season for figs. Jesus said, 'Let no one eat fruit from you ever again.'

"That curse chilled me, Mark. It was as if the tree were a person who had disappointed the Lord. I determined that I would never be guilty of such an offense. I would have staked my life on my loyalty to my friend."

TWENTY-TWO

Mark had finagled his way into Paul's welcoming party at the port, but he quickly disabused himself of the notion that he would get a chance to confide in Paul what had been going on in Antioch: Barnabas was also along.

When Paul and his small party disembarked, Mark waited tentatively at the back of the small gathering, prepared to help carry whatever they had brought. Paul greeted each with an embrace and a kiss, but his face brightened when he saw Mark, and it seemed to the younger man that the apostle hugged him tighter and longer than he had any of the others. This did not result in pride but rather gratitude, for it told Mark that perhaps Paul had put the past behind them.

"I have heard so many good reports about you, John Mark. I greet you in the matchless name of Jesus the Christ."

"Greetings, rabbi. It is so good to see you again."

Paul, in his usual manner, began directing his people and the greeters into the wagon, pointing out where each should sit. He had Barnabas and Mark join him directly behind the driver, Paul on the left and Barnabas in the middle. He wasted no time coming directly to the point. "Now then," he said, "Barnabas, the truth."

"The truth?"

"That Peter no longer associates with the uncircumcised and that you and many others of the elders have joined him in this travesty."

"Well, I wouldn't call it a travesty, nor would I say that he 'no longer associates' with them."

"Then it *is* true! But you would go only as far as saying that he refuses to break bread with them."

"I will concede that."

"I expected more from you, Barnabas. I really did. As for Peter, he is without excuse and I will deal with him face-to-face. But you. I can barely comprehend it. In fact, I am puzzled beyond words. What possible justification—"

"To avoid offense!"

"And whose feelings are you so earnestly protecting? Men who are wrong! Heretics!"

"Well, I wouldn't call it heresy."

"You wouldn't? What would you call it then, man? If you require a man to be circumcised in order that you may associate with him even over a meal, you are implying that he is not Jewish enough for you, even though he is an adopted son of God because of Christ's sacrifice on the cross."

"Peter and I have never even hinted that the Gentile believer is any less worthy of sal—"

"What, then? No less worthy of salvation, but not worthy to break bread with you." He tapped the driver on the shoulder. "Straight to the church and drop us there before taking the cargo to the inn. Barnabas, I hope Peter is there when I arrive."

"He awaits you with great anticipation, sir."

"His mood may change once I have reached him."

"Many of the brothers and sisters will be there for a meal, followed by a meeting where we hoped you would speak. I hate to have given you no warning."

"I need no notice to be able to hold forth for the word of God and the gospel of Christ. I shall be prepared."

"Good."

"And there had better be Gentiles at this meal."

"I'm not sure that there will be, sir."

"In fact, you know there will not be, am I right?"

Barnabas nodded miserably.

Paul leaned past him to address Mark. "I understand you have opposed this heresy."

"Yes, sir, I have made my opposition clear."

"Bless you. Now, Barnabas, I should save this for Peter, for I perceive it is he who has led you and others astray, but you know better too. Do you not remember that some seventeen years after my own conversion, you and I went to Jerusalem and also took Titus with us? At that time Peter and James and John extended to us the right hand of fellowship, even after I, by revelation, communicated to them that gospel which I preach among the Gentiles, privately to those who were of reputation. Not even Titus, a Greek, was compelled to be circumcised. Didn't that tell you something?

"I surmise that what has happened here is due to false brethren secretly brought in to spy out our liberty which we have in Christ Jesus, that they might bring us into bondage. No one should have yielded submission to them even for an hour, that the truth of the gospel might continue.

"I know you remember clearly that from those who seemed to be something—whatever they were, it makes no difference to me (God shows personal favoritism to no man)—nothing was added to me. On the contrary, when Peter and James and John saw that the gospel for the uncircumcised had been committed to me, as the gospel for the circumcised had been committed to Peter (for He who worked effectively in Peter for the apostleship to the circumcised also worked effectively in me toward the Gentiles), and when they perceived the grace that had been given to me, they blessed us and exhorted you and me to go to the Gentiles and they to the circumcised. They desired only that we should remember the poor, the very thing which I also was eager to do. You remember that, Barnabas, do you not?"

Barnabas nodded and seemed grateful that Paul appeared to have spent himself and had nothing more to say. That proved only temporary, for they soon arrived at the church to find Peter waiting outside with a tentative smile of welcome. Paul burst from the wagon and embraced and kissed him. "We have much to discuss," Paul said. "As you must imagine, I am not happy. Indeed I am vexed with you."

"I presumed as much. But first, you must be famished."

"I am!" And the two entered the church arm in arm. "I warn you, my friend, I intend to speak my mind."

"I would expect nothing less, but I propose we keep this between us and discuss it forthrightly at a convenient time."

"Oh, on the contrary, brother. This issue lies before us in its full stench, and I intend to deal with it forthwith."

"Now, Paul, no. Let us not bring discord before the brethren before we've had the chance to—"

"You believe *I* would be causing this discord? It is you who have brought this upon yourself and your congregation."

Several hundred from the body of believers rose from their seats at dining tables and waited until Paul had sat. Peter had prepared a place of honor for him near Peter and Barnabas and Mark, along with others of the elders and prophets. As the aroma of freshly cooked meats and vegetables and bread permeated the sanctuary, Peter stood and said, "Now let us ask our esteemed colleague and brother and guest to give thanks."

Paul stood and Peter sat, looking miserable, and the assembled bowed their heads. But all eyes jerked back to Paul when he said, "All in good time, my brother, but before I pray, I would like to know how many among us are of the uncircumcised."

No one stirred. Peter whispered, "Paul, please, I beseech you—"

"Not one Gentile. For shame! Where are they?"

"They have their own gathering not far away," Peter said, having to clear his throat.

"Send for them."

"No doubt they are already—"

"Now!" Paul shouted, and Peter fell silent, signaling some to summon the Gentiles.

"Perhaps you would like to pray so these can begin," Peter whispered.

"No, we shall wait. You shall remain seated, and I shall remain standing, and when the entire body of believers is here, then we will carry on with our customary mealtime activities."

For several minutes it seemed to Mark that no one knew where to look. Certainly no one dared catch Paul's angry gaze. He appeared ready to wait until nightfall if it took that long to bring together the entire congregation. Meanwhile Barnabas marshaled help to arrange a few hundred more places.

But when the Gentiles arrived, cautiously making their way inside, Paul insisted that everyone spread out and "welcome our brethren among us, with us, next to us."

At that Peter rose and began to leave, Barnabas with him, followed by some of the other elders and many Jews from the congregation.

"Stop!" Paul shouted, and they all halted and turned to face him. "Peter, you are to be blamed! I must usurp your authority as father of this church to remind you that before certain men came claiming to be of James, you would eat with the Gentiles. But when these men came, you withdrew and began separating yourself, fearing the disapproval of those who were of the circumcision. And the rest of the Jews here also played the hypocrite with you, so that even Barnabas has been carried away with your two-facedness.

"It pains me to confront you like this, my brother, but you have failed to remain straightforward about the truth of the gospel. Think, man! If you, being a Jew, live in the manner of Gentiles and not as the Jews, why do you compel Gentiles to live as Jews? We who are Jews by nature, and not sinners of the Gentiles, knowing that a man is not justified by the works of the law but by faith in Jesus Christ, even we have believed in Christ Jesus, that we might be justified by faith in Christ and not by the works of the law; for by the works of the law no flesh shall be justified.

"But if, while we seek to be justified by Christ, we ourselves also are found sinners, is Christ therefore a minister of sin? Certainly not! For if I build again those things which I destroyed—all the rules and regulations that cannot contribute to salvation—I make myself a transgressor. For I through the law died to the law that I might live to God. I have been crucified with Christ; it is no longer I who live, but Christ lives in me; and the life which I now live in the flesh I live by faith in the Son of God, who loved me and gave Himself for me. I do not set aside the grace of God; for if righteousness comes through the law, then Christ died in vain."

Any eyes not focused on Paul or on the floor were upon Peter. Mark—though he could not have agreed more with Paul and wished he could be so eloquent and passionate and persuasive—actually felt sorry for his old friend. Peter stood ashen-faced and trembling, as if he wished the earth might swallow him.

"Repent of this hypocrisy and sacrilege, my brother!" Paul called out.

"I repent!" Peter cried, falling to his knees. "When I am wrong, I am wrong, and I know better! God, forgive me. My brethren, Gentile and Jew, forgive me."

Paul rushed to him, embracing him, kissing him on both cheeks, and helping him stand. He led Peter back to his place next to him and turned to the assemblage again. "There will be no more discussion, no more debate about this. If there are any among you who still hold to the view that the Jew and the Gentile are not equal brothers in Christ, now is the time to separate yourselves from us. And you who came claiming to be of James and began spreading this treachery, confess and repent of it now, or go your way."

Several rushed from the church while Barnabas, flushed and also appearing humiliated, quickly returned to his seat.

"Any more?" Paul said, pausing. "No one? Then I will assume that we are one in Christ, united in common purpose, and that we love and serve the gospel of salvation, free to all who believe and call upon His name."

Paul then led in prayer and a hymn as the food was served, and Mark decided he had never more enjoyed a meal.

TWENTY-THREE

Within an hour of the sumptuous meal, the Antiochan church was reassembled for a service of worship and preaching by the apostle Paul. Word had spread quickly of his public chastisement of Peter, so the place was soon overflowing with people, many of whom had left over the controversy.

Mark was deeply impressed that when Paul gathered the meeting leaders before advancing to the platform, he insisted that Peter join them. Paul asked him to lead in prayer, and Peter said, "I am not worthy."

"None of us is worthy, beloved friend," Paul said, wrapping his arm around the bigger man. "But hear me. You have acknowledged you were wrong, and you have repented. To now wallow in your sin is to deny the forgiving power of the risen Christ you serve. The sobriety of your regret is understandable and likely to be profitable, but do not let it distract you from your service. I would that you pray for us who will lead this meeting, and for me that I speak the very message of God. And then I beseech you to lead the entire assembly in prayer as we begin as well. Would you do that?"

Peter tearfully nodded.

Mark was warmed by the singing, moved by Peter's humble prayer, and emboldened by Paul's dynamic preaching. Never one to tiptoe around issues, Paul spoke on the very topic that had divided the church. "I am a bondservant of Jesus Christ," he began, "called to be an apostle, separated to the gospel of God which He promised through His prophets in the Holy Scriptures, concerning His Son Jesus Christ our Lord, who was born of the seed of David according to the flesh, and declared to be the Son of God with power according to the Spirit of holiness, by the resurrection from the dead.

"Through Him we have received grace and apostleship to call for obedience to the faith among all nations for His name, among whom you also are the called of Jesus Christ, beloved of God, called to be saints. Grace to you and peace from God our Father and the Lord Jesus Christ. I thank my God through Jesus Christ for you all, for as God is my witness—whom I serve with my spirit in the gospel of His Son—without ceasing I make mention of you always in my prayers.

"I consider you part of my flock, just as I do all other believers, Jews and Gentiles. I have been obligated by God to preach the gospel of Christ to both Jew and Gentile, educated and unschooled, Greek and barbarian, wise and unwise. So, as much as is in me, I am ready to preach the gospel anywhere at any time.

"For I am not ashamed of the gospel of Christ, for it is the power of God to salvation for everyone who believes, for the Jew first and also for the Gentile. For in it the righteousness of God is revealed; as it is written, *'The just shall live by faith.'*

"For the wrath of God is revealed from heaven against all ungodliness and unrighteousness of men, who suppress the truth in unrighteousness, because what may be known of God is manifest in them, for God has shown it to them.

"For since the creation of the world His invisible attributes—even His eternal power and Godhead—are made clear by the things that are made, so that men and women are without excuse. Although they saw enough to know God, they did not glorify Him as God, nor were thankful, but became futile in their thoughts, and their foolish hearts were darkened.

"Professing to be wise, they became fools, and changed the glory of the incorruptible God into an image made like corruptible man—and birds and four-footed animals and creeping things.

"Therefore God also gave them up to uncleanness, in the lusts of their hearts, to dishonor their bodies among themselves, who exchanged the truth of God for the lie, and worshiped and served the creature rather than the Creator, who is blessed forever. Amen."

Where, Mark wondered, *does a man learn to think and speak like this?* He knew Paul had been a brilliant student and a schoolmate of Barnabas's under Gamaliel, but that now he was using his intellect for, rather than against, Christ.

Paul continued, "For this reason God gave them up to vile passions. And even as they do not like to think about God, God has given them over to a debased mind, to do those things which are not fitting; they are filled with all unrighteousness, sexual immorality, wickedness, covetousness, maliciousness; filled with envy, murder, strife, deceit, evil-mindedness; they are whisperers, backbiters, haters of God, violent, proud, boasters, inventors of evil things, disobedient to parents, undiscerning, untrustworthy, unloving, unforgiving, unmerciful; who, knowing full well they risk the righteous judgment of God, because those who practice such things are deserving of death, not only do the same but also approve of those who practice them.

"God *'will render to each one according to his deeds'*: eternal life to those who by patient continuance in doing good seek for glory, honor, and immortality; but indignation and wrath, tribulation and anguish to those who are self-seeking and do not obey the truth, but obey unrighteousness, on every soul of man who does evil; but glory, honor, and peace to everyone who works what is good. For there is no partiality with God."

Mark could tell that the entire congregation was as stirred and encouraged by Paul's logic and eloquence as he was. This was what these wounded people needed. Paul, speaking as a man born and raised and educated a Jew, was addressing primarily Gentiles, and as he continued, he proved he was sensitive to the issue at the forefront of all their minds.

"What advantage then have we, the Jews? Much in every way! Chiefly because to us was committed the word of God. But what if some do not believe what is taught and prophesied therein? Will their unbelief render the faithfulness of God ineffective? Certainly not! Indeed, if every man said God's Word was untrue, it would make them all liars and God true. As it is written: *'That You may be justified in Your words, and may overcome when You are judged.'*

"For we have previously charged both Jews and Gentiles that they are all under sin. As it is written: *'There is none righteous, no, not one; there is none who understands; there is none who seeks after God. They have all turned aside; they have together become unprofitable; there is none who does good, no, not one.' 'Their throat is an open tomb; with their tongues they have practiced deceit'; 'the poison of asps is under their lips'; 'whose mouth is full of cursing and bitterness.' 'Their feet are swift to shed blood; destruction and misery are in their ways; and the way of peace they have not known.' 'There is no fear of God before their eyes.'*

"By the deeds of the law no flesh will be justified in His sight, for the law provides only the knowledge of sin. But now the righteousness of God apart from the law is revealed, through faith in Jesus Christ, to all and on all who believe. For there is no difference; for all have sinned and fall short of the glory of God, being justified freely by His grace through the redemption that is in Christ Jesus, whom God put forth as a propitiation by His blood, through faith, to demonstrate His righteousness.

"Therefore we conclude that a man is justified by faith apart from the deeds of the law. Or is He the God of the Jews only? Is He not also the God of the Gentiles? Yes, of the Gentiles also, since there is one God who will justify both the circumcised and the uncircumcised through faith.

"Therefore, having been justified by faith, we have peace with God through our Lord Jesus Christ, through whom also we have access by faith into this grace in which we stand, and rejoice in hope of the glory of God. And not only that, but we also glory in tribulations, knowing that tribulation produces perseverance; and perseverance, character; and character, hope.

"Now hope does not disappoint, because the love of God has been poured out in our hearts by the Holy Spirit who was given to us. For when we were still without strength, in due time Christ died for the ungodly. It is barely conceivable that someone would die for a righteous man, let alone a good man. But God demonstrates His own love toward us, in that while we were still sinners, Christ died for us.

"Much more then, having now been justified by His blood, we shall be saved from wrath through Him. For if when we were His enemies we were reconciled to God through the death of His Son, much more, having been reconciled, we shall be saved by His life.

"Where sin abounded, grace abounded much more, so that as sin reigned in death, even so grace might reign through righteousness to eternal life through Jesus Christ our Lord."

Paul moved out from behind the lectern and looked lovingly upon the huge gathering. "What shall we say then? Shall we continue in sin that grace may abound? Certainly not! How shall we who died to sin live any longer in it? Just as Christ was raised from the dead by the glory of the Father, even so we also should walk in newness of life.

"Reckon yourselves dead indeed to sin, but alive to God in Christ Jesus our Lord. Therefore do not let sin reign in your mortal body, that you should obey its lusts. And do not use your members as instruments of unrighteousness to sin, but present yourselves to God as being alive from the dead, and your members as instruments of righteousness to God. For sin shall not have dominion over you; you are not under law but under grace.

"What then? Shall we sin because we are not under law but under grace? Certainly not! Do you not know that to whom you present yourselves to obey, you are that one's slave? Will you be a slave to that which leads to sin and death, or to obedience leading to righteousness? For the wages of sin is death, but the gift of God is eternal life in Christ Jesus our Lord.

"Now don't get the idea that I put myself above you. The law is spiritual, but I am carnal, sold under sin. Often I do not understand why I do the things I do. For what I will and want to do, that I do not practice; but what I hate, that I do. If, then, I do what I will not to do, it is no longer I who do it, but rather the sin that dwells in me.

"For I know that in me (that is, in my flesh) nothing good dwells; for to will is present with me, but how to perform what is good I do not know. I find then that evil is present with me, despite that I am one who wills to do good. For inwardly I delight in the law of God. But I see another law in my flesh, warring against the law of my mind, and bringing me into captivity to the law of sin which is in my flesh."

Here Paul stretched his arms wide, as if pleading with his hearers to understand. "O wretched man that I am! Who will deliver me from this body of death? I thank God—through Jesus Christ our Lord!

"Now if anyone does not have the Spirit of Christ, he is not Christ's. And if Christ is in you, your body may be dead because of sin, but the Spirit gives life because of righteousness. If the Spirit of Him who raised Jesus from the dead dwells in you, He will also give life to your mortal bodies through His Spirit who dwells in you.

"You need no longer doubt and wonder, for the Spirit Himself bears witness with our spirit that we are children of God, and if children, then heirs—heirs of God and joint heirs with Christ, that we may also be glorified together.

"And we know that all things work together for good to those who love God, to those who are the called according to His purpose."

Stepping back behind the lectern, Paul held up his hands and sighed. "What then shall we say to these things? If God is for us, who can be against us? He who did not spare His own Son, but delivered Him up for us all, how shall He not with Him also freely give us all things? Who dares bring a charge against ones God has chosen? It is God who justifies. Who then could possibly condemn? It is Christ who died, and furthermore is also risen, who is even at the right hand of God, who also makes intercession for us."

Paul's voice dropped to just above a whisper, but Mark was certain no one had trouble hearing him. No one stirred.

"Who shall separate us from the love of Christ? Shall tribulation, or distress, or persecution, or famine, or nakedness, or peril, or sword? In all these things we are more than conquerors through Him who loved us. For I am persuaded that neither death nor life, nor angels nor principalities nor powers, nor things present nor things to come, nor height nor depth, nor any other created thing, shall be able to separate us from the love of God which is in Christ Jesus our Lord.

"And so now, brethren, it is time for this body of believers to be reconciled to one another and healed in the Spirit of Christ. If you have had ought with your brother or sister, Jew or Gentile, now is the time to seek forgiveness and restoration."

Without further word from Paul, people stood all over the room and rushed to one another, embracing, weeping, confessing, forgiving, and praying together. To Mark it seemed as miraculous a turn of events as the very signs and wonders of Jesus Peter had recounted.

Paul and Mark moved through the crowd with others of the elders, helping, counseling, praying as needed. And when the throng finally began to part, Paul sought out Mark and thanked him. "I will be asking Peter to establish a leader here and to then accompany me to Rome, where gatherings of believing Gentiles are multiplying. There is great need there, so I will ask that he take over, as my travels take me elsewhere frequently. When you return from your mission to Jerusalem, please join him to aid in the work."

"I am honored to be asked, sir," Mark said, "and will come in haste at my first opportunity."

SADLY, the Jerusalem visit took much less time than Mark had hoped. He took along a party of mostly young people, who made short work of the trip by quickly distributing foodstuffs, clothing, and money to the needy of Judea. While Mark had hoped to spend a couple of weeks with his mother, she died the morning after he arrived, and he stayed long enough only to see to her burial and the disposition of the estate.

He sent his aides directly back to Antioch when he left for Rome. On the journey he mulled precious memories of his godly mother and thanked the Lord for the privilege of having seen her one last time. It had allowed him to express his love and thanks for her having served for so long as both mother and father to him. And it allowed her the chance to tell him how pleased she was with his choice to give his life in service to God.

TWENTY-FOUR

Mark found himself ministering with Peter and sometimes Paul in Rome until more than thirty years had passed since the crucifixion and resurrection of Christ. Paul had not overstated the explosive growth of the church in the capital of the empire that boasted more than a million residents. Every day was filled with teaching and preaching, evangelizing and then equipping the saints. Bodies of believers sprang up all over the city, and Mark and the apostles labored to train leaders for each. In the midst of all that, Paul continued to travel widely and frequently write letters to the churches he had started or helped build.

On his travels, Paul reported falling under such abuse that Mark wondered whether word would one day come that he had been martyred. He was arrested, imprisoned, shipwrecked, stoned nearly to death, and generally hauled before authorities nearly everywhere he went. Often he had to employ his rank as a Roman citizen to avoid even harsher sentences.

The level of persecution in Rome itself seemed to ebb and flow depending on which emperor was on the throne. Nero, who had become the youngest emperor in Roman history several years before at the age of seventeen, seemed to slowly become aware of what many termed an eastern sect called Christianity. Paul, on his frequent stops in Rome between missionary journeys, warned Mark and Peter to beware the emperor and to do their best to keep low profiles. Many of the early Roman Christians had come from the Jewish community, which consisted of tens of thousands of slaves and merchants with connections to Jerusalem.

Peter gave Mark more and more authority and occasionally sent him also on forays far from Rome. But Mark's most rewarding work during this season of his life came when he was able to spend extended blocks of time with Peter. Not that he found much opportunity to simply sit and listen. To get Peter to tell him more of his eyewitness story of the Christ took a very unusual request from Gentile believers in Rome.

As Mark traveled throughout the area preaching and teaching, he often used Peter's accounts of Jesus to make his points. Soon, everywhere he went, people clamored for more of the same. "You are rarely with us," one said. "And it is rare indeed that we see Peter. His memories must be recorded so we can know the entire story."

Mark had to admit to himself that he repeated that conversation in more than one section of Rome, hoping that others would echo the request. Which they did. And with that ammunition, he persuaded Peter to tell him more.

He admitted to his old mentor that he had stacks of papyrus sheets of his notes from their conversations over the years, and somehow this seemed to intrigue Peter and fuel him with a peculiar urgency to see the task through.

"It falls to you, Mark, as I am no scholar, neither am I skilled with the quill. But if you are to do this, to spread abroad a written record of the gospel of Christ, I must supervise it and examine every word."

Mark could barely contain himself. "Of course, master. Whatever you say. We have been so successful in developing leaders for our churches that we should be able to afford the luxury of time to make an accurate account from my notes and from what more you have to tell me."

"It must be so much more than that," Peter said, and Mark was amused that suddenly the once reluctant apostle now seemed to see the idea as his own. So much the better.

"How do you envision it, sir?"

"Well, as you say that demand for such has come from the bodies of believers in and around Rome, it should be directed at them. Others may read it if we can employ scribes to copy it, but it should be intended for local eyes, Gentile Roman Christians. And as I have told it to you over the years, it is less a life story of Jesus than an account of his ministry in Judea and Galilee."

"It is shaping up that way, Peter, yes, but in my mind—from what you have told me already—it is more than an account of His activities. It is the story of the Son of God, the King, the Messiah, but primarily a servant."

Peter got that faraway look again. "Yes, yes, I can see that. He was above all a Servant. I told you, did I not, that He once said that 'whoever desires to become great among you shall be your servant. And whoever of you desires to be first shall be slave of all. For even the Son of Man did not come to be served, but to serve, and to give His life a ransom for many.' "

Mark nodded. "You told me. Let me get my papyrus."

For days the men used every spare moment to pore over the scribblings Mark had made—mostly at night after having listened to Peter during their travels. Now the old man sat studying them, advising, rearranging, correcting. "I can see there is more I need tell you to make it complete."

"Nothing would please me more."

"Picking up where we left off so long ago, let me tell you of our next entry into Jerusalem."

"This could not have been terribly long before you came to our house for Passover."

"Correct, although much happened before that. Jesus went directly to the temple and was furious to see men buying and selling there. We watched in horror as he overturned the tables of the money changers and the seats of those who sold doves. We feared the religious leaders, of course, and that they might involve the Romans in trying to stop Him. But He was not concerned about them. His mind was on not allowing anyone to carry wares through the temple.

"He shouted, 'Is it not written, *"My house shall be called a house of prayer for all nations"*? But you have made it a *"den of thieves."* ' "

"He did this publicly, right there at the temple?"

"Yes! And as we expected, the scribes and chief priests heard it. We knew they would seek to destroy Him, for they feared Him because all the people were astonished at His teaching. They left Him alone then, which made us only the more wary.

"That evening, He led us out of the city. The next morning, on the same route back to Jerusalem from Bethany, we passed the same fig tree as the day before. I said, 'Rabbi, look! The tree You cursed has withered away.'

"Jesus stopped and studied it, then gazed to the hills. 'Have faith in God,' he said. 'For assuredly, I say to you, whoever says to this mountain, "Be removed and be cast into the sea," and does not doubt in his heart, but believes that those things he says will be done, he will have whatever he says. Therefore I say to you, whatever things you ask when you pray, believe that you receive them, and you will have them.

" 'And whenever you stand praying, if you have anything against anyone, forgive him, that your Father in heaven may also forgive you your trespasses. But if you do not forgive, neither will your Father in heaven forgive your trespasses.' "

"Seeing the fig tree again spurred all that?" Mark said.

"I do not understand the connection myself," Peter said. "But I have never forgotten his words."

"And I suppose when you returned to Jerusalem the religious leaders were lying in wait."

"Indeed they were. When Jesus walked into the temple, the chief priests, the scribes, and the elders came to Him and said, 'By what authority are You doing these things? And who gave You this authority to do these things?'

"Jesus said, 'I also will ask you one question; then answer Me, and I will tell you by what authority I do these things: The baptism of John–was it from heaven or from men? Answer Me.'

"Now, Mark, they huddled away from Him to reason among themselves, but I could hear them. They were saying, 'If we say, "From heaven," He will say, "Why then did you not believe him?" But if we say, "From men" '—they feared the people, for everyone believed the baptizer John to have been a prophet. So they said to Jesus, 'We do not know.'

"Jesus said, 'Then neither will I tell you by what authority I do these things.' And with that He immediately told them a story. He said, 'A man planted a vineyard and set a hedge around it, dug a place for the wine vat and built a tower. And he leased it to vinedressers and went into a far country. Now at vintage-time he sent a servant to the vinedressers, that he might receive some of the fruit of the vineyard. But the vinedressers took him and beat him and sent him away empty-handed.

" 'He sent them another servant, and they threw stones at him, wounded him in the head, and sent him away. And again he sent another, and him they killed; and many others, beating some and killing some. Therefore still having one son, his beloved, he sent him to them last, saying, "They will respect my son."

" 'But those vinedressers said among themselves, "This is the heir. Come, let us kill him, and the inheritance will be ours." So they took him and killed him and cast him out of the vineyard. Therefore what will the owner of the vineyard do? He will come and destroy the vinedressers, and give the vineyard to others. Have you not even read this Scripture: *"The stone which the builders rejected has become the chief cornerstone. This was the Lord's doing, and it is marvelous in our eyes"*?'

"They knew He had spoken the parable against them, Mark, and it was obvious they wanted to lay hands on Jesus and arrest him. But they feared the multitude, so they went away. Soon some of the Pharisees and the Herodians arrived, clearly hoping to catch Him saying something for which they could charge Him.

"They said, 'Teacher, we know that You are true and show no partiality to anyone, for You do not regard the station of men but teach the way of God in truth. Is it lawful to pay taxes to Caesar, or not? Shall we pay, or shall we not pay?'

"It was almost amusing, Mark, their flattery while trying to embarrass Him. But He, knowing they were hypocrites, said, 'Why do you test Me? Bring Me a denarius that I may see it.' So they brought it. And He said, 'Whose image and inscription is this?'

"They said, 'Caesar's.'

"And Jesus said, 'Render to Caesar the things that are Caesar's, and to God the things that are God's.'

"They were amazed at His wisdom and had nothing to say. Then some Sadducees, who say there is no resurrection, came to Him and said, 'Teacher, Moses wrote to us that if a man's brother dies, and leaves his wife behind, and leaves no children, his brother should take his wife and raise up offspring for his brother. Now there were seven brothers. The first took a wife; and dying, he left no offspring. And the second took her, and he died; nor did he leave any offspring. And the third likewise. So the seven had her and left no offspring. Last of all, the woman died also. Therefore, in the resurrection, when they rise, whose wife will she be?'

"Jesus said, 'Are you not mistaken, because you do not know the Scriptures nor the power of God? For when they rise from the dead, they neither marry nor are given in marriage, but are like angels in heaven. But concerning the dead, that they rise, have you not read in the book of Moses, in the burning bush passage, how God spoke to him, saying, *"I am the God of Abraham, the God of Isaac, and the God of Jacob"*? He is not the God of the dead, but the God of the living. You are therefore greatly mistaken.'

"Then one of the scribes came, and having heard them reasoning together, perceiving that He had answered them well, asked Him, 'Which is the first commandment of all?'

"Jesus said, 'The first of all the commandments is: *"Hear, O Israel, the Lord our God, the Lord is one. And you shall love the Lord your God with all your heart, with all your soul, with all your mind, and with all your strength."* This is the first commandment. And the second, like it, is this: *"You shall love your neighbor as yourself."* There is no other commandment greater than these.'

"So the scribe said to Him, 'Well said, Teacher. You have spoken the truth, for there is one God, and there is no other but He. And to love Him with all the heart, with all the understanding, with all the soul, and with all the strength, and to love one's neighbor as oneself, is more than all the whole burnt offerings and sacrifices.'

"Now when Jesus saw that he had answered wisely, He said, 'You are not far from the kingdom of God.' After that no one dared question Him.

"Then Jesus taught in the temple, saying, 'How is it that the scribes say that the Christ is the Son of David? For David himself said by the Holy Spirit: *"The Lord said to my Lord, 'Sit at My right hand, till I make Your enemies Your footstool.' "* Therefore David himself calls Him "Lord"; how is He then his Son?'

"Well, the common people heard Him gladly because He spoke against the legalists when he said, 'Beware of the scribes, who desire to go around in long robes, love greetings in the marketplaces, the best seats in the synagogues, and the best places at feasts, who devour widows' houses, and for a pretense make long prayers. These will receive greater condemnation.'

"Jesus was sitting opposite the treasury and saw how the people put money into the collection box. Many who were rich put in much. Then one poor widow came and threw in two mites, which amounts to one sixty-fourth of a day's wage. He called us disciples to Himself and said, 'Assuredly, I say to you that this poor widow has put in more than all those who have given to the treasury; for they all put in out of their abundance, but she out of her poverty put in all that she had, her whole livelihood.'

"As we followed Him out of the temple, I said, 'Teacher, see what manner of stones and what buildings are here!' For they were beautiful.

"Jesus said, 'Do you see these great buildings? Not one stone shall be left upon another, that shall not be thrown down.' I had no idea what He was talking about.

"Soon we made our way to the Mount of Olives opposite the temple, where James, John, Andrew, and I asked Him privately, 'Tell us, when will these things be? And what will be the sign when all these things will be fulfilled?'

"Did he tell you?"

Peter appeared deep in thought, looking past Mark and speaking in a monotone. He furrowed his brow, then closed his eyes and said, "Lord, fill my memory and give me utterance. And then he recited Jesus' entire answer:

" 'Take heed that no one deceives you. For many will come in My name, saying, "I am He," and will deceive many. But when you hear of wars and rumors of wars, do not be troubled; for such things must happen, but the end is not yet. For nation will rise against nation, and kingdom against kingdom. And there will be earthquakes in various places, and there will be famines and troubles. These are the beginnings of sorrows.

" 'But watch out for yourselves, for they will deliver you up to councils, and you will be beaten in the synagogues. You will be brought before rulers and kings for My sake, for a testimony to them. And the gospel must first be preached to all the nations. But when they arrest you and deliver you up, do not worry beforehand, or premeditate what you will speak. But whatever is given you in that hour, speak that; for it is not you who speak, but the Holy Spirit.

" 'Now brother will betray brother to death, and a father his child; and children will rise up against parents and cause them to be put to death. And you will be hated by all for My name's sake. But he who endures to the end shall be saved.

" 'So when you see the *"abomination of desolation,"* spoken of by Daniel the prophet, standing where it ought not, then let those who are in Judea flee to the mountains. Let him who is on the housetop not go down into the house, nor enter to take anything out of his house. And let him who is in the field not go back to get his clothes.

" 'But woe to those who are pregnant and to those who are nursing babies in those days! And pray that your flight may not be in winter. For in those days there will be tribulation, such as has not been since the beginning of the creation which God created until this time, nor ever shall be.

" 'And unless the Lord had shortened those days, no flesh would be saved; but for the elect's sake, whom He chose, He shortened the days. Then if anyone says to you, "Look, here is the Christ!" or, "Look, He is there!" do not believe it. For false christs and false prophets will rise and show signs and wonders to deceive, if possible, even the elect. But take heed; see, I have told you all things beforehand.

" 'But in those days, after that tribulation, the sun will be darkened, and the moon will not give its light; the stars of heaven will fall, and the powers in the heavens will be shaken. Then they will see the Son of Man coming in the clouds with great power and glory. And then He will send His angels, and gather together His elect from the four winds, from the farthest part of earth to the farthest part of heaven.

" 'Now learn this parable from the fig tree: When its branch has already become tender, and puts forth leaves, you know that summer is near. So you also, when you see these things happening, know that it is near—at the doors! Assuredly, I say to you, this generation will by no means pass away till all these things take place. Heaven and earth will pass away, but My words will by no means pass away."

"*This* generation?" Mark said.

"I believe He meant the generation that sees the signs in the heavens when He returns as He promised."

" 'But of that day and hour no one knows, not even the angels in heaven, nor the Son, but only the Father. Take heed, watch and pray; for you do not know when the time is. It is like a man going to a far country, who left his house and gave authority to his servants, and to each his work, and commanded the doorkeeper to watch. Watch therefore, for you do not know when the master of the house is coming—

in the evening, at midnight, at the crowing of the rooster, or in the morning—lest, coming suddenly, he find you sleeping. And what I say to you, I say to all: "Watch!" ' "

Peter's breath came in short bursts and he appeared to need to recline.

"Are you all right, master?" Mark said, putting down his quill.

Peter raised a hand to indicate he was fine. "I feel as if I have worked an entire day."

Mark chuckled. "So do I. I pray I will be able to read my own handwriting tomorrow."

"There is not much more," Peter said, "so let me finish. I will tell what happened right up to when Jesus sent us to follow you to your home, for you yourself were eyewitness to the rest. You must write that, and then I will peruse it."

"Very well. If you are sure you are up to continuing."

"Two days later Passover began and the Feast of Unleavened Bread. The Lord told us that He knew the chief priests and the scribes were devising how they might take Him by trickery and put Him to death, but they knew better than to do it during the feast, lest there be an uproar of the people.

"Now, Mark, let me tell you of something which occurred a few days before that, on the previous Saturday. We were in Bethany at the house of Simon, a leper Jesus had healed. He was treating us to a generous meal as an expression of his gratitude. Jesus' friends, Lazarus and his sisters—Mary and Martha—were there from their nearby home, the women helping serve.

"As Jesus sat at the table, Mary brought an alabaster flask of very costly oil of spikenard. She broke the flask and poured it on His head. Sadly, there were some among us who were indignant and agreed with Judas Iscariot when he said, 'Why was this fragrant oil wasted? It might have been sold for more than three hundred denarii and given to the poor.' Others also criticized her sharply.

"But Jesus said, 'Let her alone. Why do you trouble her? She has done a good work for Me. For you have the poor with you always, and whenever you wish you may do them good; but Me you do not have always. She has done what she could. She has come beforehand to anoint My body for burial. Assuredly, I say to you, wherever this gospel is preached in the whole world, what this woman has done will also be told as a memorial to her.' "

"I have heard you tell that story when you preach," Mark said.

"Yes, and I often remind my hearers that at the time I did not know what Jesus meant about His burial.

"We learned later that this was the very night when Judas went to the chief priests and offered to betray Jesus to them for thirty pieces of silver. And when they heard it they were glad and promised the money."

TWENTY-FIVE

Mark spent the next few years preaching, teaching, discipling, and traveling from Rome to various cities throughout Asia Minor and even Egypt, laboring with both Peter and Paul. All the while he carefully penned his gospel of Jesus Christ, according to the personal memories of Peter, of course, and Peter carefully studied the documents, clarifying, adjusting, correcting.

Mark then primarily traveled with Paul for a few years, because Peter expressed a deep loneliness for his wife, and Paul urged him to send for her.

"Your children are grown, and others are running the fishing business, are they not?"

"They are."

"Then are you not free to have her with you? I know her to be devout and industrious, and she will be of great help to you."

Peter was soon a new man, invigorated and seeming more youthful than he had in years. It was plain that Esther admired and respected him, besides sharing his passion for the spread of the gospel. He preached, Mark knew, for the Lord and for the hearts and souls of the listeners, but he seemed more animated with Esther in the audience. Peter exulted that she also offered helpful suggestions, which might have threatened him coming from anyone else.

Peter commended Mark to the believers in the city of Colossi, and for a few years Mark served as their pastor and bishop. It was during this time that word came to him concerning Paul's arrest in Jerusalem and his imprisonment in Caesarea. Fellow Jews had accused him of defiling the temple by including Gentile Christians, and to rally Rome to their side, they revealed that he refused to recognize Roman deities. The news spread that Paul was appealing to Rome that, because of his citizenship there, he should be allowed to defend himself before the emperor.

Peter and Esther were abroad, ministering to churches throughout the world and establishing new ones, and Mark felt compelled to replace himself at the church in Colossi. He did not know where God would lead him next, but he wanted to be ready, especially if he could somehow aid Paul. The man had proved a tireless, effective, and brilliant apologist for Christianity, and even despite his many trials and imprisonments, he continued to write to believers and argue for the faith.

As Mark finished his work in Colossi and tried to shepherd in the new leadership before his departure, he waited anxiously, sometimes for weeks at a time, for news of his beloved compatriots. One evening an aide delivered a scroll. "Master," the young woman said, "a messenger brought this from Antioch."

An old acquaintance of Mark's and a protégé of Barnabas, young Ignatius, had recently been installed as the new head of the church there.

The woman took her leave and Mark sat to read.

My dear brother, John Mark:

It is with a heavy heart that I greet you in the matchless name of Jesus the

Christ, in whom we have been bestowed all things in the heavenlies. I have just been brought awful news, and it falls to me to bear it on to you. Your beloved cousin, Joses, whom we all came to know as Barnabas for his most generous spirit, has met his end.

The worst of it is that his death occurred in his hometown, Salamis on Cyprus, while he was there holding forth the truth of the gospel of salvation through Jesus Christ. Local Jews took offense and stoned him to death. The best of it is that your loved one fulfilled the highest calling a servant of God can attain. He was martyred for the cause of the gospel, an achievement we should all strive to achieve.

I regret to say that though I know you would want to make the sojourn here for his memorial, the body has already been disposed of, and according to tradition we felt it only right to have already officially honored him.

In your grief you may take comfort in knowing that—largely due to the ministry of your cousin—I have inherited here some of the finest young students and servants of Christ I could wish for. As they boldly carry the torch he bore for his lifetime, his influence will be felt here and abroad for as long as men and women remember his name.

Be assured that the prayers and condolences and best wishes of all the believers here attend you during this time of mourning on the one hand for the loss of your loved one, and rejoicing on the other for his life, his service, and his new home with the One with whom he so longed to reunite.

The beloved apostle John, who visited here briefly a fortnight ago, sends his greetings and sympathy as well.

With deep affection and love in Christ, the Messiah, I remain your friend,

Ignatius
Bishop of Antioch

Soon word came from Paul himself requesting that Mark meet him in Rome. The message—surprising in that it came from the apostle while en route to Italy in chains—informed Mark that the invitation came not only with the approval and blessing of Peter, but also with the news that Peter and Esther would be returning to Rome.

Mark, you and Peter have both been wonderful friends and great comrades in the work, and now I fear I have need of you more than ever. I pray that my appeal to Rome will result in my freedom and the ability to again minister to the saints there. But should it result in a sentence for me, you and Peter and his wife will be all the more critical to the work of the gospel in Rome.

Who else but Paul could be transported from Jerusalem to Caesarea and all the way to Rome, using all manner of contrivance, in chains, shipwrecked, nearly deserted, and bound for a hearing that might result in his death, and yet have such influence on his guards that they allowed him to correspond with his friends all over the world?

Mark officially installed the new leadership in Colossi and made his way to Rome even before Peter and Esther arrived. When the couple joined him, finding modest lodging through local believers, they worked together closely, planning for Paul's arrival and intending to support him in whatever way they could—short of exposing the church to further harassment from Rome.

One morning a messenger arrived at a church where Mark had just finished teaching and told him Peter had beckoned. Mark hurried to Peter's abode, where Esther met him with a smile and a cup. Peter's face bore a mixture of bemusement and amusement. "Only Paul," was all he could say, handing Mark a scroll from the prisoner's own hand.

"It begins with his customary greetings and other details, which you can read later. Start here, where he tells of the voyage."

When it was decided that we should sail to Italy, I was delivered with other prisoners to Julius, a centurion of the Augustan Regiment. We put out to sea, meaning to sail along the coasts of Asia. When we landed at Sidon, Julius treated me kindly and allowed me to visit friends there and receive care.

When we had put to sea from there, we sailed under the shelter of Cyprus, because the winds were contrary. And when we had sailed over the sea which is off Cilicia and Pamphylia, we came to Myra, a city of Lycia. There Julius found an Alexandrian ship sailing to Italy. With us the ship totaled 276 passengers.

Sailing was now dangerous because of the season, so I advised Julius that I perceived the voyage would end with disaster and much loss, not only of the cargo and ship, but also our lives.

But Julius was persuaded by the helmsman and the owner of the ship that the harbor was not suitable to winter in, and most on board agreed we should set sail from there for Phoenix, a harbor of Crete opening toward the southwest and northwest, and try to winter there. A soft south wind blew, so, supposing that they had obtained their desire, they put out to sea and sailed close by Crete. But not long after, a terrible east wind arose, and the ship was caught.

Unable to head into the wind, they ran under the shelter of an island called Clauda. When in the driving storm they had pulled the dinghy skiff on board and secured it, they used cables to undergird the ship. Fearing they should run aground, they lowered the sails and so were driven by the wind. And because we were exceedingly tempest-tossed, the next day they threw overboard anything they could do without.

Neither sun nor stars appeared for many days, and no small tempest beat on us, so we gave up all hope that we would be saved. But after long abstinence from food, I stood in the midst of them and said, "Men, you should have listened to me and not sailed from Crete. But now I urge you to take heart, for there will be no loss of life among you, but only of the ship. For there stood by me this night an angel of the God to whom I belong and whom I serve, saying, 'Do not be afraid, Paul; you must be brought before Caesar; and indeed God has granted you all those who sail with you.' Therefore take heart, men, for I believe God that it will be just as it was told me. However, we must run aground on a certain island."

Now when the fourteenth night had come, as we were driven up and down in the Adriatic Sea, about midnight the sailors sensed that they were drawing near land. And they took soundings and found the depth to be twenty fathoms; and when they had gone a little farther, they took soundings again and found it to be fifteen fathoms. Then, fearing lest we should run aground on the rocks, they dropped four anchors from the stern and prayed for day to come.

I noticed that the sailors had let down the skiff into the sea under pretense of putting out anchors from the prow, so I told Julius and his soldiers, "Unless these men stay in the ship, you cannot be saved." So the soldiers cut the ropes of the skiff and let it fall off.

As day was about to dawn, I said, "Today is the fourteenth day you have waited and continued without food. Therefore I urge you to take nourishment." I took bread and gave thanks to God in the presence of them all; and when I had broken it I began to eat. Then they were all encouraged, and also took food themselves.

When it was day, they did not recognize the land, but they observed a bay with a beach, onto which they planned to run the ship if possible. They let go the anchors and left them in the sea, meanwhile loosing the rudder ropes; and they hoisted the mainsail to the wind and made for shore. But striking a place where two seas met, they ran the ship aground; and the prow stuck fast and remained immovable, but the stern was being broken up by the violence of the waves.

I knew the soldiers planned to kill us prisoners, lest any of us should swim away and escape. But Julius, wanting to save me, commanded that those who could swim should jump overboard first and get to land, and the rest should float on boards and parts of the ship. And so it was that we all escaped safely to land.

We found that the island was called Malta, and the people there showed us unusual kindness. They kindled a fire and made us all welcome, despite the cold rain. When I gathered a bundle of sticks and laid them on the fire, a viper came out because of the heat and fastened onto my hand. When the people saw it they said, "No doubt this man is a murderer, whom, though he has escaped the sea, yet justice does not allow to live."

But I shook off the creature into the fire and suffered no harm. I'm sure they expected that I would swell up or suddenly fall dead. But after they saw no harm come to me, they changed their minds and said I was a god.

In that region sat the estate of the leading citizen of the island, Publius, who received us and entertained us courteously for three days. It happened that his father lay sick of a fever and dysentery. I went in to him and prayed and laid hands on him and healed him. When word of this spread, the rest of those on the island who had diseases also came and were healed.

They also honored us in many ways; and when we departed, they provided such things as were necessary. After three months we sailed in an Alexandrian ship which had wintered at the island. And landing at Syracuse on Sicily, we stayed three days.

From there we circled round and reached Rhegium on the southern tip of Italy. And after one day the south wind blew; and the next day we came to Puteoli, the great port where we witnessed the offloading of the Egyptian grain fleets. Here we also found brethren and have been invited to stay with them seven days. I shall send this missive to you from here, informing you that I expect to arrive in Rome soon after this finds you.

Julius, who has become a friend, has informed me that while the other prisoners will be delivered to the captain of the guard, he has arranged for me to stay in private quarters with only the guard who has been with me on the trip. My hope is that they will let me rent the space and be allowed to come and go freely, but that will depend on the success of my defense.

"So he's close by," Mark said.

"Or he will be soon. We must see if we can welcome him, but you understand the danger."

"That we will be identified as fellow believers? I will proudly associate with him."

"You know what they are calling us now, Mark."

"Of course. The Nazarene sect. And that we are."

MARK MADE IT his mission to discover the whereabouts of Julius, and through him was able to greet the apostle in his private chambers. Peter and Esther came later, and the guard assigned to Paul paid them no mind.

Paul looked older and more haggard, no surprise after all he had endured. But he was clearly regarded as little threat to the empire, at least for now. While he awaited the court date for his defense before Caesar, he plotted with Mark and Peter how he could call the leaders of the Jews together. "If you could somehow summon them, I have much to discuss with them."

It took Mark three days, but he was able to deliver the invitation to the Jewish leaders, and he was there when they came together in Paul's small dwelling. Paul thanked them for coming and said, "Men and brethren, though I have done nothing against our race or the customs of our fathers, yet I have been sent here, delivered as a prisoner from Jerusalem into the hands of the Romans. When they examined me they wanted to let me go, because they found no cause for putting me to death. But when the Jews spoke against me, I was compelled to appeal to Caesar. I am accusing my race of nothing; I merely desire to be acquitted.

"For this reason therefore I have called for you, to see you and speak with you, because for the hope of Israel—the coming of Jesus as the Messiah and the resurrection of the dead—I am bound with these chains."

Mark recognized that everyone in the room understood the obvious: that the Nazarenes were lumped with the Jews in the eyes of the Romans. Both groups were considered seditious, lazy, rebellious, and pagan, as neither bowed to Caesar or the Roman gods. It seemed, however, that as long as they didn't become rabble-rousers, they would be largely ignored. Only when they turned on one another and exposed one another to authorities did persecution result. Paul was, in essence, pleading his case to his Jewish counterparts so he would not suffer in Rome what he had in Jerusalem.

The leaders of the Roman Jews said, "We neither received letters from Judea concerning you, nor have any of the brethren who came reported or spoken any evil of you. But we desire to hear from you what you think; for concerning this sect of yours, we know that it is spoken against everywhere."

Mark knew Paul had to find it as hard as he did to believe that Jewish leaders in Rome would not be more aware of the Christians among them. But Paul thanked them for their interest and curiosity and offered to answer whatever questions they or their colleagues had. And they settled on another date when even more could be present.

Many came to Paul and he was able to explain the gospel and solemnly testify of the kingdom of God, persuading them concerning Jesus from both the Law of Moses and the Prophets. He spent all day doing this, from morning till evening, and some were persuaded and some disbelieved.

Mark saw Paul flush and grow agitated when they could come to no consensus. "Before you leave," he said, "I feel compelled to tell you that I believe the Holy Spirit spoke rightly through Isaiah the prophet to our fathers, saying, *'Go to this people and say: "Hearing you will hear, and shall not understand; and seeing you will see, and not perceive. For the hearts of this people have grown dull. Their ears are hard of hearing, and their eyes they have closed, lest they should see with their eyes and hear with their ears, lest they should understand with their hearts and turn, so that I should heal them."'*

"Therefore let it be known to you that the salvation of God has been sent to the Gentiles, and they will hear it!"

With that the Jewish leaders left Paul's place, loudly disputing among themselves.

WHETHER THROUGH THE influence of Julius the centurion or simply because of other more pressing concerns of the government, eventually all charges against Paul were dropped. His guard was removed, along with his chains, and Paul dwelt the next two years in his own rented house. There he plied his trade of tentmaking to support himself while receiving all who came to him. As he wrote to his friends in churches abroad, he was able to "preach the kingdom of God and teach the things which concern the Lord Jesus Christ with all confidence, no one forbidding me."

That last troubled Mark the most, for he feared Paul was being set up for arrest. Mark was certain the authorities would allow the beloved apostle just enough freedom to wholly incriminate himself. During this time Mark and Peter and Paul labored tirelessly together while Rome seemed to deteriorate under its young Caesar Nero, and for some reason the Nazarenes were now viewed with fear, skepticism, and even hatred by both their Jewish counterparts and the Roman citizenry. Mark prayed he would be able to understand this, for without knowing the cause, he felt at a loss to counter it.

The Christians had long been considered part of the larger Jewish community in Rome and had not suffered persecution to speak of in more than fifteen years. Mark worried that the body of believers, rapidly growing as ever—especially under the leadership of Paul and

Peter—would become complacent with their role in society. Paul often taught that followers of Christ were "not of this world," but were rather aliens, longing for their eternal home. The question was whether it was prudent to trumpet this in their day-to-day lives.

Rumors abounded about what was going on behind the palace walls. Nero was accused of everything from incest with his own mother to rape, sodomy, and even the murders of his mother and sister and many others who opposed him. He was said to have insatiable appetites and an insufferable ego that convinced him he was not only a ruler and a god, but also an artist in several disciplines.

It soon became obvious that Nero was hated even by his own countrymen. Many were convinced he had gone insane and planned to raze the entire city and rebuild it, named after himself. When public criticism arose against him, it seemed the emperor sought a scapegoat. Because the populace already suspected and hated the Jews and, even more, the so-called Nazarenes, it wasn't long before harassment became the order of the day. It began as mere nuisances, arrests for petty violations, then difficulty getting official approval for anything the church or its people wanted to do.

For months the believers simply tried to accept the status quo and stay out from under the scrutiny of the Romans. Many house churches that had become known as meeting places of the Nazarenes shut down and combined, finding new, more clandestine places to gather. Having largely enjoyed indifference on the part of the ruling class, believers now began to live as a secret society. Their leaders, especially Paul and Peter, were well known to the authorities, of course, and they were constantly forced to answer for any appearance of impropriety on the part of the adherents of the faith.

While not eager to be earmarked for persecution, Mark felt slighted that he was not considered part of the leadership, at least in the eyes of the Romans. It wasn't that he sought honor—and eventual torture or even death—for himself, but rather that he worried he was not being forthright enough in his witness. But both Paul and Peter urged him to view this as a blessing, an advantage. "God and the church are fully aware of your commitment. When the day comes that the Romans make an example of us, the body will still have you and the other elders who have not become exposed. Enjoy the honor bestowed upon you by those who know—believers old and new—and especially that the favor of God Himself rests on you."

That counsel soon proved ominously prescient.

TWENTY-SIX

Late on a hot summer night in Rome, a young boy rapped on Mark's door as he was readying himself for bed. Breathlessly the lad reported, "Master Paul has need of you and asks that you bring Rabbi Peter and his wife."

"At this hour? Are you sure? They'll certainly have retired by now." The boy nodded, and Mark added, "The apostle is not ill, is he?"

"No sir, but he said to tell you that he does have a centurion with him."

More trouble? Mark thanked the boy and hurried off to wake Peter and Esther. They appeared none too pleased to have been roused, but they did not hesitate in splashing water on their faces and pulling on their light cloaks as they followed Mark out into the night.

Making their way through the narrow streets, crowded on either side by rows of wood frame apartments and the occasional private home, they passed through the Jewish community and its dark business district, finally reaching Paul's chambers well after midnight.

There was no sign of a contrivance to have borne a centurion to his place. The torch outside his door was unlit, but Paul had apparently been watching for them and cracked the door just wide enough for them to slip in. There in the candlelight sat Julius, whom Mark had met two years before upon Paul's arrival in chains. Mark had to look twice to recognize him, for the man was not in uniform. He rose from a small table when the visitors entered and warmly greeted them.

Mark, like Peter and Esther, was wary. Paul pointed them to the sparse seats and said to Julius, "Tell them what you have told me. Mark has been searching for just this sort of information for months."

While Paul poured water for everyone, Julius said, "I am in Rome from Caesarea with another load of prisoners and will be heading back tomorrow. I came from the barracks tonight in disguise and under cover of darkness, for the favor with which my superiors once viewed our friend here has been exhausted. As you know, during the voyage with Paul two years ago I came to see clearly that he was no criminal, no threat to the empire, and certainly no threat to the Jews. Clearly the hand of His God was upon him, for he both prophesied of our welfare and healed the sick in my presence. I was pleased to see that his credibility became evident to the authorities here and that he has been largely left alone since. However, I sense a new atmosphere in the city now, much of it engendered by the people's hatred of the emperor."

"What has that to do with us?" Peter said.

"Well, the Jews—and some Roman authorities too—have been talking about your sect. For a long time they didn't seem to know or care much about you, and it didn't matter to them what you did as long as it did not affect them."

"It still doesn't affect them except that we often urge them to decide to become believers," Peter said. "But we don't—we can't—force them. Some believe and some don't. But our numbers are growing."

"Oh, believe me, I know. That has become a topic of great concern to the empire. They, or I should say Nero himself, feels threatened by you."

"By us?" Mark said. "We have little interest in doing harm to Rome, except that we would choose to ignore their pagan deities."

"And that is a serious crime," Julius said.

"And one we will continue to commit," Mark said. "But how does Nero's lack of esteem with the populace reflect on us?"

"I believe he is looking for someone else for them to despise so he might be elevated in their eyes."

"And so somehow rumors and stories about us are beginning to spread?"

"Not beginning, sir. They are rampant. If you have not felt the hostility of the people for you—"

"We have!" Mark said. "That is why I have been, as Paul said, trying to find the root of it for some time now. What are they saying about us?"

"I will tell you, but you need to know first that this is not coming from me. I am hearing it on the streets, within the government, and within the military. You have become a hated sect, and I cannot fathom it."

"Nor can I," Mark said. "I hate the religion of the state, but I choose to ignore it. Why can they not do the same?"

"They fear you. And, as I say, I believe Nero himself would like to cast you as the enemy so he may again appear the hero."

"He has never been seen as a hero," Peter said.

"But the office of Caesar has," Julius said. "He seeks that glory for himself, but of course it will never come, regardless what he or anyone else says about you Nazarenes."

"I have tried to be forthright and logical and persuasive," Paul said. "Sometimes confrontational, but rarely. I tried to use reason and simply tell the truth of Jesus that we have all seen and experienced."

"Then why," Julius said, "do some say you are cannibals? Do you eat human flesh?"

"What?" Esther said, gasping. "That's ridicu—"

"Oh, that," Paul said, holding up a hand. "I have had that charge leveled before. This some say because we partake of the Lord's Supper, remembering as He commanded, to view the bread and wine as His flesh and blood."

"Perhaps that's it," Julius said. "I can only hope. But you know the imaginations of people's hearts. This has grown into stories of your sacrificing babies and eating their flesh."

"Preposterous!" Peter said.

"Sir!" Esther said. "You must believe us! We would no more harm a child—"

"Oh, you don't have to persuade me, ma'am. I have never seen anything from a Nazarene that would make me even suspect such a thing."

"The Master Himself visited our home many times," she said, near tears. "And my children and their cousins and all the young ones from the area loved Him! And He loved them."

"Of that I have no doubt. I am just telling you what people say."

"And what else *do* they say?"

"Well," Julius said, hesitating and glancing about, "some of what they say is true, and I have seen it."

"Such as?"

"You refuse to worship the emperor."

"Guilty," Paul said, "and I will go to the gallows before I bow to him. Tell me, Julius, do *you* worship the emperor?"

The man appeared to be fighting a smile despite his obvious fear. Whenever he heard even the wind, he put a finger to his lips. Once he asked whether half the candles could be extinguished. "I must appear to, sir, to keep my job. We bow in the presence of the emperor, yes."

"But do you worship him, in your heart?"

Julius leaned forward and whispered. "Of course not. None of us do. We despise the man. How could one not?"

"What else?" Paul said. "What other things are held against us?"

"That you do not follow the traditions, nor do you acknowledge our gods."

"Guilty again," Paul said. "But neither do we speak out against them, as well we could. We avoid this to protect our flock from the vehemence of Rome."

"Some say you are uncouth and that you hate the normal joys of life."

"If they are referring to worldly pleasures and revelry that elevates the physical over the spiritual, perhaps we are. I don't see how that makes us uncouth, but we are not gluttons, we wage war in our flesh against lust, we take no pleasure in sports and games that result in violence to humans or animals. Is that a reason to hate us?"

"Honored sir," Julius said, peering at Peter, "I trust you realize that if I hated you, I would not be risking my life by being here right now. You have no quarrel with me. I simply care for your friend here and believed it would be profitable for him—and he thought for you—to know how you are viewed in the capital these days."

"Forgive me, Julius," Peter said. "You are right, of course, that my quarrel is not with you. You are merely the messenger, and we appreciate more than we can say the risk and sacrifice you have made to bring this word to us."

"I must not stay long," Julius said, "so let me finish. Another charge against you is that you do not seem to honor the memories of your own ancestors."

"What?" Paul said. "I rarely preach a sermon without harking back to the ancient Scriptures and prophecies and our fathers."

"But, as you know, many of your own Jews consider your claim of Jesus' Messiahship as anathema. In my culture we hold in great esteem the authority of greater men, the certainty of our ancestors. We worship the same gods we have always worshiped, and the reason the Jews have been tolerated despite their aversion to our gods is that at least they have remained true to their own heritage and ancestors. You are new and seem to go against both Rome *and* the Jews, which many see as a double offense. You do realize, do you not, that the worst thing a person can be called in Rome is a Christian?"

Esther shook her head. "We don't hope to have favor, I suppose, but why should we be hated so?"

"Because of what is happening to the empire, ma'am," Julius said. "There is trouble on every side. Our enemies threaten. The palace is in upheaval. We fight among ourselves. The people hate the emperor. And in the middle of all this arises a religion that seems to spit in the face of everything we have been about for centuries. My associates in the palace guard tell me that Nero rages against the Nazarene sect and calls you irrational and perverse, mischievous even. He has even said that you are perverting what was once Rome, laying waste our traditions, breaking the peace of the gods, and corrupting our morals."

"Corrupting your morals!" Esther said. "What morals? We and the Jews seem the only moral people left in this wicked city. Who is Nero to talk about morality?"

"He says you claim that your God is the only God."

"We do," Paul said. "And so do the Jews. Does that not upset Nero?"

"My friends tell me it is hard to know from one day to the next what might vex him. His anger is kindled against you because, if it were true that the God of Abraham, Isaac, and Jacob—"

"And the Father of our Lord and Savior—" Esther said.

"—Yes, if He is the one true God, that fact denies the existence of the very gods who founded Rome. Nero, like all Romans, believe Romulus, offspring of Mars, the god of war, founded our city some eight hundred years ago. That gives him divine authority for his power. When you deny the existence of Mars, you attack the state. True or not, most of Rome believes that our troubles stem from the fact that the gods are not at peace, and that they are not at peace because you and yours refuse to sacrifice to them. In their eyes, you are atheists."

"If the definition of an atheist is one who does not believe in the Roman gods," Mark said, "call me an atheist."

"I really must go," Julius said. "I trust my information at least allows you to be prudent enough to stay safe."

"We thank you, my friend," Paul said. "But I pray your affection for me would translate to belief in and love for the Lord, the Son of the true and living God."

Julius stood and moved to the door. "I feel like King Agrippa," he said. "I was there when you nearly persuaded him. But I have a young family that awaits me in Caesarea. Should I become convinced that I should adopt your life, it would mean the end of everything we have ever known."

"And well it should," Paul said. "Enjoying privileges in an empire as wicked as you have described seems little recompense for raising your children in it."

"Perhaps you are right," Julius said. "But the decision will not be made tonight."

"Know that we will be praying for you, sir," Esther said.

MARK FOUND PETER and his wife as sobered as he as they strolled back to their own lodging in the wee hours of the morning. "I had sensed a renewed resistance," he said, "but I had no idea."

"I don't even want to believe it," Esther said. "I thought we had come so far since the Romans and the Jews put Jesus to death."

"They were just pawns in God's plan, dear," Peter said weakly. "You know that. It would not have made a difference who was in power. We didn't know it, but He had come from Heaven to die."

"And to rise again," she said.

"Amen. Of one thing I am certain, Mark. It is time for you to finish your account."

"*Your* account, you mean," Mark said. "Anything of value on my papyrus has come from you."

"But now the church needs it more than ever, here and abroad. Plus, I need you to finish so you can help me with messages I would like to write."

"It would be my honor."

They agreed Mark would shape the gospel of Jesus from all the material he had and that Peter would be the final arbiter before showing it to Paul and beginning to read and distribute it to the believers.

THREE DAYS LATER, Paul arrived alone at one of the house churches, where Mark and Peter were meeting with the leadership. Mark excused himself and rushed to him. "You look crestfallen, rabbi. What is it?"

"Awful news."

Paul handed the small scroll to Mark, who opened it to find that the ship returning to Caesarea, the one carrying Roman soldiers and Julius, the centurion, had been lost at sea. No survivors. "We can only pray he made his decision for Christ before he perished," Mark said, his voice thick.

"Perhaps even as he breathed his last," Paul said.

TWENTY-SEVEN

It was the middle of July a little more than thirty years since Jesus' death, burial, and resurrection. Mark had spent a long night tossing and turning on his cot, throwing off his cover and wishing for some movement of the steamy air. He had finally dozed off just before dawn when he was startled awake by cries and shouts in the streets.

He squinted against the harsh light pouring through his window, stunned that the sun had already risen.

But it hadn't.

As he rushed out he saw the source of the orange glow in the distance. In the area of the Circus Maximus, raging flames sliced the sky and black smoke billowed. The conflagration seemed to create its own windstorm, which soon brought fire racing into the most populated areas of the city. It appeared the whole of Rome would soon be ablaze.

Barefoot, Mark sprinted toward Peter and Esther's apartment, only to meet them on the street. They looked terrified and out of breath, but Peter said, "The manuscripts! Rescue your manuscripts!"

"But are you all right?"

"We will be fine! Don't worry after us. We will try to gather the believers in this area, but you must protect your writings!"

Mark hurried back toward his place, hearing Esther call after him, "And get your shoes on!"

At the end of the street on which Mark lived, buildings burst into flames from the heat alone. He charged into his place, dancing from foot to foot as he pulled on his sandals. He found the leather bag containing his papyrus and quills, and he was grabbing for other belongings when someone hollered through his door. "Get out now! The entire block is going!"

Mark dived outside as fire swept in, and his hair and even eyebrows were singed. But the writings were safe.

With the bag slung over his shoulder, Mark hurried to help children, the elderly, the infirm. All were seeking breathable air and open spaces where the fire would not kindle everything around them. After hours of exhausting work he finally reached a clearing and was able to reunite with Peter and Esther. "Any news of Paul?" he said.

They shook their heads and looked across the city. "His area will be laid waste within the hour. We should head that way to look for him."

"He remains robust," Mark said. "He will know what to do and be able to do it."

"Fortunately," Peter said, "many of our people come from the Transtiberum region of Trastevere, on the other side of the Tiber. It seems to have been spared. Perhaps we can find shelter there."

Everyone else seemed to have the same idea, but as Mark and Peter and Esther slowly joined the long lines crossing the bridge, thousands seemed to have changed their minds and were heading back. "What news?" Peter said.

"We're not seeking refuge with Jews!" someone spat. "Not even a spark in their region. They must have started the fire!"

Mark and Peter and Esther united with several other elders and believers and set about building a small tent city from whatever scraps they could find. Meanwhile, the fire would rage for more than a week, destroying almost all of Rome. Only four of the fourteen regions of the city were spared. While the loss of life was relatively small for the epic proportion of the disaster, homes, apartments, businesses, shops, livestock, and great works of art and architecture were lost. The cultural headquarters of the Western world had been decimated.

On the second day, word came that Paul was safe, and two days later he located Mark and Peter and Esther. "Already they are blaming the Christ followers," he said. "We need to find someone in one of the surviving regions to hide us."

"If anyone torched this city," Mark said, "it is more likely to be Nero himself."

"That's what many are saying," Paul said. "But he was not even here. He was reportedly at his villa at the seaside in Anzio."

"Still," Mark said, "this looks like his handiwork. He could have had it done. People around here say it started in a shop near the Circus Maximus in the perfect location to spread. Others are saying the city will be rebuilt and named for him."

"Just as Julius predicted."

The four Christians were carrying through the city their bundles of all they had left when Roman soldiers swept through, calling out for the identities of any Nazarenes. Mark and his friends kept their heads down and kept moving as soldiers on horseback cried, "The emperor sees the Christians as utter reprobates and aims to exterminate them! You will be rewarded for information! Do not offer succor to these incendiaries who have destroyed our city!"

Hidden on the spacious estate of a new believer who had not yet become known to authorities, Mark and Paul, along with Peter and

Esther, busied themselves trying to keep abreast of the disposition of their various flocks. While many Christ followers wanted to help in the relief effort, Paul warned against this, as Nero seemed determined to ferret them out and kill them.

The owner of the estate reported that the emperor had delayed his return from his vacation home, further infuriating the populace. "Some say he immediately began planning the rebuilding and that he was happy for the opportunity at worst and indifferent at best. The people are calling for his neck. He is trying to turn the attention on us."

Paul said, "We thought we had it bad years ago under Claudius when he banished some for creating a ruckus in the synagogues. Oh, for that kind of persecution now."

Occasionally Mark disguised himself and made forays into the city to see for himself the unspeakable devastation. Once he followed an angry mob to the Forum, where they chanted and demanded answers from the emperor himself. One shouted, "Deny that you did this!" and to the amazement of the crowd, Caesar himself appeared on his balcony.

"Not only did I have nothing to do with the near death of my beloved city," he cried, "but I know who did! My people tell me that this was the hideous work of the new religionists, the superstitious Nazarene sect, which we all know engages in all manner of the macabre in their pagan rituals. I pledge to rid this city, and indeed this empire, of all such infidels."

The crowd suddenly roared, and Mark realized that—at least for a time—Nero had succeeded in taking the focus off himself and putting it squarely on innocent parties. "Death to the Christians!" they shouted. "Exterminate the infidels!"

"I shall do better than that!" Nero hollered, seeming all the more encouraged by their support. "I shall make a spectacle of their destruction!"

Now the crowd roared lustily.

"I shall have my people prepare my gardens and our arenas to host the executions of these rebels! They shall serve as examples to revolutionaries all over the world that no one is to trifle with the life and future of the Roman Empire, especially not its pagan enemies!"

NIGHT AFTER NIGHT for months, Mark toiled on his manuscript with Peter's supervision. During the day he ventured into the city to witness yet more heinous crimes of the state against the followers of Christ. Hundreds had been rounded up and commanded to renounce their faith. Those who refused, and there were many, were put to death in horrible fashion, the creativity and bloodlust of the emperor himself seeming to know no bounds.

As Nero watched and laughed and cackled and roared, Christians were tortured to within inches of their lives, forced to tell where they had gathered and who else was involved, and offered their freedom for the renouncement of their faith. Some wilted under the pressure, some broke. But even those who gave up their compatriots were extended no leniency. They suffered the double blow of having crumbled under the pressure and still being put to death.

With almost every execution, the announcement of the crime included some offense against the empire other than arson, like "hatred of the human race."

"No one loves the human race more than the followers of the Christ," Paul lamented.

And yet every day Christians had animal skins attached to them and were set in the middle of an arena where packs of wild dogs attacked them and tore them to shreds. Sometimes Nero would have dozens of such victims delivered at once to a vast gaming field, and as they desperately ran to elude the beasts, charioteers would run them down, to the delight of the emperor and the crowds.

Executions that took place near sundown involved dipping the condemned in vats of wax, nailing them to crosses, and setting them afire. Nero took pride in thus lighting his garden so more could be executed while the citizenry watched. Once, after impaling Christians on poles surrounding his garden, he had them set ablaze and crowed, "Now you truly are the lights of the world!"

The more he reveled in the torturous deaths, the more creative he became. It was as if he could not get enough of the carnage. When the dogs had had their fill, he brought in lions, and when the crowd grew weary of the repetition, he hung the victims on crosses and reenacted the death of Christ before setting them afire.

In the midst of all this, Nero took the time to push through a heavy tax on the workers and the wealthy, citing the need to rebuild the city. That, along with the unusual cruelty of his executions, resulted in the opposite of what he had hoped for. Rather than rallying the people around him and giving them what he thought they wanted—the massacre of nearly an entire sect—he succeeded in stirring their sympathy toward the victims.

Soon Mark heard Roman citizens claim they had seen the emperor dressed as a charioteer and himself riding about the execution scenes for a closer look. Many grumbled that he took too perverse a delight in these gruesome deaths and that this sect was being sacrificed because of his own brutality rather than for the good of the public.

Of course, by now the believers who survived were meeting in deep secret, protecting one another, some fleeing the city and many the entire country. Mark and Paul and Peter and his wife surreptitiously made the rounds of the meeting places, desperately, urgently teaching and preaching and trying to embolden everyone.

Meanwhile, Mark finished his gospel and told Peter he was ready to serve as his secretary for his mentor's own letter to believers.

TWENTY-EIGHT

Devastating for the followers of Christ in Rome under the brutality of Caesar Nero was that they had few options. Hardly any had the means to flee, and some who tried—by bribing Romans to get them to ships—found that a Roman's reward from the government for their capture was greater than what they could afford for the bribe. And so their "rescuers" wound up profiting from both the bribe and the bounty when they were arrested at the harbor.

Mark and Paul and Peter and Esther had to split up when word came that their protector had been found out and was on the list to have his estate searched. They cleared out in the middle of the night, promising to reconnect with one another when they had found shelter. Paul wound up in an enclave on the northern edge of the city, while Peter and Esther were able to settle beneath a shop that had somehow survived the inferno in the middle of one of the otherwise burned-out central districts. Over the next several months many peasants and slaves, Jews, and Christians slowly made their way back into the area, which was largely ignored by authorities.

No one trying to elude detection and arrest was able to move about freely, of course, so the old couple counted on Mark to ferry supplies in to them after dark. He had found shelter with the elders of a small congregation on the west side of the city. His life had come to consist of desperately making the rounds of terrified underground believers, teaching them and encouraging them, and motivating them to stay at the task of helping all the unfortunates in the capital.

Mark was conflicted, however, about what had become his life's mission. Like Paul and Peter, he longed to preach regularly and to argue for the gospel in the synagogues and public squares. That was, of course, now suicidal. And he wanted to bear witness to the truth of the saving power of the gospel everywhere he went, to anyone with whom he came in contact. That was also verboten now.

The young men and women believers despaired for their lives and seemed paralyzed with fear. How could Mark blame them? They were cooped up behind closed doors, many underground, scavenging in the darkness for food, hearing horrid stories every day about friends and loved ones who had been arrested, tortured for sport, and executed, and wondering when their time would come.

Mark could only dread the same fate, but in his constant prayer and worship and seeking the face of God, he felt compelled to spend the rest of his days—regardless how many or few—doing all humanly possible for the sake of the gospel. No human, especially a despicable one of the ilk of Nero, should be able to do so much damage to the cause. Sadly, if the scant reports from the outside could be believed, the persecution was spreading throughout the empire, even as far as Jerusalem, where Christians were being crucified. Their crosses lined the roadways in and out of the city.

Strangest to Mark was that in his times of deep prayer and supplication, pleading with the Lord for some sort of relief—not just for himself but for all his brothers and sisters—it seemed God was nudging him about some future ministry of, in all places, Africa. It felt so bizarre to even think of a future, let alone somewhere else.

Mark could barely remember the last time he had seen the sun. The light of day had become the enemy of safety.

One night, after a particularly horrifying day of news of more executions, Mark made the rounds of all the believers he knew in the area and pressed them for money or goods he could use to keep Peter and Esther alive. Many resisted and said they had only enough for themselves and their families.

"We must all sacrifice. This man has been your spiritual father, and he is too old now to get about or work or even beg. And we should not expect him to. I do it gladly in his stead, for I feel I owe him so much."

Mark put what he had been able to scrape together in the way of meager foodstuffs and cash in his leather bag along with his manuscripts and quills. He had learned to be sure to bribe different Roman citizens each time for food and goods, because he knew they would go directly from the transaction to a Roman soldier who would be on the lookout for him. And he never traded near where he was lodging.

The only hope for many in the underground church was being able to pass as a normal Roman citizen looking for work in the rebuilding of the city. The few who were able to secure such labor had to share their income with the rest.

When Mark had been able to buy meal and grain from a peasant, he stole into the district where Peter and Esther resided and found them meeting quietly with a half dozen other believers, including the prophet Silvanus, also known as Silas, who had traveled much with Paul. Only as he reached the door did he hear the low, beautiful humming of a psalm, and his heart tore within him at the sweet sadness of it. How he and these fellow believers had once enjoyed lifting their voices in praise to God, and now they were relegated to wordless humming just above a whisper to avoid drawing the attention of Nero's minions.

Mark used the special knock that silenced the music and allowed him entrée to the tiny candlelit chamber. He greeted the brethren and Peter and Esther with a holy kiss, prompting Silvanus to mutter, "Don't let a Roman see you and charge us with lechery."

Mark urged the faithful to continue the meeting.

"Do you and Silas not need to meet with Peter?" a young man said.

"We do, but it is not as if we have other obligations," Mark said, smiling sadly. "Please."

"We were almost finished, Mark," Esther said. "Perhaps after another tune you would lead us in prayer."

Many wept as they hummed a familiar melody, reminding them of a favorite psalm of David. When the music faded they looked to Mark, then bowed their heads. He didn't know why the Lord prompted him to think of the Shema, the traditional Jewish prayer, but he could not shake the urging.

"Hear, O Israel: The Lord our God, the Lord is one! You shall love the Lord your God with all your heart, with all your soul, and with all your strength.

"And these words which I command you today shall be in your heart. You shall teach them diligently to your children, and shall talk of them when you sit in your house, when you walk by the way, when you lie down, and when you rise up. You shall bind them as a sign on your hand, and they shall be as frontlets between your eyes. You shall write them on the doorposts of your house and on your gates."

Several looked up and whispered their thanks, but Mark held up a hand. "If I may," he said. "Some of you know that years ago, around the time I met Peter, I was a diligent student of the ancient texts. Our Father God is urging me in my spirit to tell you what comes after this passage in the Pentateuch. Do not be alarmed by how it ends, but heed its counsel for the predicament in which we find ourselves.

" 'So it shall be, when the Lord your God brings you into the land of which He swore to your fathers, to Abraham, Isaac, and Jacob, to give you large and beautiful cities which you did not build, houses full of all good things, which you did not fill, hewn-out wells which you did not dig, vineyards and olive trees which you did not plant—when you have eaten and are full—then beware, lest you forget the Lord who brought you out of the land of Egypt, from the house of bondage. You shall fear the Lord your God and serve Him, and shall take oaths in His name. You shall not go after other gods, the gods of the peoples who are all around you (for the Lord your God is a jealous God among you), lest the anger of the Lord your God be aroused against you and destroy you from the face of the earth.'

"Now I cautioned you against concentrating on that final part, because you might be prompted to wonder if God's anger has somehow been aroused against us and He is using this evil regime to remove us from the earth. I do not believe that. I quoted this passage to remind us that we do right to ignore the gods of the people around us. Let us trust in the promise of the rest of it that there is a Promised Land for us as well. It may not be on this earth, but we shall again reach paradise if we remain true."

As the gathering broke up and the others—save for Silas—left one by one to return to their own hovels, Mark presented Peter and Esther with food and supplies. "You are too good to us," Esther said.

"Not at all. But I do worry about you."

"*We* worry about *you,* Mark," she said. "But if you don't mind and will forgive my lack of hospitality, I will do my worrying in bed."

"Please, feel free. Silas and I plan to keep your man here up late."

When Esther had moved to her cot in the other room, Mark asked Peter if he was up to working.

"Nothing would please me more," he said. "I feel as if I am in prison again. I love to teach the young people, but I miss addressing the whole church. Through your gospel and my letter, we can influence many more believers."

When the men had pored over the manuscript of the ministry of Jesus one more time, Peter declared it ready to be read publicly and copied privately. "Mark, we must enlist many with legible handwriting so this can be spread abroad. And it must not fall into the hands of the Romans until we have our own copies. I pray it will influence even them, should anyone of import read it before destroying it."

"So I have my orders," Mark said. "Now then, you wanted Silas to write a letter for you if I could find the supplies. It wasn't easy, but here they are. I ask only that I be allowed to sit in."

"It's certainly all right with me, rabbi," Silas said, "if it's all right with you."

"Of course."

Mark spread fresh papyrus on a small table and set out his quills before Silas in the dim light.

"First," Silas said, "let's identify you. 'Peter, an apostle of Jesus Christ . . .' "

He looked up. "To whom?"

"Well, Silas, I want to communicate what we have been teaching here to all the pilgrims who have been dispersed to various parts of the Roman Empire. They suffer much as we do, and I want to identify them further as well. Call them the elect according to the foreknowledge of God the Father, in sanctification of the Spirit, for obedience and sprinkling of the blood of Jesus Christ."

And Peter continued to dictate as Mark listened and Silas quickly wrote:

"Grace to you and peace be multiplied. Blessed be the God and Father of our Lord Jesus Christ, who according to His abundant mercy has begotten us again to a living hope through the resurrection of Jesus Christ from the dead, to an inheritance incorruptible and undefiled and that does not fade away, reserved in heaven for you, who are kept by the power of God through faith for salvation ready to be revealed in the last time. In this you greatly rejoice, though now for a little while, if need be, you have been grieved by various trials, that the genuineness of your faith, being much more precious than gold that perishes, though it is tested by fire, may be found to praise, honor, and glory at the revelation of Jesus Christ, whom having not seen you love."

Mark held up a hand as Silas finished the paragraph. "Rabbi, you are more eloquent than you know. That is just thrilling."

"Stop, Mark. I am warmed by your enthusiasm, but it is the Lord who gives utterance, and I daresay being in the presence of scholars like you two makes me concentrate all the more. Anyway, all three of us have benefited from hearing our brother Paul express such sentiments for years now. I don't expect my letters to compare with his, except as the Lord blesses, but it is the Spirit who gives utterance. Most of all, I long to fill the fearful with courage during such a time as this."

"Then let me hear what else the Spirit is telling you."

Peter rubbed his eyes and cleared his throat.

"Though now you do not see Him, yet believing, you rejoice with joy inexpressible and full of glory, receiving the end of your faith—the salvation of your souls. Of this salvation the prophets have inquired and searched carefully, who prophesied of the grace that would come to you, searching what, or what manner of time, the Spirit of Christ who was in them was indicating when He testified beforehand the sufferings of Christ and the glories that would follow. To them it was revealed that, not to themselves, but to us they were ministering the things which now have been reported to you through those who have preached the gospel to you by the Holy Spirit sent from heaven—things which angels desire to look into."

"How true, how true," Mark said.

"Yes, and now let me try to fill them with boldness. Ready, Silas?"

The prophet nodded.

"Therefore gird up the loins of your mind, be sober, and rest your hope fully upon the grace that is to be brought to you at the revelation of Jesus Christ; as obedient children, not conforming yourselves to the former lusts, as in your ignorance; but as He who called you is holy, you also be holy in all your conduct, because it is written, *'Be holy, for I am holy.'*

"And if you call on the Father, who without partiality judges according to each one's work, conduct yourselves throughout the time of your stay here in fear; knowing that you were not redeemed with corruptible things, like silver or gold, from your aimless conduct received by tradition from your fathers, but with the precious blood of Christ, as of a lamb without blemish and without spot.

"He indeed was foreordained before the foundation of the world, but was manifest in these last times for you who through Him believe in God, who raised Him from the dead and gave Him glory, so that your faith and hope are in God. Since you have purified your souls in obeying the truth through the Spirit in sincere love of the brethren, love one another fervently with a pure heart, having been born again, not of corruptible seed but incorruptible, through the word of God which lives and abides forever, because *'All flesh is as grass, and all the glory of man as the flower of the grass. The grass withers, and its flower falls away, but the word of the Lord endures forever.'* Now this is the word which by the gospel was preached to you."

"Peter," Mark said, sighing, "you must never again discount your own scholarship. This will be so encouraging to its hearers."

"Let me also teach them," Peter said.

"Therefore, laying aside all malice, all deceit, hypocrisy, envy, and all evil speaking, as newborn babes, desire the pure milk of the word, that you may grow thereby, if indeed you have tasted that the Lord is gracious. Coming to Him as to a living stone, rejected indeed by men, but chosen by God and precious, you also, as living stones, are being built up a spiritual house, a holy priesthood, to offer up spiritual sacrifices acceptable to God through Jesus Christ."

Peter quoted more of the ancient Scriptures, then exhorted his readers: ". . . [Y]ou are a chosen generation, a royal priesthood, a holy nation, His own special people, that you may proclaim the praises of Him who called you out of darkness into His marvelous light; who once were not a people but are now the people of God, who had not obtained mercy but now have obtained mercy.

"Beloved, I beg you as sojourners and pilgrims, abstain from fleshly lusts which war against the soul, having your conduct honorable among the Gentiles, that when they speak against you as evildoers, they may, by your good works which they observe, glorify God in the day of visitation."

Peter stood and stretched. "Mark and Silas, this next is going to clang in their ears at first, but I believe it from the core of my being."

"Then speak it, sir."

"Therefore submit yourselves to every ordinance of man for the Lord's sake, whether to the king as supreme, or to governors, as to those who are sent by him for the punishment of evildoers and for the praise of those who do good. For this is the will of God, that by doing good you may put to silence the ignorance of foolish men—as free, yet not using liberty as a cloak for vice, but as bondservants of God."

"Oh, my, Peter, you're right," Mark said. "You realize this will be read and heard first by the body here in Rome."

"Babylon, you mean. Has any city on earth better fit the description of Babylon from the ancient word?"

"I agree, but you're suggesting that we submit ourselves to evil rulers?"

"Let's say it this way: Honor all people. Love the brotherhood. Fear God. Honor the king. Servants, be submissive to your masters with all fear, not only to the good and gentle, but also to the harsh. For this is commendable, if because of conscience toward God one endures grief, suffering wrongfully. For what credit is it if you take it patiently when you are beaten for your faults? But when you do good and suffer, if you take it patiently, this is commendable before God.

"For to this you were called, because Christ also suffered for us, leaving us an example, that you should follow His steps: '*Who committed no sin, nor was deceit found in His mouth*'; who, when He was reviled, did not revile in return; when He suffered, He did not threaten, but committed Himself to Him who judges righteously; who Himself bore our sins in His own body on the tree, that we, having died to sins, might live for righteousness—by whose stripes you were healed.

"For you were like sheep going astray, but have now returned to the Shepherd and Overseer of your souls."

After exhorting believing husbands and wives how to conduct themselves within the bonds of marriage, Peter discussed suffering for Christ and serving others. He closed by addressing church leaders directly.

"The elders who are among you I exhort, I who am a fellow elder and a witness of the sufferings of Christ, and also a partaker of the glory that will be revealed: Shepherd the flock of God which is among you, serving as overseers, not by compulsion but willingly, not for dishonest gain but eagerly; nor as being lords over those entrusted to you, but being examples to the flock; and when the Chief Shepherd appears, you will receive the crown of glory that does not fade away."

He urged younger people to submit themselves to their elders and for all to be submissive to one another, clothed with humility, "for *'God resists the proud, but gives grace to the humble.'*

"Therefore humble yourselves under the mighty hand of God, that He may exalt you in due time, casting all your care upon Him, for He cares for you. Be sober, be vigilant; because your adversary the devil walks about like a roaring lion, seeking whom he may devour. Resist him, steadfast in the faith, knowing that the same sufferings are experienced by your brotherhood in the world.

"But may the God of all grace, who called us to His eternal glory by Christ Jesus, after you have suffered awhile, perfect, establish, strengthen, and settle you. To Him be the glory and the dominion forever and ever. Amen.

"By Silvanus, our faithful brother as I consider him, I have written to you briefly, exhorting and testifying that this is the true grace of God in which you stand. She [the church] who is in Babylon [Rome], elect together with you, greets you; and so does Mark my son. Greet one another with a kiss of love. Peace to you all who are in Christ Jesus. Amen."

TWENTY-NINE

"Perhaps we should have left separately, Mark," Silas said as the men crept through the deserted streets of Rome.

"I do not mind the threat," Mark said. "When will you leave with the letter?"

"At dawn. I wish I could stay and help copy your gospel. I pray God will use it widely."

"Do you need a place to stay tonight?" Mark said.

"No, but my dwelling is past your district. I'll accompany you as far as that."

But when they came within several streets of Mark's place, they hesitated at the sound of excited voices and agreed to split up. As they embraced, Mark said, "I bid you Godspeed. Greet all the brothers for me."

"Be careful, Mark. And be safe."

As Silas disappeared into the shadows, Mark took the long way around his block and entered from the west side, only to find bands of his friends and brothers and sisters in Christ being bound and led away by soldiers on horseback. "Spare yourselves!" a centurion shouted. "Give us Peter and you may return to your beds!"

"They don't even live near here!" a woman wailed, and Mark grimaced.

Offer nothing! he wished. *They leap on every clue.*

"They?" the centurion said. "Who is with him?"

"No one!"

"Then what did you mean by *they*? Give me one name and I will reunite you with your children."

"Esther, his wife!"

"And where do they lodge?"

Please, woman, say no more.

"I do not know. But not near here."

Thank God!

"Now, sir, you promised. My children."

The centurion laughed.

If these poor people were so quick to give up their spiritual father, how long would it be before Mark himself was revealed? Slinking back the way he had come, he moved slowly and quietly until he knew he was out of range of the soldiers. Then he sprinted back to Peter's place.

"You must leave and soon!" he told the old couple. "Stay on the move. Don't alight in any one place too long."

"I am wearying of fleeing, Peter," Esther said. "Sometimes I feel we should just resign ourselves to our fate."

"Never!" Mark said. "We need you. We need you both."

"I fear she is right, Mark," the old man said. "As things stand now, we are a burden on the people. How can they be expected to continue to hide us, to lodge us, to feed us, to help us stay on the move? At some point we become much more trouble than we are worth."

Fortunately no one else in the church agreed with Peter and Esther, and for the next several months they were shuttled from place to place every few days. Even Mark, on the move himself, found it difficult to keep track of all the places they were hidden. Somehow, however, enough members of the church body were able to find them and show up at all hours to sit under his teaching. Peter had lost much of his strength and energy, but none of his passion.

"Most troubling to me, Mark," he said late one night, "is the word coming back from Silas that false teachers seem to have sneaked in to many of our fellowships abroad. They teach heresy. He is fighting it for all he is worth, but he fears the leadership needs to hear directly from me. Would you be willing to help me with a second letter to the churches?"

"Of course."

Remaining covert while still able to trade on the streets was becoming much more difficult, but in his search for more papyrus, quills, and ink, Mark came upon a group of Christ followers from the northern district who brought him greetings from Paul. "He wants to see you," they said.

"Are you sure? We had agreed to keep our distance so as not to give him away."

"That was his specific request."

When Mark found him near midnight one night, Paul pulled him into a tiny room that served as both sleeping chamber and workshop, where he appeared to be plying his old tentmaking trade. "What could people need more than these right now?" he said. "I have had even Romans bring me materials in exchange for crafting them a dwelling. I tell you, Mark, the city remains in an uproar over Nero. He had better watch himself or he will be assassinated. He is hated within and without the palace."

Paul reminded Mark that he had always had the ability to make friends, even endearing himself to his enemies. "Not always, of course, as my scars prove. But being a Roman citizen has its advantages. Do you know that even if I am arrested and convicted for being an enemy of the state because of my work for the gospel, I cannot be tortured?"

"Is that so?"

"Absolutely. As fate would have it, I could be executed, but it must be humanely."

"Forgive me for smiling, rabbi, but is there a humane way to kill a man?"

"Of course there is! I am willing to die for my Lord, Mark, but I am human. I wouldn't choose it. And when that day comes, I would certainly rather my end come swiftly and without unbearable torture and pain."

"I pray it never happens, but that if it does, you are granted your wish."

"I pray I will in some way honor my Lord in it."

Mark brought Paul up to date on all that was happening among the believers to whom he and Peter had been ministering. "When I met you I was searching for the materials necessary to aid Peter in his second letter to the churches."

"He should have written as many as I have by now," Paul said. "He is wise and deep with much to say, and his earnestness comes through. But listen, I told you of my ability to befriend my enemies because I have done just that with some old friends and acquaintances of Julius. They say that he told them of seeing me heal the sick and prophesy based on words from an angel, and he convinced them that I am a man of God. They are not so persuaded, but they trust me, and on occasion they tell me what is happening at the palace. They are apparently not brave enough to plot an assassination or even to support an insurrection, but they feel they are doing their part by aiding me with information."

"What kind of information?"

"Who is targeted for arrest. What the centurions and soldiers know. That kind of thing."

Mark told Paul how he and others had been keeping Peter and Esther on the run. "Any surprises? We know Peter is one of their prime targets."

"*The* prime target, as it turns out," Paul said. "The empire seems to view me as damaged goods, a man with no influence or audience or impact. I am no threat."

"If they only knew."

"Were it not for my pen, I would feel the same as they do. I am but a feeble old tentmaker, of some value even to them. When they learn of my epistles being spread abroad, my days will be numbered. But there is good news."

"Tell me. It's been a long time."

"You are entirely unknown to them, Mark. I have been given lists of names and meeting places. If you keep your distance from known believers, you can easily spare yourself arrest."

"I don't know if I could do that, master. It sounds cowardly."

"On the contrary. Everyone knows you are no coward. I believe you could be much more effective for the church because of your ability to move about freely in society. Disguise yourself as someone from a specific trade. As no one in authority is looking for you, you will have access to places most believers cannot go."

"Such as?"

"Anywhere, man! You can shop in the markets. You can visit the prisons. You could be a messenger. You can't stand there and embrace friends or pray with them, but you can seem to be impartially bearing news back and forth. Of course, you would have to do the same for all, brothers and sisters and foes alike, but imagine the possibilities."

THIRTY

Taking Paul's advice, Mark moved out of the Christian ghetto into a tiny apartment near the Forum, identifying himself as a scribe and seeking work. Soon he had enough to buy food and pay his rent. When he had extra, he bought meal and grain and bread in large quantities, and under the cover of darkness smuggled it into the city and delivered it to secret believers. They kept him up on the news, especially on who had been arrested, imprisoned, tortured, or put to death. Generally, those were the fates—and in that order—of anyone who had been caught and identified as part of the Nazarene sect.

While the populace had tired of Nero's macabre shows of death, apparently the emperor himself remained bloodthirsty. Hardly a victim was executed without his watching from his private boxes at the arenas or from his balcony when these were carried out in his garden or at the Circus on his grounds.

Mark, dressed in the garb of a Roman citizen so as not to give himself away, forced himself to attend many of these spectacles, horrifying as they were. Sometimes it was all he could do to keep from hiding his eyes and bursting into tears, whether he knew the victim personally or not—and ofttimes he did. He believed it his duty to witness these atrocities and to pray for each saint as he or she was humiliated and interrogated.

All were asked why they believed in a dead Man, and nearly all testified that they believed Jesus was alive. All were given the chance to recant their allegiance to Him and bow to the gods of Rome and specifically to the emperor. But even those who did were then found guilty of arson and put to death in no less ignoble fashion.

Mark tried to spread the word among the faithful that they must not acknowledge him if they saw him at any of these venues, for he was occasionally finding his way even into the prisons to serve as amanuensis to prisoners who could afford it. Often he would pretend to be working for hire for a believer he knew had no money, but in this way he was able to trade news and encourage the condemned.

Mark had not realized how exhausting was his work and the alertness he had to maintain in order to succeed in his double life until he found himself so exhausted one afternoon that he had to retire to his quarters. There he collapsed on his cot and slept through his afternoon mealtime and into the evening.

He was roused near midnight by urgent knocking and worried that perhaps he had been found out and was being hauled in for sentencing himself. But the knock, fast as it was, did not carry the boom of the Roman soldiers, who wanted to bring attention to themselves and awaken everyone around.

Mark hurriedly padded to the door and opened it to two young men he had known from Silas's congregation. "We risked our lives coming here," they said, peeking out from hooded cloaks. "It's Peter and Esther. They have been arrested and several with them."

"Where have they been taken?"

"To Mamertime Prison."

"And has Paul been informed?"

"No, and we dare not venture out any farther."

"I will tell him and try to get to them as soon as possible."

MARK KNEW IT would arouse suspicion if he showed up at the prison near the Capitoline Hill in the middle of the night, but there was no going back to bed. He grabbed some fruit and rushed north to see Paul. He hated to wake the apostle, but he would want to know.

It took so long for Paul to answer his knock that Mark feared he too had been taken, or was lying ill—or worse, had passed. But eventually the diminutive man, now in his sixties, appeared at the door. Mark quickly spilled the news, and Paul urged him to move on. "You must not risk being seen with me," he said. "So far your disguise has proved a success. But here, let me give you a brief message for our friends. I hope it will encourage them."

He quickly scribbled a greeting assuring them of his prayers, but of course he did not sign it.

MARK WAS GRATEFUL that he had fallen asleep so early in the day, because he could not even attempt to doze the rest of the night. As soon as it made sense for him to be seen out and about, he made his way to Mamertime Prison and strolled through the cell blocks and dungeons as he frequently had.

He didn't dare arouse suspicion by asking after Peter, and with hundreds of prisoners incarcerated, he feared finding him might take all day. Mark wondered how long they would allow Peter to linger before his execution.

As Mark descended a stone stairway he passed a jailer on his way up. "Guess who we've got down there," the jailer said, nodding toward the dungeon. "Peter of the Nazarenes himself. They've got his wife in the women's section too."

Mark merely nodded. When he reached the underground compound he spotted Peter almost immediately, sitting, his head in his hands. The only light came from torches mounted on the walls outside the cells.

"Anyone need anything written?" Mark said, and he noticed Peter's head jerk up. He knew the old man would know enough not to give him away.

"I do, young man," Peter said, and he slowly stood and moved to the bars. Other prisoners were gnawing on stale bread for their breakfast and talking among themselves.

Mark pretended to be arranging his writing materials as they whispered, and he passed the note from Paul.

"I really do need something written, Mark," Peter rasped. "It's urgent that I get this second letter out to the churches. Can you do it?"

"Of course, sir," Mark said, loudly enough for guards and other prisoners to hear. "But it will cost you."

They pretended to haggle over the price until everyone else lost interest. "I don't know whether they'll let you into the women's section, but—"

"I will bring any news I can find, Peter, you know that."

During the next several days they toiled over the letter. Mark was not allowed into the women's area, but from what he could gather, Esther was alive and unharmed, though she was growing thin. No wonder, because Peter was doing the same. The prisoners were given bread and water twice a day, and all soon began to look gaunt, their cheekbones protruding.

"I am the only believer in this area," Peter said. "Except for those two guards."

"Really?"

"They fear for their lives, but they are now believers. I would not tell them about yourself, however. Too much is at stake. They could be forced to tell anything they have heard. I finally got them to find out about my disposition. I feared Nero would let me rot to death in here, but they assure me that he knows exactly who I am and intends to make the most of my demise."

"Unless we can devise some way out of here."

"Don't be ridiculous, Mark. Prisoners don't escape from here. And anyway, if this is God's will, this is where I want to be."

"Have they told you what form your, uh, end is supposed to take?"

Peter nodded. "Apparently he wants Esther and me together at the end. I know she is as willing as I to die for the cause, but it pains me to think of her enduring any discomfort, let alone torture."

Mark slipped Peter a chunk of bread, and he immediately shared it with his cellmate on the condition that he keep it hidden. If word got out that Mark was smuggling food in, all would be lost.

Mark was amazed that Peter's mind could be clear enough to result in the letter to the churches that he felt privileged to write. The old man was so eager to see it through to completion and for Mark to get it on its way that he worked until he could barely keep his eyes open.

Much older than even Paul, Peter impressed Mark with his ability to use metaphor to make his points. At one point early in the missive he referred to his mortal body as his tent that he would soon have to put off. He dictated, ". . . an entrance will be supplied to you abundantly into the everlasting kingdom of our Lord and Savior Jesus Christ. For this reason I will not be negligent to remind you always of these things, though you know and are established in the present truth. Yes, I think it is right, as long as I am in this tent, to stir you up by reminding you, knowing that shortly I must put off my tent, just as our Lord Jesus Christ showed me.

"Moreover I will be careful to ensure that you always have a reminder of these things after my decease. For we did not follow cunningly devised fables when we made known to you the power and coming of our Lord Jesus Christ, but were eyewitnesses of His majesty. For He received from God the Father honor and glory when such a voice came to Him from the Excellent Glory: 'This is My beloved Son, in whom I am well pleased.'

"And we heard this voice which came from heaven when we were with Him on the holy mountain. And so we have the prophetic word confirmed, which you do well to heed as a light that shines in a dark place, until the day dawns and the morning star rises in your hearts; knowing this first, that no prophecy of Scripture is of any private interpretation, for prophecy never came by the will of man, but holy men of God spoke as they were moved by the Holy Spirit.

"But there were also false prophets among the people, even as there will be false teachers among you, who will secretly bring in destructive heresies, even denying the Lord who bought them, and bring on themselves swift destruction. And many will follow their destructive ways, because of whom the way of truth will be blasphemed."

After lengthy warnings and exhortations, Peter finished his letter with encouragement, as always.

"Therefore, beloved, looking forward to these things, be diligent to be found by Him in peace, without spot and blameless; and consider that the longsuffering of our Lord is salvation—as also our beloved brother Paul, according to the wisdom given to him, has written to you, as also in all his epistles, speaking in them of these things, in which are some things hard to understand, which untaught and unstable people twist to their own destruction, as they do also the rest of the Scriptures.

"You therefore, beloved, since you know this beforehand, beware lest you also fall from your own steadfastness, being led away with the error of the wicked; but grow in the grace and knowledge of our Lord and Savior Jesus Christ. To Him be the glory both now and forever. Amen."

PETER URGED MARK to get the letter past Paul first, and then to make sure it was copied and circulated in Rome, while the original was to go to the churches abroad. Mark was in the middle of all these chores when the dreadful announcement came from the palace. Word quickly spread throughout Rome of the day and time of the so-called trial of the ringleader of the Nazarenes.

At four o'clock in the afternoon, in two days, the apostle Peter and his wife would be processed, as the official notice put it. And the whole of Rome was welcome to witness with joy the justice meted out to this enemy of the state, the empire, and the gods.

THIRTY-ONE

"All is under way as you wish," Mark told Peter the morning of his execution.

"You will be there this afternoon, will you not?"

"I don't know whether I can bear it."

"You must, for my sake, and for Esther's. You have been like a son to us."

"Then why require me to see it? I wish to remember you as you are."

"It will give us comfort to know that you stand with us. Now, please."

Mark said, "As you wish," but it was as hard a promise as he had ever had to make.

That afternoon, under an unforgiving sun, he joined tens of thousands in Nero's Circus as Peter and Esther were brought in chains from their respective cells. The emperor had left the palace and was prominent in his royal box.

Mark's heart ached as Peter and Esther stared into each other's eyes, not allowed to get near each other or talk with each other. They were forced to kneel about ten feet apart, and the chief executioner asked questions. Remarkably, for Mark knew they had not had opportunity to plot together, they answered every inquiry the same, in unison.

"Are you members of the Nazarene sect?"

"We are."

"Are you guilty of destroying the city of Rome by fire, either by your own hands or by those you hired?"

"We are not."

"Do you worship the emperor, Caesar Nero, as your god?"

"We do not."

"Do you acknowledge the gods of Rome and bow to them and sacrifice to them?"

"We do not."

"Will you renounce your allegiance to Jesus, whom you call the Christ and the Messiah and the Son of God?"

"We will not."

"Then by the power vested in me by the empire and by Caesar, I sentence you to death."

Esther was unbound and led a hundred feet to the center of the arena, where she was wrapped with freshly cut animal skins. Mark could only imagine how the bloody things felt and smelled. Vicious wild dogs were let loose from cages at one end of the ring, and Esther was prodded and commanded to run, but she would not.

Peter cried out, "Esther, my beloved! Remember the Lord!"

And as the beasts closed on her, she slowly knelt and raised her hands toward heaven. The crowd stood and roared as the dogs tore at her limbs and at her neck, ripping her to pieces and devouring her flesh.

Peter raised his face toward the sun and wept aloud, and Mark stood in the midst of a frenzied crowd that ignored him as he sobbed.

As Peter's chains were removed, he appeared pale, as if about to topple. Mark wished he had the power to rescue him, to stop his captors and abscond with him to the sea where the beloved apostle could be delivered to the saints who so revered him.

But to Mark's horror, and certainly to Peter's, as he was lifted and guided forward, slaves passed him with a rough-hewn cross that took Mark's mind back more than three decades. Peter began to resist, to fight and pull away. Mark was surprised. He had expected Peter to maintain his dignity to the end the way his wife had.

But this was not about fear of death. Plainly Peter had resigned himself to that. No, he was violently protesting the manner of his execution. "Anything but that!" he cried out. "I am not worthy to suffer the same end as my precious Savior!"

But the cross was laid out on the ground and he was forced upon it. Still he fought and screamed and raged. As the spikes were driven into his hands and feet, Peter turned to the executioner, his ancient gravelly voice as desperate as Mark had ever heard it.

"If you have an ounce of humanity left in you, sir, do not, do not suspend me in the way my Jesus was put to death! I beg you! I beg you! At least hang me upside down!"

The crowd began to roar, "Let the man die however he wishes!"

The executioner looked to the emperor's box and lifted his hands, palms up.

Nero called out, "What is it to me if he dies sideways? Just finish him!"

And so the executioner directed the slaves to turn the cross, with Peter pinned to it, upside down and drop the top of it into the hole in the ground first. Peter let out a great groan when it violently settled in.

"My Lord and my God," he managed, his voice constricted, "into Thy hands I commend my spirit."

And within seconds, Peter was dead.

EPILOGUE

Just under a year later, the missionary Paul was dragged from his quarters by Roman soldiers and hauled along the Via Ostia. Because of his Roman citizenship, the law prohibited torturing him, but he was also so well known to the authorities as a champion of the gospel of the Nazarene that he was not even proffered the courtesy of an interrogation.

Mark watched from the road as the great apostle and apologist for the faith spoke clearly of his belief.

"Silence!" the executioner shouted, but Paul would not be dissuaded.

"What is your plan if I continue to testify, sir?" Paul said, almost as if amused. "Do I risk death?"

"A quicker death," the man growled, handing the great blade to a muscled, black-hooded man.

Paul's head was also covered, but he continued to speak, only louder. "I declare the gospel I preached, which I also received: that Christ died for our sins according to the Scriptures, and that He was buried, and that He rose again the third day according to the Scriptures."

Even as Paul's head was forced down onto the chopping block, he said, "I am not ashamed of the gospel of Christ, for it is the power of God to salvation for everyone who believes. The just shall live by faith."

MARK HAD SEEN more than enough violence and bloodshed for one lifetime, and yet in the sobriety that permeated him after the losses of so many dear friends, he found one truth ironic: Christianity had been little more than a small sect, a nuisance to Rome, before Nero blamed the inferno on believers. His garish displays of brutal torture and execution were so extreme that he engendered pity for and then sympathy with the martyrs even on the part of the Roman citizens.

That people were devout enough to be willing to die rather than to renounce their faith in Christ made people all over the world take notice and want to know more about their beliefs.

Nero was soon deposed, and he committed suicide to avoid execution, but a pattern of persecuting Christians had begun.

MARK EVENTUALLY WAS led by the Holy Spirit to leave Rome and believed God had called him to plant churches more than twelve hundred miles away in the great Egyptian city of Alexandria, which lay northwest of the Nile Delta and along a narrow strip between the Mediterranean Sea and Lake Mareotis.

By the time he reached Alexandria, he had traveled by horse, wagon, ship, and camel, and on foot, and had ministered everywhere he went. Church bodies had sprung up and people had come to faith in Christ. Finally reaching the city gates of Alexandria, Mark realized he had broken a strap on one of his sandals. A curious child directed him to a cobbler whose shop was set up in a large tent off the city square. The ruddy man wore a leather apron, and sweat poured from him.

"It appears you've gotten more than your money's worth out of these," the cobbler said, introducing himself as Atef, a family man. It made Mark smile to hear him mention his loved ones, reminding Mark of his own family. He told Mark, "You would be better off to invest in new ones, rather than pay me to fix these."

"Unfortunately," Mark said, "I am currently without means. I have only enough to pay you to perhaps reattach this strap."

"If you're sure."

"I am, but I will make you a solemn promise. Because you showed concern for my expense, when I have settled and have my affairs in order, I will return and buy sandals from you."

"I sell only used and remade ones, sir, but if that is your wish, I will accommodate you."

"Do you mind if I watch while you work?"

"Not at all! Was it your hope I would repair this right now?"

"Oh, pardon me. I am sure you have other work ahead of it. I am willing to wait."

"No! I can do it!"

The good-natured Atef grabbed an awl from his rack and pulled a small piece of metal from a bin. "If I pierced it right there and fastened it with this, how would that be?"

"I wouldn't begin to tell you your trade, sir, but I envision it being more than adequate."

Atef lay the strap over his wood workbench, placed the point of the awl carefully over the leather, and smacked it three times. He held the strap up to the sunlight and asked Mark to move close. "See the light peeking through?" he said. "You don't want it too big before the brad is forced through. Let the metal stretch the leather, and it will hold longer."

"You should be a teacher, Atef."

"Ach!" Atef pressed the metal close to the tiny hole and attempted to push it through. "Sometimes I make the hole too small."

He sat and pressed his elbows close to his body, steadying the leather while pressing hard on the metal with his thumbs. Still it would not budge. Atef grabbed the awl and held the top to one end of the brad, slowly increasing the pressure. Mark saw the veins in his neck and forehead stand out, and he watched with interest to see how much force it would take to press the metal through.

But suddenly the awl slipped and the point tore all the way through the web of skin between the man's thumb and index finger. He leapt from his chair as blood spattered everywhere, holding the wound with his good hand and hopping about, swearing by every Egyptian god Mark had ever heard of.

"Oh, my!" Mark said. "Atef! Let me see it!"

"No! It has torn all the way through! Oh, my business will be ruined!"

"Please, sit down and let me see."

"Go get me some help!"

"I will, but you must show me first."

Grimacing, his eyes pressed shut, Atef finally sat and Mark knelt next to him. He gently put his hands over Atef's and urged him to release his fingers so he could assess the wound. It was worse than Mark feared. The tool had not just pierced him, but it had also ripped the skin apart. Blood poured onto the ground.

"Now please, sir, get me some help!"

"Be still," Mark said quietly, surprised himself by the calm in his tone. He held the man's wounded hand in his own, then spat in the dirt next to where the blood was pooling. He reached with his free hand and mixed the spittle and blood and dirt to make a paste.

Atef stiffened and tried to pull away when Mark brought the cool mixture up. Mark held the man's wrist tight and pressed the clay directly into the wound, saying, "In the name of Jesus Christ who lives eternally, be whole."

Mark let go and leaned back, and Atef leapt to his feet, staring at his hand and turning it this way and that in the sunlight. There was no wound, not even the hint of a scar.

"Who are you?" he demanded. "And who is this Jesus Christ you speak of?"

"If you will introduce me to your family, I will tell you all about Him, from the first time I met Him until today."

"I will do better than that, sir! You shall have the best sandals I have available, free! And you shall have dinner with me and my family this very night."

Atef and his entire household listened raptly to the story of Jesus' death, burial, resurrection, and return to heaven, and then to the story of the spread of the gospel. They all became believers and helped Mark start a church in Alexandria that soon grew so large it attracted the attention, and the ire, of local pagan leaders who specialized in idol worship.

The church of Christ grew so large that its worship services conflicted with a festival honoring the pagan god Serapis. The local leaders led a mob into the sanctuary and seized Mark, binding him with ropes and dragging him through the streets. His captors exulted, "We're taking the ox to the stall!"

Mark was thrown into prison with deep lacerations all over his body from the stones over which he had been pulled. That night an angel appeared to him and told him that he would soon "rejoice on with the powers on high."

The next morning he had a rope thrown around his neck and was again dragged through the streets. When finally the rope cut off his breath, Mark surrendered to death. But the pagan leaders were not satisfied. They built a bonfire to consume his body.

Before they could incinerate him, however, lightning flashed, thunder rolled, and the earth shook as God sent a hailstorm to snuff out the flames. As his tormentors scattered, Atef led a group of Christians who gathered up his remains and ensured he would be properly buried and his bones preserved.

THE WORDS OF MARK

MARK

John the Baptist Prepares the Way

1 The beginning of the gospel of Jesus Christ, the Son of God. 2As it is written in the Prophets:[a]

"Behold, I send My messenger
before Your face,
Who will prepare Your way
before You."[b]
3 *"The voice of one crying in the*
wilderness:
'Prepare the way of the
LORD;
Make His paths straight.'"[a]

4John came baptizing in the wilderness and preaching a baptism of repentance for the remission of sins. 5Then all the land of Judea, and those from Jerusalem, went out to him and were all baptized by him in the Jordan River, confessing their sins.

6Now John was clothed with camel's hair and with a leather belt around his waist, and he ate locusts and wild honey. 7And he preached, saying, "There comes One after me who is mightier than I, whose sandal strap I am not worthy to stoop down

---

1:2 [a]NU-Text reads *Isaiah the prophet.* [b]Malachi 3:1 1:3 [a]Isaiah 40:3

and loose. [8]I indeed baptized you with water, but He will baptize you with the Holy Spirit."

John Baptizes Jesus

[9]It came to pass in those days *that* Jesus came from Nazareth of Galilee, and was baptized by John in the Jordan. [10]And immediately, coming up from[a] the water, He saw the heavens parting and the Spirit descending upon Him like a dove. [11]Then a voice came from heaven, "You are My beloved Son, in whom I am well pleased."

Satan Tempts Jesus

[12]Immediately the Spirit drove Him into the wilderness. [13]And He was there in the wilderness forty days, tempted by Satan, and was with the wild beasts; and the angels ministered to Him.

Jesus Begins His Galilean Ministry

[14]Now after John was put in prison, Jesus came to Galilee, preaching the gospel of the kingdom[a] of God, [15]and saying, "The time is fulfilled, and the kingdom of God is at hand. Repent, and believe in the gospel."

Four Fishermen Called as Disciples

[16]And as He walked by the Sea of Galilee, He saw Simon and Andrew his brother casting a net into the sea; for they were fishermen. [17]Then Jesus said to them, "Follow Me, and I will make you become fishers of men." [18]They immediately left their nets and followed Him.

[19]When He had gone a little farther from there, He saw James the *son* of Zebedee, and John his brother, who also *were* in the boat mending their nets. [20]And immediately He called them, and they left their father Zebedee in the boat with the hired servants, and went after Him.

Jesus Casts Out an Unclean Spirit

[21]Then they went into Capernaum, and immediately on the Sabbath He entered the synagogue and taught. [22]And they were astonished at His teaching, for He taught them

1:10 [a]NU-Text reads *out of.* **1:14** [a]NU-Text omits *of the kingdom.*

as one having authority, and not as the scribes.

23 Now there was a man in their synagogue with an unclean spirit. And he cried out, 24 saying, "Let *us* alone! What have we to do with You, Jesus of Nazareth? Did You come to destroy us? I know who You are—the Holy One of God!"

25 But Jesus rebuked him, saying, "Be quiet, and come out of him!" 26 And when the unclean spirit had convulsed him and cried out with a loud voice, he came out of him. 27 Then they were all amazed, so that they questioned among themselves, saying, "What is this? What new doctrine *is* this? For with authority[a] He commands even the unclean spirits, and they obey Him." 28 And immediately His fame spread throughout all the region around Galilee.

Peter's Mother-in-Law Healed

29 Now as soon as they had come out of the synagogue, they entered the house of Simon and Andrew, with James and John. 30 But Simon's wife's mother lay sick with a fever, and they told Him about her at once. 31 So He came and took her by the hand and lifted her up, and immediately the fever left her. And she served them.

Many Healed After Sabbath Sunset

32 At evening, when the sun had set, they brought to Him all who were sick and those who were demon-possessed. 33 And the whole city was gathered together at the door. 34 Then He healed many who were sick with various diseases, and cast out many demons; and He did not allow the demons to speak, because they knew Him.

Preaching in Galilee

35 Now in the morning, having risen a long while before daylight, He went out and departed to a solitary place; and there He prayed. 36 And Simon and those *who were* with Him searched for Him. 37 When they found Him, they said to Him, "Everyone is looking for You."

38 But He said to them, "Let us go into the next towns, that I may preach there also, because for this purpose I have come forth."

1:27 [a] NU-Text reads *What is this? A new doctrine with authority.*

39 And He was preaching in their synagogues throughout all Galilee, and casting out demons.

Jesus Cleanses a Leper

40 Now a leper came to Him, imploring Him, kneeling down to Him and saying to Him, "If You are willing, You can make me clean."

41 Then Jesus, moved with compassion, stretched out *His* hand and touched him, and said to him, "I am willing; be cleansed." 42 As soon as He had spoken, immediately the leprosy left him, and he was cleansed. 43 And He strictly warned him and sent him away at once, 44 and said to him, "See that you say nothing to anyone; but go your way, show yourself to the priest, and offer for your cleansing those things which Moses commanded, as a testimony to them."

45 However, he went out and began to proclaim *it* freely, and to spread the matter, so that Jesus could no longer openly enter the city, but was outside in deserted places; and they came to Him from every direction.

Jesus Forgives and Heals a Paralytic

2 And again He entered Capernaum after *some* days, and it was heard that He was in the house. 2 Immediately[a] many gathered together, so that there was no longer room to receive *them,* not even near the door. And He preached the word to them. 3 Then they came to Him, bringing a paralytic who was carried by four *men.* 4 And when they could not come near Him because of the crowd, they uncovered the roof where He was. So when they had broken through, they let down the bed on which the paralytic was lying.

5 When Jesus saw their faith, He said to the paralytic, "Son, your sins are forgiven you."

6 And some of the scribes were sitting there and reasoning in their hearts, 7 "Why does this *Man* speak blasphemies like this? Who can forgive sins but God alone?"

8 But immediately, when Jesus perceived in His spirit that they reasoned thus within themselves, He said to them, "Why do you reason

---

2:2 [a] NU-Text omits *Immediately.*

about these things in your hearts?
9Which is easier, to say to the paralytic, '*Your* sins are forgiven you,' or
to say, 'Arise, take up your bed and
walk'? 10But that you may know that
the Son of Man has power on earth
to forgive sins"—He said to the paralytic, 11"I say to you, arise, take up
your bed, and go to your house."
12Immediately he arose, took up the
bed, and went out in the presence of
them all, so that all were amazed and
glorified God, saying, "We never saw
anything like this!"

Matthew the Tax Collector

13Then He went out again by the
sea; and all the multitude came to
Him, and He taught them. 14As He
passed by, He saw Levi the *son* of Alphaeus sitting at the tax office. And
He said to him, "Follow Me." So he
arose and followed Him.

15Now it happened, as He was
dining in *Levi's* house, that many tax
collectors and sinners also sat together with Jesus and His disciples;
for there were many, and they followed Him. 16And when the scribes
and[a] Pharisees saw Him eating with
the tax collectors and sinners, they
said to His disciples, "How *is it* that
He eats and drinks with tax collectors
and sinners?"

17When Jesus heard *it,* He said to
them, "Those who are well have no
need of a physician, but those who are
sick. I did not come to call *the* righteous, but sinners, to repentance."[a]

Jesus Is Questioned About Fasting

18The disciples of John and of
the Pharisees were fasting. Then they
came and said to Him, "Why do the
disciples of John and of the Pharisees
fast, but Your disciples do not fast?"

19And Jesus said to them, "Can
the friends of the bridegroom fast
while the bridegroom is with them?
As long as they have the bridegroom
with them they cannot fast. 20But the
days will come when the bridegroom
will be taken away from them, and
then they will fast in those days. 21No
one sews a piece of unshrunk cloth
on an old garment; or else the new
piece pulls away from the old, and
the tear is made worse. 22And no one
puts new wine into old wineskins; or

2:16 [a]NU-Text reads *of the.* **2:17** [a]NU-Text omits *to repentance.*

else the new wine bursts the wineskins, the wine is spilled, and the
wineskins are ruined. But new wine
must be put into new wineskins."

Jesus Is Lord of the Sabbath

23Now it happened that He went
through the grainfields on the Sabbath; and as they went His disciples
began to pluck the heads of grain.
24And the Pharisees said to Him,
"Look, why do they do what is not
lawful on the Sabbath?"

25But He said to them, "Have you
never read what David did when
he was in need and hungry, he and
those with him: 26how he went into
the house of God *in the days* of Abiathar the high priest, and ate the
showbread, which is not lawful to eat
except for the priests, and also gave
some to those who were with him?"

27And He said to them, "The Sabbath was made for man, and not man
for the Sabbath. 28Therefore the Son
of Man is also Lord of the Sabbath."

Healing on the Sabbath

3 And He entered the synagogue
again, and a man was there who had
a withered hand. 2So they watched Him
closely, whether He would heal him on
the Sabbath, so that they might accuse
Him. 3And He said to the man who had
the withered hand, "Step forward."
4Then He said to them, "Is it lawful on
the Sabbath to do good or to do evil, to
save life or to kill?" But they kept silent.
5And when He had looked around at
them with anger, being grieved by the
hardness of their hearts, He said to the
man, "Stretch out your hand." And
he stretched *it* out, and his hand was restored as whole as the other.[a] 6Then the
Pharisees went out and immediately
plotted with the Herodians against
Him, how they might destroy Him.

A Great Multitude Follows Jesus

7But Jesus withdrew with His disciples to the sea. And a great multitude
from Galilee followed Him, and from
Judea 8and Jerusalem and Idumea and
beyond the Jordan; and those from
Tyre and Sidon, a great multitude,
when they heard how many things He
was doing, came to Him. 9So He told
His disciples that a small boat should be
kept ready for Him because of the

3:5 [a]NU-Text omits *as whole as the other.*

multitude, lest they should crush
Him. 10For He healed many, so that as
many as had afflictions pressed about
Him to touch Him. 11And the unclean
spirits, whenever they saw Him, fell
down before Him and cried out, saying, "You are the Son of God." 12But
He sternly warned them that they
should not make Him known.

The Twelve Apostles

13And He went up on the mountain and called to *Him* those He
Himself wanted. And they came to
Him. 14Then He appointed twelve,[a]
that they might be with Him and that
He might send them out to preach,
15and to have power to heal sicknesses
and[a] to cast out demons: 16Simon,[a] to
whom He gave the name Peter;
17James the *son* of Zebedee and John the
brother of James, to whom He gave
the name Boanerges, that is, "Sons of
Thunder"; 18Andrew, Philip, Bartholomew, Matthew, Thomas, James the *son*
of Alphaeus, Thaddaeus, Simon the
Canaanite; 19and Judas Iscariot, who
also betrayed Him. And they went into
a house.

A House Divided Cannot Stand

20Then the multitude came together again, so that they could not
so much as eat bread. 21But when His
own people heard *about this,* they went
out to lay hold of Him, for they said,
"He is out of His mind."

22And the scribes who came
down from Jerusalem said, "He has
Beelzebub," and, "By the ruler of the
demons He casts out demons."

23So He called them to *Himself* and
said to them in parables: "How can
Satan cast out Satan? 24If a kingdom
is divided against itself, that kingdom
cannot stand. 25And if a house is divided against itself, that house cannot stand. 26And if Satan has risen up
against himself, and is divided, he
cannot stand, but has an end. 27No
one can enter a strong man's house
and plunder his goods, unless he first
binds the strong man. And then he
will plunder his house.

The Unpardonable Sin

28"Assuredly, I say to you, all sins
will be forgiven the sons of men,

3:14 [a]NU-Text adds *whom He also named apostles.* **3:15** [a]NU-Text omits *to heal sicknesses and.* **3:16** [a]NU-Text reads *and He appointed the twelve: Simon. . . .*

and whatever blasphemies they may
utter; 29but he who blasphemes
against the Holy Spirit never has
forgiveness, but is subject to eternal condemnation"— 30because they
said, "He has an unclean spirit."

Jesus' Mother and Brothers Send for Him

31Then His brothers and His
mother came, and standing outside
they sent to Him, calling Him. 32And
a multitude was sitting around Him;
and they said to Him, "Look, Your
mother and Your brothers[a] are outside seeking You."

33But He answered them, saying,
"Who is My mother, or My brothers?" 34And He looked around in a
circle at those who sat about Him,
and said, "Here are My mother and
My brothers! 35For whoever does the
will of God is My brother and My sister and mother."

The Parable of the Sower

4 And again He began to teach by
the sea. And a great multitude
was gathered to Him, so that
He got into a boat and sat *in it* on the
sea; and the whole multitude was
on the land facing the sea. 2Then
He taught them many things by parables, and said to them in His teaching:

3"Listen! Behold, a sower went out
to sow. 4And it happened, as he sowed,
that some *seed* fell by the wayside; and
the birds of the air[a] came and devoured
it. 5Some fell on stony ground, where
it did not have much earth; and immediately it sprang up because it had
no depth of earth. 6But when the sun
was up it was scorched, and because it
had no root it withered away. 7And
some *seed* fell among thorns; and the
thorns grew up and choked it, and it
yielded no crop. 8But other *seed* fell on
good ground and yielded a crop that
sprang up, increased and produced:
some thirtyfold, some sixty, and some
a hundred."

9And He said to them,[a] "He who
has ears to hear, let him hear!"

The Purpose of Parables

10But when He was alone, those
around Him with the twelve asked
Him about the parable. 11And He said

3:32 [a]NU-Text and M-Text add *and Your sisters.* **4:4** [a]NU-Text and M-Text omit *of the air.* **4:9** [a]NU-Text and M-Text omit *to them.*

to them, "To you it has been given to
know the mystery of the kingdom of
God; but to those who are outside,
all things come in parables, 12so that

'Seeing they may see and not
perceive,
And hearing they may hear
and not understand;
Lest they should turn,
And their sins be forgiven
them.'"[a]

The Parable of the Sower Explained

13And He said to them, "Do you
not understand this parable? How
then will you understand all the
parables? 14The sower sows the word.
15And these are the ones by the wayside where the word is sown. When
they hear, Satan comes immediately
and takes away the word that was
sown in their hearts. 16These likewise
are the ones sown on stony ground
who, when they hear the word,
immediately receive it with gladness; 17and they have no root in
themselves, and so endure only for a
time. Afterward, when tribulation or
persecution arises for the word's sake,
immediately they stumble. 18Now
these are the ones sown among
thorns; *they are* the ones who hear the
word, 19and the cares of this world,
the deceitfulness of riches, and the
desires for other things entering in
choke the word, and it becomes
unfruitful. 20But these are the ones
sown on good ground, those who
hear the word, accept *it,* and bear
fruit: some thirtyfold, some sixty,
and some a hundred."

Light Under a Basket

21Also He said to them, "Is a lamp
brought to be put under a basket or
under a bed? Is it not to be set on a
lampstand? 22For there is nothing
hidden which will not be revealed,
nor has anything been kept secret
but that it should come to light.
23If anyone has ears to hear, let
him hear."

24Then He said to them, "Take
heed what you hear. With the same
measure you use, it will be measured
to you; and to you who hear, more
will be given. 25For whoever has, to
him more will be given; but whoever

4:12 [a]Isaiah 6:9, 10

does not have, even what he has will be taken away from him."

The Parable of the Growing Seed

[26]And He said, "The kingdom of God is as if a man should scatter seed on the ground, [27]and should sleep by night and rise by day, and the seed should sprout and grow, he himself does not know how. [28]For the earth yields crops by itself: first the blade, then the head, after that the full grain in the head. [29]But when the grain ripens, immediately he puts in the sickle, because the harvest has come."

The Parable of the Mustard Seed

[30]Then He said, "To what shall we liken the kingdom of God? Or with what parable shall we picture it? [31]*It is* like a mustard seed which, when it is sown on the ground, is smaller than all the seeds on earth; [32]but when it is sown, it grows up and becomes greater than all herbs, and shoots out large branches, so that the birds of the air may nest under its shade."

Jesus' Use of Parables

[33]And with many such parables He spoke the word to them as they were able to hear *it.* [34]But without a parable He did not speak to them. And when they were alone, He explained all things to His disciples.

Wind and Wave Obey Jesus

[35]On the same day, when evening had come, He said to them, "Let us cross over to the other side." [36]Now when they had left the multitude, they took Him along in the boat as He was. And other little boats were also with Him. [37]And a great windstorm arose, and the waves beat into the boat, so that it was already filling. [38]But He was in the stern, asleep on a pillow. And they awoke Him and said to Him, "Teacher, do You not care that we are perishing?"

[39]Then He arose and rebuked the wind, and said to the sea, "Peace, be still!" And the wind ceased and there was a great calm. [40]But He said to them, "Why are you so fearful? How *is it* that you have no faith?"[a] [41]And they feared exceedingly, and

4:40 [a]NU-Text reads *Have you still no faith?*

said to one another, "Who can this be, that even the wind and the sea obey Him!"

A Demon-Possessed Man Healed

5 Then they came to the other side of the sea, to the country of the Gadarenes.[a] [2]And when He had come out of the boat, immediately there met Him out of the tombs a man with an unclean spirit, [3]who had *his* dwelling among the tombs; and no one could bind him,[a] not even with chains, [4]because he had often been bound with shackles and chains. And the chains had been pulled apart by him, and the shackles broken in pieces; neither could anyone tame him. [5]And always, night and day, he was in the mountains and in the tombs, crying out and cutting himself with stones.

[6]When he saw Jesus from afar, he ran and worshiped Him. [7]And he cried out with a loud voice and said, "What have I to do with You, Jesus, Son of the Most High God? I implore You by God that You do not torment me."

[8]For He said to him, "Come out of the man, unclean spirit!" [9]Then He asked him, "What *is* your name?"

And he answered, saying, "My name *is* Legion; for we are many." [10]Also he begged Him earnestly that He would not send them out of the country.

[11]Now a large herd of swine was feeding there near the mountains. [12]So all the demons begged Him, saying, "Send us to the swine, that we may enter them." [13]And at once Jesus[a] gave them permission. Then the unclean spirits went out and entered the swine (there were about two thousand); and the herd ran violently down the steep place into the sea, and drowned in the sea.

[14]So those who fed the swine fled, and they told *it* in the city and in the country. And they went out to see what it was that had happened. [15]Then they came to Jesus, and saw the one *who had been* demon-possessed and had the legion, sitting and clothed and in his right mind. And they were afraid. [16]And those who saw it told them how it happened to him *who had been* demon-possessed, and about the swine. [17]Then they began to plead with Him to depart from their region.

5:1 [a]NU-Text reads *Gerasenes.* **5:3** [a]NU-Text adds *anymore.* **5:13** [a]NU-Text reads *And He gave.*

18 And when He got into the boat, he who had been demon-possessed begged Him that he might be with Him. 19 However, Jesus did not permit him, but said to him, "Go home to your friends, and tell them what great things the Lord has done for you, and how He has had compassion on you." 20 And he departed and began to proclaim in Decapolis all that Jesus had done for him; and all marveled.

A Girl Restored to Life and a Woman Healed

21 Now when Jesus had crossed over again by boat to the other side, a great multitude gathered to Him; and He was by the sea. 22 And behold, one of the rulers of the synagogue came, Jairus by name. And when he saw Him, he fell at His feet 23 and begged Him earnestly, saying, "My little daughter lies at the point of death. Come and lay Your hands on her, that she may be healed, and she will live." 24 So *Jesus* went with him, and a great multitude followed Him and thronged Him.

25 Now a certain woman had a flow of blood for twelve years, 26 and had suffered many things from many physicians. She had spent all that she had and was no better, but rather grew worse. 27 When she heard about Jesus, she came behind *Him* in the crowd and touched His garment. 28 For she said, "If only I may touch His clothes, I shall be made well."

29 Immediately the fountain of her blood was dried up, and she felt in *her* body that she was healed of the affliction. 30 And Jesus, immediately knowing in Himself that power had gone out of Him, turned around in the crowd and said, "Who touched My clothes?"

31 But His disciples said to Him, "You see the multitude thronging You, and You say, 'Who touched Me?'"

32 And He looked around to see her who had done this thing. 33 But the woman, fearing and trembling, knowing what had happened to her, came and fell down before Him and told Him the whole truth. 34 And He said to her, "Daughter, your faith has made you well. Go in peace, and be healed of your affliction."

35 While He was still speaking, *some* came from the ruler of the synagogue's *house* who said, "Your daughter is dead. Why trouble the Teacher any further?"

36 As soon as Jesus heard the word
that was spoken, He said to the ruler of
the synagogue, "Do not be afraid; only
believe." 37 And He permitted no one to
follow Him except Peter, James, and
John the brother of James. 38 Then
He came to the house of the ruler of
the synagogue, and saw a tumult and
those who wept and wailed loudly.
39 When He came in, He said to them,
"Why make this commotion and weep?
The child is not dead, but sleeping."

40 And they ridiculed Him. But
when He had put them all outside,
He took the father and the mother of
the child, and those *who were* with Him,
and entered where the child was
lying. 41 Then He took the child by the
hand, and said to her, "Talitha, cumi,"
which is translated, "Little girl, I say to
you, arise." 42 Immediately the girl
arose and walked, for she was twelve
years *of age.* And they were overcome with great amazement. 43 But
He commanded them strictly that no
one should know it, and said that
something should be given her to eat.

Jesus Rejected at Nazareth

6 Then He went out from there
and came to His own country,
and His disciples followed Him. 2 And
when the Sabbath had come, He
began to teach in the synagogue. And
many hearing *Him* were astonished,
saying, "Where *did* this Man *get* these
things? And what wisdom *is* this
which is given to Him, that such
mighty works are performed by His
hands! 3 Is this not the carpenter, the
Son of Mary, and brother of James,
Joses, Judas, and Simon? And are not
His sisters here with us?" So they
were offended at Him.

4 But Jesus said to them, "A
prophet is not without honor except
in his own country, among his own
relatives, and in his own house."
5 Now He could do no mighty work
there, except that He laid His hands
on a few sick people and healed *them.*
6 And He marveled because of their
unbelief. Then He went about the villages in a circuit, teaching.

Sending Out the Twelve

7 And He called the twelve to *Himself,* and began to send them out two
by two, and gave them power over
unclean spirits. 8 He commanded
them to take nothing for the journey except a staff—no bag, no bread,

no copper in *their* money belts— 9but
to wear sandals, and not to put on
two tunics.

10Also He said to them, "In whatever place you enter a house, stay
there till you depart from that place.
11And whoever[a] will not receive you
nor hear you, when you depart from
there, shake off the dust under your
feet as a testimony against them.[b]
Assuredly, I say to you, it will be
more tolerable for Sodom and
Gomorrah in the day of judgment
than for that city!"

12So they went out and preached
that *people* should repent. 13And they
cast out many demons, and anointed
with oil many who were sick, and
healed *them.*

John the Baptist Beheaded

14Now King Herod heard *of Him,*
for His name had become well
known. And he said, "John the Baptist is risen from the dead, and therefore these powers are at work in him."

15Others said, "It is Elijah."

And others said, "It is the Prophet,
or[a] like one of the prophets."

16But when Herod heard, he said,
"This is John, whom I beheaded; he
has been raised from the dead!" 17For
Herod himself had sent and laid hold
of John, and bound him in prison for
the sake of Herodias, his brother
Philip's wife; for he had married her.
18Because John had said to Herod, "It
is not lawful for you to have your
brother's wife."

19Therefore Herodias held it
against him and wanted to kill him,
but she could not; 20for Herod feared
John, knowing that he *was* a just and
holy man, and he protected him.
And when he heard him, he did
many things, and heard him gladly.

21Then an opportune day came
when Herod on his birthday gave a
feast for his nobles, the high officers,
and the chief *men* of Galilee. 22And
when Herodias' daughter herself
came in and danced, and pleased
Herod and those who sat with him,
the king said to the girl, "Ask me
whatever you want, and I will give *it*
to you." 23He also swore to her,
"Whatever you ask me, I will give
you, up to half my kingdom."

24So she went out and said to her
mother, "What shall I ask?"

6:11 [a]NU-Text reads *whatever place.* [b]NU-Text omits the rest of this verse. **6:15** [a]NU-Text and M-Text omit *or.*

And she said, "The head of John the Baptist!"

25 Immediately she came in with haste to the king and asked, saying, "I want you to give me at once the head of John the Baptist on a platter."

26 And the king was exceedingly sorry; *yet,* because of the oaths and because of those who sat with him, he did not want to refuse her. 27 Immediately the king sent an executioner and commanded his head to be brought. And he went and beheaded him in prison, 28 brought his head on a platter, and gave it to the girl; and the girl gave it to her mother. 29 When his disciples heard *of it,* they came and took away his corpse and laid it in a tomb.

Feeding the Five Thousand

30 Then the apostles gathered to Jesus and told Him all things, both what they had done and what they had taught. 31 And He said to them, "Come aside by yourselves to a deserted place and rest a while." For there were many coming and going, and they did not even have time to eat. 32 So they departed to a deserted place in the boat by themselves.

33 But the multitudes[a] saw them departing, and many knew Him and ran there on foot from all the cities. They arrived before them and came together to Him. 34 And Jesus, when He came out, saw a great multitude and was moved with compassion for them, because they were like sheep not having a shepherd. So He began to teach them many things. 35 When the day was now far spent, His disciples came to Him and said, "This is a deserted place, and already the hour *is* late. 36 Send them away, that they may go into the surrounding country and villages and buy themselves bread;[a] for they have nothing to eat."

37 But He answered and said to them, "You give them something to eat."

And they said to Him, "Shall we go and buy two hundred denarii worth of bread and give them *something* to eat?"

38 But He said to them, "How many loaves do you have? Go and see."

And when they found out they said, "Five, and two fish."

39 Then He commanded them to make them all sit down in groups on

---

6:33 [a] NU-Text and M-Text read *they.* **6:36** [a] NU-Text reads *something to eat* and omits the rest of this verse.

the green grass. 40So they sat down in
ranks, in hundreds and in fifties. 41And
when He had taken the five loaves and
the two fish, He looked up to heaven,
blessed and broke the loaves, and gave
them to His disciples to set before them;
and the two fish He divided among
them all. 42So they all ate and were
filled. 43And they took up twelve baskets full of fragments and of the fish.
44Now those who had eaten the loaves
were about[a] five thousand men.

Jesus Walks on the Sea

45Immediately He made His disciples get into the boat and go before
Him to the other side, to Bethsaida,
while He sent the multitude away.
46And when He had sent them away,
He departed to the mountain to
pray. 47Now when evening came, the
boat was in the middle of the sea;
and He *was* alone on the land. 48Then
He saw them straining at rowing,
for the wind was against them. Now
about the fourth watch of the night
He came to them, walking on the
sea, and would have passed them by.
49And when they saw Him walking
on the sea, they supposed it was a
ghost, and cried out; 50for they all
saw Him and were troubled. But
immediately He talked with them
and said to them, "Be of good cheer!
It is I; do not be afraid." 51Then He
went up into the boat to them, and
the wind ceased. And they were
greatly amazed in themselves beyond
measure, and marveled. 52For they
had not understood about the loaves,
because their heart was hardened.

Many Touch Him and Are Made Well

53When they had crossed over,
they came to the land of Gennesaret
and anchored there. 54And when they
came out of the boat, immediately
the people recognized Him, 55ran
through that whole surrounding region, and began to carry about on
beds those who were sick to wherever
they heard He was. 56Wherever He
entered, into villages, cities, or the
country, they laid the sick in the
marketplaces, and begged Him that
they might just touch the hem of His
garment. And as many as touched
Him were made well.

6:44 [a]NU-Text and M-Text omit *about.*

Defilement Comes from Within

7 Then the Pharisees and some of the scribes came together to Him, having come from Jerusalem. 2 Now when[a] they saw some of His disciples eat bread with defiled, that is, with unwashed hands, they found fault. 3 For the Pharisees and all the Jews do not eat unless they wash *their* hands in a special way, holding the tradition of the elders. 4 *When they come* from the marketplace, they do not eat unless they wash. And there are many other things which they have received and hold, *like* the washing of cups, pitchers, copper vessels, and couches.

5 Then the Pharisees and scribes asked Him, "Why do Your disciples not walk according to the tradition of the elders, but eat bread with unwashed hands?"

6 He answered and said to them, "Well did Isaiah prophesy of you hypocrites, as it is written:

'This people honors Me with
their lips,
But their heart is far from Me.
7 *And in vain they worship Me,*
Teaching as doctrines the
commandments of men.'[a]

8 For laying aside the commandment of God, you hold the tradition of men[a]—the washing of pitchers and cups, and many other such things you do."

9 He said to them, "*All too* well you reject the commandment of God, that you may keep your tradition. 10 For Moses said, *'Honor your father and your mother'*;[a] and, *'He who curses father or mother, let him be put to death.'*[b] 11 But you say, 'If a man says to his father or mother, "Whatever profit you might have received from me *is* Corban"—' (that is, a gift *to God*), 12 then you no longer let him do anything for his father or his mother, 13 making the word of God of no effect through your tradition which you have handed down. And many such things you do."

14 When He had called all the multitude to *Himself*, He said to them, "Hear Me, everyone, and understand: 15 There is nothing that enters a man

---

7:2 [a]NU-Text omits *when* and *they found fault*. **7:7** [a]Isaiah 29:13 **7:8** [a]NU-Text omits the rest of this verse.
7:10 [a]Exodus 20:12; Deuteronomy 5:16 [b]Exodus 21:17

from outside which can defile him;
but the things which come out of
him, those are the things that defile
a man. 16If anyone has ears to hear,
let him hear!"[a]

17When He had entered a house
away from the crowd, His disciples
asked Him concerning the parable.
18So He said to them, "Are you thus
without understanding also? Do you
not perceive that whatever enters a
man from outside cannot defile him,
19because it does not enter his heart
but his stomach, and is eliminated,
thus purifying all foods?"[a] 20And He
said, "What comes out of a man, that
defiles a man. 21For from within, out
of the heart of men, proceed evil
thoughts, adulteries, fornications,
murders, 22thefts, covetousness,
wickedness, deceit, lewdness, an evil
eye, blasphemy, pride, foolishness.
23All these evil things come from
within and defile a man."

A Gentile Shows Her Faith

24From there He arose and went
to the region of Tyre and Sidon.[a] And
He entered a house and wanted no
one to know *it,* but He could not be
hidden. 25For a woman whose young
daughter had an unclean spirit heard
about Him, and she came and fell at
His feet. 26The woman was a Greek, a
Syro-Phoenician by birth, and she
kept asking Him to cast the demon
out of her daughter. 27But Jesus
said to her, "Let the children be filled
first, for it is not good to take the
children's bread and throw *it* to the
little dogs."

28And she answered and said to
Him, "Yes, Lord, yet even the little
dogs under the table eat from the
children's crumbs."

29Then He said to her, "For this
saying go your way; the demon has
gone out of your daughter."

30And when she had come to
her house, she found the demon
gone out, and her daughter lying on
the bed.

Jesus Heals a Deaf-Mute

31Again, departing from the region
of Tyre and Sidon, He came through

7:16 [a]NU-Text omits this verse. **7:19** [a]NU-Text ends quotation with *eliminated,* setting off the final clause as Mark's comment that Jesus has declared all foods clean. **7:24** [a]NU-Text omits *and Sidon.*

the midst of the region of Decapolis
to the Sea of Galilee. 32Then they
brought to Him one who was deaf and
had an impediment in his speech, and
they begged Him to put His hand on
him. 33And He took him aside from
the multitude, and put His fingers in
his ears, and He spat and touched his
tongue. 34Then, looking up to heaven,
He sighed, and said to him, "Eph-
phatha," that is, "Be opened."

35Immediately his ears were
opened, and the impediment of his
tongue was loosed, and he spoke
plainly. 36Then He commanded
them that they should tell no one;
but the more He commanded them,
the more widely they proclaimed *it.*
37And they were astonished beyond
measure, saying, "He has done all
things well. He makes both the deaf
to hear and the mute to speak."

Feeding the Four Thousand

8 In those days, the multitude
being very great and having nothing to eat, Jesus called His disciples *to
Him* and said to them, 2"I have compassion on the multitude, because
they have now continued with Me
three days and have nothing to eat.
3And if I send them away hungry to
their own houses, they will faint on
the way; for some of them have come
from afar."

4Then His disciples answered
Him, "How can one satisfy these people with bread here in the wilderness?"

5He asked them, "How many
loaves do you have?"

And they said, "Seven."

6So He commanded the multitude to sit down on the ground. And
He took the seven loaves and gave
thanks, broke *them* and gave *them* to
His disciples to set before *them;* and
they set *them* before the multitude.
7They also had a few small fish; and
having blessed them, He said to set
them also before *them.* 8So they ate
and were filled, and they took up
seven large baskets of leftover fragments. 9Now those who had eaten
were about four thousand. And He
sent them away, 10immediately got
into the boat with His disciples, and
came to the region of Dalmanutha.

The Pharisees Seek a Sign

11Then the Pharisees came out
and began to dispute with Him, seek-

ing from Him a sign from heaven, testing Him. [12]But He sighed deeply in His spirit, and said, "Why does this generation seek a sign? Assuredly, I say to you, no sign shall be given to this generation."

Beware of the Leaven of the Pharisees and Herod

[13]And He left them, and getting into the boat again, departed to the other side. [14]Now the disciples[a] had forgotten to take bread, and they did not have more than one loaf with them in the boat. [15]Then He charged them, saying, "Take heed, beware of the leaven of the Pharisees and the leaven of Herod."

[16]And they reasoned among themselves, saying, "*It is* because we have no bread."

[17]But Jesus, being aware of *it,* said to them, "Why do you reason because you have no bread? Do you not yet perceive nor understand? Is your heart still[a] hardened? [18]Having eyes, do you not see? And having ears, do you not hear? And do you not remember? [19]When I broke the five loaves for the five thousand, how many baskets full of fragments did you take up?"

They said to Him, "Twelve."

[20]"Also, when I broke the seven for the four thousand, how many large baskets full of fragments did you take up?"

And they said, "Seven."

[21]So He said to them, "How *is it* you do not understand?"

A Blind Man Healed at Bethsaida

[22]Then He came to Bethsaida; and they brought a blind man to Him, and begged Him to touch him. [23]So He took the blind man by the hand and led him out of the town. And when He had spit on his eyes and put His hands on him, He asked him if he saw anything.

[24]And he looked up and said, "I see men like trees, walking."

[25]Then He put *His* hands on his eyes again and made him look up. And he was restored and saw everyone clearly. [26]Then He sent him away to his house, saying, "Neither go into the town, nor tell anyone in the town."[a]

8:14 [a]NU-Text and M-Text read *they.* **8:17** [a]NU-Text omits *still.* **8:26** [a]NU-Text reads *"Do not even go into the town."*

Peter Confesses Jesus as the Christ

27 Now Jesus and His disciples went out to the towns of Caesarea Philippi; and on the road He asked His disciples, saying to them, "Who do men say that I am?"

28 So they answered, "John the Baptist; but some *say,* Elijah; and others, one of the prophets."

29 He said to them, "But who do you say that I am?"

Peter answered and said to Him, "You are the Christ."

30 Then He strictly warned them that they should tell no one about Him.

Jesus Predicts His Death and Resurrection

31 And He began to teach them that the Son of Man must suffer many things, and be rejected by the elders and chief priests and scribes, and be killed, and after three days rise again. 32 He spoke this word openly. Then Peter took Him aside and began to rebuke Him. 33 But when He had turned around and looked at His disciples, He rebuked Peter, saying, "Get behind Me, Satan! For you are not mindful of the things of God, but the things of men."

Take Up the Cross and Follow Him

34 When He had called the people to *Himself,* with His disciples also, He said to them, "Whoever desires to come after Me, let him deny himself, and take up his cross, and follow Me. 35 For whoever desires to save his life will lose it, but whoever loses his life for My sake and the gospel's will save it. 36 For what will it profit a man if he gains the whole world, and loses his own soul? 37 Or what will a man give in exchange for his soul? 38 For whoever is ashamed of Me and My words in this adulterous and sinful generation, of him the Son of Man also will be ashamed when He comes in the glory of His Father with the holy angels."

Jesus Transfigured on the Mount

9 And He said to them, "Assuredly, I say to you that there are some standing here who will not taste death till they see the kingdom of God present with power."

2 Now after six days Jesus took Pe-

ter, James, and John, and led them up on a high mountain apart by themselves; and He was transfigured before them. 3His clothes became shining, exceedingly white, like snow, such as no launderer on earth can whiten them. 4And Elijah appeared to them with Moses, and they were talking with Jesus. 5Then Peter answered and said to Jesus, "Rabbi, it is good for us to be here; and let us make three tabernacles: one for You, one for Moses, and one for Elijah"— 6because he did not know what to say, for they were greatly afraid.

7And a cloud came and overshadowed them; and a voice came out of the cloud, saying, "This is My beloved Son. Hear Him!" 8Suddenly, when they had looked around, they saw no one anymore, but only Jesus with themselves.

9Now as they came down from the mountain, He commanded them that they should tell no one the things they had seen, till the Son of Man had risen from the dead. 10So they kept this word to themselves, questioning what the rising from the dead meant.

11And they asked Him, saying, "Why do the scribes say that Elijah must come first?"

12Then He answered and told them, "Indeed, Elijah is coming first and restores all things. And how is it written concerning the Son of Man, that He must suffer many things and be treated with contempt? 13But I say to you that Elijah has also come, and they did to him whatever they wished, as it is written of him."

A Boy Is Healed

14And when He came to the disciples, He saw a great multitude around them, and scribes disputing with them. 15Immediately, when they saw Him, all the people were greatly amazed, and running to *Him,* greeted Him. 16And He asked the scribes, "What are you discussing with them?"

17Then one of the crowd answered and said, "Teacher, I brought You my son, who has a mute spirit. 18And wherever it seizes him, it throws him down; he foams at the mouth, gnashes his teeth, and becomes rigid. So I spoke to Your disciples, that they should cast it out, but they could not."

19He answered him and said, "O faithless generation, how long shall I be with you? How long shall I bear with you? Bring him to Me." 20 Then they brought him to Him. And when he saw Him, immediately the spirit convulsed him, and he fell on the ground and wallowed, foaming at the mouth.

21 So He asked his father, "How long has this been happening to him?"

And he said, "From childhood. 22 And often he has thrown him both into the fire and into the water to destroy him. But if You can do anything, have compassion on us and help us."

23 Jesus said to him, "If you can believe,[a] all things *are* possible to him who believes."

24 Immediately the father of the child cried out and said with tears, "Lord, I believe; help my unbelief!"

25 When Jesus saw that the people came running together, He rebuked the unclean spirit, saying to it, "Deaf and dumb spirit, I command you, come out of him and enter him no more!" 26 Then *the spirit* cried out, convulsed him greatly, and came out of him. And he became as one dead, so that many said, "He is dead." 27 But Jesus took him by the hand and lifted him up, and he arose.

28 And when He had come into the house, His disciples asked Him privately, "Why could we not cast it out?"

29 So He said to them, "This kind can come out by nothing but prayer and fasting."[a]

Jesus Again Predicts His Death and Resurrection

30 Then they departed from there and passed through Galilee, and He did not want anyone to know *it.* 31 For He taught His disciples and said to them, "The Son of Man is being betrayed into the hands of men, and they will kill Him. And after He is killed, He will rise the third day." 32 But they did not understand this saying, and were afraid to ask Him.

Who Is the Greatest?

33 Then He came to Capernaum. And when He was in the house He asked them, "What was it you disputed among yourselves on the road?" 34 But they kept silent, for on the road they had disputed among

9:23 [a]NU-Text reads "*'If You can!' All things. . . .*" **9:29** [a]NU-Text omits *and fasting.*

themselves who *would be the* greatest.
35 And He sat down, called the twelve,
and said to them, "If anyone desires
to be first, he shall be last of all and
servant of all." 36 Then He took a little child and set him in the midst of
them. And when He had taken him
in His arms, He said to them, 37 "Whoever receives one of these little children in My name receives Me; and
whoever receives Me, receives not Me
but Him who sent Me."

Jesus Forbids Sectarianism

38 Now John answered Him, saying, "Teacher, we saw someone who does not follow us casting out demons in Your name, and we forbade him because he does not follow us."

39 But Jesus said, "Do not forbid
him, for no one who works a miracle
in My name can soon afterward
speak evil of Me. 40 For he who is not
against us is on our[a] side. 41 For whoever gives you a cup of water to drink
in My name, because you belong to
Christ, assuredly, I say to you, he will
by no means lose his reward.

Jesus Warns of Offenses

42 "But whoever causes one of these
little ones who believe in Me to stumble, it would be better for him if a millstone were hung around his neck, and
he were thrown into the sea. 43 If your
hand causes you to sin, cut it off. It is
better for you to enter into life
maimed, rather than having two
hands, to go to hell, into the fire that
shall never be quenched— 44 where

'Their worm does not die
And the fire is not quenched.'[a]

45 And if your foot causes you to sin, cut it off. It is better for you to enter life lame, rather than having two feet, to be cast into hell, into the fire that shall never be quenched—
46 where

'Their worm does not die
And the fire is not quenched.'[a]

47 And if your eye causes you to sin, pluck it out. It is better for you to enter the kingdom of God with one eye, rather than having two eyes, to
be cast into hell fire— 48 where

9:40 [a] M-Text reads *against you is on your side.* **9:44** [a] NU-Text omits this verse. **9:46** [a] NU-Text omits the last clause of verse 45 and all of verse 46.

‘Their worm does not die
And the fire is not quenched.’[a]

Tasteless Salt Is Worthless

49“For everyone will be seasoned
with fire,[a] and every sacrifice will be
seasoned with salt. 50Salt *is* good, but
if the salt loses its flavor, how will you
season it? Have salt in yourselves, and
have peace with one another.”

Marriage and Divorce

10 Then He arose from there and
came to the region of Judea by
the other side of the Jordan. And
multitudes gathered to Him again,
and as He was accustomed, He taught
them again.

2The Pharisees came and asked
Him, “Is it lawful for a man to divorce *his* wife?” testing Him.

3And He answered and said
to them, “What did Moses command you?”

4They said, “Moses permitted *a
man* to write a certificate of divorce,
and to dismiss *her.*”

5And Jesus answered and said to
them, “Because of the hardness of
your heart he wrote you this precept.
6But from the beginning of the creation, God *‘made them male and
female.’*[a] 7*‘For this reason a man shall
leave his father and mother and be
joined to his wife,* 8*and the two shall
become one flesh’*;[a] so then they are
no longer two, but one flesh. 9There-
fore what God has joined together,
let not man separate.”

10In the house His disciples also
asked Him again about the same *matter.* 11So He said to them, “Whoever
divorces his wife and marries another
commits adultery against her. 12And
if a woman divorces her husband
and marries another, she commits
adultery.”

Jesus Blesses Little Children

13Then they brought little children to Him, that He might touch
them; but the disciples rebuked those
who brought *them.* 14But when Jesus
saw *it,* He was greatly displeased and
said to them, “Let the little children
come to Me, and do not forbid them;
for of such is the kingdom of God.
15Assuredly, I say to you, whoever
does not receive the kingdom of God

9:48 [a]Isaiah 66:24 **9:49** [a]NU-Text omits the rest of this verse. **10:6** [a]Genesis 1:27; 5:2 **10:8** [a]Genesis 2:24

as a little child will by no means enter it." 16 And He took them up in His arms, laid *His* hands on them, and blessed them.

Jesus Counsels the Rich Young Ruler

17 Now as He was going out on the road, one came running, knelt before Him, and asked Him, "Good Teacher, what shall I do that I may inherit eternal life?"

18 So Jesus said to him, "Why do you call Me good? No one *is* good but One, *that is,* God. 19 You know the commandments: *'Do not commit adultery,' 'Do not murder,' 'Do not steal,' 'Do not bear false witness,' 'Do not defraud,' 'Honor your father and your mother.'* "[a]

20 And he answered and said to Him, "Teacher, all these things I have kept from my youth."

21 Then Jesus, looking at him, loved him, and said to him, "One thing you lack: Go your way, sell whatever you have and give to the poor, and you will have treasure in heaven; and come, take up the cross, and follow Me."

22 But he was sad at this word, and went away sorrowful, for he had great possessions.

With God All Things Are Possible

23 Then Jesus looked around and said to His disciples, "How hard it is for those who have riches to enter the kingdom of God!" 24 And the disciples were astonished at His words. But Jesus answered again and said to them, "Children, how hard it is for those who trust in riches[a] to enter the kingdom of God! 25 It is easier for a camel to go through the eye of a needle than for a rich man to enter the kingdom of God."

26 And they were greatly astonished, saying among themselves, "Who then can be saved?"

27 But Jesus looked at them and said, "With men *it is* impossible, but not with God; for with God all things are possible."

28 Then Peter began to say to Him, "See, we have left all and followed You."

29 So Jesus answered and said, "Assuredly, I say to you, there is no one

---

10:19 [a] Exodus 20:12–16; Deuteronomy 5:16–20 **10:24** [a] NU-Text omits *for those who trust in riches.*

who has left house or brothers or sisters or father or mother or wife[a] or
children or lands, for My sake and
the gospel's, 30 who shall not receive a
hundredfold now in this time—
houses and brothers and sisters and
mothers and children and lands,
with persecutions—and in the age to
come, eternal life. 31 But many *who are*
first will be last, and the last first."

Jesus a Third Time Predicts His Death and Resurrection

32 Now they were on the road,
going up to Jerusalem, and Jesus was
going before them; and they were
amazed. And as they followed they
were afraid. Then He took the twelve
aside again and began to tell them the
things that would happen to Him:
33 "Behold, we are going up to Jerusalem, and the Son of Man will be betrayed to the chief priests and to the
scribes; and they will condemn Him
to death and deliver Him to the Gentiles; 34 and they will mock Him, and
scourge Him, and spit on Him, and
kill Him. And the third day He will
rise again."

Greatness Is Serving

35 Then James and John, the sons
of Zebedee, came to Him, saying,
"Teacher, we want You to do for us
whatever we ask."

36 And He said to them, "What do
you want Me to do for you?"

37 They said to Him, "Grant us
that we may sit, one on Your right
hand and the other on Your left, in
Your glory."

38 But Jesus said to them, "You do
not know what you ask. Are you able
to drink the cup that I drink, and be
baptized with the baptism that I am
baptized with?"

39 They said to Him, "We are able."

So Jesus said to them, "You will
indeed drink the cup that I drink,
and with the baptism I am baptized
with you will be baptized; 40 but to sit
on My right hand and on My left is
not Mine to give, but *it is for those* for
whom it is prepared."

41 And when the ten heard *it,* they
began to be greatly displeased with
James and John. 42 But Jesus called
them to *Himself* and said to them,
"You know that those who are con-

10:29 [a] NU-Text omits *or wife.*

sidered rulers over the Gentiles lord it over them, and their great ones exercise authority over them. 43Yet it shall not be so among you; but whoever desires to become great among you shall be your servant. 44And whoever of you desires to be first shall be slave of all. 45For even the Son of Man did not come to be served, but to serve, and to give His life a ransom for many."

Jesus Heals Blind Bartimaeus

46Now they came to Jericho. As He went out of Jericho with His disciples and a great multitude, blind Bartimaeus, the son of Timaeus, sat by the road begging. 47And when he heard that it was Jesus of Nazareth, he began to cry out and say, "Jesus, Son of David, have mercy on me!"

48Then many warned him to be quiet; but he cried out all the more, "Son of David, have mercy on me!"

49So Jesus stood still and commanded him to be called.

Then they called the blind man, saying to him, "Be of good cheer. Rise, He is calling you."

50And throwing aside his garment, he rose and came to Jesus.

51So Jesus answered and said to him, "What do you want Me to do for you?"

The blind man said to Him, "Rabboni, that I may receive my sight."

52Then Jesus said to him, "Go your way; your faith has made you well." And immediately he received his sight and followed Jesus on the road.

The Triumphal Entry

11 Now when they drew near Jerusalem, to Bethphage[a] and Bethany, at the Mount of Olives, He sent two of His disciples; 2and He said to them, "Go into the village opposite you; and as soon as you have entered it you will find a colt tied, on which no one has sat. Loose it and bring *it.* 3And if anyone says to you, 'Why are you doing this?' say, 'The Lord has need of it,' and immediately he will send it here."

4So they went their way, and found the[a] colt tied by the door out-

---

11:1 [a]M-Text reads *Bethsphage.* **11:4** [a]NU-Text and M-Text read *a.*

side on the street, and they loosed it. 5But some of those who stood there said to them, "What are you doing, loosing the colt?"

6And they spoke to them just as Jesus had commanded. So they let them go. 7Then they brought the colt to Jesus and threw their clothes on it, and He sat on it. 8And many spread their clothes on the road, and others cut down leafy branches from the trees and spread *them* on the road. 9Then those who went before and those who followed cried out, saying:

"Hosanna!
'Blessed is He who comes in the
name of the LORD!'[a]
10 Blessed *is* the kingdom of our
father David
That comes in the name of the
Lord![a]
Hosanna in the highest!"

11And Jesus went into Jerusalem and into the temple. So when He had looked around at all things, as the hour was already late, He went out to Bethany with the twelve.

The Fig Tree Withered

12Now the next day, when they had come out from Bethany, He was hungry. 13And seeing from afar a fig tree having leaves, He went to see if perhaps He would find something on it. When He came to it, He found nothing but leaves, for it was not the season for figs. 14In response Jesus said to it, "Let no one eat fruit from you ever again."

And His disciples heard *it.*

Jesus Cleanses the Temple

15So they came to Jerusalem. Then Jesus went into the temple and began to drive out those who bought and sold in the temple, and overturned the tables of the money changers and the seats of those who sold doves. 16And He would not allow anyone to carry wares through the temple. 17Then He taught, saying to them, "Is it not written, *'My house shall be called a house of prayer for all nations'*[a] But you have made it a *'den of thieves.'*"[b]

18And the scribes and chief priests heard it and sought how they might destroy Him; for they feared Him, be-

11:9 [a]Psalm 118:26 **11:10** [a]NU-Text omits *in the name of the Lord.* **11:17** [a]Isaiah 56:7 [b]Jeremiah 7:11

cause all the people were astonished at His teaching. 19 When evening had come, He went out of the city.

The Lesson of the Withered Fig Tree

20 Now in the morning, as they passed by, they saw the fig tree dried up from the roots. 21 And Peter, remembering, said to Him, "Rabbi, look! The fig tree which You cursed has withered away."

22 So Jesus answered and said to them, "Have faith in God. 23 For assuredly, I say to you, whoever says to this mountain, 'Be removed and be cast into the sea,' and does not doubt in his heart, but believes that those things he says will be done, he will have whatever he says. 24 Therefore I say to you, whatever things you ask when you pray, believe that you receive *them,* and you will have *them.*

Forgiveness and Prayer

25 "And whenever you stand praying, if you have anything against anyone, forgive him, that your Father in heaven may also forgive you your trespasses. 26 But if you do not forgive, neither will your Father in heaven forgive your trespasses."[a]

Jesus' Authority Questioned

27 Then they came again to Jerusalem. And as He was walking in the temple, the chief priests, the scribes, and the elders came to Him. 28 And they said to Him, "By what authority are You doing these things? And who gave You this authority to do these things?"

29 But Jesus answered and said to them, "I also will ask you one question; then answer Me, and I will tell you by what authority I do these things: 30 The baptism of John— was it from heaven or from men? Answer Me."

31 And they reasoned among themselves, saying, "If we say, 'From heaven,' He will say, 'Why then did you not believe him?' 32 But if we say, 'From men' "—they feared the people, for all counted John to have been a prophet indeed. 33 So they answered and said to Jesus, "We do not know."

And Jesus answered and said to them, "Neither will I tell you by what authority I do these things."

11:26 [a] NU-Text omits this verse.

The Parable of the Wicked Vinedressers

12 Then He began to speak to them in parables: "A man planted a vineyard and set a hedge around *it,* dug *a place for* the wine vat and built a tower. And he leased it to vinedressers and went into a far country. 2 Now at vintage-time he sent a servant to the vinedressers, that he might receive some of the fruit of the vineyard from the vinedressers. 3 And they took *him* and beat him and sent *him* away empty-handed. 4 Again he sent them another servant, and at him they threw stones,[a] wounded *him* in the head, and sent *him* away shamefully treated. 5 And again he sent another, and him they killed; and many others, beating some and killing some. 6 Therefore still having one son, his beloved, he also sent him to them last, saying, 'They will respect my son.' 7 But those vinedressers said among themselves, 'This is the heir. Come, let us kill him, and the inheritance will be ours.' 8 So they took him and killed *him* and cast *him* out of the vineyard.

9 "Therefore what will the owner of the vineyard do? He will come and destroy the vinedressers, and give the vineyard to others. 10 Have you not even read this Scripture:

'The stone which the builders rejected
Has become the chief cornerstone.
11 *This was the LORD's doing,*
And it is marvelous in our eyes'?"[a]

12 And they sought to lay hands on Him, but feared the multitude, for they knew He had spoken the parable against them. So they left Him and went away.

The Pharisees: Is It Lawful to Pay Taxes to Caesar?

13 Then they sent to Him some of the Pharisees and the Herodians, to catch Him in *His* words. 14 When they had come, they said to Him, "Teacher, we know that You are true, and care about no one; for You do not regard the person of men, but teach the way of God in truth. Is it lawful

---

12:4 [a] NU-Text omits *and at him they threw stones.* **12:11** [a] Psalm 118:22, 23

to pay taxes to Caesar, or not? [15]Shall
we pay, or shall we not pay?"

But He, knowing their hypocrisy,
said to them, "Why do you test Me?
Bring Me a denarius that I may see
it." [16]So they brought *it.*

And He said to them, "Whose
image and inscription *is* this?" They
said to Him, "Caesar's."

[17]And Jesus answered and said to
them, "Render to Caesar the things
that are Caesar's, and to God the
things that are God's."

And they marveled at Him.

The Sadducees: What About the Resurrection?

[18]Then *some* Sadducees, who say
there is no resurrection, came to
Him; and they asked Him, saying:
[19]"Teacher, Moses wrote to us that if
a man's brother dies, and leaves *his*
wife behind, and leaves no children,
his brother should take his wife and
raise up offspring for his brother.
[20]Now there were seven brothers.
The first took a wife; and dying, he
left no offspring. [21]And the second
took her, and he died; nor did he
leave any offspring. And the third
likewise. [22]So the seven had her and
left no offspring. Last of all the
woman died also. [23]Therefore, in
the resurrection, when they rise,
whose wife will she be? For all seven
had her as wife."

[24]Jesus answered and said to
them, "Are you not therefore mistaken, because you do not know the
Scriptures nor the power of God?
[25]For when they rise from the dead,
they neither marry nor are given in
marriage, but are like angels in
heaven. [26]But concerning the dead,
that they rise, have you not read in
the book of Moses, in the *burning*
bush *passage,* how God spoke to
him, saying, *'I am the God of Abraham, the God of Isaac, and the
God of Jacob'*?[a] [27]He is not the God
of the dead, but the God of the
living. You are therefore greatly
mistaken."

The Scribes: Which Is the First Commandment of All?

[28]Then one of the scribes came, and
having heard them reasoning together,
perceiving[a] that He had answered

12:26 [a]Exodus 3:6, 15 **12:28** [a]NU-Text reads *seeing.*

them well, asked Him, "Which is the first commandment of all?"

[29]Jesus answered him, "The first of all the commandments *is*: *'Hear, O Israel, the* LORD *our God, the* LORD *is one.* [30]*And you shall love the* LORD *your God with all your heart, with all your soul, with all your mind, and with all your strength.'*[a] This *is* the first commandment.[b] [31]And the second, like *it, is* this: *'You shall love your neighbor as yourself.'*[a] There is no other commandment greater than these."

[32]So the scribe said to Him, "Well *said*, Teacher. You have spoken the truth, for there is one God, and there is no other but He. [33]And to love Him with all the heart, with all the understanding, with all the soul,[a] and with all the strength, and to love one's neighbor as oneself, is more than all the whole burnt offerings and sacrifices."

[34]Now when Jesus saw that he answered wisely, He said to him, "You are not far from the kingdom of God."

But after that no one dared question Him.

Jesus: How Can David Call His Descendant Lord?

[35]Then Jesus answered and said, while He taught in the temple, "How *is it* that the scribes say that the Christ is the Son of David? [36]For David himself said by the Holy Spirit:

'The LORD *said to my Lord,*
"Sit at My right hand,
Till I make Your enemies Your footstool."'[a]

[37]Therefore David himself calls Him *'Lord'*; how is He *then* his Son?"

And the common people heard Him gladly.

Beware of the Scribes

[38]Then He said to them in His teaching, "Beware of the scribes, who desire to go around in long robes, *love* greetings in the marketplaces, [39]the best seats in the synagogues, and the best places at feasts, [40]who devour widows' houses, and for a pretense make long prayers. These will receive greater condemnation."

12:30 [a]Deuteronomy 6:4, 5 [b]NU-Text omits this sentence. **12:31** [a]Leviticus 19:18
12:33 [a]NU-Text omits *with all the soul.* **12:36** [a]Psalm 110:1

The Widow's Two Mites

41Now Jesus sat opposite the treasury and saw how the people put money into the treasury. And many *who were* rich put in much.
42Then one poor widow came and threw in two mites,[a] which make a quadrans.
43So He called His disciples to *Himself* and said to them, "Assuredly, I say to you that this poor widow has put in more than all those who have given to the treasury;
44for they all put in out of their abundance, but she out of her poverty put in all that she had, her whole livelihood."

Jesus Predicts the Destruction of the Temple

13 Then as He went out of the temple, one of His disciples said to Him, "Teacher, see what manner of stones and what buildings *are here!*"

2And Jesus answered and said to him, "Do you see these great buildings? Not *one* stone shall be left upon another, that shall not be thrown down."

The Signs of the Times and the End of the Age

3Now as He sat on the Mount of Olives opposite the temple, Peter, James, John, and Andrew asked Him privately,
4"Tell us, when will these things be? And what *will be* the sign when all these things will be fulfilled?"

5And Jesus, answering them, began to say: "Take heed that no one deceives you.
6For many will come in My name, saying, 'I am *He,*' and will deceive many.
7But when you hear of wars and rumors of wars, do not be troubled; for *such things* must happen, but the end *is* not yet.
8For nation will rise against nation, and kingdom against kingdom. And there will be earthquakes in various places, and there will be famines and troubles.[a] These *are* the beginnings of sorrows.

9"But watch out for yourselves, for they will deliver you up to councils, and you will be beaten in the synagogues. You will be brought[a] before rulers and kings for My sake, for a testimony to them.
10And the gospel must first be preached to all the na-

12:42 [a]Greek *lepta,* very small copper coins worth a fraction of a penny. 13:8 [a]NU-Text omits *and troubles.*
13:9 [a]NU-Text and M-Text read *will stand.*

tions. [11]But when they arrest *you* and deliver you up, do not worry beforehand, or premeditate[a] what you will speak. But whatever is given you in that hour, speak that; for it is not you who speak, but the Holy Spirit. [12]Now brother will betray brother to death, and a father *his* child; and children will rise up against parents and cause them to be put to death. [13]And you will be hated by all for My name's sake. But he who endures to the end shall be saved.

The Great Tribulation

[14]"So when you see the *'abomination of desolation,'*[a] spoken of by Daniel the prophet,[b] standing where it ought not" (let the reader understand), "then let those who are in Judea flee to the mountains. [15]Let him who is on the housetop not go down into the house, nor enter to take anything out of his house. [16]And let him who is in the field not go back to get his clothes. [17]But woe to those who are pregnant and to those who are nursing babies in those days! [18]And pray that your flight may not be in winter. [19]For *in* those days there will be tribulation, such as has not been since the beginning of the creation which God created until this time, nor ever shall be. [20]And unless the Lord had shortened those days, no flesh would be saved; but for the elect's sake, whom He chose, He shortened the days.

[21]"Then if anyone says to you, 'Look, here *is* the Christ!' or, 'Look, *He is* there!' do not believe it. [22]For false christs and false prophets will rise and show signs and wonders to deceive, if possible, even the elect. [23]But take heed; see, I have told you all things beforehand.

The Coming of the Son of Man

[24]"But in those days, after that tribulation, the sun will be darkened, and the moon will not give its light; [25]the stars of heaven will fall, and the powers in the heavens will be shaken. [26]Then they will see the Son of Man coming in the clouds with great power and glory. [27]And then He will send His angels, and gather together His elect from the four winds, from the farthest part of earth to the farthest part of heaven.

13:11 [a]NU-Text omits *or premeditate.* **13:14** [a]Daniel 11:31; 12:11 [b]NU-Text omits *spoken of by Daniel the prophet.*

The Parable of the Fig Tree

28“Now learn this parable from the fig tree: When its branch has already become tender, and puts forth leaves, you know that summer is near. 29So you also, when you see these things happening, know that it[a] is near—at the doors! 30Assuredly, I say to you, this generation will by no means pass away till all these things take place. 31Heaven and earth will pass away, but My words will by no means pass away.

No One Knows the Day or Hour

32“But of that day and hour no one knows, not even the angels in heaven, nor the Son, but only the Father. 33Take heed, watch and pray; for you do not know when the time is. 34*It is* like a man going to a far country, who left his house and gave authority to his servants, and to each his work, and commanded the doorkeeper to watch. 35Watch therefore, for you do not know when the master of the house is coming—in the evening, at midnight, at the crowing of the rooster, or in the morning—36lest, coming suddenly, he find you sleeping. 37And what I say to you, I say to all: Watch!”

The Plot to Kill Jesus

14 After two days it was the Passover and *the Feast* of Unleavened Bread. And the chief priests and the scribes sought how they might take Him by trickery and put *Him* to death. 2But they said, “Not during the feast, lest there be an uproar of the people.”

The Anointing at Bethany

3And being in Bethany at the house of Simon the leper, as He sat at the table, a woman came having an alabaster flask of very costly oil of spikenard. Then she broke the flask and poured *it* on His head. 4But there were some who were indignant among themselves, and said, “Why was this fragrant oil wasted? 5For it might have been sold for more than three hundred denarii and given to the poor.” And they criticized her sharply.

6But Jesus said, “Let her alone. Why do you trouble her? She has done a good work for Me. 7For you

---

13:29 [a]Or *He*

have the poor with you always, and
whenever you wish you may do
them good; but Me you do not have
always. 8 She has done what she
could. She has come beforehand to
anoint My body for burial. 9 Assuredly, I say to you, wherever
this gospel is preached in the whole
world, what this woman has
done will also be told as a memorial
to her."

Judas Agrees to Betray Jesus

10 Then Judas Iscariot, one of the
twelve, went to the chief priests to
betray Him to them. 11 And when
they heard *it,* they were glad, and
promised to give him money. So he
sought how he might conveniently
betray Him.

Jesus Celebrates the Passover with His Disciples

12 Now on the first day of Unleav-
ened Bread, when they killed the
Passover *lamb,* His disciples said to
Him, "Where do You want us to go
and prepare, that You may eat the
Passover?"

13 And He sent out two of His disciples and said to them, "Go into the
city, and a man will meet you carrying a pitcher of water; follow him.
14 Wherever he goes in, say to the
master of the house, 'The Teacher
says, "Where is the guest room in
which I may eat the Passover with My
disciples?"' 15 Then he will show you
a large upper room, furnished *and*
prepared; there make ready for us."

16 So His disciples went out, and
came into the city, and found it just
as He had said to them; and they prepared the Passover.

17 In the evening He came with the
twelve. 18 Now as they sat and ate, Jesus
said, "Assuredly, I say to you, one of
you who eats with Me will betray Me."

19 And they began to be sorrowful, and to say to Him one by one, "*Is*
it I?" And another *said,* "*Is* it I?"[a]

20 He answered and said to them,
"*It is* one of the twelve, who dips with
Me in the dish. 21 The Son of Man indeed goes just as it is written of Him,
but woe to that man by whom the
Son of Man is betrayed! It would have
been good for that man if he had
never been born."

14:19 [a] NU-Text omits this sentence.

Jesus Institutes the Lord's Supper

22 And as they were eating, Jesus
took bread, blessed and broke *it,* and
gave *it* to them and said, "Take, eat;[a]
this is My body."

23 Then He took the cup, and
when He had given thanks He gave
it to them, and they all drank from it.
24 And He said to them, "This is My
blood of the new[a] covenant, which is
shed for many. 25 Assuredly, I say to
you, I will no longer drink of the fruit
of the vine until that day when I
drink it new in the kingdom of God."

26 And when they had sung a
hymn, they went out to the Mount
of Olives.

Jesus Predicts Peter's Denial

27 Then Jesus said to them, "All of
you will be made to stumble because
of Me this night,[a] for it is written:

'I will strike the Shepherd,
And the sheep will be
scattered.'[b]

28 "But after I have been raised, I
will go before you to Galilee."

29 Peter said to Him, "Even if all
are made to stumble, yet I *will* not *be.*"

30 Jesus said to him, "Assuredly, I
say to you that today, *even* this night,
before the rooster crows twice, you
will deny Me three times."

31 But he spoke more vehemently,
"If I have to die with You, I will not
deny You!"

And they all said likewise.

The Prayer in the Garden

32 Then they came to a place
which was named Gethsemane; and
He said to His disciples, "Sit here
while I pray." 33 And He took Peter,
James, and John with Him, and He
began to be troubled and deeply dis-
tressed. 34 Then He said to them, "My
soul is exceedingly sorrowful, *even* to
death. Stay here and watch."

35 He went a little farther, and fell
on the ground, and prayed that if it
were possible, the hour might pass
from Him. 36 And He said, "Abba,
Father, all things *are* possible for You.
Take this cup away from Me; nevertheless, not what I will, but what You *will.*"

37 Then He came and found them
sleeping, and said to Peter, "Simon,

14:22 [a] NU-Text omits *eat.* **14:24** [a] NU-Text omits *new.* **14:27** [a] NU-Text omits *because of Me this night.* [b] Zechariah 13:7

are you sleeping? Could you not watch one hour? [38]Watch and pray, lest you enter into temptation. The spirit indeed *is* willing, but the flesh *is* weak."

[39]Again He went away and prayed, and spoke the same words. [40]And when He returned, He found them asleep again, for their eyes were heavy; and they did not know what to answer Him.

[41]Then He came the third time and said to them, "Are you still sleeping and resting? It is enough! The hour has come; behold, the Son of Man is being betrayed into the hands of sinners. [42]Rise, let us be going. See, My betrayer is at hand."

Betrayal and Arrest in Gethsemane

[43]And immediately, while He was still speaking, Judas, one of the twelve, with a great multitude with swords and clubs, came from the chief priests and the scribes and the elders. [44]Now His betrayer had given them a signal, saying, "Whomever I kiss, He is the One; seize Him and lead *Him* away safely."

[45]As soon as he had come, immediately he went up to Him and said to Him, "Rabbi, Rabbi!" and kissed Him.

[46]Then they laid their hands on Him and took Him. [47]And one of those who stood by drew his sword and struck the servant of the high priest, and cut off his ear.

[48]Then Jesus answered and said to them, "Have you come out, as against a robber, with swords and clubs to take Me? [49]I was daily with you in the temple teaching, and you did not seize Me. But the Scriptures must be fulfilled."

[50]Then they all forsook Him and fled.

A Young Man Flees Naked

[51]Now a certain young man followed Him, having a linen cloth thrown around *his* naked *body.* And the young men laid hold of him, [52]and he left the linen cloth and fled from them naked.

Jesus Faces the Sanhedrin

[53]And they led Jesus away to the high priest; and with him were assembled all the chief priests, the elders, and the scribes. [54]But Peter followed Him at a distance, right into

the courtyard of the high priest. And he sat with the servants and warmed himself at the fire.

55Now the chief priests and all the council sought testimony against Jesus to put Him to death, but found none. 56For many bore false witness against Him, but their testimonies did not agree.

57Then some rose up and bore false witness against Him, saying, 58"We heard Him say, 'I will destroy this temple made with hands, and within three days I will build another made without hands.'" 59But not even then did their testimony agree.

60And the high priest stood up in the midst and asked Jesus, saying, "Do You answer nothing? What *is it* these men testify against You?" 61But He kept silent and answered nothing.

Again the high priest asked Him, saying to Him, "Are You the Christ, the Son of the Blessed?"

62Jesus said, "I am. And you will see the Son of Man sitting at the right hand of the Power, and coming with the clouds of heaven."

63Then the high priest tore his clothes and said, "What further need do we have of witnesses? 64You have heard the blasphemy! What do you think?"

And they all condemned Him to be deserving of death.

65Then some began to spit on Him, and to blindfold Him, and to beat Him, and to say to Him, "Prophesy!" And the officers struck Him with the palms of their hands.[a]

Peter Denies Jesus, and Weeps

66Now as Peter was below in the courtyard, one of the servant girls of the high priest came. 67And when she saw Peter warming himself, she looked at him and said, "You also were with Jesus of Nazareth."

68But he denied it, saying, "I neither know nor understand what you are saying." And he went out on the porch, and a rooster crowed.

69And the servant girl saw him again, and began to say to those who stood by, "This is *one* of them." 70But he denied it again.

And a little later those who stood by said to Peter again, "Surely you are *one* of them; for you are a Galilean, and your speech shows *it*."[a]

14:65 [a]NU-Text reads *received Him with slaps.* **14:70** [a]NU-Text omits *and your speech shows it.*

71 Then he began to curse and swear, "I do not know this Man of whom you speak!"

72 A second time *the* rooster crowed. Then Peter called to mind the word that Jesus had said to him, "Before the rooster crows twice, you will deny Me three times." And when he thought about it, he wept.

Jesus Faces Pilate

15 Immediately, in the morning, the chief priests held a consultation with the elders and scribes and the whole council; and they bound Jesus, led *Him* away, and delivered *Him* to Pilate. 2 Then Pilate asked Him, "Are You the King of the Jews?"

He answered and said to him, "*It is as* you say."

3 And the chief priests accused Him of many things, but He answered nothing. 4 Then Pilate asked Him again, saying, "Do You answer nothing? See how many things they testify against You!"[a] 5 But Jesus still answered nothing, so that Pilate marveled.

Taking the Place of Barabbas

6 Now at the feast he was accustomed to releasing one prisoner to them, whomever they requested. 7 And there was one named Barabbas, *who was* chained with his fellow rebels; they had committed murder in the rebellion. 8 Then the multitude, crying aloud,[a] began to ask *him to do* just as he had always done for them. 9 But Pilate answered them, saying, "Do you want me to release to you the King of the Jews?" 10 For he knew that the chief priests had handed Him over because of envy.

11 But the chief priests stirred up the crowd, so that he should rather release Barabbas to them. 12 Pilate answered and said to them again, "What then do you want me to do *with Him* whom you call the King of the Jews?"

13 So they cried out again, "Crucify Him!"

14 Then Pilate said to them, "Why, what evil has He done?"

But they cried out all the more, "Crucify Him!"

15 So Pilate, wanting to gratify the crowd, released Barabbas to them;

15:4 [a] NU-Text reads *of which they accuse You.* **15:8** [a] NU-Text reads *going up.*

and he delivered Jesus, after he had scourged *Him,* to be crucified.

The Soldiers Mock Jesus

16 Then the soldiers led Him away into the hall called Praetorium, and they called together the whole garrison. 17 And they clothed Him with purple; and they twisted a crown of thorns, put it on His *head,* 18 and began to salute Him, "Hail, King of the Jews!" 19 Then they struck Him on the head with a reed and spat on Him; and bowing the knee, they worshiped Him. 20 And when they had mocked Him, they took the purple off Him, put His own clothes on Him, and led Him out to crucify Him.

The King on a Cross

21 Then they compelled a certain man, Simon a Cyrenian, the father of Alexander and Rufus, as he was coming out of the country and passing by, to bear His cross. 22 And they brought Him to the place Golgotha, which is translated, Place of a Skull. 23 Then they gave Him wine mingled with myrrh to drink, but He did not take *it.* 24 And when they crucified Him, they divided His garments, casting lots for them *to determine* what every man should take.

25 Now it was the third hour, and they crucified Him. 26 And the inscription of His accusation was written above:

THE KING OF THE JEWS.

27 With Him they also crucified two robbers, one on His right and the other on His left. 28 So the Scripture was fulfilled[a] which says, *"And He was numbered with the transgressors."*[b]

29 And those who passed by blasphemed Him, wagging their heads and saying, "Aha! *You* who destroy the temple and build *it* in three days, 30 save Yourself, and come down from the cross!"

31 Likewise the chief priests also, mocking among themselves with the scribes, said, "He saved others; Himself He cannot save. 32 Let the Christ, the King of Israel, descend now from the cross, that we may see and believe."[a]

15:28 [a] Isaiah 53:12 [b] NU-Text omits this verse. **15:32** [a] M-Text reads *believe Him.*

Even those who were crucified with Him reviled Him.

Jesus Dies on the Cross

33 Now when the sixth hour had come, there was darkness over the whole land until the ninth hour. 34 And at the ninth hour Jesus cried out with a loud voice, saying, "Eloi, Eloi, lama sabachthani?" which is translated, *"My God, My God, why have You forsaken Me?"*[a]

35 Some of those who stood by, when they heard *that,* said, "Look, He is calling for Elijah!" 36 Then someone ran and filled a sponge full of sour wine, put *it* on a reed, and offered *it* to Him to drink, saying, "Let Him alone; let us see if Elijah will come to take Him down."

37 And Jesus cried out with a loud voice, and breathed His last.

38 Then the veil of the temple was torn in two from top to bottom. 39 So when the centurion, who stood opposite Him, saw that He cried out like this and breathed His last,[a] he said, "Truly this Man was the Son of God!"

40 There were also women looking on from afar, among whom were Mary Magdalene, Mary the mother of James the Less and of Joses, and Salome, 41 who also followed Him and ministered to Him when He was in Galilee, and many other women who came up with Him to Jerusalem.

Jesus Buried in Joseph's Tomb

42 Now when evening had come, because it was the Preparation Day, that is, the day before the Sabbath, 43 Joseph of Arimathea, a prominent council member, who was himself waiting for the kingdom of God, coming and taking courage, went in to Pilate and asked for the body of Jesus. 44 Pilate marveled that He was already dead; and summoning the centurion, he asked him if He had been dead for some time. 45 So when he found out from the centurion, he granted the body to Joseph. 46 Then he bought fine linen, took Him down, and wrapped Him in the linen. And he laid Him in a tomb which had been hewn out of the rock, and rolled a stone against the door of the tomb. 47 And Mary Magdalene and Mary *the mother* of Joses observed where He was laid.

15:34 [a] Psalm 22:1 **15:39** [a] NU-Text reads *that He thus breathed His last.*

He Is Risen

16 Now when the Sabbath was
past, Mary Magdalene, Mary
the mother of James, and Salome
bought spices, that they might come
and anoint Him. 2Very early in the
morning, on the first *day* of the week,
they came to the tomb when the sun
had risen. 3And they said among
themselves, "Who will roll away the
stone from the door of the tomb for
us?" 4But when they looked up, they
saw that the stone had been rolled
away—for it was very large. 5And entering the tomb, they saw a young
man clothed in a long white robe sitting on the right side; and they were
alarmed.

6But he said to them, "Do not be
alarmed. You seek Jesus of Nazareth,
who was crucified. He is risen! He is
not here. See the place where they
laid Him. 7But go, tell His disciples—
and Peter—that He is going before
you into Galilee; there you will see
Him, as He said to you."

8So they went out quickly[a] and
fled from the tomb, for they trembled and were amazed. And they said
nothing to anyone, for they were
afraid.

Mary Magdalene Sees the Risen Lord

9Now when *He* rose early on the
first *day* of the week, He appeared first
to Mary Magdalene, out of whom He
had cast seven demons. 10She went
and told those who had been with
Him, as they mourned and wept.
11And when they heard that He was
alive and had been seen by her, they
did not believe.

Jesus Appears to Two Disciples

12After that, He appeared in another form to two of them as they
walked and went into the country.
13And they went and told *it* to the rest,
but they did not believe them either.

The Great Commission

14Later He appeared to the eleven
as they sat at the table; and He rebuked their unbelief and hardness of
heart, because they did not believe
those who had seen Him after He had
risen. 15And He said to them, "Go
into all the world and preach the

16:8 [a]NU-Text and M-Text omit *quickly*.

gospel to every creature. [16]He who believes and is baptized will be saved; but he who does not believe will be condemned. [17]And these signs will follow those who believe: In My name they will cast out demons; they will speak with new tongues; [18]they[a] will take up serpents; and if they drink anything deadly, it will by no means hurt them; they will lay hands on the sick, and they will recover."

Christ Ascends to God's Right Hand

[19]So then, after the Lord had spoken to them, He was received up into heaven, and sat down at the right hand of God. [20]And they went out and preached everywhere, the Lord working with *them* and confirming the word through the accompanying signs. Amen.[a]

16:18 [a]NU-Text reads *and in their hands they will.* **16:20** [a]Verses 9–20 are bracketed in NU-Text as not original. They are lacking in Codex Sinaiticus and Codex Vaticanus, although nearly all other manuscripts of Mark contain them.

I PETER

Greeting to the Elect Pilgrims

1 Peter, an apostle of Jesus Christ,
To the pilgrims of the Dispersion
in Pontus, Galatia, Cappadocia, Asia,
and Bithynia, [2]elect according to the
foreknowledge of God the Father, in
sanctification of the Spirit, for obedience and sprinkling of the blood of
Jesus Christ:

Grace to you and peace be multiplied.

A Heavenly Inheritance

[3]Blessed *be* the God and Father of
our Lord Jesus Christ, who according
to His abundant mercy has begotten
us again to a living hope through the
resurrection of Jesus Christ from the
dead, [4]to an inheritance incorruptible and undefiled and that does not
fade away, reserved in heaven for
you, [5]who are kept by the power of
God through faith for salvation ready
to be revealed in the last time.

[6]In this you greatly rejoice,
though now for a little while, if need
be, you have been grieved by various
trials, [7]that the genuineness of your
faith, *being* much more precious than
gold that perishes, though it is tested
by fire, may be found to praise,
honor, and glory at the revelation of
Jesus Christ, [8]whom having not seen[a]
you love. Though now you do not

1:8 [a]M-Text reads *known*.

see *Him,* yet believing, you rejoice with joy inexpressible and full of glory, 9receiving the end of your faith—the salvation of *your* souls.

10Of this salvation the prophets have inquired and searched carefully, who prophesied of the grace *that would come* to you, 11searching what, or what manner of time, the Spirit of Christ who was in them was indicating when He testified beforehand the sufferings of Christ and the glories that would follow. 12To them it was revealed that, not to themselves, but to us[a] they were ministering the things which now have been reported to you through those who have preached the gospel to you by the Holy Spirit sent from heaven—things which angels desire to look into.

Living Before God Our Father

13Therefore gird up the loins of your mind, be sober, and rest *your* hope fully upon the grace that is to be brought to you at the revelation of Jesus Christ; 14as obedient children, not conforming yourselves to the former lusts, *as* in your ignorance; 15but as He who called you *is* holy, you also be holy in all *your* conduct, 16because it is written, *"Be holy, for I am holy."*[a]

17And if you call on the Father, who without partiality judges according to each one's work, conduct yourselves throughout the time of your stay *here* in fear; 18knowing that you were not redeemed with corruptible things, *like* silver or gold, from your aimless conduct *received* by tradition from your fathers, 19but with the precious blood of Christ, as of a lamb without blemish and without spot. 20He indeed was foreordained before the foundation of the world, but was manifest in these last times for you 21who through Him believe in God, who raised Him from the dead and gave Him glory, so that your faith and hope are in God.

The Enduring Word

22Since you have purified your souls in obeying the truth through the Spirit[a] in sincere love of the brethren, love one another fervently with a pure heart, 23having been born

1:12 [a]NU-Text and M-Text read *you.* 1:16 [a]Leviticus 11:44, 45; 19:2; 20:7 1:22 [a]NU-Text omits *through the Spirit.*

again, not of corruptible seed but incorruptible, through the word of God which lives and abides forever,[a]
24because

"*All flesh is as grass,*
And all the glory of man[a] *as*
the flower of the grass.
The grass withers,
And its flower falls away,
25 *But the word of the* LORD
endures forever."[a]

Now this is the word which by the gospel was preached to you.

2 Therefore, laying aside all malice, all deceit, hypocrisy, envy, and all evil speaking, 2as newborn babes, desire the pure milk of the word, that you may grow thereby,[a] 3if indeed you have tasted that the Lord *is* gracious.

The Chosen Stone and His Chosen People

4Coming to Him *as to* a living stone, rejected indeed by men, but chosen by God *and* precious, 5you also, as living stones, are being built up a spiritual house, a holy priesthood, to offer up spiritual sacrifices acceptable to God through Jesus Christ. 6Therefore it is also contained in the Scripture,

"*Behold, I lay in Zion*
A chief cornerstone, elect,
precious,
And he who believes on Him
will by no means be put to
shame."[a]

7Therefore, to you who believe, *He is* precious; but to those who are disobedient,[a]

"*The stone which the builders*
rejected
Has become the chief
cornerstone,"[b]

8and

"*A stone of stumbling*
And a rock of offense."[a]

1:23 [a]NU-Text omits *forever.* **1:24** [a]NU-Text reads *all its glory.* **1:25** [a]Isaiah 40:6–8 **2:2** [a]NU-Text adds *up to salvation.* **2:6** [a]Isaiah 28:16 **2:7** [a]NU-Text reads *to those who disbelieve.* [b]Psalm 118:22 **2:8** [a]Isaiah 8:14

They stumble, being disobedient to the word, to which they also were appointed.

[9]But you *are* a chosen generation, a royal priesthood, a holy nation, His own special people, that you may proclaim the praises of Him who called you out of darkness into His marvelous light; [10]who once *were* not a people but *are* now the people of God, who had not obtained mercy but now have obtained mercy.

Living Before the World

[11]Beloved, I beg *you* as sojourners and pilgrims, abstain from fleshly lusts which war against the soul, [12]having your conduct honorable among the Gentiles, that when they speak against you as evildoers, they may, by *your* good works which they observe, glorify God in the day of visitation.

Submission to Government

[13]Therefore submit yourselves to every ordinance of man for the Lord's sake, whether to the king as supreme, [14]or to governors, as to those who are sent by him for the punishment of evildoers and *for the* praise of those who do good. [15]For this is the will of God, that by doing good you may put to silence the ignorance of foolish men— [16]as free, yet not using liberty as a cloak for vice, but as bondservants of God. [17]Honor all *people.* Love the brotherhood. Fear God. Honor the king.

Submission to Masters

[18]Servants, *be* submissive to *your* masters with all fear, not only to the good and gentle, but also to the harsh. [19]For this *is* commendable, if because of conscience toward God one endures grief, suffering wrongfully. [20]For what credit *is it* if, when you are beaten for your faults, you take it patiently? But when you do good and suffer, if you take it patiently, this *is* commendable before God. [21]For to this you were called, because Christ also suffered for us,[a] leaving us[b] an example, that you should follow His steps:

2:21 [a]NU-Text reads *you.* [b]NU-Text and M-Text read *you.*

22 *"Who committed no sin,*
Nor was deceit found in His
mouth";[a]

[23]who, when He was reviled, did not
revile in return; when He suffered,
He did not threaten, but committed
Himself to Him who judges righteously; [24]who Himself bore our sins
in His own body on the tree, that we,
having died to sins, might live for
righteousness—by whose stripes
you were healed. [25]For you were like
sheep going astray, but have now returned to the Shepherd and Overseer[a] of your souls.

Submission to Husbands

3 Wives, likewise, *be* submissive to
your own husbands, that even if
some do not obey the word, they,
without a word, may be won by the
conduct of their wives, [2]when they
observe your chaste conduct *accompa-*
nied by fear. [3]Do not let your adorn-
ment be *merely* outward—arranging
the hair, wearing gold, or putting
on *fine* apparel— [4]rather *let it be* the
hidden person of the heart, with
the incorruptible *beauty* of a gentle and
quiet spirit, which is very precious in
the sight of God. [5]For in this manner,
in former times, the holy women
who trusted in God also adorned
themselves, being submissive to their
own husbands, [6]as Sarah obeyed
Abraham, calling him lord, whose
daughters you are if you do good and
are not afraid with any terror.

A Word to Husbands

[7]Husbands, likewise, dwell with
them with understanding, giving
honor to the wife, as to the weaker
vessel, and as *being* heirs together of
the grace of life, that your prayers
may not be hindered.

Called to Blessing

[8]Finally, all *of you be* of one mind,
having compassion for one another;
love as brothers, *be* tenderhearted, *be*
courteous;[a] [9]not returning evil for
evil or reviling for reviling, but on the
contrary blessing, knowing that you
were called to this, that you may inherit a blessing. [10]For

2:22 [a]Isaiah 53:9 2:25 [a]Greek *Episkopos* 3:8 [a]NU-Text reads *humble.*

"He who would love life
And see good days,
Let him refrain his tongue from evil,
And his lips from speaking deceit.
11 *Let him turn away from evil and do good;*
Let him seek peace and pursue it.
12 *For the eyes of the* LORD *are on the righteous,*
And His ears are open *to their prayers;*
But the face of the LORD *is against those who do evil."*[a]

Suffering for Right and Wrong

13And who *is* he who will harm
you if you become followers of what
is good? 14But even if you should suffer for righteousness' sake, *you are*
blessed. *"And do not be afraid of their*
threats, nor be troubled."[a] 15But sanc-
tify the Lord God[a] in your hearts, and
always *be* ready to *give* a defense to
everyone who asks you a reason for
the hope that is in you, with meek-
ness and fear; 16having a good conscience, that when they defame you
as evildoers, those who revile your
good conduct in Christ may be
ashamed. 17For *it is* better, if it is the
will of God, to suffer for doing good
than for doing evil.

Christ's Suffering and Ours

18For Christ also suffered once for
sins, the just for the unjust, that He
might bring us[a] to God, being put to
death in the flesh but made alive by
the Spirit, 19by whom also He went
and preached to the spirits in prison,
20who formerly were disobedient,
when once the Divine longsuffering
waited[a] in the days of Noah, while *the*
ark was being prepared, in which a
few, that is, eight souls, were saved
through water. 21There is also an an-
titype which now saves us—baptism
(not the removal of the filth of the
flesh, but the answer of a good conscience toward God), through the
resurrection of Jesus Christ, 22who
has gone into heaven and is at the

3:12 [a]Psalm 34:12–16 **3:14** [a]Isaiah 8:12 **3:15** [a]NU-Text reads *Christ as Lord.* **3:18** [a]NU-Text and M-Text read *you.*
3:20 [a]NU-Text and M-Text read *when the longsuffering of God waited patiently.*

right hand of God, angels and authorities and powers having been made subject to Him.

4 Therefore, since Christ suffered for us[a] in the flesh, arm yourselves also with the same mind, for he who has suffered in the flesh has ceased from sin, 2 that he no longer should live the rest of *his* time in the flesh for the lusts of men, but for the will of God. 3 For we *have spent* enough of our past lifetime[a] in doing the will of the Gentiles—when we walked in lewdness, lusts, drunkenness, revelries, drinking parties, and abominable idolatries. 4 In regard to these, they think it strange that you do not run with *them* in the same flood of dissipation, speaking evil of *you*. 5 They will give an account to Him who is ready to judge the living and the dead. 6 For this reason the gospel was preached also to those who are dead, that they might be judged according to men in the flesh, but live according to God in the spirit.

Serving for God's Glory

7 But the end of all things is at hand; therefore be serious and watchful in your prayers. 8 And above all things have fervent love for one another, for *"love will cover a multitude of sins."*[a] 9 *Be* hospitable to one another without grumbling. 10 As each one has received a gift, minister it to one another, as good stewards of the manifold grace of God. 11 If anyone speaks, *let him speak* as the oracles of God. If anyone ministers, *let him do it* as with the ability which God supplies, that in all things God may be glorified through Jesus Christ, to whom belong the glory and the dominion forever and ever. Amen.

Suffering for God's Glory

12 Beloved, do not think it strange concerning the fiery trial which is to try you, as though some strange thing happened to you; 13 but rejoice to the extent that you partake of Christ's sufferings, that when His glory is revealed, you may also be glad with exceeding joy. 14 If you are reproached for the name of Christ, blessed *are you*, for the Spirit of glory and of God rests upon you.[a] On their

---

4:1 [a]NU-Text omits *for us*. **4:3** [a]NU-Text reads *time*. **4:8** [a]Proverbs 10:12 **4:14** [a]NU-Text omits the rest of this verse.

part He is blasphemed, but on
your part He is glorified. 15But let
none of you suffer as a murderer, a
thief, an evildoer, or as a busybody in
other people's matters. 16Yet if *anyone*
suffers as a Christian, let him not be
ashamed, but let him glorify God in
this matter.[a]

17For the time *has come* for judgment to begin at the house of
God; and if *it begins* with us first,
what will *be* the end of those who
do not obey the gospel of God? 18Now

> *"If the righteous one is scarcely*
> *saved,*
> *Where will the ungodly and*
> *the sinner appear?"*[a]

19Therefore let those who suffer according to the will of God commit
their souls *to Him* in doing good, as to
a faithful Creator.

Shepherd the Flock

5 The elders who are among you I
exhort, I who am a fellow elder
and a witness of the sufferings of
Christ, and also a partaker of the
glory that will be revealed: 2Shepherd
the flock of God which is among you,
serving as overseers, not by compulsion but willingly,[a] not for dishonest
gain but eagerly; 3nor as being lords
over those entrusted to you, but being examples to the flock; 4and when
the Chief Shepherd appears, you will
receive the crown of glory that does
not fade away.

Submit to God, Resist the Devil

5Likewise you younger people,
submit yourselves to *your* elders.
Yes, all of *you* be submissive to one
another, and be clothed with humility, for

> *"God resists the proud,*
> *But gives grace to the*
> *humble."*[a]

6Therefore humble yourselves
under the mighty hand of God, that
He may exalt you in due time, 7cast-
ing all your care upon Him, for He
cares for you.

8Be sober, be vigilant; because[a]
your adversary the devil walks about

4:16 [a]NU-Text reads *name.* **4:18** [a]Proverbs 11:31 **5:2** [a]NU-Text adds *according to God.* **5:5** [a]Proverbs 3:34 **5:8** [a]NU-Text and M-Text omit *because.*

like a roaring lion, seeking whom he may devour. 9Resist him, steadfast in the faith, knowing that the same sufferings are experienced by your brotherhood in the world. 10But may[a] the God of all grace, who called us[b] to His eternal glory by Christ Jesus, after you have suffered a while, perfect, establish, strengthen, and settle *you.* 11To Him *be* the glory and the dominion forever and ever. Amen.

Farewell and Peace

12By Silvanus, our faithful brother as I consider him, I have written to you briefly, exhorting and testifying that this is the true grace of God in which you stand.

13She who is in Babylon, elect together with *you,* greets you; and *so does* Mark my son. 14Greet one another with a kiss of love.

Peace to you all who are in Christ Jesus. Amen.

5:10 [a]NU-Text reads *But the God of all grace . . . will perfect, establish, strengthen, and settle you.* [b]NU-Text and M-Text read *you.*

2 PETER

Greeting the Faithful

1 Simon Peter, a bondservant and apostle of Jesus Christ,

To those who have obtained like precious faith with us by the righteousness of our God and Savior Jesus Christ:

[2]Grace and peace be multiplied to you in the knowledge of God and of Jesus our Lord, [3]as His divine power has given to us all things that *pertain* to life and godliness, through the knowledge of Him who called us by glory and virtue, [4]by which have been given to us exceedingly great and precious promises, that through these you may be partakers of the divine nature, having escaped the corruption *that is* in the world through lust.

Fruitful Growth in the Faith

[5]But also for this very reason, giving all diligence, add to your faith virtue, to virtue knowledge, [6]to knowledge self-control, to self-control perseverance, to perseverance godliness, [7]to godliness brotherly kindness, and to brotherly kindness love. [8]For if these things are yours and abound, *you* will be neither barren nor unfruitful in the knowledge of our Lord Jesus Christ. [9]For he who lacks these things is shortsighted, even to blindness, and has forgotten that he was cleansed from his old sins.

[10]Therefore, brethren, be even
more diligent to make your call and
election sure, for if you do these
things you will never stumble; [11]for
so an entrance will be supplied to you
abundantly into the everlasting kingdom of our Lord and Savior Jesus
Christ.

Peter's Approaching Death

[12]For this reason I will not be negligent to remind you always of these
things, though you know and are established in the present truth. [13]Yes,
I think it is right, as long as I am in
this tent, to stir you up by reminding
you, [14]knowing that shortly I *must* put
off my tent, just as our Lord Jesus
Christ showed me. [15]Moreover I will
be careful to ensure that you always
have a reminder of these things after
my decease.

The Trustworthy Prophetic Word

[16]For we did not follow cunningly devised fables when we made
known to you the power and coming
of our Lord Jesus Christ, but were
eyewitnesses of His majesty. [17]For He
received from God the Father honor
and glory when such a voice came to
Him from the Excellent Glory: "This
is My beloved Son, in whom I am
well pleased." [18]And we heard this
voice which came from heaven when
we were with Him on the holy
mountain.

[19]And so we have the prophetic
word confirmed,[a] which you do well
to heed as a light that shines in a dark
place, until the day dawns and the
morning star rises in your hearts;
[20]knowing this first, that no
prophecy of Scripture is of any private interpretation,[a] [21]for prophecy
never came by the will of man, but
holy men of God[a] spoke *as they were*
moved by the Holy Spirit.

Destructive Doctrines

2 But there were also false prophets
among the people, even as there
will be false teachers among you,
who will secretly bring in destructive
heresies, even denying the Lord who
bought them, *and* bring on themselves swift destruction. [2]And many
will follow their destructive ways, because of whom the way of truth will

1:19 [a]Or *We also have the more sure prophetic word.* 1:20 [a]Or *origin* 1:21 [a]NU-Text reads *but men spoke from God.*

be blasphemed. [3]By covetousness
they will exploit you with deceptive
words; for a long time their judgment has not been idle, and their
destruction does[a] not slumber.

Doom of False Teachers

[4]For if God did not spare the angels who sinned, but cast *them* down
to hell and delivered *them* into chains
of darkness, to be reserved for judgment; [5]and did not spare the ancient
world, but saved Noah, *one of* eight
people, a preacher of righteousness,
bringing in the flood on the world of
the ungodly; [6]and turning the cities
of Sodom and Gomorrah into ashes,
condemned *them* to destruction, making *them* an example to those who afterward would live ungodly; [7]and
delivered righteous Lot, *who was* oppressed by the filthy conduct of the
wicked [8](for that righteous man,
dwelling among them, tormented *his*
righteous soul from day to day by
seeing and hearing *their* lawless
deeds)— [9]*then* the Lord knows how
to deliver the godly out of tempta-
tions and to reserve the unjust under
punishment for the day of judgment,
[10]and especially those who walk according to the flesh in the lust of
uncleanness and despise authority.
They are presumptuous, self-willed.
They are not afraid to speak evil of
dignitaries, [11]whereas angels, who are
greater in power and might, do not
bring a reviling accusation against
them before the Lord.

Depravity of False Teachers

[12]But these, like natural brute
beasts made to be caught and destroyed, speak evil of the things they
do not understand, and will utterly
perish in their own corruption, [13]*and*
will receive the wages of unrighteousness, *as* those who count it pleasure to carouse in the daytime. *They*
are spots and blemishes, carousing in
their own deceptions while they feast
with you, [14]having eyes full of adultery and that cannot cease from sin,
enticing unstable souls. They have a
heart trained in covetous practices,
and are accursed children. [15]They have
forsaken the right way and gone
astray, following the way of Balaam
the *son* of Beor, who loved the wages
of unrighteousness; [16]but he was re-

2:3 [a]M-Text reads *will not.*

buked for his iniquity: a dumb donkey speaking with a man's voice restrained the madness of the prophet.

[17]These are wells without water, clouds[a] carried by a tempest, for whom is reserved the blackness of darkness forever.[b]

Deceptions of False Teachers

[18]For when they speak great swelling *words* of emptiness, they allure through the lusts of the flesh, through lewdness, the ones who have actually escaped[a] from those who live in error. [19]While they promise them liberty, they themselves are slaves of corruption; for by whom a person is overcome, by him also he is brought into bondage. [20]For if, after they have escaped the pollutions of the world through the knowledge of the Lord and Savior Jesus Christ, they are again entangled in them and overcome, the latter end is worse for them than the beginning. [21]For it would have been better for them not to have known the way of righteousness, than having known *it,* to turn from the holy commandment delivered to them. [22]But it has happened to them according to the true proverb: *"A dog returns to his own vomit,"*[a] and, "a sow, having washed, to her wallowing in the mire."

God's Promise Is Not Slack

3 Beloved, I now write to you this second epistle (in *both of* which I stir up your pure minds by way of reminder), [2]that you may be mindful of the words which were spoken before by the holy prophets, and of the commandment of us,[a] the apostles of the Lord and Savior, [3]knowing this first: that scoffers will come in the last days, walking according to their own lusts, [4]and saying, "Where is the promise of His coming? For since the fathers fell asleep, all things continue as *they were* from the beginning of creation." [5]For this they willfully forget: that by the word of God the heavens were of old, and the earth standing out of water and in the water, [6]by which the world *that* then existed perished, being flooded with water. [7]But the heavens and the earth *which* are now preserved by the same word, are reserved for fire

---

2:17 [a]NU-Text reads *and mists.* [b]NU-Text omits *forever.* **2:18** [a]NU-Text reads *are barely escaping.* **2:22** [a]Proverbs 26:11
3:2 [a]NU-Text and M-Text read *commandment of the apostles of your Lord and Savior* or *commandment of your apostles of the Lord and Savior.*

until the day of judgment and perdition of ungodly men.
[8]But, beloved, do not forget this
one thing, that with the Lord one day
is as a thousand years, and a thousand
years as one day. [9]The Lord is not
slack concerning *His* promise, as
some count slackness, but is longsuffering toward us,[a] not willing that
any should perish but that all should
come to repentance.

The Day of the Lord

[10]But the day of the Lord will
come as a thief in the night, in which
the heavens will pass away with a
great noise, and the elements will
melt with fervent heat; both the
earth and the works that are in it will
be burned up.[a] [11]Therefore, since all
these things will be dissolved, what
manner *of persons* ought you to be in
holy conduct and godliness, [12]look-
ing for and hastening the coming of
the day of God, because of which the
heavens will be dissolved, being on
fire, and the elements will melt with
fervent heat? [13]Nevertheless we, according to His promise, look for new
heavens and a new earth in which
righteousness dwells.

Be Steadfast

[14]Therefore, beloved, looking
forward to these things, be diligent
to be found by Him in peace, without spot and blameless; [15]and
consider *that* the longsuffering of our
Lord *is* salvation—as also our
beloved brother Paul, according to
the wisdom given to him, has written to you, [16]as also in all his epistles,
speaking in them of these things, in
which are some things hard to understand, which untaught and unstable *people* twist to their own
destruction, as *they do* also the rest of
the Scriptures.
[17]You therefore, beloved, since
you know *this* beforehand, beware lest
you also fall from your own steadfastness, being led away with the
error of the wicked; [18]but grow in the
grace and knowledge of our Lord and
Savior Jesus Christ.

To Him *be* the glory both now and forever. Amen.

3:9 [a]NU-Text reads *you*. **3:10** [a]NU-Text reads *laid bare* (literally *found*).

Following is a special excerpt from

LUKE'S STORY

BY

TIM LAHAYE

and

JERRY B. JENKINS

Part One

THE SLAVE

ONE

Syrian Antioch, A.D. *20*

Having just turned fifteen, Loukon was not even required on the errand that would shape the rest of his life.

As the son of slaves under the charge of Theophilus, he could just as easily have remained tending the animals at the master's vast estate in Daphne, near the outskirts of the city.

But, as usual, Loukon's insatiable curiosity had gotten the better of him. That same sense of wonder that had spurred him to learn to read as a child and beg scrolls from the master's house staff made him sprint to the flatbed wood wagon as the thick driver secured the horses to it.

"Where to this morning, Lippio?" he said, as adult slaves climbed aboard, rimming the back, legs dangling.

"Through the city to the river, lad. Picking up a shipment of marble."

"Marble! No wonder so many men. Last time you brought papyrus by yourself."

"I must make haste, Loukon," Lippio said, settling behind the horses.

"I've never been all the way into Antioch. Let me come?"

"You know that's not up to me, and I don't have time to wait till you get permission."

"One minute! Please!"

"One."

Loukon raced to ask his father, tilling the gardens with his mother and others.

"If you'll help us upon your return," his father said.

"Of course!" he said over his shoulder. "Lippio! Wait!"

"You're not coming to watch, Luke," Lippio said as the boy mounted the wagon and sat next to him. "We'll need every pair of hands."

"I hoped you would say that. May I drive the horses?"

"No! Now, just sit still until we reach the Orontes."

Sitting still was no small task on the heavy rig. The wagon bounced and jostled, its wood and iron wheels rattling through ruts until the dirt road led to stone streets that would take them into the city proper. Loukon held on, feeling the pressure in his thighs as he pressed his sandals to the floorboard. Inches away, Lippio's hairy arms strained to keep the horses moving slow and steady.

The only slave his age who could read, Loukon had been studying the history of this very area and badgering adults with questions about it. Now he took to instructing Lippio, who gave him a look as if he needed no teaching.

"This is the center of the Imperial Province of Syria!" Loukon exulted.

"And you can thank Caesar Augustus for that," Lippio said, *"Quiescat in pace."*

"Yes, may he rest in peace. What? You don't think I know Latin too?"

Lippio shook his head. "It shouldn't surprise me, but that is all *I* know in Latin. I'd wager you are fluent."

"Not quite, but someday."

"You realize how privileged you are, Luke."

"I'm learning."

It was true. Loukon had been slow to recognize that the slaves under Theophilus were treated unlike anyone else's. But a trip like this made that even more obvious.

Antioch was militarily strategic to Rome, located at the foot of a mountain range. It also served the trade routes into Egypt and India and Parthia. And of course the Orontes River led to the Mediterranean. Lippio steered them through the Eastern Gate, decorated with a statue of a wolf nursing Romulus and Remus.

"Do you believe in the gods?" Loukon said.

Lippio gave him a look.

"What?" the young man said. "Are you not religious?" Loukon pretended to be teasing, but such things intrigued him. Some of his fellow slaves worshiped the God of the Jews, but most either believed in the Roman gods or none at all.

"You know better than to discuss such things," Lippio said. "Especially with your elders."

"You're saying it's none of my concern?"

"Of course it isn't! It's personal. And there are enough other things to be thinking and talking about."

"Such as?"

"You're the educated one. Aren't you interested in all the cultures that come together in this city?"

Loukon saw people of seemingly every race bustling about. The slaves were obvious. Many were branded and marked, even shackled. All went about their work quickly, eyes cast down, followed by masters with sticks and whips. No wonder strangers who learned that Loukon was the son of slaves seemed to wince or even grimace, as if discovering he had been stricken by some plague.

"I've never seen our master treat his slaves like that," Loukon said.

"And you won't," Lippio said, pulling into a line that included velvet-draped carriages bearing dignitaries, covered trailers laden with who knew what kinds of imported goods, and pedestrians. "Theophilus is most excellent in that regard. What other master would allow the likes of us such freedom?"

"Why does he?"

Lippio kept his eyes on the vehicle ahead and pulled the reins. "It has to do with his stoicism. Don't ask me to explain it, because unlike you I do not deem it polite to discuss it with him. But I believe he sees all men as equals, even though clearly we are not. Yet isn't it nice to be treated that way?"

The broad expanse of stone pavement extended nearly thirty feet across and was lined on either side by tiled roofed porticoes twenty feet high and thirty feet thick. Hundreds milled beneath these, sheltering themselves from the sun. Loukon stared at the decorations of marble and mosaics, along with the statues under the colonnades, as the wagon slowly and noisily made its way past temples. One was gold-paneled, and there was a circus, Roman baths, and several theaters. The majesty of the city finally began to give way to plainness and eventually squalor. This Loukon found fascinating.

"Look at all the soldiers, Lippio. You know the Roman legion commander here is second in power to only the emperor himself."

"Well, he has his hands full in this district, doesn't he?"

Lippio made a clicking noise and yanked the horses until they sidled into a narrow side street, lined with five-story buildings pressed close together. Each had row upon row of shuttered windows, behind which, Loukon knew, the poorest of the population lived.

Not far from the river they rumbled past a synagogue. As the wagon slowed to a crawl and Lippio navigated yet another tight turn, Loukon overheard men praying.

One thanked God he had not been born "a Greek, a slave, or a woman."

"Why would he say that?" Loukon said.

"Don't ask me," Lippio said. "Like you, I was born two of those three, but I would rather be a slave under Theophilus than live here a freeman, wouldn't you?"

Loukon nodded. "I *am* grateful I was not born a woman, though."

Lippio laughed. "Me too, Luke. That would be too great a burden."

When finally they reached the Orontes, Loukon saw small craft laden with oil and wine and cloth and spices and grain and nuts. These would be transported to larger ships at the harbor on the Mediterranean for trade around the world.

Lippio steered the wagon toward a man standing in the sand by huge pallets stacked with marble slabs. The man looked relieved. "I let the ship sail on with the rest of its cargo," he said, "praying you would arrive and I would not be left here guarding this all day while finding no other buyer."

"Do not fret, friend," Lippio said. "My master is trustworthy."

While Lippio was completing the transaction, the slaves clambered down and began loading the marble onto the wagon. Loukon helped the best he could, but the loads were so heavy, he knew he wasn't making much of a difference.

Presently Lippio joined them and lent his weight and his back to the task, moving the loads about until all but two stacks had been secured. "These will be the biggest challenge, men," he said. "Make sure each stays level as we put them atop. If they shift, there will be no righting them, and don't try to be a hero. If the load tips, just clear out or you will be crushed."

"But the marble will surely break," Loukon said.

"Much of it would, yes. But I'd rather return to the master with all my men and less of the marble than the other way around."

The agent who had sold the goods was clearly no slave and obviously not about to help. He seemed to watch dispassionately as the crew painstakingly maneuvered the several-hundred-pound loads into position. They had the second-to-last pallet in place to be lifted above their shoulders and slid onto the top when Lippio instructed them to pause and inhale.

"Together now!" he said.

Luke helped lift, but when the load was raised beyond his reach, he moved out of the way, only to watch in horror as the pallet tilted. The men strained to keep it steady, sweating in the sun. With a sickening scrape, the top slab of marble began to slowly slide.

"We're good!" Lippio called out. "We're good! Let it go!"

As the men ducked, still trying to keep the rest of the weight level, the slab slipped free and slid directly toward Lippio. Loukon could see that if the man merely followed his own advice he could have leapt out of the way, which, of course, would have caused the entire load to fall.

But there he stood, glistening muscled arms shaking with the effort, and the corner of the slab ripped into his right biceps, tearing a huge gash all the way to the bone. As he screamed and fell, the rest of the men were somehow able to wrestle the load to the ground and save the rest.

Lippio writhed, blood shooting from his riven arm with each beat of his heart. Loukon quickly knelt next to him and tore a strip of the hem off his own garment. He tied tight above the wound.

"I'm going to die!" Lippio cried.

"You're not!" Loukon said, turning to the men, who looked pale and frozen in place. "Help me get him up! He must sit with his arm raised! Now! You and you, help him up! I'll drive the horses." He turned to the marble agent. "You guard the rest of this until we return."

"I'm not responsible! I have other duties!"

"You'll deal directly with my master if any of this is lost!"

The men loaded Lippio into the seat next to Loukon, and the lad told one to squeeze in beside him and make sure the man kept his arm elevated. "It will keep him from losing more blood!"

Loukon wrangled the horses through the deep sand and back onto the street, the going slower than ever now with thousands of pounds of marble on board.

"Don't let me die, Luke!" Lippio said, his eyes wide, voice thin.

Luke finally got the wagon moving at a steady clip, pushing through the narrow streets and back onto the wide thoroughfare. There he passed curious traffic where people at first scowled and shouted and shook their fists, then fell silent as they saw the injured man and gave way.

The worst part of the journey was the last mile of rutted dirt road, where Loukon was forced to slow to keep Lippio from pitching off his perch and the marble from shifting and falling. A couple of hundred yards from the estate, Loukon enlisted one of the men in the back to take over the driving. Then he leaped down and ran all the way, quickly outdistancing the wagon.

Loukon flew into the main house, apologizing to one and all and demanding to know where the physician was. Someone pointed him to the parlor, where the elderly man was teaching the master's grandchildren.

"Lippio has been seriously injured and will be here shortly!"

The physician, who had evolved into more instructor than doctor over the last few years, hobbled behind Loukon, breathlessly asking the details. As soon as the wagon breached the gate, three men carried Lippio in, his arm still raised.

The mistresses of the house gathered the children as the physician ordered the men to deliver Lippio directly to his own chambers and called for water to be heated and aides to attend him.

"If this man survives, Loukon," the physician said, "you will have saved him."

Printed in the United States
by Baker & Taylor Publisher Services